D0777215

BAD MAGIC

stephan zielinski

 A TOM DOHERTY ASSOCIATES BOOK
NEW YORK

BAD MAGIC

Copyright © 2004 by Stephan Zielinski

This book is printed on acid-free paper.

A Tor Book
Published by Tom Doherty Associates, LLC
175 Fifth Avenue
New York, NY 10010

www.tor.com

Tor® is a registered trademark of Tom Doherty Associates, LLC.

Library of Congress Cataloging-in-Publication Data

Zielinski, Stephan.
    Bad magic / Stephan Zielinski.—1st ed.
        p. cm.
    "A Tor book."
    ISBN 0-312-87862-1 (acid-free paper)
    EAN 978-0312-87862-7
    1. Magicians—Fiction. I. Title.

    PS3626.I485B33 2004
    813'.6—dc22
                            2004050015

First Edition: December 2004

Printed in the United States of America

0 9 8 7 6 5 4 3 2 1

for my parents

BAD MAGIC

part one

Rider watches her root for aluminum in overflowing trash cans. Lawyers and marketers in their daytime finery pass by without seeing—perfect. He can approach without difficulty.

Cracked eyes meet his. Grime lips croak "Spare change?" He draws his wallet and hands her a ten-dollar bill. She squints at it. While she tries to think of something to say, Rider reaches out with a metaphor and takes her invisibility from her. She can tell something has happened—looks around, realizes the suits are staring with sick horror. As Rider slips away, teeth gritted with the effort of holding on, he watches their faces. There will be many glasses of pill-chased delicate wine lifted tonight; many this-is-the-City anecdotes, and killing bouts of depression.

Rider waves down a cab. Sweat covers his forehead. Finally, he enters his loft and hurries to his workroom, where his special clamp is ready. He is still proud of it. It holds the raw invisibility securely, and Rider can relax. He runs fingers through his beard; flattens his mustache nervously.

An hour ginning and spinning the invisibility, another hour at the loom, and Rider has a cloak. It will crumble at sunrise; the street person is, in part, defined by her invisibility, and so it must return to her.

Summer night has fallen; warm breezes, sounds of patio barbecues. Rider would rather take his Goldwing, but he has too much to carry. So he loads his panel truck and motors to Twenty-third and Potrero. The great brick buildings of San Francisco General loom, dwarfing the walking wounded dragging themselves through the grounds. Narrow windows like a medieval castle, forbidding. Rider parks, unloads, crosses the street, and wraps himself in his cloak. Makes his way to the burn wards.

His paraphernalia is bulky—a Dewar flask of liquid nitrogen, a brazier, a staff—and even with the cloak, the night nurses can tell something is in the air. A young woman asks her supervisor if she has the shivers. "No, I do not," she answers, staring her down, "and neither do you." Rider smiles. In Berkeley, there is a graduate student writing her thesis about the ghost tales wrought by Rider's visits to the hospital.

Acres of bandages and gallons of raw alcohol; patients in troubled, drugged sleep. Rider can't cure them but he can make things easier. He slips into a room. The chart says nine-year-old girl, small but multiple full-thickness burns to the lower body, vaginal abrasion. Rider makes a note of her name. He sets the brazier on a telescoping camera tripod, burns incense, waves the staff around, muttering. The girl sleeps deeply. Rider unwraps the bandages. He takes silvery-translucent ectoplasmic tweezers from beneath his cloak; uses them to draw threads of pain from her wounds. They twist and squirm as Rider pulls them free, thrashing in search of flesh like lampreys until he drops them into the chill fluid.

The next patient was in a car wreck and his face will never be the same. The next knocked over a deep fat fryer. The next ran into a burning house to save the cat. The next is the fireman who went in after him.

And the next patient, and the next . . .

Fanning vapors from the Dewar, Rider can see slivers break the surface as they try to escape. Time to go. But as he packs his gear he realizes that something is jarring; something is not as it should be.

The burn ward is a terrible hall, full of the dreadfully injured; nothing to do for them but pour in liters of morphine. . . .

He snaps his fingers. Enters the rooms he hasn't inspected: not a single goner. Not that there is any lack of work, but . . .

A quick distraction isn't hard to arrange. Rider sneaks down to the end of a corridor, lights three cigarettes, balances them in a bedpan, drops in a coin for the clatter, quickslides down the wall as the young nurse rounds the corner to investigate. She is goose-pimpled and hesitant. She calls to the head nurse; the two of them approach slowly. Patients sneak cigarettes, but never have either seen three burning at once with nobody nearby . . . giving Rider time enough to vault behind the counter of the floor station and yank bright knots of information from the stacks of records and the filing cabinet. More staff-waving and Sumerian chants and he has copies. Releases the originals and hotfoots it away.

All three eyes, two concrete and one abstract, hurt. No surgeon ever worked harder, and he still needs to stabilize the shards of raw pain lest they burst free and return to their wounds—or worse, swarm into him. Once, Rider knocked over the Dewar; he spent the night in a refrigerator suit and respirator, frantically spraying the floor with nitrogen and grabbing at fragments. He didn't get them all; a square foot of scald snapped into his leg and Rider screamed himself raw before he could dig it out.

Home. Once a great raw concrete space in a factory converted to artists' lofts, but Rider has put in drywall to make rooms—and mortared cinder block around his laboratory. He pours the contents of his little Dewar into his big, squat, silver Dewar; adds more liquid nitrogen; affixes the penta-grammed lid. The slivers are restive, despite the cold; he can hear the bigger ones dragging themselves over the bottom of the flask. Stabilizing them will take four hours. "Four painstaking hours, that is," mutters Rider. Smiles weakly at his own old pun.

As he works, dawn comes and the cloak unravels. Under the fluorescents Rider is oblivious.

At ten o'clock, the doorbell rings the chime that means the button knows whose finger is on it and likes him. (There is a different chime for a her. Not that he hears it much.) Rider looks up with red eyes, yells at the door to let him in. Listens to the footsteps; hears the cane tapping jauntily up the stairs to the loft. "In here, Perry."

Pericles Whitlomb makes a disdainful entrance, looks askance at the alembics and strings of dried gunk hanging on the walls. "No prettier than usual. I still think the bulk of these accoutrements are merely for show," he sniffs. Rider does not turn.

"Says the man who carries a cane when it matches the color of his suit. I need about another hour here, Perry. Is something up?"

"No, just came by to chat. Brought a paper. I'll wait."

"With you in a little while, then. . . ."

Whitlomb goes into the living room. Glances at himself in the mirror. "The cane does match this suit, after all," he mutters. He'd found that dressing like Abraham Lincoln with spectacles by Benjamin Franklin made people treat him like a grandfather. He'd given up trying to look young forty years ago, when his hair went from black to white on the eve of his twenty-first birthday—and a long coat can hide a big gun. Turning from the mirror, he notices a new sculpture, carved of moonbeams and dusted with the menace of a spider. Studies it from all angles. Shudders.

His task done, Al Rider finally turns from the workbench and stretches. His scuffed leather jacket is too old to creak. He holds the Erlenmeyer of powdered agony to the light, hefts it in his hand. He can feel it snarling defiance at him. "Relax," he mutters. "You'll be back in action soon enough." It is mollified a little. He shelves it and heads into the kitchen, scratching his beard.

Leaving the workroom, he suddenly smells coffee and bacon. His stomach rumbles. Whitlomb smiles at him. "Your self-management is frightful; you go entirely too long without food."

"With this stuff, I'm just another kind of chemist. You don't eat in a laboratory. Thanks."

Whitlomb beams, makes a show of checking his heavy pocket watch. "How long have you been at it?"

"Since about four yesterday."

"Tsk tsk. I would suggest you take yourself to bed straightaway."

"Too keyed up. I'll crash early tonight."

"Hrm. A productive night?"

"Point four three kilograms. Keep me in beer and skittles for a while."

"Euthanize anybody?" asks Whitlomb, in a studiously peaceful tone of voice.

"No need. Not a single goner in the ward."

"Remarkable. Suspicious, even, perhaps."

"Yep. Grabbed some records but I haven't transcribed 'em yet. Want to have a look?"

Whitlomb sighs. "I was rather hoping to speak to you about next season's football pool, but I suppose needs must."

Rider fetches a few reams of paper, pulls knots of information from his pocket, and scatters them over the stack. A few passes and they format themselves back into visible words. He gives one ream to Whitlomb, opens the other himself and begins scanning the text.

They munch companionably for a while, a professor of archaeology and a synesthetic mage. The occult makes for strange bedfellows.

Rider stretches. "You been working on anything?"

"Just the regular patrols. There has been a veritable rash of anemia among members of the UC Berkeley band, but not a trace of the occult."

"Are you sure?"

Whitlomb lowers his glasses and gazes over the rims. "Whom are you addressing?"

"Still."

"No neck wounds; no allergic reaction to hawthorn, ash, silver, garlic, salt, holy water, holy oil, ultraviolet, the Host, white rose, raw sunlight—"

"All right, all right."

"Apology accepted." Whitlomb reads on. "Hmn. A Mr. John Doe; third-degree burns over much of his body; critical condition. Transferred to the 'Holy Cross Hospice.'"

Rider turns to the in-out logs. "Holy Cross . . . here's another Doe transferred there . . . and another one. Are they all goners?"

Whitlomb combs the papers. "Doe . . . yes, this one inhaled flame, it seems. Two code blues yesterday. Doe . . . different Doe, he's still at SF General . . . and a third Doe, also with a code."

"That's impossible."

"Perhaps a building fire? Trapping the squatters within?"

"That's not what I mean. Why would they transfer a burn case to a hospice at all? And three Does' worth?"

"If they are not expected to survive—"

"You don't move a goner. It could kill him, and if the relatives ever turn up, they sue." Rider stares at the papers. He pulls a whistle from his pocket, blows it; the noise pulls the white pages from the shelf and to his hand.

"Show-off."

"Practice . . . No Holy Cross Hospice that I can see." Plucks the phone from its cradle. "San Francisco . . . Holy Cross Hospice . . . No? How about Marin? Yes? Thanks. . . ." Writes a number on a pad and hangs up. He turns on the tape recorder and the voice distorter; punches in the number.

"Hi there! This is Tim Harris, I'm with the *San Jose Mercury*. Hi! Listen, could you transfer me to your public-relations folks? I'm doing a piece on innovations in health care. . . . Sure, I'll hold. Thanks!" Rider stares off into space. "Yes, I'm here. Uh-huh. Hi! Yes, I'm Tim Harris, with the *San Jose Mercury* . . ."

Whitlomb polishes his glasses. The PR-media dance goes on quite a long time. If they were birds, the eggs would be en route.

"And yes," blathers Rider, "we're particularly interested in innovative patient-management techniques. Now, I was down at San Francisco General just now, and they mentioned . . ."

Eventually Rider hangs up. "According to the flack, the hospice managed to bung something through the ethics board—I've got the date of the decision, we can verify it—on the grounds that the hospice has more experience with intense pain and large doses of narcotics. They argued that they can do a better job of caring for the patient, so it's actually *unethical* to leave them in the burn ward. They do the transfer in an ambulance with one of their own code teams aboard. If the patient lives long enough, they transfer him back; it hasn't happened yet, and probably won't." Rider stops. "Now, I wonder why a hospice would have a code team?"

"A hospice is not merely an annex to the funeral home, Al."

"You're right. Anyway, so far they're only doing it with Does, and I'll bet you a nickel SF General wouldn't even suggest it to a regular patient's next of kin."

"The ethics do sound questionable."

"If the board passes it, it's ethical. Besides, SF General gets a bed, and the hospice gets money from the state. If it's mundane, it's mild corruption at the absolute worst. We'll have to check for the occult ourselves."

"Shall we knock them up, swing by this afternoon?"

"Mmm. I've been going for quite a while. Tomorrow?"

"Tomorrow, I have promised to tutor a gentleman at Oakland High School on the finer points of system administration. Perhaps I could just examine this anomaly solo."

"Against doctrine, Perry. Maybe you could catch Chloe on her lunch hour?" Whitlomb scratches the back of his neck.

"We need to get her out in the field more often," says Rider.

"Max may think otherwise."

"Or not. Actually, he'll probably want to shepherd her himself."

Whitlomb nods. "In any event, it's most likely nothing to be concerned with."

. ▪ ▪

There is a tangle of hooves and a jockey struggling to get away from her mount in that eternal two seconds of a collapsing horse. Before the beast slams to the ground, Maggie-Sue Percy is running for the golf cart, her blond tresses streaming behind. The horse slides along the track from sheer momentum, three good legs fighting to get up and continue the race.

The crowd is standing, straining to see. Only the fanatics are still watching the race and Maggie-Sue hates each and every one of them. Off the cart, black bag in hand—the jockey is soothing the horse as best she can, tears on her face.

The knee is shattered. Maggie-Sue take a syringe from her bag, fills it from a livid purple bottle. The jockey knows that color; turns away. Maggie-Sue cradles the velvety head as the poison does its work and the jerking legs still and the great eyes stop rolling in their sockets. Finally she lets herself cry.

But then the hair stands up on the back of her neck. She stands and whirls, slaps a hand onto the talisman tattooed onto her breast, opens her third eye. In a flash, sees an old man, neck forward, drinking the spectacle with his eyes, grotesque sexual arousal scrawled across his features. . . . He sees her, starts; is on his feet and elbowing his way to the aisle . . .

▪ ▪ ▪

"Yes, Perry, Max told me to call you and get the details. Mmm-hmm . . . Mmm-hmm . . . You're right, doesn't sound like much."

Chloe Lee pivots in her swivel chair. Brunette pocket Venus; with her snub nose, she looks like a twelve-year-old girl with tissue stuffed in her bodice.

"But it can't hurt to check. What say we all get together for dinner? See if you can get Rider to show up, too; I haven't scanned him in a while. Yes, I know I'm a heathen paranoid. Yes, I do. Um—how about Goat Hill? Sound good? Great. See you at eight. Bye." She hangs up, goes back to reviewing inventory. A twenty-by-forty container of wicker chairs seems to be missing. She glares at her terminal. For the next hour, the machine happily refuses to do what she means it to do. She types in one more command. The screen freezes solid. She beats her head against her desk. From neighboring offices she hears curses.

She grabs her purse, steps into the corridor, and high-heel taps her way down to Geek Central. A man is typing gibberish on a screen already full of it. He looks up. Pinks. "I'm working on it. . . . I'm working on it. . . . It's the patch for the year 2000 problem; it has some bugs in it. . . ."

"Jones, the Port of Oakland would run a bit more smoothly, if you can just get it up and keep it up for a *little* longer this time," she purrs. Bucks his elbow with her hip. He turns bright red and she sashays out, leering over her shoulder.

A six-foot-six bear of a man is marching around the corner. "Great timing, Max. Let's go," she simpers, pressing against him.

"Please, show some respect for the uniform," he grins. His naval whites are immaculate, and his lieutenant's shoulder boards go well with his RAF mustache and lantern jaw. He leans down and kisses her forehead.

"Oh, I *hate* when you do that." She slips her arm part of the way around him and they depart.

Once they gain the parking lot she stops giggling. They climb into Sturgeon's Ford and head for the Bay Bridge. "I'll want to stop off and get out of uniform," he says. "What do you need to get ready?"

"Anywhere I can reach the water." They chat about his base and her work as they drive. Stop at the Alameda Marina; quick jaunt to the waterfront.

Max Sturgeon watches as she bounces down the pier, takes off her shoes, and dangles her feet into the Bay. He can't see her face, but knows her eyes are closed and she is reaching out to her totem, the spirit animal her rite of passage revealed to her. He has known her for over a year, now, and thus can keep a straight face when she speaks of Seattle's mighty patron, the Mollusk of Glory: the geoduck clam.

He wonders, not for the first time, just where on her body her totemic tattoo is.

She jerks her feet from the water, walks down the exact center of the pier, quivering from an overwhelming desire to run. She shakes water from her feet and climbs in.

"What was that all about?"

"The barnacles on that pier—some of them are from San Diego. Spies. If I'm lucky, they didn't taste me after I opened my third eye; otherwise, I could have some unwelcome company."

Sturgeon studiously avoids rolling his eyes. He starts the car, and they head for the Bay Bridge. "So, you were having computer trouble?"

"Yes. I *wish* you'd have a look at it."

"Sorry. I just keep 'em safe—I don't fix 'em. Perry may be able to help."

"Maybe it's a hacker."

"Cracker. And I doubt it—you don't have any information worth stealing." Chloe is staring at a Mercedes that just whipped past. She takes a pad from her purse and writes down the license number.

"What was that?"

"Nothing much—two-headed driver. We can add it to your list." She sighs. "I should do this more often. It's not like I'm ever far from the water in this city." She mock-frowns at him. "You should spend more time with *your* third eye open, too, Max."

"I've been busy," he mutters. "Besides, you know I hate seeing things I can't do anything about. Anyway. Any idea why Rider didn't want to do this?"

"No. Probably out spinning sunbeams into gold."

"Can he do that?"

"He's working on it. Remember when he had his hands all bandaged up? The metal didn't hold and he got burns all over." She watches the view out the window for a while. They have just passed through the tunnel on Treasure Island and San Francisco has come into view. The Transamerica Pyramid, Coit Tower, postcard views.

She sighs and returns her attention to the traffic. "Don't follow that guy too close—there's a poltergeist in the car with him."

"Thanks. You working on anything weird?"

"No. Things have been quiet." She grins at him. The two of them chorus, "Too quiet." She continues, "So I figure Al may well be on to something."

"Just as well it's us doing this, anyway. What's our story?"

They plot and rehearse, stop off at the San Francisco Marina. Sturgeon goes onto his sailboat—a tremendous Formosa 51, fifty-one feet long with teak decks—and changes. They drive north, take the Golden Gate Bridge to Marin County. Each steals glances west, to the Pacific and the deep water. And finally, arrive in San Rafael. They find the hospice without any trouble, and park.

"How's it look, Chloe?"

"Clean from out here."

Sturgeon takes a few deep breaths. "Let's do it." He climbs from the Ford—slow, deliberate, his face a mask. Looks at the entrance. Chloe takes his arm; he pats her hand, and they funeral-march through the front door.

The receptionist smiles at them. "Hello. Are you here for a visit?"

"Ah, no," heaves Sturgeon. "I was wondering . . . do you have anyone who could . . . er . . ."

"I understand, sir. Please, have a seat; I'll see if Dr. Gray is available." They sit. Sturgeon picks up an old *Time* magazine and examines it assiduously, running his eyes over the same paragraph repeatedly. Chloe divides her attention between *House and Garden* and him.

When a man in a white coat enters, Sturgeon stands quickly and swallows.

"Hello. I'm Dr. Gray. Please, let's go to my office."

Pleasantries, and then the awful story—mother sick with liver cancer, chemotherapy and radiotherapy as likely to kill her as slow down the disease, nobody at home to take care of her, senile dementia and depression . . . looking for somewhere . . . Gray is professionally understanding. They tour the facility. The very picture of ongoing grief and wifely support.

The tour over, they take a card and brochure, manage to avoid leaving any documentation themselves—dangerous and memorable, but if there is something afoot, best to make the villains work for their ID.

They regain the car, cross the bridge, and stop at Golden Gate Park, not saying a word. Sturgeon draws a map; Chloe waits until he is done. Finally, he says, "Anything?"

"Nothing obviously wrong," she says, "no constructs, undead, chimera, or anything like that. One of the patients was chanting to the Tiger totem—they can get violent when they get old, but she was too frail to do much."

"Didn't see anything either, but I don't know what I'd see."

"Well, I think we can stop worrying about this one."

"There is one more fellow we could call in—"

"No. No way. We don't need Arbeiter, either."

"Okay." He checks his watch. "Shall we eat, or do you need to get back?"

"Let's eat. Oh, we're meeting at Goat Hill Pizza at eight."

"Deal."

■　　■　　■

That evening, Maggie-Sue is assaulting Chinese takeout in her Belmont one-bedroom apartment. Peninsula bedroom community; apartment buildings you can hear the freeway from at night. One can hardly see the walls for the potted ferns and hanging plants. Kerosene lanterns provide light, but do not smoke or stink; the fish tanks hum.

Her cut-off jeans show off her long, tanned, thin legs; broad hips and a wasp waist. Her mostly rayon top (blood-red, like her elegant fingernails) struggles to contain her bosom; torrents of blond hair whisper below her shoulders and lie curling around a sweet, gently pulsing throat. No chin; china blue eyes set entirely too close together in a face too small by half for her skull; microscopic mouth twisted into a perpetual snarl. Gazing upon her visage is like jabbing six live centipedes into your eye sockets. One could rib her about the practice of bagging one's head, if one felt one could get along with a few feet less colon.

Knock on door. Nobody visible through eyehole. Knock comes again. She opens the door. A white-haired black dwarf with yellow scleras looks up at her. She huffs and jerks the door open enough for him to enter. "Thought you might like some company," he drones.

"Why? Mystic fucking voodoo connectivity?"

"Close. Six-o'clock news. Sports. They caught you looking up at heaven with rage, too. Very dramatic."

"I was not. Somebody in the stands looking at me. Some dirty old man."

"Hmn. You want to talk about it?"

"No."

"Dumb question. You never do. How'd you spot him?"

"I don't know. I just did. Caught up to him in the parking lot, kicked him in the balls a few times. Just another creep. What do you care?"

"No reason. Just thought I'd check, see how you were doing."

"Well, you could have done that over the phone. So you can go back and open up your shop again, for all I care."

"You want me to go?"

"I don't care one way or the other." She seizes a carton, yanks out a pot sticker. The chopsticks twist in her hand. The pot sticker drops into her lap.

Joseph Washington whoops laughter. She glares. A mosquito, blundering between the two of them, turns to stone and drops to the table. A fern behind him wilts. The fish hide in the gravel. Washington keeps laughing. Her hand moves like lightning as she grabs the pot sticker and bounces it off his head.

．　．　．

Kristof Arbeiter is not eating. He's hunched over a motorcycle, ripped out of his mind on a compound made of rattlesnake venom and black-widow-spider webbing, hauling his backside the hell away from a neighborhood in Oakland he should never have set foot in. He's cursing in German as he pulls around a truck piled high with cardboard. Switches to English as he runs a red light. "Every August," he snarls. "Every August, like clockwork,

Creedon watches that damn documentary about Hiroshima, and is he around to watch my back? No, he is not. And every August I say I can do it alone and—" He stops to lay the bike down long enough to slide under a semi trailer. "—every August I get in over my head and have to—" He switches to the sidewalk and weaves through foot traffic. "—bust my ass just to get a hold of the one lousy ingredient I don't have in the lab just so I can"—back to street, jumps an open manhole—"make up a batch of some stupid recipe I get off of some stupid promotional calendar"—goes *around* a fruit stand—"spend half the night running from some thousand-year-old aboriginal Eskimo whale hunter with a guilty conscience. . . . When the Wall came down, I should have stayed on my side where I belonged. . . ."

■   ■   ■

"Garlic?"

"Yes. I love garlic."

"Hey, here's a special. Look at this, Chloe!" says Rider. Chloe frowns at him. "Oh, come on, there's more than one kind of clam. Oh, miss?" A passing waitress turns. "Are the clams you use here geoduck clams?"

"Ah . . . I could check?" The waitress smiles hesitantly over the checked oilskin tablecloth; the table candle flickers.

"Never mind." Whitlomb smiles, kicking Rider. The waitress leaves to collect a pitcher of beer, and the piano player launches into another piece.

"Anyway," says Sturgeon, "we didn't see anything. Although I am surprised that the hospice is taking burn patients—that's a very specialized field of care. Of course, we could get Arbeiter and company to check for parts-raiding and unusual deaths, but I don't think it's worth the—ah—hassle involved."

"Wouldn't be so bad," says Rider. "Might even be justified. Perry hit the library; this hospice opened up without a whole lot of press. That's always a bad sign." He looks around the table. "Oh come on, y'all look like I just suggested summoning one of the Four Horsemen."

"And you know as well as I which one I have in mind," growls Chloe.

Rider shrugs. The sun is setting; he is framed in a window of pink skyscrapers.

Whitlomb gestures to the waitress; they give up and order the same pizza they always do. "I had to wonder, when I left you, what you planned to spend the rest of the day on?" he asks Rider.

"Oh, there's this project I'm working on."

"Really," says Chloe, widening her eyes. "What is it?"

"Don't give me that breathless I-never-saw-magic-before look."

"What look?"

"If you must know . . . I'm trying to take the carcinogenic properties out of cigarettes."

"Ye gods, man," says Sturgeon, "whom do you hate enough to give cancer to?"

"Nobody. I just don't want lung cancer to catch up with me."

"You could quit," murmurs Chloe.

"Bite me."

"How would you dispose of the cancer-stuff if you got it out, anyway? Sell it to the same people you sell pain to?"

"Yeah, probably. Although I suppose Puget Sound could probably afford to be taken down a peg or two. Not that there are many pegs left to go."

"Well, that's probably the right answer. We could at least seal it up into pearls."

"Thought that was oysters."

"*We* have *friends.*"

"You do?"

Eyes lock. Sturgeon coughs; Whitlomb tugs at his collar. Rider deliberately looks away, reaches for his beer; Chloe rummages in her purse and checks her makeup in a compact.

Sip. Sip. "Anyway," say Rider. "Everything else I'm worried about is pretty far away. Germany looks nasty, as always; the Balkans and the Middle East, of course, and if we get bored, we can always get behind one of Seattle's San Diego projects. Can't fault their ability to organize, at least. Don't know about you all, but I'm not that bored yet."

"Naturally. You're not one to burn yourself out saving the world," mutters Chloe.

Thankfully, food arrives, and soon they chatter happily about the summer movies. Rider even manages to make an incisive crack at exactly the right moment to make Coke come out Chloe's nose.

．　．　．

The girls of the Tenderloin are sweetly anxious. The first two weeks of August always see a rise in violence—johns are found with bullet holes, pimps lie in alleys with gashes in terrible, terrible places—but for some reason, the prostitutes are untouched. Mostly. Were it not for the spectral sobbing, the wails of grief coming from the sky, they could almost be calm.

．　．　．

Maggie-Sue rises early, feeds the fish, waters the plants, takes a shower. The black lump on the couch is still snoring. She takes a stick, prods his foot. He sits up very, very fast. "It's morning," she snaps.

"Thank you."

"If you're dead, how come you snore? It's annoying."

Washington grunts.

"You want breakfast?" she asks.

"I'll cook."

"No, I'll cook. I can't stand to see you clambering around in my kitchen like some kind of monkey."

"You think I like seeing you cooking eggs over hellfire?"

"It's not hellfire. It's perfectly natural."

Washington grunts and heads for the bathroom.

She has food ready when he emerges. "Here's your damned paper," she hisses, flinging it at his head.

He reaches up and takes it. "Thank you."

He hauls himself up to the chair, unfolds the business section. She eyeballs the paper resentfully.

"If you scorch a hole in NASDAQ again I'll put you over my knee."

"What knee?"

They eat. "Hurry up," she says. "I have to leave soon."

"Afraid if you leave me here alone I'll steal the stereo?"

"Fuck you."

Munch, munch. "Have we any more toast?" asks Washington. Scrape. Bang, clatter clatter. Whoosh. Slam. "Thank you, Maggie-Sue."

"I suppose you'll want to come by again tonight."

"Not particularly."

"Good. I have things to do."

"Me too."

Munch munch. Washington mops up egg with toast, finishes the paper, glances at his watch. "Have to open up soon. See you later."

She points at the door. Slam. She hurls dishes into the sink.

.   .   .

"Ja?"

"You know me."

"Hallo?"

"I have a name for your friend."

"You've been reading Vachss again, haven't you, Rider? Go ahead."

"Heh. I guess wiretaps aren't high on the list of things we have to worry about, eh? The clown in question is named James Evingine; foster father of one Jennifer Will." Reads off an address.

"What's the trouble?"

"Child abuse."

"Drop in the ocean, then. He probably won't even bother."

"Yeah, I know."

"And this is a bad time to ask him to work."

"I know, Kris."

"Did you know her?"

"She was in the burn ward at SF General, that's all."

"You *have* been reading Vachss."

"Look, you want to tell him, or not?"

"I'll blind-drop it, but I don't know when he'll pick it up. Maybe tomorrow."

"Thanks, Kris. Keep an eye on him."

"Ha. Talk to you."

"Bye."

Click.

. . .

Max Sturgeon's job is to watch over electronic security for the Treasure Island Naval Station. Sturgeon walks with an emission patrol, sniffing the ether for unauthorized transmissions.

He strolls along, feeling the wind on his face. Perfectly ordinarily day; no leviathans rising from the water, no haruspecoid mutants.

The Bay Area is a land of microclimates and sudden change. Today, on Treasure Island, the sky is tropical as the Caribbean and the ocean seems to go on forever. But in a few hours, the sun will touch horizon and it's the North Sea, bone-cutting fog and cold enough to kill. And thus, Sturgeon wonders about his double life.

Chloe and Whitlomb tell him that things simply are not as they seem—there are monsters and demons and undead all around, and always have been. But if you can't see it, it has a hard time giving a damn about you. So humanity evolved a selective inability to comprehend certain things. Some people can "open their third eye" and watch all the goofy things actually going on, but this is dangerous as hell. On the other hand, they can do things that others can't, like shoot scorpions out of their navels.

Sturgeon was nonplussed to learn that "natural" deaths are nothing of the sort. And he can't vacation in San Diego anymore.

His companions' insistence on describing things in mystical terms annoys him. Totems and souls and spirits and Tibetan eschatology and gods—phooey. His pet theory is that there is a parallel universe that leaks over every now and then. When Sturgeon advanced it, Whitlomb pinched his nose and said it was as good an explanation as any.

Still, dollars aren't much of an issue anymore. Sometimes he feels guilty about all the counterfeit he throws around. But according to Arbeiter it's all Monopoly money anyway; the things that honestly are scarce can't be bought with currency. All in all, being aware of things as they really are is a good deal.

When a K-9 rushes at him and Sturgeon pitches into the drink with teeth sunk into his calf, he changes his mind. He has time to think, "Well, *this* isn't supposed to happen to the leaders," before the water closes over his head.

. . .

Washington blinks. The first joint of his left hand's ring finger burns. He scurries into the back and opens a floor safe. There are seven small bundles of herbs and dried blood. Washington takes five and throws them into a brazier, following up with a squirt of lighter fluid and a match.

Chloe knocks over her chair. Arbeiter spills coffee onto a painting. Maggie-Sue sets her Rolodex on fire. Whitlomb drops a three-thousand-year-old tablet. Rider fumbles a microgram of cancer and an innocent flea bloats with sudden tumors. Many feet pound pavement.

Arbeiter ties off, injects a savage substance into his veins. The world becomes slow and rectilinear—headlights appear square, trees are twisting nests of jagged green lightning bolts. He makes sure he has the antidote and burns off toward the Bay Bridge at well over a hundred miles an hour. Weaves through traffic. He curses as he goes; probably another false alarm. On the other hand, the system saved his thymus, once, so he really can't complain. It almost makes up for the irritation of the constant drills where everybody makes for some arbitrary point on the map. Switches on his throat mike. "Status?"

"Washington here; Sturgeon down on Treasure Island. Chloe, Whitlomb, and Rider are en route. I'm eastbound, but won't be there any time soon. Maggie-Sue is fifteen minutes out."

"Okay. I'll do a recon, then. Just reached the Treasure Island off-ramp." He slows to the base speed limit—shore police are not people he wants to argue with. Soon enough, he reaches the pierlet and sees forms thrashing in the water. "Looks like a thin dog—the SPs pretty much have it under control, they're getting him out of the water."

"Joe, this is Chloe. I've got trouble. Westbound on the Bay Bridge, and there's a whole pack of dogs behind me, maybe ten. They're following and sixty miles an hour is too fast to be natural."

"Those aren't dogs; those are thin dogs. Don't turn off at Treasure Island. Make for Rider's. Rider, Whitlomb, go back to the loft and get ready."

"Rider here, I copy."

"Whitlomb?"

"Loaded for bear; be at Al's in a moment."

"Arbeiter here, Sturgeon's on land, bleeding, they're working on his leg—oh, shit. Thin dog pack, fifty meters." They hear gunshots and the sound of an engine.

> (From the San Diego Institute of Necromancy Cookbook: THIN DOG: Take one dog. Feed for three months on human flesh. Eviscerate with bone knife; loop intestines around neck as beast perishes. Insert subdermal armor, if desired. Stuff with mastiff pelt and powdered wolf teeth. Bake at 200 degrees and zero humidity, basting regularly with fresh blood and rosemary, for seven days or until the hide is flaky and brittle to the touch. Reanimate under open sky when Sirius is above horizon. Slaughters four, or more if your enemies are weak. Keep away from salt.)

Arbeiter points the fairing of his BMW at the center of the pack; pops a wheelie as he accelerates and draws a sawed-off shotgun. The SPs are confused. The dog that knocked Sturgeon into the water has bitten all half-dozen of them; two are holding it down as a third empties a magazine of bullets into its head. That slows it down a little. They start stomping on it; that works better.

Arbeiter whoops as he arrows for the pack. In a half instant he sees the lead dog brace and turn its head to bite his tire—notices metal teeth aglint. Realizes that he is going to need a new tire and, in all likelihood, Extreme Unction. Forces himself to bail off the bike as it mashes to a halt. One of his gloves comes off as he rolls down the pavement and soon his left hand is a sponge of road rash. Loses the shotgun. Watches the world spin and listens to his brains bounce off the sides of his skull. Wonders where the first bite will come.

Sturgeon recovers consciousness in time to hear an SP screaming with his last breath. Sturgeon is close enough to death for his third eye to have come open; he can hear the hoarse, dustthroat barking as the pack circles, planning the charge. He notices Valkyries riding overhead but he's pretty sure that's just a conventional hallucination.

. . .

Meanwhile, in San Francisco proper, Rider is shouting obscenities as he counts his dog skulls—six. Well, it's a start. Carries the box downstairs, runs outside, slashes his palm with his bone knife, and drips blood over the skulls, chanting like a lunatic.

"Whitlomb to Rider, I'm five blocks out—"

"Rider, this is Chloe, I'm a block away. Should I stop, or go by and have you guys take 'em out as they follow?"

Rider can't answer either of them—he's busy screaming in a polyglot of Tibetan, Sumerian, and Haitian. Sees Chloe drift around the corner and zoom toward him. And skidding behind her Toyota, ten nightmares.

. . .

Back on Treasure Island, Arbeiter manages to sit up, and wonders where the dogs are. Turns—sees them circling the SPs. They've managed to pepper one to fragments; the others are jumping and dodging around to spoil their aim. The SPs will soon run out of ammunition. Arbeiter hobbles toward his shotgun, dripping blood from his hand.

. . .

Rider grins as Chloe blasts past. The dogs are dead, not stupid—to one with an open third eye, Rider's staff is a beacon shouting I AM BEING HELD BY A VERY PISSED MAGE. Threat management dictates they rip his throat out.

. . .

Arbeiter has his shotgun. The SPs are down to truncheons. The dogs are making darting passes. An SP loses his calf and bleeds profusely. Arbeiter raises his helmet's visor. "Yoo hoo, puppy dogs!"

One turns and looks at him. Mummified dog faces don't have much expression, but this one seems to say, "I'll be happy to tear your kidneys out as soon as I get a chance, but I'll have to get back to you on it." Arbeiter points the shotgun at the thing's face and pulls the trigger.

Lead does not vomit from the bores. Nor silver. The beast gets a load of rock salt. It cocks its head at him, shrugs, and goes back to circling. Arbeiter pumps the action.

．　■　■

Rider waves his staff around. The dogs bark at him. He barks back. They snarl and charge. Rider crushes a dog skull with his bleeding hand. The lead dog's skull collapses into dust. The body runs a little farther and disassembles into a jumble of ancient hide and brittle bones. Rider crushes another skull. Wonders vaguely what he'll do when he runs out.

■　■　■

Arbeiter shoots another dog. Another SP is down.

■　■　■

Rider runs out of skulls.

■　■　■

One of the dogs circling Sturgeon stops in its tracks, cocks its head. Wanders off. The other dogs bark at it. The dog trots to a tree and sits. Scratches a flea. Jumps as it hears bone scrape on leathery hide. Stares at its foot. Remembers having a glossy coat, chasing Frisbees, getting its hair brushed. Wags its tail; hears vertebrae grind against each other. Cranes its head back and studies its hindquarters.

Tibetan salt works much faster on reanimated humans; humans can think and remember faster. It rarely takes more than a second for a human zombie to realize what it is and how much it has lost. Humans also have hands and can use tools, so it is very seldom one sees a human zombie trying to end its suddenly unbearable existence by biting itself to pieces.

■　■　■

Rider decides to try blind panic—turns and runs screaming. There is an Oldsmobile coming fast down the street. Rider makes a complicated set of gestures intended to inquire if Whitlomb might be able to do something about the creatures behind him. Whitlomb has seen Rider panic before, so he gets the gist of the question. Whitlomb has one of the only Oldsmobiles in San Francisco with a gun rack. Extreme terror gets Rider around and behind the car as it skids to a halt and Whitlomb jumps out with a very large rifle.

· · ·

The dogs have figured out that Arbeiter is doing something bad to them. Two peel off and rush him. He catches one point-blank before the other bodyslams. Arbeiter goes down. His helmet is too massive for the creature to rip out his throat, so it bites his arm right through the leather and Arbeiter can feel teeth scratching deep grooves into his bone.

About then Maggie-Sue's tornado reaches from the sky and pulls the dog into pieces. From it leaps a white-haired black man, about three foot eight. Fifty kilograms of dehydrated Rottweiler figures this should be easy enough to deal with; jumps for the throat. Washington does something complicated and fast, the sort of thing Bruce Lee used to do, and the dog's head goes in one direction and the body in the other.

Four thin dogs rush Whitlomb, who knows that most people use Tibetan salt to dispatch zombies. He prefers the direct approach. His father's estate provided him with a Holland & Holland Nitro Express. Dad used it to kill elephants. It has two barrels. Two extremely loud noises occur. There are only two dogs remaining. They look at each other in consternation. Chloe's Toyota blindsides one and skids in a perfect bootlegger's reverse as Rider recovers from his panic and charges the last infernal canine, waving his staff.

· · ·

The jaws are still locked on Arbeiter's arm, but the rest of the dog has been scattered by the four winds. He pries the skull loose, watching a pine tree climb right up out of the ground, leap onto a dog, and hypocotylate the devilment out of it. Another is dragged howling into the bay by ropes of seaweed. "If I know Maggie-Sue," he thinks, "that one over there is about to—"

Big noise. Burning bits of fur and bone rain down over a surprisingly large area. The last dog's charge at Washington is redirected into a power-slam into the asphalt. One moment, an implacable revenant pit bull; the next, a mere sack of powdered bone.

.   .   .

Whitlomb's engine is still running. As the dog leaps for Rider, he points his finger at the engine block and his staff at the dog. It lands, and tries to figure out why the world seems to be spinning at several thousand rpm. Rider two-hands his staff across its back. The dog is no longer wondering about much of anything.

The people of Sturgeon's cell begin panting and wondering if anybody noticed.

.   .   .

The one surviving SP, though uninjured, goes into shock—a common occurrence when the occult attacks one with a closed third eye. The SP's brain literally cannot hold the idea that a pack of undead hounds ripped great holes in his friends' flesh, so within minutes he is forgetting everything. All the base commander knows is that much gunfire occurred, and his men are down with terrible wounds and amnesia. Sturgeon has been through this before; he feigns confusion. He uses the SP as a model.

And when the questioning gets too intense, Sturgeon holds a zombie dog skull before his interrogator. Bits of the enchantment remain; the jaw works, the sockets track the officer's throat without the benefit of eyes. The questioner's mind cannot hold what his senses are trying to tell him, so he gets very uncomfortable and changes the subject. Every now and then, he manages to write down something like "Zombie dogs," but then crosses it out as clearly impossible. Sturgeon's military record has a lot of strange holes in it.

.   .   .

Washington's car—a Pontiac specially modified to accommodate a three-foot-eight driver—is parked in the base lot. He drives Maggie-Sue and Arbeiter to Rider's loft; Arbeiter mourning his beloved motorcycle, Maggie-Sue in the backseat with him lavaging the awful wounds in his arm. Washington looks over his shoulder. "Careful with that. You get my upholstery wet, I'll take it out of your hide."

"Fuck your upholstery," hisses Maggie-Sue.

Arbeiter checks his bandoleer. "A pity regular table salt doesn't work," he mutters. "This cost me a fortune."

Washington gets Rider on the radio. "Rider, we'll need somebody to Jedi Mind Trick Sturgeon loose."

"Who'd you have in mind?"

"You and Whitlomb. Tell him to arm heavy. Wait until we get there before you leave."

The "Jedi Mind Trick" is a somewhat more sophisticated version of waving a zombie dog skull in someone's face. Rider and Whitlomb take the Olds to the hospital.

"Maxwell Sturgeon?"

"Room 302. You'll have to wait, though; he's talking to his commander and the doctor just now."

"Thanks." They head for Room 302.

"Sir, you can't go in there."

Rider sighs. Takes the H. R. Giger folio from under his arm. Chants in Sumerian and takes two monstrous faces from the pages, drapes one on Whitlomb and one on himself. Turns around. "Boo."

The nurse's eyes bug out—and then humanity's survival trait cuts in. She no longer perceives them, doesn't even know they were ever there.

They walk to Room 302. "Al, do you feel like making a late birthday present of one of those? I would benefit from an infallible way to sneak out of seminars."

"In a day or two I can make one that's semipermanent, but will fade eventually. Is that good enough? Okay, I'll get on it when I get a chance. Here we are." Rider takes off the faces and they walk in. "Hi guys!"

The doctor and officer turn. "Who the hell are you?"

"We're here to take Max home."

"You can't do that."

Rider puts on the face. Takes it off.

"Who the hell are you?"

"We're here to take Max home."

"You can't do that."

Rider puts on the face. Takes it off.

"Who the hell are you?"

"We're here to take Max home."

"You can't do that."

Face on. Face off.

"Who the hell are you?"

This goes on for about fifteen minutes.

"Who the hell are you?"

"We're here to take Max home."

Operant conditioning has set in. The officer and the doctor know (subconsciously, at least) that arguing will attract the attention of an unholy monstrosity that'd as soon convert them to blood sausage as chat. Something has to give.

"Oh, you're here to take Max home."

"Yes. You're done debriefing him and he's well enough to leave the hospital."

"Well . . . we're done debriefing him, and he's well enough to leave the hospital."

"The whole situation isn't worth investigating any further."

"I don't think we need to investigate this situation any further."

"These aren't the droids you're looking for."

"These aren't the droids we're looking for."

"Move along."

"Move along."

They fetch a wheelchair and roll Sturgeon down to the car. "Thanks, guys."

"No problem," says Rider.

"Are you sure I'm well enough to leave the hospital?"

Whitlomb scratches under his right ear. "In point of fact . . . you're not quite well enough to be discharged from the hospital, no. Your leg is rather awful and the bone is damaged."

"Ah. So, why am I leaving the hospital?"

"At a minimum, we must remove you to a location safe from the depredations of occult assassins, such as nocturnal stranglers."

"What's a nocturnal strangler?"

"Al?"

Rider frowns. "Well, it comes in the night, and it strangles people."

"That much I figured out."

"Nobody knows any more than that."

"Do I want to know why?"

"You can figure it out, if you decide you *do* want to know."

"Ah." Sturgeon looks nervously at the western horizon.

"Besides, with a thin-dog bite, there's probably a bunch of occult germs in you, too. Mummy's Curse and necrosepticemia at the least. If we left you there, you'd probably die."

"Oh."

. . .

They regroup at Rider's flat. "Al, I can't believe you don't have any lady threefinger," says Chloe. "I can't be much of an occult medic without something to be occult with, can I?"

"For the last time, I never heard of it," says Rider. "Are you sure it's not just some stupid geoduck name for oregano or something?"

"Come on. Everybody knows what lady threefinger is."

Rider looks appealingly at Washington. "Joe, tell her she's crazy."

Washington grunts, "She's not crazy. Now, Maggie-Sue, she's crazy."

"Fuck you," snaps Maggie-Sue.

"Business as usual," sighs Arbeiter.

Chloe rolls her eyes. "Joe, you do mean you *have* heard of lady threefinger, right?"

Washington nods.

"Well?"

"Some folks call it eucalyptus."

"Oh, really? I always wondered where it came from."

"My God," says Arbeiter. "Sturgeon is sitting there with his leg half bitten off and I'm checking out the scrimshaw on my radius and you're mixing cough syrup?"

Chloe snaps, "I suppose you'd rather put on your mad-scientist hat? I'm sure you and Rider could go find somebody who's just going to die soon anyway."

"Gentlemen. Ladies," says Whitlomb.

Everybody glares at everybody else. Everybody drops their eyes. Finally, Rider gets up. "You need the seeds, the leaves, what?"

"The root," says Chloe.

"Oh. So you want me to go dig up a eucalyptus tree in the middle of the night. No problem. Anybody seen my bulldozer? I had it here a minute ago."

Maggie-Sue stands up. "Shut the fuck up, Rider. How much do you need?"

Chloe rocks her hand from side to side. "About half a kilo."

Sturgeon says, "Perry, you want to go with her?"

Whitlomb stands and says, "I would be delighted." In the movies, people show their willingness to kill by pumping their shotguns, thus chambering a shell. Whitlomb doesn't do that. He did it when he got Washington's call. And he replaced the round in the magazine besides—you never know when that one extra shot might be your last chance.

They leave. And as they drive off in search of a eucalyptus tree, Whitlomb says, "You know, it's remarkable how much anxious squabbling we do when we're all wrought with concern."

"I wasn't squabbling. Fuck you."

Whitlomb sighs. "On the other hand," he thinks, "perhaps we're simply unpleasant people to be around, to a man."

.   .   .

"Thanks, Maggie-Sue," says Chloe.

Maggie-Sue jerks her head up, then down. "Good thing we have a *real* mage to fall back on," she snips.

Rider says, "I know this is Maggie-Sue's line, but still: Fuck you." Chloe heads for the workroom. Rider paces a little. "Max, don't wiggle around so much. Just because I took the pain out of your leg doesn't mean you should move it."

"Yessir."

Rider grunts. "Anybody else want a beer? Besides Arbeiter, that is."

"Yo."

Rider fetches beers. Paces.

"Sit down, Al."

Rider grunts. Goes to the doorway of the workroom. "Hey, Chloe, you need some help in there?"

"No, I'm good."

Arbeiter says, "For heaven's sake, give him some stuff to grind up or something; I'm getting exhausted just watching him."

Chloe laughs, and calls, "No, there's nothing left to do but wait for the essential oils to soak out of the glubu-wort, and then mix it with everything else."

"Glubu-wort?" asks Al.

"Oregano," says Washington.

"It is *not!*"

Rider goes into the workroom. "You need the oil to come out of those nuts, there?"

"Yeah."

Rider goes into the kitchen and grabs a can of peanuts and a bottle of cooking oil. Returns, and mixes them in a beaker. Raves in Sumerian. Pours off the oil. The oil oozes out of the glubu-wort.

"Hey, that's neat."

"Yeah. I think of all the time I spent in San Bernardino learning synesthetic magic, but sometimes I think I should've just stuck with ol' boring thaumaturgy."

"Hmn. Yeah, but you wouldn't be able to make such pretty stuff."

"Pretty? *Pretty?* My sculptures are not *pretty.*"

"Oh, you. Hey, I never looked at your hand. How is it?"

"Stings a bit."

"Why didn't you pull out the pain?"

"If you do that with your hand, you use the hand too much, and it never heals."

"You should cut your arm instead."

"That spell, it doesn't work unless you use your hand. Getting all the bits of bone out afterward is a bitch if you try to do it manually."

"Hmn. Hand me that spatula, there? Thanks. This'll just take a minute."

"Okay."

"You mind if I ask you a question?" says Chloe.

"Shoot," says Rider.

"That thing out in the living room, by your bookcase? Made out of ripples in coffee?"

"Yeah?"

"Is that . . . is that a real thing, or something you imagined?"

"It's not a real thing."

"Whew. That's a load off. I'd hate to ever run into one in a dark alley. It's beautiful, though."

"Thanks . . . I made that one right after I met Perry—you remember, when he brought me into the Van Helsing Society? She had that sort of terrible beauty you always read about, in the Romantic authors. I'd planned to make a straight sculpture of her, but that's not what ended up happening."

"I know what you mean."

"Yeah. Look, Chloe?"

"Yes?"

"This stuff you're mixing up? If they've got what people might get when a zombie reaches bone, how much is it going to help?"

"About as much as two good doses of chicken soup, Al. Kris's pills and Joe's voodoo might be enough to halt it; if not, all this'll do is slow it down a little."

"So we may have to strike a deal with somebody."

"I don't walk in the same circles you do, Al. The idea scares me."

"Chloe, the more you know about them, the more scared you get."

. . .

Chloe finishes up. Back in the living room, Sturgeon and Arbeiter choke down the resulting vials despite their reek of Satan's own cough drops.

"I think it's about time for a strategy meeting, gang," says Sturgeon.

"Good idea," says Whitlomb.

"Let's deal with the obvious first. Kris and I are messed up."

"You're not hurt that bad. I can take care of you," says Maggie-Sue.

"Of course, if you make a mistake, we'll have to be put down," says Arbeiter.

Maggie-Sue glares.

"Maggie-Sue's right," says Rider. "You'll heal. The only reason to be worried is occult infection. Kris, Chloe, and Joe have done what they can; it should be enough. You won't be out of danger for another few days, though."

"Fair enough," says Sturgeon. "Second. We're dealing with somebody who can sic two dozen thin dogs on us. Necromancers?"

"Maybe," says Chloe. "But they attacked just the two of us, after we showed our faces at that hospice."

"That is cause for hope," says Whitlomb. "Perhaps they believe the threat to consist of Chloe and Max alone."

"They may well have. But by now," says Sturgeon, "they know better. We all fought back. They know how tough we are and how many of us there are; we put all our cards on the table."

"Not all our cards," says Rider. Everybody looks down, then at Arbeiter.

Arbeiter shrugs. "Creedon Thiebaud is just a person, like any of us. You seem to think he's some sort of irresistible natural force—you don't even use his name, just like you wouldn't say the name of a demon without a pentagram around you. It's ridiculous. And the voices in his head should taper off in at most a day or two."

. . .

Just about the time Arbeiter makes this speech, a spidery hand is running itself over the bed of one Jennifer Will. It moves through the room, fingering clothing, a bigletter looped diary, a stuffed panda.

He moves into the hall. He touches doorknobs. Into the kitchen—he sifts silently through trash. Finds cigarette butts. Fingers them. Back to the hall. He eases open a bedroom door.

A man sits up with a start. Looks around the room. Reaches for the lamp. Hits the switch—nothing. Scrabbles on the bedside table.

A light flares in the room. The man sees his cigarette lighter in a gloved hand. There is a disembodied elongated face above it. Two eyes over streaks of tears. The hand moves—the light goes out. The man doesn't quite have time to scream.

■ ■ ■

Midnight. Rider's loft doesn't look like it can sleep six guests in comfort. Nor can it. One would expect bickering in the bathrooms, curses over morning coffee. The first time everybody holed up there, such things did occur. This time, each sleeps better for hearing the others' breathing.

Whitlomb is on watch; Arbeiter just handed off the night-vision goggles and stumbled to his cot. Whitlomb is reminded of the Second World War, somehow—bodies packed together in the Underground over floors of concrete, the enemy circling overhead. Not that he was in London at the time. He lied about his age and island-hopped through the Pacific in early 1945. When he saw the movie Iwo Jima, years later, he hurled his Coke at the screen and stormed out. It wasn't like that.

Arbeiter can joke about the things he's seen, laugh at the way the dogs jerked and rattled and clicked as they lunged. Whitlomb doesn't want to shut his eyes for fear he'll see them again. "This nonsense is unacceptable at my time of life," he thinks. "Would that I'd never learned to open my third eye."

He knows he doesn't mean it. Remembers when his eccentric old friend Erik Johanson came out of the fog like a dervish, hurling holy water and Latin curses, wrestling with the woman who'd promised eternal life. Remembers being sent to San Francisco to bring Rider into the Society; remembers Maggie-Sue with flames pouring off her body, immolating vampires with bear hugs. Remembers his bout of necromalaria, Arbeiter preparing leaves that Chloe laid on his brow in his delirium. Remembers Joe Washington's lips on his skin as he sucked poisons out of his body.

Pericles Whitlomb straightens his back, sits like a lion and sweeps his eyes over these people young enough to be his children, or maybe even his grandchildren. Cradles his father's elephant gun. If Satan himself rose from the pit of Hell to take them, he would have to step over Whitlomb's dead body to do it.

· · ·

Sunrise comes and goes; people rise and shower in shifts. Rider's water heater could boil the snows of Yellowstone—and, in fact, operates on the same general principles. Around ten, Maggie-Sue shoves Rider out of his kitchen and makes breakfast with much clattering of pans and banging of dishes. Stomps downstairs to fetch the paper, guns it at Washington's head. He wakes up in time to catch it—flips it open and barricades himself behind the front page.

After she does the dishes, she slaps a test-tube rack on the table. It holds eight samples. Two are blood-red. The other six are sickly yellow.

Arbeiter frowns, adjusts his octagonal-frame glasses. "Is that a test for what I think it is?"

She nods.

Sturgeon puffs his cheeks. Addresses a pixie's face framed by short, dark hair, a bearded nebbish with a failing grin, a tanned elderly gentleman with a shock of white hair, a pinch-faced frowning blonde, a handsome German with a haircut that Dr. Strangelove would envy, and the business section. "Bad news. But I seem to recall that test is prone to false positives."

"Control negative. Our five negative," bites Maggie-Sue.

"Still, exposure is not necessarily infection. Suggestions for who does what today?" says Sturgeon.

The business section rattles. "Trip to Haiti. Only question is, who goes?"

"Well, you'd better take me, to keep your ugly black ass out of trouble."

"Don't need you for this, Maggie-Sue. Stay here and keep your eye on the other blancs."

"I don't think that's what we need," says Sturgeon. "I know the Haitians practice necromancy, but it's not the style we need."

"Maybe. Maybe not. But loa, at least, we can trust."

"Look," says Arbeiter, "the only question is how far we go. Now, I'm not saying Texas is the right answer, and if it is, it's still a bad idea 'cause once they get their hooks into you, it's a long time before you can get free. But we should consider it."

Chloe shudders. "If we need to go that far, are you ready to do it?"

Arbeiter shrugs. "Not for me, no. But better one of us makes it."

"Eh?" says Sturgeon.

"Well, if we're looking at extreme measures, one solution is to simply find an immune-system donor. We don't want to take down somebody else. But I cut up enough people for spare parts in my day. Only karma that be the way I go. I may not have enough antibodies to fight off the infection in myself, but take them out and pump them into Max—"

"Absolutely not!" shouts Sturgeon. His mustache bristles; his shoulders are squared.

"If it was Chloe or Whitlomb or anybody else but you, would you say the same thing? Got a martyr complex, want to die?"

"Martyr? You stupid fool, you're the one talking about being butchered!"

"Only fair."

Deep, dark silence.

Maggie-Sue reaches across the table, takes Arbeiter's chin in her hand. Glares into his eyes. "Fuck you."

"I concur," says Whitlomb.

"Ditto." Washington.

"Hear, hear." Chloe.

"I don't know, pretty little face like that, look kinda sexy bolted onto some bloated plutocrat," grins Rider. "Sure, let's cut our losses. Shucks, we can do it six more times after this! It's not *that* much blood to have on your hands in the Bardo!"

"You jackasses. What else are you going to do? Haiti doesn't have the throw. You going to send Rider down south? Bungling incompetent like him, they'd have his blood out of him the minute he got off the plane."

"Correct in one respect, Mr. Arbeiter."

Goose pimples appear on arms. Sturgeon turns, careful not to make any sudden moves. Creedon Thiebaud is seated at the breakfast bar, watching a spider crawl up the wall. Then he is in the eighth chair at the table—still watching the spider.

"May I ask a favor?" he murmurs.

"Er . . . what can we do for you?" says Sturgeon.

"Have we any more toast?"

． ． ．

Maggie-Sue jerks to her feet like an automaton, fumbles the bread out of the wrapper. Drops a slice. The air catches it. Lifts two more slices up; glares at them. Slathers on butter—swish-slash with a knife; onto a plate. She sets it before Thiebaud—gently.

He's not much to look at, really. Gray overcoat, broad-brimmed gray hat, long face. Except people can never quite remember what color his eyes are. They're gray in photographs, for what little that's worth.

He picks up a triangle of rye toast and nods at Arbeiter. "This morning I woke from a nightmare. I foresaw Mr. Rider exiting an American Airways 727. The karma detectors revealed his nature, and he was torn limb from limb." Crunch.

"So I'll take United," says Rider, weakly.

"Mr. Rider, I must advise you against flying to San Diego."

"Terrific."

"We will take the train."

"Okay, the train, fine, that ma—wait a minute. Did you just say 'we'?" Crunch.

"Now, just jump right in and let me know if I'm wrong; but thirsty as they are for *mage's* blood, aren't they, oh, say, maybe a little more interested in *yours*? You've got DNA sequences that'd make an alchemist cream in his jeans, no pun intended, ha ha. Eh? Look at me. Hey, Creedon—"

Thiebaud is standing, examining a cloudscape made of the scent of thunder, ruminatively chewing his toast.

Rider shakes his head. "He can't be serious, Max."

Sturgeon says, "You ever know him to make a wisecrack without killing all the witnesses afterward?"

"What's wrong, Al?" says Chloe. "Scared to sleep in the same compartment with him?"

Rider snorts. "I'm scared to sleep in the same *state* with him."

Thiebaud says, "I will withdraw my offer if you like, Mr. Rider."

"I was being facetious, Creedon. Humor, you know, jokes? The things that Maggie-Sue doesn't understand?"

"Fuck you," mutters Maggie-Sue.

"Hey, Sturgeon, you have a headache, or is it just me?" says Arbeiter.

Rider clears his throat loudly. "Look, blazehead, what's is going on here?"

Creedon Thiebaud takes a black frying pan from the nail on the kitchen wall, runs his fingers over it while people try to remember when he went around the breakfast bar. He scratches the cast iron with a fingernail; sniffs the scratch. "Mr. Sturgeon and Mr. Arbeiter will become ill soon."

Arbeiter breaks in. "So let's the two of us go down, ja? It'll be just like the yard. Watching each other's back?" There is something wrong with Arbeiter's voice. Tight, like he's tense. Real tense. People look at him.

Sturgeon's glass of orange juice shatters in his hand.

"Oh, no," says Chloe. "It's—"

"*Necroclostridium oedipia*—" gapes Whitlomb as Arbeiter pitches out of his chair.

"Lockjaw of Doom," finishes Washington, catching Sturgeon as he goes into convulsions.

Maggie-Sue's needle flickers as she injects massive doses of curare. She hisses. Sturgeon and Arbeiter's chests begin rising and falling in a precise rhythm. They foul themselves as all their muscles, voluntary and involuntary, relax. The alternative is having them contract until they tear themselves from the bone.

"I guess we're going to San Diego," murmurs Rider.

· · ·

"Well, this is a fine how'd-you-do," Chloe flares. "You planning to wear the same set of shorts for the next two weeks?"

"It won't take that long."

"It might."

"It's Lockjaw of Doom. There won't be any point in staying any longer than a week."

"So pack at least a little bag of clothes, huh?"

"Chill the sorority-den-mother act, will you? I need the space for my stuff. I'm going to burn any clothing I wear down there, anyway."

"It's not that bad. My father says the Opposition consistently exaggerates how dangerous San Diego is."

"Then you inherited your fucking naïveté from him." Slam. Stomp. Stomp. "Hey, Lamont Cranston, let's get it in gear, eh?"

"The Shadow used .45s, Mr. Rider," whispers Thiebaud into his ear.

"Jesus, Creedon, don't do that. Come on, we've got a train to catch."

"You recall, of course, the meaning Mr. Freud ascribed to the symbolism of missing a train?"

"Creedon, if you think it's apropos and worth remembering, I don't want it in my head."

■   ■   ■

The conductor has four arms. Their fellow passengers on the San Diego Express are quite beyond description. The injections looted from Arbeiter's gear have given Thiebaud and Rider the delicate waxy complexion of the newly embalmed. They sit woodenly across from each other and practice blank stares. A cigarette girl pulses down the aisle to them, swaying. "Candy? Cigarettes? Sushi?"

Rider turns unfocused eyes her way. "One . . . tray . . . sushi . . . please. . . ."

"Five-fifty trade units, please."

"Do . . . you . . . have . . . change . . . for . . . a . . . mage's . . . penis . . . ?"

"Let me check. . . . Er, do you have anything smaller?"

"Lawyer's . . . heart . . . ?"

"Tee hee."

"How . . . about . . . the . . . preserved . . . gall . . . bladder . . . of . . . a . . . water . . . demon . . . ?"

"Sounds good . . . and two grams of malignant uterine whale tumor is your change. Thank you!"

"Thank . . . you . . ." The cigarette girl slithers away, leaving a faintly luminous trail of slime.

· ■ ·

They collect their baggage, step into the famed San Diego sunlight. Rider's eyes try to crawl into the damp cool of his brain. He pries open his lids about the time the smog starts spraying graffiti onto the inner side of his breastbone. Recovers from that—is hit with a wall of Muzak. "Whargh," he says.

A concerned porter slips his tentacle around Rider's shoulders. "You all right, sir?"

"Just . . . fine. . . . Good . . . to . . . be . . . home . . ."

"You sure? You looked awfully healthy, for a minute there. . . . Course, a lotta folks comin' off that train look shook up. Frisco does that to a fella. Maggot?"

"No . . . thank . . . you . . . I . . . ate . . . on . . . the . . . train. . . ."

· ■ ·

"Look, Maggie-Sue. Ever seen clumping like that?"

"Joseph Moses, you stop fucking around and tell me what it means."

"Things are getting weird."

"They're in San Diego. Of course things are getting weird."

"No. I mean weird."

· ■ ·

"Alexander! Alexander Rider!"

This, thinks Rider, *has got to be the* SHORTEST *undercover mission ever undertaken by a journeyman synesthetic mage. Let's see, four days in a swoon, hold on to the moment of perfection like a rolling needle balanced on a thread; if that doesn't work, I come awake in the Bardo and head for the bright scary lights, not the dim ones. . . .*

"Alexander, over here! Over here!"

Of all the times to run into an old flame . . . Maybe Creedon will have time to shoot me. Well, may as well turn around and look my death in the face.

"Oh, Alexander! Are you *dead*?"

Not yet. Soon. "Hello . . . Janet. . . . Small . . . world . . ." *Where the hell did Creedon go off to? Did they get him already?*

.   .   .

Thin horses speed the hearse along the way; *Todten reite schnell* and all that. Rider is grateful for the padding of the coffin, although he gags occasionally from the funk of the last passenger.

A ghost oozes in through the crack of the lid. "Hello, traveler."

"Hello."

"Do you happen to bear the quivering heart of a fellow yclept Johan Groth?"

" 'Fraid not."

"More's the pity. That's all I need to free my tortured spirit from this earth and go on to the afterlife, you see."

"Ah."

"Look, if you run across it, could you bring it by this stretch of the road? I'd appreciate it very much."

"How do you spell that last name?"

"G-R-O-T-H."

"I'll keep it in mind."

"Thanks awfully. Oh, and would you mind if I possessed you and sought my bloody revenge?"

"Sorry."

"Oh, no, not at all. Perhaps next time."

"Okay."

"Well, then, I'll be off. The best of luck to you on your journey, sir!"

"Yours, too."

.   .   .

Rider opens the coffin and carefully plummets to the blood-soaked earth. He'd much rather have eased down, but zombies aren't known for agility. He

stands and clomps behind Janet toward her house. The door yawns open and
Rider steps onto the house's tongue, is drawn within. He is extremely grateful
for the ten milligrams of Valium he downed in the coffin. Blood drips from
his nose as he surveys the interior—hide wallpaper, cage of bones confining
a mummified winged lizard, girlhair couch. "Homey," he says.

"You like it? I had Yawson's Interior Decorating and Abattoir do it. I
think it's just provincial enough to keep from being a slave to fashion, don't
you?"

Rider allows as it is.

"So what brings you down here after all these years?"

Rider has considered and discarded numerous tissues of lies, looking for
one with enough truth in it to confuse the dickens out of all concerned. Fo-
cuses his eyes and grins. "Well, Janet, it's pretty complicated."

She gapes. "Alexander . . . You're not dead after all!"

"No, I'm not. And therein lies a story. You have any bourbon?"

"Sure! You know I own stock in Old Liver Plasma! They ship it to me by
the cask!"

Mistake. "Oops, don't get up; I forgot, I have a bottle right here in my
bag!" Fortunately, Rider was clever enough to pour Wild Turkey 101 into an
Old Liver Plasma bottle and carefully reclose it. He strips the seal (made
from the finest coffin lead), yanks the cork with his teeth, and takes a heroic
slug. "Well, you remember the circumstances under which we parted."

"That's a sweet way to refer to my scraping you off my leg with a tire
iron."

"My passion for you burned in my breast for many moons."

"Was that when you mailed me those letters with all the subtle references
to suicide?"

"I became angry with you."

"Hence the bomb threat."

"I decided to get even with you."

"Hence the bomb. I had an awful time getting matching eyes the right
color after that. I must admit I'm still a little peeved."

"No, that wasn't it."

"What?"

"I did that . . . but that was an act of passion. No, I decided to do something that would rankle for a long, long time."

"Alexander . . . you didn't volunteer for the Democrats, did you?"

"That, too. No, I did . . . something . . . Janet, it's been so long since we were together, I can remember like it was yesterday, but still, I don't know . . ." He looks mutely at her.

"Alexander, a lot of water has passed under a lot of bridges in the last few years. But you're here now. Please—you can tell me. I won't be angry."

Rider carefully relaxes all major muscle groups. "Janet—I joined the Opposition."

Getting slammed into the wall doesn't hurt any less for his being prepared for it. Janet's jaws gape open in a razortoothed trefoil and her suckered flippers inflict innumerable tiny hickeys all over his body. The fangs on her nipples gnaw through her blouse. "Those TERRORISTS?! I can give you a medium-slow death, Rider, for old times' sake."

"Janet, would I come to San Diego if I were still with them?"

"The Sun only knows what monsters like you think."

"Janet, listen to me. I'm a spy."

"I know that."

"For *us*, Janet. Not the Opposition."

"And I suppose you've burrowed deep into the heart of some Opposition cell in Seattle and you're here to come clean?"

"Close. I'm not with a cell anymore, and it's in San Francisco, and it's a little more complicated than that."

"I'm listening."

"Could you take your spines away from my groin?"

"Okay."

"Thanks. . . . Look, after we parted I went home and walked into the San Bernardino desert. I wanted to die, and I almost made it. But they found me and saved my life. Then they taught me more thaumaturgy, until I was ready, and then they taught me still more. I'm a journeyman synesthetic mage, Janet. I moved to San Francisco, found a cell and joined them. We staked vampires, shot zombies with Tibetan salt, disassembled organ harvesters . . . I was young, I was angry, I wasn't in my right mind, I'm not proud of anything I did. But then they went too far."

"What?"

"You remember about a year ago, when the San Diego navy was moving up the coast?"

She presses against him. "You were involved with that?"

"Aaugh . . ."

"Give me the names of the others in your cell and I'll give you a moderately quick death."

"Aauugh . . . spines . . ."

She retracts the spines.

"It won't do you any good. They all died when they cut the pentagram. Why do you think you haven't seen hide nor hair of them since? But listen. I have a lead on the Dolphin totem."

"Uh-huh. And the address of the Orca high priest and a few acres of swampland, right?"

"Listen to me. There are six Dolphin totemists up north who were hit by a pack of thin dogs from the Oil Slick. Four of them lived but the teeth got to the bone and the totemists are rotten with Lockjaw of Doom. They're scared stiff, no pun intended, ha ha. They're willing to spill their guts to me, but only if I can get the Lockjaw out of them first."

"How do I know you're telling the truth?"

"That's the beauty of it. It doesn't really matter whether I'm lying or not. I'm not here to beg, I'm here to buy."

"With what? Money? San Diego is a strict barter economy."

"I'm a synesthetic mage, right?"

"So?"

"Twenty kilograms of powdered agony."

Janet's seven eyes light up. "I thought that bag looked a little heavy."

"It is. But that's not where it is."

Janet almost conceals her disappointment. "So where?"

"Offshore, about two and a half miles. I had it night-dropped."

"I assume this is about one of the complications you mentioned."

"Yes. Keep in mind that the totemists think I'm still trying to *look* like a loyal member of the Opposition. So I can't come down here, walk into a clinic, buy what I need, and take the next flight north. I need to look like a spy. It has to look illicit. That's why I took the train. By the way, how did you happen to be at the station?"

"My horoscope said I would encounter a man who failed to avoid death. It didn't make any sense to me until I remembered my Freud; trains are death, and missing a train is avoiding death. I played the hunch. But anyway, why do you need to act like a spy now that you're already here?"

"Double agents. If any undercover Opposition types see me acting like a legitimate traveler, my cover is blown to shreds."

"So why do you trust me?"

He smiles at her.

"I'm flattered."

"You never did anything to hurt me. I thought you did, thought you planned it all out, but you didn't."

"I thought about it a lot . . . but I never gave in. I was about to, right after the bomb went off, but I realized you knew it wouldn't kill me when you planted it—you were just throwing a tantrum."

"That's true." Boy, is it ever untrue.

"So, Mr. Secret Agent Man, what do we do now?"

"Well, I figure twenty keys is about right for four topflight occult antibiotic / antiviral shots. I don't mean a specific, I mean something that'll knock out *anything,* I don't know what else they might have been infected with. But it would appear I was too trusting if I didn't see good faith on your part, so this is the plan: You get me two shots now. We charter a boat, go out to the spot. I raise the container; you verify it is what it is, and give me the other two shots. I take a Zodiac and make for the three-mile limit—I'll drift until I can get a message out for a pickup."

"I don't like it. If I get two shots to you before anything else, you can find a way to vanish. I have no knowledge that there's anything out there."

"How can I vanish?"

"Heat shimmer."

"Check my bags. Besides, I'm a Journeyman, not a Master."

She runs her tongues over her lips. "Were you planning on contacting me all along?"

"No. I figured I'd make an underground connection, somehow. I considered looking you up, but I had no way to know you're not still angry with me."

"Hmn . . . Alexander, I'll have to think about it. Have you eaten?"

Thankfully, Rider is too terrified to think of food, so his stomach does not rumble. Besides, he knows what they put on the pizza here. "Yes. I ate on the train."

"Okay. Maybe we can just have a little nightcap and call it a day. Or do you want to go out?"

Buddha's navel, no. "Wouldn't be in character." Rider suddenly realizes that if he offers his bottle to Janet, he'll be dead of blood loss in moments—if he's lucky.

"Okay. Oh, you put that away; that's your traveling bourbon. Let me fetch you some of mine."

"Twist my arm. I ain't gotten any cheaper in my old age." She gets up and heads for the kitchen. Rider dumps two more shots down his throat. The Old Liver Plasma and the Wild Turkey will fight it out in his system—it'll be painful, but he'll live through the heartburn and philosophical ambivalence.

They drink, chat about old times. Rider becomes extremely drunk—five drinks on an empty stomach is no fun at all. The Old Liver Plasma fumes on his lips and trifurcates his vision, so he sits and watches Janet's twenty-one eyes flash over and under nine flapping jaws. Tries to pretend he's playing with a kaleidoscope.

Janet stands, stretches luxuriously. "You've changed, Alexander."

"We all do."

She smiles at him. Her stripes ripple as the muscle underneath shifts. The smile broadens. Four eyes wink. "But I bet you're still the same about one or two things."

Rider's brain figures out what's going on, sends a message down his spine to the little cluster of neurons just over the pelvis that handles sexual arousal. The little cluster considers it. Rider's penis tries to retract into his abdomen. He's doomed. *I came this close . . .* he thinks.

"Why don't you bring your stuff upstairs and we can . . . do a little more catching up." Her nipples lick their lips suggestively.

Doom. Flippers. Spines. Fangs. Doom. "I haven't had an offer I was more astonished at in years." Many tonguelike organs. Doom. Unusual articulation. Doom. Vagina dentata and bodily fluids not found in nature. Doom. Doom. His testicles kiss each other goodbye.

"I think I owe it to you. And you owe it to me."

Rider has a straight razor in his ditty bag. He can slash his jugular and head straight for the Bardo. His brain begins chanting the Mantra of Chenrazee as he gathers his stuff. They wander up the stairs with his arm around her thorax. Reach the bedroom. "Just let me brush my teeth first; I'll be right with you."

Enters the bathroom—shuts the door. Takes out the razor. Turns on the sink tap. Sits down in the tub. The black jade mocks.

Of course, death isn't always the end. He wonders if he has the strength to come back. Thinks about it. Men slain by treachery sometimes rise as *Zombi revenant,* corpses animated by their burning desire for revenge. But suicides come back as ghosts, if at all. No way out. He steels himself and fixes his eyes on the mandala in his ditty bag. Lifts the razor to his throat—

—and freezes.

Remembers dumping every potion Arbeiter had on him into his bag before leaving the loft.

Arbiter, the *alchemist.*

Arbeiter, the alchemist, who trained in Texas and is not quite as squeamish as some of his *other* friends.

Scrabble scrabble. Three vials of a substance sold primarily to elderly men who cannot sustain an erection. The label says:

Rhinoceros horn, sea turtle egg, tiger semen in buffered thaumaqueous suspension.
LEVEL THREE THEOTOXIN (TOTEMIC)—*not to exceed two doses in fourteen years.*

Rider drinks the three doses down. Shuts off the water. Opens the door. "Darling," he says.

．　．　．

Well, the morning is no fun at all. His back hurts and his metabolism is like the fields of Shilo. Janet, thank heaven, is in the kitchen cooking breakfast. He can hear her singing and giggling as the kittens caterwaul on the chopping board. He grabs a robe and rises in a lurch, casting the duvet to the floor; it begins creeping back onto the bed as he staggers downstairs.

"Hello, sleepyhead," trills Janet.

"Hello yourself, cutie." Rider pretends he's in Special Forces training, reminds himself that if you put enough salsa on something, it doesn't really matter what it is. He hopes she's not still fond of long-pig sausage. She is. Rider reminds himself that he led Creedon Thiebaud to his death, he's selling armaments to the Incumbents, and last night he enraged three powerful totems just to get a woody to save his pathetic heinie—and therefore is going straight to Hell, anyway. He chows down.

"You know it's almost noon, Sandy?"

The tile underfoot bears a delicate scarab pattern, the better to conceal San Diego's contribution to automatic kitchen maintenance. Even as he looks, they roll minute balls of kitchen scrap out to the garden. Rider says, "I've been keyed up like you wouldn't believe since I don't know when. It felt good to sleep and know I'm safe."

This inspires a maternal hug. "Janet's been a good girl."

"I'll just bet she has."

"Why don't you see if you can find what Janet has for you?"

I'm not doing what I'm about to do, thinks Rider. *Actually, I'm sifting through a spare parts heap looking for evidence.* We will draw a veil on what, exactly, Rider does as Janet coos and wriggles under his hands. Eventually, in a place so unlikely as to have no name, even in Latin, he discovers two small, glowing vials.

"My goodness. So fast?"

"Janet believes in moving quickly. Besides, if it's Lockjaw of Doom, you need to get back north as soon as possible. More's the pity, lover."

"Hmn." Rider achieves a convincing semblance of a leer.

"Actually, it may already be too late. But I should warn you—there's a catch."

"There always is."

"I had to get these from—well, an old mutual friend."

"Oh, no. Not—"

"Now, Sandy, you know as well as I how things turned out. . . ."

Rider does not have to act. No, the bitterness and loathing comes straight from the spleen. "I can't believe it. That *hack*? That excuse for a mage? You know he once came to me and asked how many sides pentagrams have?"

"Alexander Rider, you stop that. He finished his medical degree—"

"Where? Doctor Mbogo's Medical School and Bait Shop?"

"—and he has done very well for himself. He made up that batch of antibiotic personally."

"Who, *him*? Why not just give me four vials of polyacrylamide? The totemists *might* be able to survive *that!*"

"Ho ho, still the razor-tongued little thaumaturge," booms Bartholomew "Call me Biff" Stern, sweeping through the doorway. "Hi, Janet." Peck, peck. "C'mere, boy, let me look at you." Dripping pseudopodia over a leering face a meter across lift Rider into the air and amoeba-hug him.

Rider struggles ineffectually. "Put me down!"

"Janet rung me up this morning with your little business proposal and I thought to myself, 'Biff—' ('Biff,' 'cause that's my name—) 'Biff, now what you're hearing is this ol' pard of yours, he needs some bug juice and a boat,' and I plumb busted out and said, 'Well, HELL, little lady, you done come to the right place.' Now I just happen to have a forty-foot day cruiser parked right down by the marina and I surely do think we can get you a Zodiac in time for tonight."

"I smell a fucking rat. Even if I *did* trust you to not to try to sell me eight milliliters of radioactive goose lymph, you flunked O-chem three times."

"Yep, that is the truth, no doubt, no doubt at all. But I done passed it eventually. You tutored me in occult chemistry yourself, the time I did make it. I owe you one."

Glower.

"Look, boy, I know we've had our little disagreements in the past—"

"Yeah, like whether you should be broken up for parts, or burned alive."

"—and so I can see how you'd be a wee bit nervous. So I say we just go down and do a little ass-ay, somewhere's you trust."

"Trust? Trust? In this town, I couldn't so much as find a thaumopharmacist I *don't* trust. Let alone one I *would* trust."

"I know a place," says Janet.

"Great, somewhere where one of his incompetent asshole buddies just happens to have a script all laid out."

Janet heaves a sigh. "Alexander, be reasonable. We'll visit two or three places, if you want, get some names out of the Black Pages. We've got all afternoon."

"All afternoon? If I *must* breathe the same smog he does I'd just as soon get this over with right now."

Biff shakes his belly. "Well, that's not likely to be possible, boy."

"What, the assassin isn't free until nine?"

"Now you just *sit* down and let me *explain,* son." Biff drops Rider into his chair and holds him in place with thirty kilograms of throbbing protoplasm. "Now, in case your brain cells are firing just as slow as they used to, you came in this town with the stink of the Opposition on you. Police knew *somebody* come in on the Frisco–San Diego Express, but they can't track it any further. Happens all the time; they warned the navy patrols. Only chance we have is to do this under cover of night, when even inside the three-mile limit, they don't have the Sun in the sky to give 'em strength."

"There's an angle you're not telling. With you, there has to be."

"I am hurt and disappointed, my friend."

"And you are at this very moment trying to come up with a plausible lie."

"Now, there is one other factor—"

"Ha!"

"—and that is, the stuff you're selling is subject to an import tax. Or didn't you know you were evading a tariff, too?"

"Hah?"

"City Crypt's got to have its ten percent. Now, if they catch us smuggling, well, ordinarily it'd just be a little fine, maybe an eye or two, and community service. But they'd also do a pretty thorough background check on everybody on the boat. If your cover as a double agent is any good, they'll find you're linked to the Opposition, sure as shit, and then all three of us find ourselves floating around in a big jar with all the other brains San Diego uses to try out new forms of torture. I ain't particularly sure I'd like to try that trick at my age."

"Oh."

"So you just sit tight. I got the other two doses here. We'll assay all four and spend a nice afternoon down at Horton Plaza and then we'll take our little sea cruise. That all right with you, Mr. Journeyman Synesthetic Mage, sir?"

·   ·   ·

Amazing heat and scanty clothing. Muzak. Rider sits with Janet and Biff outside of Macy's; sips a not quite passable espresso, watches the zombies. Horton Plaza: two square blocks of mall, rising from Old Town like a terracotta cyst in rotting meat.

All four vials seem all right, even with Rider peering suspiciously over everybody's shoulders and insisting on reading the assay procedure before the pharmacists so much as cracked the seals. Biff just leaned up against the wall and laughed, chatted with Janet.

Rider has even managed to enjoy himself a little, shopping; bought T-shirts with some unthinkable credos emblazoned across the breast. The jolly "pushcarts" yielded candles incorporating certain ingredients neither he nor Arbeiter can bring themselves to harvest personally. "All in a good cause," he thinks. "Good intentions, ha ha."

By seven, they're at the marina. The Zodiac semi-inflatable sits on the stern of the yacht. Rider inspects it, checks the fuel tank and the twenty-horsepower motor. Mutters and raves in Sumerian—it still looks good. Biff spends his time pointing out bathing beauties. Biff is an ass man, so the hexapods inspire him to mating calls rivaling that of the Irish elk.

·   ·   ·

They quiet as night comes. Rider sits and talks football with Biff and Janet. Biff gestures floridly as they talk, and Janet coos at the both of them, stretches more often than she needs to; just as they should. Rider's not paying attention; he's watching for watchers. When he realizes his, he feels an ugly thump, and falters. This is just how the three of them used to watch for potential foes, back in school; the old patterns are still there. Rider clams up and stares at the bow.

Rider is cold despite the tropic night.

At twenty hundred hours they set out. The night is inky; the lights of downtown stand over the black water like the walls of Dis. The jets over the sea are birds crying, swooping home to nest; tail and wing lights blink like tearing eyes. Rider has a compass in his hand, tells Biff where to point the bow. It doesn't take long to leave the city behind, to travel two and a half miles.

San Diego glitters behind them.

"Have a gaff ready," says Rider. "I'm going to bring it up. Leave the motor going in neutral, stand by on the throttle." Rider takes a tiny chip of plastic, ties a string around it. Dips seawater into a graduated cylinder. Drops in the chip. Sumerian. Slowly pulls the chip up through the cylinder. The motor groans and slows. "Throttle. More. Good."

As the plastic chip reaches the meniscus, there is a sudden upwelling off the bow. The engine speeds up; Janet throttles off. Biff whoops as a netting-wrapped aluminum suitcase surfaces. He gaffs it, hauls it on board. "What's the combo, partner?"

"Do *not* try to open it until *both* dials are set. 1424 on the left, 0776 on the right. Give me my vials." They are shadows under the moonless sky.

"Not so fast, boy, just need to make one other check . . ." Biff runs a combination bomb-sniffer and aura-reader over the suitcase. Strokes up the combination. Opens it. Takes out a wax-sealed beaker, hefts it. Stumbles through a few phrases of Sumerian. Nothing happens. Tries again. Advances on Rider, curling and uncurling his protuberances.

Rider shakes his head. "Still can't pronounce Sumerian worth a damn. Repeat after me."

Biff does so. The contents of the beaker and suitcase glow briefly, a phosphorescent firefly flare. "Looks right, looks right. Twenty kilograms of pure unadulterated suffering!"

"Great, great, let me get out of here before the patrol wanders by."

"Well, we need to have a little chat, first."

Rider stares at Biff. Janet's jaws yawn open. The face on Biff's belly leers. "Oh, no."

"Oh yes, my little double-agent triple-agent friend."

Rider slumps. "You two could at least have the decency to pull a gun on me."

"I don't think it's necessary. Do you, my little sugarplum?"

"Little boy like that?"

Rider spits in their general direction. "Thanks loads, Janet. How'd you know?"

"Tell the truth, we had to go all the way to our agents in Frisco."

"*Agents? In the City? Oh, shit.*"

"You did it right; mixed lies and truth like cream into coffee. But thin dogs are pretty distinctive, and you shouldn't have lied about the number of sick. Would've made more sense to tell the truth about that, bring up ten keys and bargain for two doses."

Rider holds his head in his hands. "I was trying to get my hands on two vials in a good-faith move and get out without handing over the agony. Janet spotted that right off, but twenty keys for four doses was still an acceptable deal."

"And there was no reason to lie about who got hit."

"Needed to convince you I'd use the antibiotics to serve the Incumbents."

"So why'd you tell her it was Oil Slick instead of the Vulture cult who did it?"

"I was pretty sure even San Diego couldn't put an agent into Oil Slick."

Janet speaks up, slipping into the shrill, echoing voice that Rider remembers so well. "I knew something had to be up the minute I saw you. Would've been a sweet deal; rip us off, get one final screw out of me. I hope you enjoyed yourself. I could smell the Wild Turkey on your breath all night. It was disGUSting."

Rider leers at her. "My love for you, I made into a clamp for my journeyman piece. Spent six months, working with it every day, wondering if I should let it back into my heart. I had to take three doses of aphrodisiac just to get myself into that charnel you call a cunt."

Janet is moving at Mach 2 for his groin, stripes barely visible under the spangled sky. Biff catches her. "Easy, now, honey, easy. He's just trying to get you to kill him quick."

"Y'know, Janet, Biff's right. Actually, I didn't even know I had the aphrodisiac on me when I went into the head. I went in there planning to kill myself."

Janet struggles and screams horrible oaths. The night air swallows them.

Biff says, "Well, the only thing I'm wondering is how you expected to get away with this scam in the first place. Janet ain't dumb, and even if you could fool her, you should've known I'd be around to back her up."

Rider shrugs. "I've been improvising since I heard Janet call my name, back at the station. I was telling the truth when I said I didn't expect to meet her. I had planned to cruise the barrios and make a black-market connection."

"I'm also wondering why you don't try to leap over the side and try to save yourself."

"And get away how? If I tried that, you'd get my blood and twenty kilograms of agony."

"Hell, if that's all you're worried about, we've got all that either way. So why don't you at least try to die with your boots on? Al? Al, Al, come on. You still freezing up when the chips are down?"

"Yeah, I still freeze up. I still panic, too. But as it turns out, I'm just stalling. I'm hoping against hope for a deus ex machina."

"A what?"

Rider smiles. "You knew, once. I taught it to you. You remembered it just long enough to pass Classical Literature."

The Glock 17 holds seventeen rounds in the magazine and one in the chamber, and will fire as fast as the gunman can pull the trigger. In two seconds, as Rider dives for cover and starts chanting, six sharp reports occur. Janet and Biff stagger briefly but the muzzle flash reveals a gray, elongated face, dripping with tears. They reach tentacles and jaws for it. Rider takes a beaker from the suitcase, bellows Sumerian as he throws it hard at the deck before them. The stabilized pain destabilizes—seeks its natural habitat. "Biff" Stern and Janet Walker each absorb the pain of three full-body second-degree burns. They cannot even scream.

Thiebaud shuts his eyes. The flow of tears redoubles. He points his guns at them. Rider screams, "Creedon, don't! For the love of God!"

Thiebaud opens his eyes. "These are incorrigibles, Mr. Rider."

Rider approaches him, hands wide, supplicating. "Please. Please, Creedon." Thiebaud shakes his head.

"Creedon—I don't mean what we usually mean."

Thiebaud lifts a brow over an eye flooding tears.

"Creedon. Give me one of your guns."

A long instant; a short eternity. Thiebaud looks nervous, but hands over a Glock. He says, "Please be very careful, Mr. Rider. This has been extensively modified to disconnect the safety and have a short trigger pull."

"Shut up, Creedon." Rider stands over Biff. "See you in Hell," whispers Rider, and starts pulling the trigger. Brain. Upper spine. Lower spine. Liver. Right kidney. Left kidney. Heart. He loots the body for the two vials.

Moves to Janet. Brain. Upper spine. Lower spine. Liver. Right kidney. Left kidney. Heart. Heart. Click. Click. The open action mocks Rider. Black blood spreads over the deck. The running lights pick up highlights; there is a starry sky underfoot to match the one overhead. "Clip! Give me another fucking clip!"

A second's pause. A magazine comes from the darkness. Rider reloads. Five eyes open. Rider realizes that even a master thaumaturge can't take away all of a certain thing from somebody's soul.

"Alexander . . . It wasn't like I said it was, just now. Stern, he doesn't understand, he never understood, I thought you had changed, come back to me . . . Alexander . . ."

Rider drops the slide. Heart. Heart. Heart. Heart. Heart. Heart. Heart. Heart.

Rider's trigger finger drips blood. He retches and steps away to be alone with what his master couldn't take from him.

"Sandy, do what you have to do. But please . . . forgive me."

Rider whirls around, looks down at her. Somehow she is still alive. Closes his third eye. Sees a woman, not the woman he once knew but still the same woman, crying. He points the gun at her. His hand shakes. Raises the Glock to his temple. Puts his finger on the trigger.

Changes his mind.

Heart. Heart. Heart. Heart. Heart. Heart. Heart. Heart. Heart. Click. Click. Click. Click.

. . .

Tens of seconds pass. Draft on Rider's hand, sudden wrench. He hears Thiebaud replace the magazine and drop the slide. "Creedon . . ." sobs Rider. "Creedon, I never had any doubt. I knew you'd save my miserable ass."

Thiebaud is watching a seabird wheel across the night sky. "Thank you, Mr. Rider."

Rider sucks snot out of his nose. "And thank *you* for not reminding me you know I'm lying through my teeth, you goddamned MUTANT! Where the FUCK have you been?"

Thiebaud leans overboard, watches the waves.

"You know how worried I've been about you?"

Thiebaud watches water run off the side of the fiberglass hull. "I must doubt you had time to worry, Mr. Rider."

"Yeah? Well, if I'd *had* time, I *would* have worried."

"I understand. Perhaps this would be a good time to commence."

"Huh?"

"Ten arms and an elongated body is characteristic of weresquid, is it not?"

"What? Wha—oh, shit. Shoot it! Shoot it, for crying out loud!"

Blam, blam.

"Creedon, we've got to get out of here!" Rider scrabbles toward the cockpit. "The keys! Where are the damn keys! Who turned off the fucking engine?!" Rider dithers and waves his hands. "Right. Don't panic. Not a patrol. Just a scout."

"Duck."

Rider is something of a chowderhead, but he and his friends train for many hours to acquire the "duck" conditioned reflex. A kamikaze sea urchin sails over his head, squeaking.

"Keys! Keys! Wait; I'm a thaumaturge . . . I don't need keys . . ." Rider whirls like a dervish and the engine turns over. The boat blunders ahead. Rider heaves the wheel over and they turn toward the west.

"Destroyer, Mr. Rider."

"Creedon! You dri—" Thiebaud is at the wheel. "Jesus, Creedon, don't do that." Thiebaud heels the wheel hard to port. "Wrong way, Creedon! Not sou—" A shell hits off the starboard bow, kicking up barrels of seawater. "Never mind. Just warn me next time, okay?" Rider bounces off various annoying nautical accouterments as he gibbers towards his pack.

"RESISTANCE IS USELESS," booms the destroyer's PA system.

"You stole that line from Douglas Adams," shouts Rider.

"RESISTANCE IS FUTILE," booms the destroyer's PA system.

"*Star Trek: The Next Generation,* you sodsucking catamites!"

"WE ARE NOT CATAMITES," booms the destroyer's PA system. Rider can hear the Muzak oozing from the destroyer: a gutted, bleached, and deflavored *Yellow Submarine.* Tracer rounds find the yacht and pieces of superstructure are chipped into the ocean.

Rider opens his pack. He can't see the labels in the dark but he can feel the Braille. "Yak butter . . . Virgin's blood . . . Grandma's fruitcake . . ."

"WE ARE ALL STRAIGHT MEN OF DIVERSE ETHNICITY WHO HAPPEN TO BE IN THE NAVY," booms the destroyer's PA system. A rocket shatters the yacht's radar boom.

"Gorgon dung . . . Yttrium needles . . . Sacramental ouzo . . . I have got to get a system one of these days. . . . Mandrake . . ."

"WELL, WE'RE NOT ALL MEN, BUT THE WOMEN ON OUR SHIP ARE ALL HETERO-SEXUAL." A surface-to-surface missile malfunctions, hitting the water off the port stern with a sound like doomsday.

"Wicker lingam . . . Nixon buttons . . . Schrödinger's cap . . . Aha! Where's the damn can opener?"

"ADMITTED, THERE MAY BE CERTAIN APPARENT SALARY DISCREPANCIES, BUT THEY ARE JUST STATISTICAL ARTIFACTS. IF YOU CORRECT FOR TIME IN SERVICE, IT ALL EVENS OUT. AT ANY RATE, YOU ARE MONDO OUTGUNNED. WE WILL BE BOARDING SOON. PLEASE THROW DOWN YOUR WEAPONS AND RAISE ALL PREHENSILE LIMBS OVER YOUR PRIMARY CLUSTER OF SENSE ORGANS."

Rider gashes his thumb in his haste to open up a king-sized can of Chicken of the Sea. Shoves all four vials of antibiotic / antiviral serum into the aluminum suitcase and lashes it to a stanchion; seizes a line, takes a deep breath, and jumps overboard. Bounces off the hull a few times but manages to hold on. Begins letting his breath go to moan certain bass notes in a language that predates mankind.

The barnacles on the hull have ripped his skin in a hundred places. Something huge and black crunches into the screws astern and a shock wave knocks all the air Rider has left out of his lungs.

■   ■   ■

Rider is in a dark temple. Doors creak around him. Staccato gun bursts. Flowers of light. Something kicks him in the crotch. It hurts a lot.

■   ■   ■

Rider thrashes on the surface, still managing to hold on to the rope. The destroyer is a mere fifty meters away, looming like death itself. The Muzak has switched to Disney's *Pirates of the Caribbean* in preparation for the boarding. It is approaching at perhaps a knot, many large guns pointing.

Rider suddenly realizes the sea sounds like hinges flexing after lying unoiled for a thousand years. There are some unusual flashes of light coming from below the surface.

"HAVE YOU DECIDED TO COME PEACEFULLY?"

Rider is watching the lights.

"WE WOULD PREFER IT. IT IS VERY COLD AND DARK OUT, AND WE'D JUST AS SOON GET BACK TO PORT."

The lights approach the surface.

Rider and Thiebaud are not going to be coming peacefully.

A mottled gray torpedo rises from the water on a pillar of fire. The flame moves with the speed of rocket exhaust, chewing deep into the water with a bass roar like an avalanche. Rider can barely hear emergency sirens going off all over the destroyer, hears the whoop-whoop-whoop of the engine room warning everybody they are going to put the ship into full reverse very, very quickly. Atop the pillar of fire, a blowhole spumes and two markedly angry cetacean eyes drip burning white phosphorous. The jaw drops—a dolphin gesture whose meaning is approximately equivalent to a human hooking his fingers into claws and screaming through a snarl.

Some bungling idiot on the destroyer reasons that dolphins are aquatic, and therefore are vulnerable to fire. Hoses it down with a flamethrower. The burning napalm looks dim and cool as it floats beside the tower of flame.

A few brainier San Diegans dive off the destroyer. Many do not surface, or if they do, they don't stay surfaced for long. Rider can just spot the totemic tattoo along the dolphin's right flank. Can't make out any details, but he knows it is a naked man, flint knife in one hand, burning torch in the other.

The pillar of fire rises another few meters. Rider can hear groans and creaks coming from the dolphin's forehead. Flippers and flukes and jaws wave. The blowhole spits a cloud of steam. The jaw snaps shut. The destroyer melts like ice dropped into molten lead, all at once glowing white and slumping into its cavity in the sea. Water explodes into steam. Steely meteors hurtle in all directions. Rider dives away from the fist-sized chunks of burning alloy. Watches twisted fragments of metal sink past him, trailing clouds of steam. Eventually, they stop coming. Rider surfaces.

The pillar of fire is gone. There is nothing but a great mushroom cloud of steam where the destroyer was. The yacht is a ways away, scorched from bow to stern and burning in a dozen places. "Creedon!" Rider starts swimming for it.

A blowhole spumes just ahead of him. A sleek head rises from the waves. Rider looks at the dolphin. She swims up and rubs against him. He hugs her. The *Stenos bredanensis* puts her flippers around her totem animal as best she can and creaks happily.

.   .   .

Rider finds Thiebaud on the fantail, calmly playing a fire extinguisher over the Zodiac. "I am afraid your pack is in rather poor condition, Mr. Rider."

"My God! The antibiotic!"

"The aluminum protected it."

"How hot was the suitcase when you got to it? That stuff is vulnerable to heat!"

"Hmn. Hot."

Rider lunges for the suitcase. Smeared along one side is a patch of smoking steel the size of a dinner plate. He grabs the case, burning his hands. Rider screams. The case hisses as he dunks it into the water.

There are more ships coming toward them; they have no time to waste. Rider tears a volume of the Congressional Record in two; the Zodiac inflates. Hurried loading, and they cast off from the yacht. Rider finds Maggie-Sue's contribution to their effort—a piece of seaweed tied in three knots. He unties the first one. A current comes up, pushing the little boat west at about two knots. He unties the second one. The current picks up to ten knots; a sudden, wide river surging through the sea. "Paddle ready?"

"Ready, Mr. Rider."

"Goggles?"

"Check."

"Here we go!" Unties the third knot. An unnatural curler six meters high looms from behind the Zodiac and Rider and Thiebaud ride a foaming mountain of water away from San Diego at a mind-boggling seventy knots.

.   .   .

Zodiacs are not speedboats. They are not even particularly hydrodynamic. Thiebaud and Rider are completely exhausted from keeping the boat heading west and bailing out water by the time the spell gives out and they heave to a halt. Rider starts the engine and they continue at a somewhat more sedate pace.

"Perhaps we should turn north, Mr. Rider."

"Nope," says Rider through chattering teeth. "The San Diego Navy may not be any great shakes at night, outside the three-mile limit, but when the sun comes up they can spot us in a heartbeat and have things coming for us that make a hammerhead shark on phencyclidine look like a fried green sea cucumber. If it comes down to minutes, I want as much distance between us and them as I can get."

They motor through the night. Neither has the energy to talk. The Zodiac is not faring well on the open ocean and they are both very wet and very cold. Rider suddenly wonders what it would be like to run out of gas and drift until they die of dehydration.

False dawn.

There is a mosquito on the horizon. It rapidly grows to become a seaplane. Rider studies it with binoculars. Grins at Thiebaud and gives a thumbs-up. The plane passes low overhead, rolling back and forth. Rider waves back. They point the Zodiac into the current, pull goggles over their eyes, and curl into balls.

The seas are too rough to land, so the seaplane drones over them, flaps down. A tornado reaches from the sky and picks up Thiebaud and the case, drags him through the sky and deposits him into the plane. Another pass for Rider and his gear. Chloe cranes around in the pilot's seat, looks at them as the plane picks up speed and turns for home. Maggie-Sue glares at them. "Well?"

"We think we've got it." Rider collapses into a seat and falls into a deep, dreamless slumber.

▪   ▪   ▪

Maggie-Sue immediately reaches over and punches him in the thigh. Rider wakes up. "What? What?"

"What is all that shit on your face? You look like you spent all night fucking an octopus."

"Zombies. Old flame. Rode in a coffin. Vengeful ghost. Lies. Tiger semen. Cannibalism. Betrayal. Deus ex machina. Destroyer. Dolphin. Big fire. I've brought gifts for all. Ugh." Rider falls back asleep and not even Maggie-Sue's repeated shaking can rouse him. She turns to Thiebaud, who is playing with a bit of string.

"That is the gist of it, Miss Percy." Goes back to making cat's cradles. Maggie-Sue yells at him for fifteen minutes before she gives up.

▪   ▪   ▪

Long flight north. Frantic but uneventful dash from SFO to the loft. Storytelling. There are two limp forms on cots in the next room.

Rider's news that the serum was possibly exposed to sufficient heat to render it worthless is not met with glee.

"And what if the serum did, in fact, overheat? Would it now be poison?" asks Whitlomb.

"No," says Rider. "It just breaks down into more or less harmless protein fragments."

"And is an overdose of this serum dangerous?"

"No, not really."

"Is a vial likely to lose, say, half its efficaciousness?"

"No, Perry. If it's warm enough to go, it goes all at once."

"And would half a dose be of any use?"

"Probably not; it's been too long."

"Then," says Whitlomb, "we have a fascinating problem." They stare at him. "Let us consider this, case by case. Postulate we somehow knew all four vials were unaffected by the heat. We inject our comrades with one apiece; they recover, and we have two doses left for future use or sale."

"I think I see where this is going," murmurs Chloe.

"Second case. Postulate we somehow knew exactly one vial is useless. We would then mix all four together, administer one and a third units apiece, and we would have one dose in reserve. Third case: two bad vials. We would mix all four vials together, and inject each with two vials' worth of mixture; two recoveries. Fifth case: all four vials are worthless, and there is nothing to do but read the Bardo Thodol." He chuckles. "Contemplation of this case is depressing in the utmost; we shall ignore it." He pauses. "But what of the fourth case?"

Maggie-Sue says, "Two vials each, no mixing. One recovers."

Whitlomb takes off his glasses and polishes them. "You would conclude, then, that the path of wisdom is to administer two vials apiece, without mixing? To ensure that we have at least one recovery, even if it is the fourth case that applies?"

Chloe says, "Perry, this is not a good time to go into Socratic-method teaching mode."

Maggie-Sue snaps, "What are you talking about?"

Chloe says, "Maggie-Sue, let's say we give them each two vials without mixing. What if there are exactly *two* bad vials, and one man happens to get both? One lives and one dies, even though we had enough medicine to save both. So what do we do? Mix them or not?"

Rider is scribbling equations and charts on a legal pad. Chloe is watching

Rider and biting her lip. Maggie-Sue is staring at Whitlomb, who has put his glasses back on and commenced to wind his pocket watch. Washington is glowering in the direction of the cots. Thiebaud is across the room with headphones on, oblivious, humming the alto line of a barbershop quartet.

"Assay," says Maggie-Sue.

"We can't do that," says Chloe. "The materials we need are in San Diego and we can't even think of going down there until the heat cools off."

"Haiti can't run tests like that. Tibet?" says Washington.

"They won't help us," says Rider. "To them, drastic life-prolonging measures are stupid, dangerous, and wrong; ruining your karma to stick to maya."

"Perhaps we should ask them," murmurs Thiebaud.

Rider says, "Look, I know these people. The Tibetan lamas will counter atrocities and export blessed salt, but that's it."

Chloe says, "Not the Tibetans. Max and Kris."

Heads turn toward the cots, then look in various directions.

Maggie-Sue snaps, "They can't even blink. I've got enough muscle relaxant in them to paralyze a horse."

Rider mutters, "Trust her on that one. She knows."

"Fuck you. So how do we know their answer?"

Whitlomb says, "Speech is impossible. But they are conscious, and Creedon will know."

Washington growls, "And if one wants to do it one way and one the other?"

"Flip a coin?" says Rider.

"Fuck you," says Maggie-Sue.

"How about straight divination? Joe?" asks Whitlomb.

"Possibility."

"Creedon," says Rider, "I don't suppose you might just happen to have had a flash of—ah—insight, you haven't mentioned?"

Thiebaud doesn't say anything.

"Thiebaud, if we ask them and you tell us what they think . . . how do we know you're telling the truth?" asks Washington.

Rider snorts. "If you examine a bucket of chicken entrails, how do we know *you're* telling the truth? Let's flip a coin. I'm serious."

Washington shakes his head. "Even Whitlomb could influence the way it falls, all the time he's spent around us, even if he never has cast a spell in his life."

"A poll may be of some utility," says Whitlomb.

"I agree. Anonymous ballot," says Chloe. "We'll just hope we don't go three-three."

Many pointless small stirrings. Nobody says anything.

Rider roots around, finds a chess set. Gives everybody one white pawn and one black pawn and sheets of paper. "Same as always. The choices are mix and separate. Alphabetical order: Black is mix. White is separate. Wrap your pawn in the paper and toss it into the middle of the floor. Usually Max would be the one who kicks the clumps around until nobody knows which one came from who, because he's the least eerie, but I suggest Perry do it. Any objections? Then, one by one, we all take one and unwrap it slowly, in full view of the others. Everybody swears an oath. Okay? Black is mix, white is separate. I'll start. I am Alexander Rider. I swear before myself, before my cellmates, and by the Eightfold Path, that I will not use sleight of hand or magic, any means mundane or occult, to unfairly influence the outcome of this vote. I will not use sleight of hand or magic, any means mundane or occult, to learn how others have voted."

It was a marathon night, a while ago, that they thrashed out the procedure. By now it is a ritual as precise as the Latin Mass.

They each speak. Chloe murmurs her oath to the Great Geoduck, Whitlomb recites one to Man, Washington grates to Baron Samedi, Maggie-Sue snaps one to the elemental balance, and Thiebaud whispers his oath to the god of the Israelites.

"Black is mix, white is separate. Everybody ready? Shall I call? Okay. Chloe." Thump. "Rider." Thump. "Perry. Joe. Maggie-Sue. Creedon. Okay, mix 'em, Perry." Whitlomb stands up and rolls paper balls around with his feet. Returns to his place.

"I'll call. Chloe." She kneels before the pile. Takes up a crumpled lump. Unwraps a black pawn. "Rider." Rider unwraps a white pawn. "Perry." White. "Joe." Black pawn. "Maggie-Sue." Black pawn.

"Okay. Do it, Creedon." Creedon borrows heavy work gloves, muffles his hands in a scarf. Takes up two pokers and pries the paper apart.

Black pawn. "All right, everybody, come with me and Chloe, make sure we really do mix them."

The deed is done. Maggie-Sue administers the injections.

■   ■   ■

It is late at night. Washington has just relieved Rider. Rider slips onto the balcony for a cigarette and a beer or three.

Maggie-Sue hisses quietly at him. Rider looks inside at her in confusion. Eventually realizes she wants to join him. He waves her out. She slides open the winter-sky doors, drifts to the railing and leans against it. She can move very quietly, on the rare occasions she wants to.

She stares at him. He looks back. "Give me a cigarette."

"Okay. You need a light? Ha ha."

Maggie-Sue spits softly at his feet. Drags on the cigarette; the tip ignites and glows. She hisses out smoke. They watch the stars for a while.

"Rider."

"Yo."

"If the serum doesn't work they're going to pick us off one by one and we'll never even know who's killing us."

"The six of us are so incompetent?"

"If they take some of us they will take all of us. We will have too much fire and too much water."

"We're not the four elements, Maggie-Sue. We're eight people. Besides, I never have been able to make sense of why you say Max and Chloe are 'earth', they're both water totems, aren't they? But tell you what, you're so worried about it—they kick off, the two of us will kamikaze and then the remaining four will be balanced."

"Don't talk like that."

"Scared to die?"

She slaps him, hard.

For a moment his eyes blaze at bright as hers and he clenches his fists. Then he relaxes. "Okay, cheap shot. I deserved that. I'm worried, too, and I don't think before I open my mouth. Forgive me?"

For once, she can't meet his eyes. There is a pause. She nods her head once like a gunshot.

"Hell, you're braver than I am, and you don't even believe in the afterlife. I'll tell you what; I don't talk kamikaze, and you stop thinking we all die if any of us die."

"Without Sturgeon's connections we'll never find them. We don't even know who wants us."

"Hmn. Maggie-Sue, did I ever tell you about the time I woke up and found Creedon sitting by my bed? Before I knew him?"

"I don't remember. Tell me again."

"I woke up. I know now he woke me up deliberately. I'd heard all the stories, and worse, I'd seen his work. He was close enough, I knew I could never get off a spell in time. He lit my cigarette lighter and looked into my eyes. I just looked back at him. He reached out and ran his finger along my cheek. That was enough; he knew I was okay."

"So what?"

"I haven't gotten to the point yet."

"So talk."

"Well, later, I asked him what would have happened if I *hadn't* been all right. He said I would have died without ever even knowing why." Rider shivers. "Anyway. It's like the old four-color comics. You ever read any, when you were a kid?"

She shakes her head.

"Um, you ever watch Batman, on TV?"

"Of course I did."

"Okay, it's just like that. The bad guy would always get ready to kill Batman and Robin, and before he did, he'd tell them what he was going to do to Gotham City. And Batman and Robin always got away, and they'd stop him. Creedon taught me that if you're going to kill somebody, you don't say so, you don't warn them. You don't breathe a word about anything at all."

"So?"

"You weren't listening when I told my story. Biff told me that the people hunting us are the Vulture cult."

. . .

Morning. Breakfast. Rider yells at Maggie-Sue to get out of his kitchen and let him wash up and put away the dishes before she has the whole place so rearranged he can't find anything. She keeps washing dishes. Rider storms up and down, waving his arms, insulting her obsessive work ethic and anachronistic attachment to "women's work," quoting Tannen loud enough to make the windows rattle. Tells her to be more like Chloe, come into the twentieth century, be a human being first and a woman second. Lays down the law. Maggie-Sue stalks back to the table. Folds her arms. Rider turns on the tap. Nothing comes out. Rider approaches apoplexy. Grabs a glass of water, pours it out, chanting in Sumerian. Water gushes out of the tap. Purple smoke comes out of Maggie-Sue's ears and the water stops. Rider starts gesturing wildly with his free hand as Maggie-Sue stands up and begins dancing and hissing and the water oscillates between full blast and zero. Then the pipes explode.

Well, frayed tempers are much in evidence as Maggie-Sue keeps the water from completely flooding the loft while Rider crawls around thaumaturging the pipes back together. When they are done, Whitlomb and Chloe shove them both out of the kitchen and tell Thiebaud to shoot them both if either so much as moves.

Finally, everybody is sitting around drinking coffee (or the espresso derivatives thereof, for the younger and trendier folks). Chloe says, "I have to say I'm surprised the Vulture totem is attacking an Opposition cell."

"Not the totem. The cult," says Washington. "Vulture totem is junkyard owners and corporate raiders. Vulture cult comes and goes in cycles. Been a long time."

"I'm not familiar with the Vulture cult."

"Find the weak and dying. Peck out their eyes. Feed."

Whitlomb clears his throat. "Or, somewhat less metaphorically, they find individuals already perishing—alcoholics, or burn victims, say—and they accelerate the process. They channel their sufferings and death to appease their god and perform magic."

Whitlomb takes off his glasses and begins to polish them. "Now, the remarkable thing is, they haven't the slightest sense of proportion. Their policies are fundamentally shortsighted. When they achieve hegemony, they commence to accelerate all manner of things. Dysfunctional families. Endemic drug abuse. Race hate. Entire civilizations fall. The Incumbents cannot be said to—hrmph—exemplify the milk of human kindness, but they seldom wax so destructive as to eliminate their supplies entirely."

Whitlomb puts his glasses back on. "An example: Perhaps you recall Hitler's betrayal and destruction of the 'Brown Shirts,' during the days the Incumbents preferred mind control to necromancy."

"I've heard of them," says Chloe.

"Recent—harrumph!—scholarship," says Whitlomb, looking at Rider, "seems to indicate many of the *Sturmabteilung* were Vulture cultists. Hitler exploited them to vault into power, and then destroyed them before their depredations tore Germany to shreds."

Chloe wrinkles her nose. "But if these Vulture clowns are so blatantly destructive, how come I've never heard of them?"

Whitlomb beams at Rider, who blushes. "Oh, go ahead and explain it yourself, Perry," says Rider, wretchedly.

Chloe cocks her head at Rider, who looks away. "What?"

Whitlomb says, "By a remarkable coincidence, Al's doctorate is in quantitative theological epidemiology."

"In *what*? And when did you get a PhD?" says Chloe in disbelief.

"It's just a toy one," says Rider, scuffing a toe.

"Nothing 'toy' about Miskatonic, my boy," retorts Whitlomb. "I was his advisor," he asides.

"Well, Dr. Rider," grates Washington, "get on with it."

Rider clears his throat. Certain cynics in the audience note how much the cadence of the sound resembles Whitlomb's. "Well, the first thing you do is postulate that ideas and religions are like germs. It's called 'memetics.' Ideas, religions, and germs all spread by parasitizing other things; germs parasitize more complex organisms, ideas and religions parasitize minds. Some are mostly benevolent. 'Leave other people alone unless they're hurting me or mine' is like the bugs in our guts that synthesize vitamins—helpful, and likely to crowd out organisms slash ideas less benign. Others are a little more dangerous—Tibetan Buddhism, as practiced in preoccupation

Tibet, provided (A) comfort to the masses and (B) power to the rulers to protect the masses. But, it could also be said to have weakened and enervated the nation by draining resources and the best minds into the monasteries. Am I making sense so far?"

"And what," sparks Chloe, "would the veneration of the Great Geoduck be?"

"Chronic cowpox," mutters Rider. "Inconvenient, but providing resistance to more dangerous things like smallpox."

Chloe folds her arms.

"These are all analogies, of course," hurries Rider. "It makes more sense with math. Anyway, the Vulture cult plays a role analogous to opportunistic infection. They can't get a toehold until the host society is weakened. The Weimar Republic just recently became—ah—a commonly referenced example." He blushes.

"Can't attack a strong society. Why?" asks Washington, becoming interested despite himself.

"Because the Vulture cult is a pathetic excuse for a belief system! Their god is uncaring, greedy; it spurs its followers to gross excess. Like a big, fat, weak germ that stomps into the bloodstream and starts attacking everything it sees. A healthy body pounces and the infection is over. So even a society on the skids, like San Francisco, can tolerate only a tiny number of cultists; any large number—like, more than ten—draws attention to itself."

"Hold on," says Chloe. "The Incumbents are excessive, too, but they show no signs of getting thrown out."

"The Incumbents get reasonable return for their atrocities. When the Vulture cult destroys somebody, the lion's share of the mana goes to their god. Er—this is where the quantitative approach becomes necessary."

Chloe scratches her head. "Okay, you say it's like epidemiology, right? If the Vulture cult is inefficient, then they should be crowded out of their 'ecological niche' by the Incumbents."

"Well, let me continue with the analogy. Take the Weimar Republic. A small group of cultists enters the nation, and the society is too weak to keep them from growing and spreading—just like an opportunistic infection. Eventually the society rallies—this would be when Hitler cracked down.

The cult is mostly wiped out. But small groups of cultists escape. This would be equivalent to sporulation. These groups scatter and lie in wait for another weak society. Most don't make it—even their small excesses draw the attention of the Incumbents or the Opposition."

Chloe says, "So we're facing no more than ten cultists? Al, just to reanimate two dozen thin dogs would take a master necromancer over a year of work. And that's with efficient magic; you're saying they lose most of their mana to their god."

"Bingo. Damn, you catch on fast. Did I ever tell you that really pisses me off?" Rider grins at her. "So what I think we have here is a *synergistic* infection. San Francisco is weakened by the struggle between us and the Incumbents, sure. But a simple thirty-member congregation performing a mass would set off our alarms like nobody's business—unless the Vulture cult has allies, either here or elsewhere, bankrolling and protecting them."

"Who?" says Maggie-Sue.

"I don't have an answer for that. Biff might have known—he knew they were present in the City, which is more than we knew—but he was in no condition for interrogation, and we can't ask him now without recovering his corpse."

Silence.

"If they're so incompetent, how'd they spot us?" says Chloe.

Rider shrugs. "Must have something to do with that hospice. Although if it is a cult HQ, or even just a shrine, it should have stood out like a sore thumb when you went through it. Unless the damned Geoduck fell down on the job again."

"I'll thank the man in the glass pentagram to not cast spells, all right?" says Chloe. "Now, we only saw it during the day. What if it's just a holding pen or something, and they move people out during the night? Maybe there was somebody watching the entrance from afar, checking out anybody who went in with their third eye open."

"Good," grunts Washington. "Means we need someone to swing by and eyeball it at night."

Everybody turns to Thiebaud, who is arranging grains of sugar with a toothpick.

Chloe says, "Now that we know what we're up against, how do we prepare to defend ourselves?"

Maggie-Sue says, "I'm not leaving until Arbeiter and Sturgeon are okay."

"Or they die," says Washington.

"Fuck you."

Washington grunts. "Vulture's just a bird. Birds can't fly with salt on their tails. I need salt. I'll go get some."

"Eh?" says Rider. He doesn't get an explanation.

"Religious gluttons. Terrific," mutters Chloe. "Religion. Religion. Well, if they're a religion, they have heresies—all religions do, even mine. And heretics know all the weaknesses of the mainstream, right? And it has even happened that they write them down to teach other heretics. So does anybody know of any Vulture-cult heresies?"

People peer at the ceiling, scratch their heads, furrow their brows. "Well," says Whitlomb, "there is one theory—rather speculative, I'm afraid—"

"Authored by somebody some of us may have met—" interrupts Rider.

"Mea culpa, thank you, Al—a theory that the philosophy whose practitioners we designate 'the Incumbents' may have originally been a heretical sect of the Vulture cult. The archaeological evidence has been reliably dated at approximately fifteen thousand BCE."

Chloe says, "That doesn't help a whole bunch, Perry. What was the heresy?"

"Moderation."

"Ah."

More chin-rubbing and touching of the back of the head.

Whitlomb shrugs. "Well, what say I review the literature Al and I gathered in pursuit of his thesis, with particular reference to heresy. Al, you could do worse than to *finally* do the follow-up work with the Chinese and Vietnamese oral traditions you've been promising."

Rider chuckles. "Yes, Professor." He turns to Chloe and adds, "The Chinese probably have some good ways to deal with them either way; Lord knows they've been through enough ups and downs."

Chloe says, "If you can get along without me for a little bit, I should fly up to Seattle and report this. They may be able to send some help."

"Oh, that's the last thing we need. *Two* of you."

Chloe rolls her eyes. "Shut up, Al."

Whitlomb says, "Seattle has more than enough troubles of its own. I doubt they will be in a position to divert resources to San Francisco."

Washington snorts. "One other thing."

"Yes, Joe?"

"Usually Sturgeon says this. He can't, so I will. Maybe we should get out, or shut our third eyes and wait for it to blow over. Or if any one of us wants out, go now. No shame."

As usual, they carefully make a show of considering it.

"Where's to run to?" murmurs Chloe.

"Closing the third eye ensures you will not see it. But it does not *guarantee* it will not see you," says Whitlomb.

"Yep yep yep. Nobody here but the usual bunch of bright-eyed guacamole-brained suicidal maniacs. I am so full of righteousness I could just spit." Rider spits.

"Okay," says Chloe. "So I'll skip Seattle, and stay here to help Maggie-Sue out."

"Sounds good," says Rider. "So, Cree—oh, rats. Creedon? You in the head or something? Did anybody see where Creedon went?"

"Does anybody, ever?"

．　■　■

"Nothing? NOTHING? You mean you spent the whole night skulking around San Rafael and you saw NOTHING?"

Another typical breakfast at Chez Rider. Thiebaud folds an origami chrysanthemum.

"Are we FOOLS? Are we on DRUGS? Have we lost our MINDS? Have all our remaining brain cells gone to LUNCH??"

"Al, take a red, huh?" Chloe says wearily.

"We are missing something OBVIOUS, here, people!"

"Joe, go sit on Al. He's becoming hysterical again." Joe grabs Al and sits on him.

Whitlomb gets up and starts pacing. "Do not panic. Panic is counterproductive at this stage, so I suggest calm. Do not panic."

"AAAUGH!"

"Nobody else panic, that is. Let's review the bidding. Creedon saw nothing suspicious at, in, or near the hospice. Maggie-Sue believes that if the fever does not break in the next two hours, we will lose Max and Kris; further, she is refusing to leave their sides, and Chloe has a small contusion attesting to her unwillingness to do so. My efforts revealed two heretical Vulture-cult outbreaks, one in the Roman Empire and one in the British Empire, but the first was coopted by the Opposition and the second by the Incumbents. Neither yielded useful insights. Joe returned with ten pounds of Haitian salt, of obvious utility should the Vulture cult continue to make use of necromancy. Al hamstrung a zygodactyl Samoan mugger—who may or may not have anything to do with this—and then spent the day's remaining hours on the phone in search of a source of vulture feathers."

"We're pretty much fucked," says Washington.

"AAAUGHmmmgmgbmh," says Rider as Washington stuffs a handkerchief in his mouth.

They hear a thin German accent say, "Chloe, I have some reds in my bag." Eight feet pound for the next room. There is a traffic jam in the doorway.

"Kris! Max! You're alive!"

"Of course we're alive. You were yammering loud enough to wake the dead."

"How long were we out? What happened?" says Sturgeon.

A babble of voices rapidly catch Arbeiter and Sturgeon up on what has occurred. Arbeiter laughs long and loud as Whitlomb tells them about Rider's overdose of aphrodisiac. Sturgeon concentrates intensely as Chloe briefs him on the Vulture cult.

Sturgeon groans. "Let me sit up . . . give me some water . . . no, beer. Can I have beer?" Maggie-Sue whipnods, fetches a Red Tail. "Thanks." Nk. Nk. Nk. "Ahhh . . . thought I might never taste that again. . . . Okay. So we're dealing with people who accelerate personal and social decay."

"Boy, that narrows it down," mutters Arbeiter.

"The obvious place to look is a *center* of personal and social decay."

"What, Los Angeles?" queries Rider.

Whitlomb snaps his fingers. "No! Of course, why didn't I think of it before? Stanford!"

"Rider, Whitlomb, shut up. Let me think a minute."

Sturgeon thinks a minute. Everybody waits with bated breath.

Sturgeon thinks another minute. Everybody starts breathing again. Chloe scratches an itch that has been driving her crazy.

"I HAVE IT!"

"What? WHAT?"

"WE'LL JUST—oh, no, wait, that won't work."

Rider beats his head against the wall. "I'm going out for a smoke. If either of these two rocket scientists comes up with anything, I'll be out on the balcony revising my will."

"You two should get some rest," says Chloe.

"Not too much. Plenty of time to rest in the grave," says Washington.

. ∎ .

Nobody can think of anything useful to do with the rest of the day; a fine miasma of cabin fever settles over the loft. Rider becomes particularly unpleasant to be around. Many people inwardly curse the fact that he has the best-defended installation of any of them, because you can't very well throw a fellow out of his own home.

Sturgeon and Arbiter become woozy and slip into a dream-racked sleep as their systems fight off the last of the Lockjaw of Doom. About two, Rider's mania mutates and he leaves the table with lunch untouched and his eyes become fixed and dilated and he starts rushing around in the lab doing things that make one's eyes hurt just to watch. Washington takes Whitlomb aside and asks what Rider is doing. Whitlomb waves his hands reassuringly. Washington sits on him. Whitlomb hems and haws for a while, and eventually admits he thinks Rider is preparing Doomsday devices against the circumstance they are cornered like rats and have to depart this plane of reality with as much noise as possible.

Night comes. Rider burns midnight oil, chattering to himself in polyglot. Washington tries to talk to him. Whitlomb tries to talk to him. Chloe tries to talk to him. Maggie-Sue screams at him for a while. They send in Thiebaud. Thiebaud comes out. He shrugs and offers to go watch the hospice again. They tell him to take first watch instead.

In the room with two cots, Arbeiter leans over and shakes Sturgeon's shoulder.

Sturgeon gets up on one elbow. "What?"

"Are you awake?"

"No, I talk in my sleep. What?"

"Do you believe in life after death?"

Sturgeon sits back and knuckles his eyes. "Of course. If there isn't life after death, then where do all the ghosts come from?"

"You don't have to have life after death for there to be ghosts. I mean, maybe souls die just like bodies do. Ghosts are living souls without a living body. That's what the necromancers say."

"I suppose so."

"And then zombies would be people with dead souls who are still walking around."

"Mhnph. You know, Perry was talking about the undead a couple weeks ago."

"Yeah?"

"He and Al were arguing about what kind was the most dangerous. Most people say lich, but Al was holding out for mummy. Then Perry snapped his fingers and said he'd just remembered the *worst* kind. He said, a lich's dead, but once he's laid to rest, he takes his chances on Judgment Day with the rest of us. The *worst* kind of undead, he said, has a mind that's never known death and a soul that's already been judged."

"That makes absolutely no sense."

"That's Perry. He said—hang on, let me think—something about desire running rampant without the brake of karma? No, desire without soul—desire taking its cue from the maya around it. I don't know. Anyway, Al looked sick and said it could never happen naturally, and then the two of them started yelling at each other in Tibetan. I tuned out."

"Hmn."

"Kris?"

"Ja."

"Why did you wake me up?"

Arbeiter leans in Sturgeon's direction, eyes gleaming. "Black pawn? Or white? I say white pawn. This time, we got lucky. We may not, next time."

Sturgeon thinks. Thinks again. "No. Black pawn. Maggie-Sue can barely tie her shoes in the morning, but there is one thing she understands better than any of us."

"Fuck you," says a voice they didn't know was there.

. . .

Arbeiter and Sturgeon manage to shuffle to the table. The serum is screeching through their systems like a thousand randy Siamese cats; which makes sense, because that's one of the ingredients.

"First order of business. Somebody get some straw. We're drawing lots to see who goes in and tries to find out what Rider is doing."

"Max, don't you think that should be a volunteer-only mission?"

"Fine, Chloe, fine. Volunteers?" Seven thumbs and thirty-six fingers reach for the sky. "Happy? Where's the straw? No cheating, anybody." Whitlomb gets the short straw. Rises with a sigh.

"While Perry tries to communicate with the head case in there, let me present some vague ideas I've been working on. . . ."

. . .

"Al!"

Rider's red eyes meet Whitlomb's spectacles. "I'm busy, Perry."

"I know, my friend, I know. Perhaps you could enlighten your aged teacher on the nature of the pursuit on which you are squandering your reserves? Or perhaps you do not feel your condition of readiness is of any concern to the other members of your cell?"

"Where are the cards?"

"What, your Tarot cards? How should I know?"

"Not my Tarot cards. The cards you wrote that speech on before you came in here. Oops, forgive me, misspoke myself. The cards Sturgeon wrote the speech on before you came in here."

"Clever, boy, clever; nobody's ever beat you at the dozens. With a proper upbringing you might well have been your generation's Lenny Bruce. Now cut the dramatics and talk."

Rider rolls his head around on his neck. Pulls over a stool with his foot. "You have any bourbon on you?"

Whitlomb holds out his flask.

"Can't take it. I've got gunk all over my gloves. . . ." Whitlomb comes across the room, holds the flask to Rider's lips. "I shouldn't drink in here at all. Not safe," says Rider, and drinks.

"Al . . . are you contemplating worst-case scenarios?"

Gurgle. Cough. "What?"

"My best guess was that you were planning one last nasty surprise for our winged associates."

"Huh? No. Well, maybe. Look, Perry, all I'm doing is distilling cancer out of cigarettes. We may need to put together a customized bullet, here."

"Cancer is not a quick death." Rider shrugs. Whitlomb says, "The only purpose such a weapon serves is to guarantee your honor guard includes a leader."

"Probably."

"Are you having any luck?"

"Yeah, one dose worth. It all came together tonight. I mean, I could *publish* this, it's a breakthrough. But I've gone through every cigarette in my stockpile and it took three-quarters of my supply of diamond to stabilize it. On the other hand, now I can smoke as much as I damn well please. Want a couple cartons?"

"Emphysema."

"Yeah, well."

"Cigarettes are carcinogenic, but not overwhelmingly so. Why not simply attack with dioxin?"

"Dioxin usually causes mundane neoplasms, which are treatable. But tobacco is special; it didn't cause cancer until the California coastal tribes were decimated and the Crab totem put a curse on the plant. That's why it's relatively easy to extract—it's not really part of it in the first place."

Whitlomb frowns. "The Crab totem has not influenced the affairs of man for at least two hundred—oh, I see. The last gasp, as it were."

"Yeah. Had a lot of psychic energy tied up in beaches and reefs." Rider rubs his hands together under a stream of phenol, another of ethanol, then water; strips off the gloves and tosses them into the incinerator. Washes up. "I'm scared, Perry."

"I, too."

"Sturgeon isn't."

"Hence his position of leadership. Someone has to keep in touch with the maya level of reality, tell occultists which fights are worth it and which aren't."

Rider shakes his head. "God, don't remind me. I still can't get a handle on that."

Whitlomb shrugs. "You have lived with it for longer than I. Your squeamishness betrays a certain lack of cynicism that I, as an aged and bitter man, find refreshing. Except when I find it infuriating. But be grateful that Sturgeon is not the *usual* Opposition coordinator."

"Yeah. Baby-faced kid new to the whole scene, too young for the odds to have sunk in . . . Like those poor bastards in Chicago; what've they had, four leaders in the last year? It's not fair, you ask me. Tell them they're the man without warning them about the turnover . . ."

"It's not just the leaders. A year ago, we could have taken Kris and Max to Dr. Garner, before the Clown Hammer caught up to him."

"Don't remind me. Did those guys out of Maine ever manage to get him?"

"Not yet, and they've lost two people trying. . . ." Whitlomb polishes his glasses. "Still. You are not one to fear death or dismemberment."

"Ha."

"Not morbidly, at least. Are you, then, isolating yourself because of our necessary status vis-a-vis Max?"

"No, it was just I could tell I was pissing everybody else off . . . I don't know. But what you're saying; hell, what we *should* do is tell Sturgeon to get out, and handle this ourselves."

Whitlomb's expression becomes very, very cold.

"I know we can't. But I don't want the temptation. If he didn't irritate me so much I would've warned him off eleven months ago. I guess that's a pretty rotten thing to say, huh?"

"I give thanks to God above for your intolerant personality, then."

"Phooey. We're going to lose him on this one, Perry."

"Perhaps. Perhaps not. And even if so, there will still be Chloe."

"What? Chloe knows the score." Whitlomb looks at him. "Perry, you said you'd fill her in!"

"I did make that statement. But I rather counted on finding a suitable replacement for Max beforehand, and so I have not done so."

Rider stares. "So what! She can still open her third eye. It's not fair to keep her in the dark!"

"Fair? Fair? It is not 'fair' to keep *anybody* in the dark. 'Fair' is not a priority an underground has the luxury to pursue—as you well know." Rider gapes. "Al, Al. She's just a totemist."

" 'Just a totemist'?! Johanson explained things to *you,* and you've never so much as drawn a pentagram in your life!"

"And that was an error of epic proportions!" thunders Whitlomb. "It is I who should be next in the line of succession. My inability to master the occult—the fact I have one foot in the grave already—were it not for his rampant sentimentality, we would not be driven to retain Chloe in my place!"

Rider stares. Whitlomb is made of iron. Rider leans back. "So this is what happens when a suicidal tendency is sublimated. You start plotting the deaths of your friends."

"It is your anger speaking, Al. You know as well as I: I wanted life, not death."

"Nobody gets tempted by a vampire unless they want death, Perry."

"Be that as it may, you cannot deny we need a backup leader. Chloe is it; there is none other available. End of discussion."

Rider sneers. "At least now I think I know where one of the white pawns came from."

"Getting old, Dr. Rider? Do you find yourself unable to meet your reflection in the eye?"

Uncomfortable pause. Rider sits down.

Whitlomb puts his hand on Rider's shoulder. "We're going to lose both of them, Al. I don't know who or what is powerful enough to cloak an entire cult without showing themselves to us. But we are going to take casualties—and you know who goes first."

"And afterward, if there is an afterward, what do we do; cruise a New Age convention and recruit some cat-and-crystal-worshipping dingbat to wear the bullseye?"

"Probably. Somebody from the Lizard totem, ideally. We're not overwhelmed with options."

Rider stares into his lap.

"Let's go, Al. Enough is enough. Time to show your face."

·   ·   ·

Sturgeon looks up. "Well?"

"Just another of Rider's adolescent snits," says Whitlomb.

"I was not in a snit. Anyway, we've got a dose of cancer to play with, now."

"Great, just great," sneers Chloe, tossing her hair. "You and Arbeiter have got to open up an abattoir one of these days."

Sturgeon clears his throat. "Anyway, you two, we've got a plan. We're getting mobile at twenty hundred hours. I'll explain, and then we'll all prep for a stalking-horse run."

"Who's the horse?" asks Whitlomb.

"Well, Joe's the one who gets ridden all the time."

·   ·   ·

Washington staggers off BART at the Oakland West station, stinking of piss and Ripple. Mumbles as he shoves his ticket into the side of the turnstile, crumpling it; painful flattening, tries to put it in backward. Rider has bolted a real street person's raw invisibility to his flesh to delude even the third-eye-open crowd. Yuppies will look away—but to urban predators, he is raw meat. In this neighborhood, there are no yuppies and plenty of predators.

And, with any luck, scavengers.

The flesh between Washington's shoulders crawls. His third eye is squeezed shut and he feels helpless. The woman on the nighttime train, the woman with the ivory skin—vampire, or just a trendy student? Fly trap or secretary? What unguessable shuggoth might there be, under the flickering mercury lamps?

Derelicts slump in doorways. Incomprehensible impassioned arguments. Fires burn in the middle of the street with nobody near. Sirens and distant gunfire. Washington's job is to stagger in a direction for a while, stop and wait—a wounded bird with no nest to flee to. Like a refugee from a sprayed and bulldozed anthill; staggering jerk-jerk, sick with almost enough Malathion to finish it off.

It's not any prettier to Arbeiter, although it is a little brighter. Will-o'-the-wisps congregate in the pools of dark, drawing in the walking wounded, hovering over them and taking little sips. But there aren't as many as usual. They do not have minds as such, and are probably sowing the seeds of their own starvation by drawing Vulture cultists to carrion.

Actually, will-o'-the-wisps never starve. They can always move on. The Opposition has given up trying to exterminate them.

If Sturgeon's cell is really lucky, there will be the wail of a Bean Sidhe. The sound is bound to draw Vulture cultists like a dinner bell—Maggie-Sue can swoop from the sky and watch for their approach. Failing that, there's Washington.

Arbeiter has borrowed Rider's 650. Hates it. Pathetic engine, sloppy suspension. Quiet as the grave, though, and that ain't just whistling Dixie. He wonders what sounds echoed in the mausoleum when Rider pulled away the silence and wadded it into his jeans. Arbeiter scans the black sky, catches a high-altitude glimmer of Maggie-Sue and Rider. Wonders amusedly if Rider is trying to cop a feel as he clings to her back in the soft hurricane. Thiebaud's arms are wrapped around Arbeiter like a band of coyote bone, ready for quick acceleration.

Washington is being harassed by a drunk. Nothing occult about it. He puts up with it until the drunk draws a cheap switchblade. Arbeiter whispers "No witnesses"; his throat mike sends these words to the Communications, Command, and Control panel truck idling just off the freeway. Chloe is at the wheel and Sturgeon is in back, hunched over the switchboard under red lights. Whitlomb sits beside Sturgeon, plotting positions on a map of the Bay Area and running periodic checks on the electronics. Three C relays the message. Washington takes the knife away and knocks out the drunk, moves on.

Adrenaline has you jumping at shadows, the first hour. It keeps you going the second. By the third hour, your eyes are scratching runnels in your lids when you blink and you know in your heart that the night will last for weeks, or perhaps the sun will never come up at all, ever. You know you can't let your attention flag for more than an instant, or else that will be when the storm comes and you'll never know what hit you.

Sturgeon and Whitlomb are pounding coal black navy coffee and scarfing antidiuretics. Rider is snuggled close to Maggie-Sue. He can even smell her: sometimes ozone, sometimes rain on parched earth, sometimes a forest fire devouring pine. Once, a bestial musk that forces him to concentrate on baseball for a while. He wonders how many people in the world have ever gotten this close to her and lived to tell the tale.

While Rider is mulling over the problem, wondering if Chloe and Maggie-Sue ever got together, Thiebaud taps Arbeiter's thigh. Points with a subtle twitch of a finger. There is a black-cloaked figure oozing around the corner and drifting toward Washington as he pisses against a wall. The figure's head bobs as it moves. Arbeiter calls it in.

Maggie-Sue hisses. Rider fingers a nylon coil as they drift down a few blocks away, glide over rooftops. The whirlwind Maggie-Sue rides is too noisy to take down to the street or stealth in close to the surveillance zone, and Rider has yet to find a way to muffle it. "Check belay."

"Check," she hisses.

"Belay off," he says, and drops through the night like a spider swinging on silk. Touches down, unhooks the line. Two long pulls, one short—the line vanishes up into the dark sky. Far away, a church sounds one bell.

"Creedon has you," says the voice in Rider's ear. "Go."

"Wilco." This is the fourth possible of the night. Rider hopes the Apache were right when they said four is the most magical number. Wonders where Creedon is; he amuses himself, sometimes, trying to spot him when he knows he's around but not showing himself.

"You're there," says Sturgeon. "Doorway on the left." Rider slips into an abandoned building, the padlock hanging open. Thiebaud is inside. Finger crooks. Up stairs to the second floor, summer wind hissing through shattered windows over filthy, splintered hardwood. Chains banging against a pipe, somewhere. Thiebaud flattens against an outside wall, side-cranes a look at the street. Waves Rider forward. Rider eases his head sideways to bring an eye to a dusty shard of glass. Feels his cheek crawling with spiderwebs and fear of a sniper's bullet.

Definitely occult, unlike the last three. Calls it in. "Please advise."

Sturgeon listens to the pitch coming in over Washington's open mike. Mission. Direct action. Twelve point program. Halfway house. "Maggie-Sue, get altitude and proceed to position over Treasure Island. Al, wait thirty seconds and do it."

Rider mentally reviews Washington's instructions. Wishes Washington could run the check himself without blowing his cover. Wishes Thiebaud could just walk up and touch the figure and know immediately, but there's too good a chance a real cultist would be too strongly shielded.

Rider drinks a bitter potion.

The sky opens and the gods lean in, dicing for souls. The earth opens up and the worms gnash their teeth in anticipation. *I hate voodoo,* thinks Rider. Behind him, he can feel Thiebaud's iron Star of David throb and hum under the gaze of the god who demands an eye for an eye. He can see that Joe's teeth have held the bits of Samedi and Erzulie. And he can see a naked head and the great wings of a shape above, gazing benevolently at the figure leaning over Washington. "Match, match, we have a match," says Rider.

"We're on. Get ready to roll," says Sturgeon.

There are too many things in the sky for Rider to concentrate on the tableau. He watches the gods. Looks from one to the other to see if any are watching him. Thiebaud hovers in the shadows, glances occasionally at Rider, whose eyes have rolled up into his head; nothing but white shows.

Washington hears "We're on." The priest leans over him; kind and gentle, helps him to his feet. Washington staggers and mumbles. They approach a van. There are others in the van—recovering street people, another priest. They smile and greet him. Sing "Amazing Grace" as the van burbles north.

· · ·

"Creedon, how's Al?"

"He is not moving, Mr. Sturgeon. And I believe he is weeping."

"Okay. Don't let him go anywhere for a couple hours. It's mostly hallucinations he's seeing—anything coming for you two, you'll have to spot yourself. And he may go crazy, start casting spells—watch your talismans."

"I remember, Mr. Sturgeon."

"Right. Kris, stay close. Three C is en route to the Richmond–San Rafael. Keep us advised."

· · ·

Washington is in a rolling box with five people who appear to be recovering alcoholics. There is also a driver, and a cassocked priest up front. In a sense, he is trapped. On the other hand, in the confined space, they would just get in each other's way. Washington is confident that jumping him would be stupid; pulling a gun, suicide. He studies the drunks, recognizes typical mundane cult trappings: songs, silly games, big baked-on smiles, and protein deficiency.

· · ·

"Arbeiter here. They're taking the Bay Bridge, not the Richmond–San Rafael. They're going to the City."

Sturgeon curses as Three C takes the off-ramp and Chloe heads for the on-ramp leading the other way. Fortunately, he sent Maggie-Sue toward Treasure Island just in case something unexpected like this happened. "Maggie-Sue. Proceed to San Francisco. Keep altitude."

Uncomfortable silence; time passing. Chloe keeps the truck in the second lane, going as fast as she can without getting too far from the off-ramps. Finally, the radio crackles, "Arbeiter here. Through the toll gate, continuing westbound."

Whitlomb is monitoring the Cal-Trans radio traffic. Accident on the City-bound upper section of the Bay Bridge, probably a drunk. Traffic toward the bridge slows to a crawl. Chloe pulls onto the frontage road and makes slightly better time. Sturgeon fumes in the back.

"Arbeiter here. They just took the Treasure Island exit."

Sturgeon pounds his thighs. Big error. Should have kept Maggie-Sue directly over the van, doctrine be hanged. "Maggie-Sue. Back to Treasure Island. Hurry. Arbeiter, stay close as you can. Washington, turn your repeater to maximum." Distance and bearing figures gain several decimal places of precision, flickering in red LED, and Whitlomb plots the reading on a more detailed map.

"Arbeiter. The van is going up the Yerba Buena residential road. Doesn't look good. Should I intervene?"

"Joe, you want extraction, let go the dead man's switch now."

Nothing. "Negative, Kris."

"Okay. There they go—into a residence, big iron gates going through a crenellated stone wall, can't follow. Looks like they're headed for the garage. Ja, garage."

Whitlomb notes distance and bearing—still good. Then the numbers oscillate wildly and flicker out. He punches up the telemetry records. "Contact cut off. Last moments show constant bearing, fast increasing distance. Broadcast attenuated, then vanished. Closing Faraday cage would be my guess."

"Maggie-Sue and Kris, meet each other at TI-9, by the numbers." Thanks the heavens for all the drills.

"Arbeiter. En route."

"Maggie-Sue. En route." She power-dives through the night, finds a certain stand of trees, drops to the earth, and runs to Arbeiter and his bike. They return to the gate the van passed through.

· · ·

It was dark in the van before. Still dark. Washington can feel the van dropping. When the radio chatter stops he knows he is cut off. The descent ends and he hears the van shift back into gear. It goes around a whole bunch of corners. Spends some time on a turntable in a completely black chamber. Back into gear. Washington casually looks out the window—rough-hewn rock, actinic lights dangling from a cable strung down the walls as they surge down a long, long tunnel that has no right to be there. There are doors, clearly waterproof, swung back against the walls every few hundred yards. They're going in a direction he cannot guess. The trip goes on for several minutes.

And, with sinking heart, Washington feels the van cutting occult force planes. They are approaching a bubble of mana, like the one covering San Diego; but since the core is smaller, the flux density delta is much more intense. Soon his third eye will be forced open, at least a little. His cover is looking very dicey and his friends are converging with all possible speed on the wrong place. If his hair hadn't turned white on a certain Haitian afternoon it would turn white now, and his three-foot-eight frame is not big enough to contain his consternation.

· ■ ■

"Arbeiter here. Please advise."

Sturgeon grimaces. Please advise, indeed. One mage down with hallucinations and Creedon the only one powerful enough to stay in the same room with him. Three C stuck in traffic. Kris and Maggie-Sue staring at cult HQ. "Three C is en route to Treasure Island. We've got all we need—go get Joe out. Maggie-Sue, you wait outside and only go in if Kris calls for help."

"What if I hear gunfire?"

"Wait."

"What if he gets hurt, can't call for help?"

"Do as I say, Margaret."

Arbeiter parks the bike. Takes off his helmet, begins digging things out of the saddlebags. His heaviest weapon is a Heckler & Koch MP5 submachinegun with an integral silencer. Arbeiter takes a little black box from a pocket, plays it up and down the exterior wall. Nothing—no motion detectors, infrared beams, or inductance sensors. He shrugs.

"Maggie-Sue, I want you to get high over the site and do a thorough recon. Don't get spotted. Radio silence."

She nods, runs far, far away into the night. Arbeiter waits.

Arbeiter watches for guards. Nothing. Fifteen minutes pass; it takes time to run, fly up, snap photographs, fly down, and run back. Maggie-Sue arrives a little out of breath, gives Arbeiter the pictures. He memorizes them.

Sturgeon says, "Three C here, Kris. We're on the Bay Bridge, almost to the exit."

.   .   .

The bubble comes closer. Washington braces himself. Opposition operatives have died, flying into San Diego, when the aura of the place suddenly overwhelmed their defenses. Unlucky ones survived the shock but absorbed the paradigm—switched sides. Rider almost went that way, once— barely made it in time to the lavatory, held on to his sanity by stuffing a Warren Zevon tape into—well, he almost didn't make it.

It hits. For all the dark, Washington is suddenly dying of heat and light and thirst, and he looks up, grateful for the buzzards circling down to release him from the earth.

The five people in the van are wearing black. Ruffled collars. Shaved heads. Perched with their hands folded before them. One pulls his head back, hissing, but then recovers his composure. "You have fallen far, brother."

"I have," says Washington.

"You have been in the grave before, haven't you?"

"Yes. Poisoned by my grandmother to take the passage and know the other side."

"And you have longed to return."

"I have."

"It will receive you."

"I know."

The van stops.

.   .   .

"I think," says Sturgeon to Whitlomb, "I know how Chloe and I were spotted, even though the hospice is clean."

Whitlomb cocks his head. "How?"

Sturgeon taps a map. "The Yerba Buena site is the HQ. Fortified, because they know when they get strong they'll be hit by both the Opposition and the Incumbents. It's a good place—central location, and people tend to forget about it. Like we did, and I take the Treasure Island exit every day. We forget that TI was built for the World's Fair and it's just bolted on to a whole natural island."

"Indeed."

"But they have both Yerba Buena and the Treasure Island base under surveillance. Eventually, they sniff out traces of the Opposition—me. My third eye is almost completely shut, most of the time, so all they know is there's a weak occultist around every now and then. They start watching the bridge."

"Yes?"

"Then I pick up Chloe to check out the hospice. She opens her third eye as wide as she can, over in Alameda. And then we take the Bay Bridge. And there are the Vulture cultists, watching. See the two of us swoop through, watching everything around us. Maybe they follow us, see us scrutinizing the hospice. Now they've got a lead on me as the source of their grief. Send the thin dogs after us when we're separated." He grins. "If I hadn't stopped at my boat in the City to change, we would have taken the Richmond–San Rafael Bridge and they would never have noticed us."

Whitlomb nods. "The theory fits the facts well. But what of Al and myself? The four of us dined together that very night; we should all have been under surveillance."

"Good question," says Sturgeon. "Well, you look pretty innocuous—you're almost as bad at this third-eye mumbo-jumbo as I am. And Al is paranoid; they probably lost him when he left the restaurant. Besides, Chloe says his aura scans pretty gray, a whole lot of bad karma—I still think he only plugs for the Opposition for esthetic reasons, not moral. Look how willing he was to deal with San Diego just to keep us going. By the way, when all this is over, we all need to have a long talk about that. In hindsight, it worked out—but I think Al panicked and everybody followed him a little blindly, when you should have been listening to Joe and tried Haiti."

Whitlomb looks at him out of the corner of his eye. "You may well have a point. But do you really consider Al so ambivalent?"

Sturgeon shrugs.

Whitlomb sighs contemplatively, puffing his cheeks. "My student is a fine blend of quick-witted responsiveness and youthful stupidity. But he's not half as dark as any member of the B team."

"Oh, come on. Can you see Maggie-Sue doing anything with an Incumbent but setting him on fire?"

Whitlomb nods. "Her loyalty is beyond reproach. But she never stirs herself unless Joe takes her by the hand; had she never encountered him, she would have spent the rest of her days in bucolic withdrawal. And speaking as Devil's advocate, one could point out that Joe is arguably one of the undead himself; similarly, Kris has a disquieting sadistic streak, and Creedon . . ."

"Yeah, well. But the four of them . . . They're all driven by whatever demons they're trying to exorcise; they've got no way to stop, ever. Rider could snap and go Incumbent any day, and they'd welcome him with open arms."

Whitlomb scratches his head.

Sturgeon suddenly frowns.

"What?"

"Ah; I don't want to, I don't mean, it's just a stray thought, mind, but— Perry, it would explain why he wasn't attacked."

Whitlomb blinks.

Just about then, telemetry from Washington's repeater comes back with a beep.

Whitlomb glances at it. The numbers are very different. "What the devil— something's wrong. Joe is not in Yerba Buena!" Dives for the map. "Saints preserve us! He's in the Farralon Islands!"

Sturgeon lunges for the radio. "Ping from the Farralons! Wrong site! Kris, abort!"

.   .   .

Arbeiter reaches up and pulls himself to the top of the wall—lots of broken glass. The grounds are not well lit and security sucks. Something is wrong. Plays with the electronics again—still clean. He is crouching when he hears Sturgeon call for an abort. Nods as he jumps down and runs for the motorcycle.

Smiles his brilliant smile at Maggie-Sue. "I knew it couldn't be this easy."

.   .   .

They step out of the van into a great concrete-floored chamber. The priest, now revealed to be bald and hunched forward, takes Washington by the hand; they walk through a doorway and into a corridor that turns ninety degrees several times.

Somehow, they step into a desert night; Washington suspects that a synesthetic mage took a trip to Death Valley and converted. The ground is sand, the air redolent with the sort of decay that sets in a little before death. The priest takes him by the hand and leads him to a patch of desert floor. Sagebrush pollen tickles his nose. "Lie down," says the priest. Joe lies down. "What do you like best, my friend? Sweet wine? Hard liquor?"

"Bourbon. Usually Wild Turkey 101, but I guess that's out of the question."

The priest smiles. "We do have some we have treated to take out all the Opposition poisons. For undercover work. They say it tastes just the same, but of course I have no way of knowing." The priest waves. A cowled figure approaches. Whispered conversation. The figure departs as Washington gazes at the moon. The priest comes back, hands a pint flask to Washington, who takes a long swallow. There is a bitter fungal aftertaste.

Washington blesses the fact that true alcoholics don't need much to get drunk—he can keep a clear head and still maintain his cover.

The priest hunkers down. "We have to wait for daylight. Would you like to be alone, in the meantime? If you'd rather have company, we can talk. I am named Violetefeld; I'd like to hear your story."

"Not much to tell."

"Please."

Washington sighs. "Happened the way it always does, with us. Drinking the bird not to counteract the stuff in the water—drinking it to forget. They're so strong, there are so many of them. Seventeen thousand years we've been fighting them, losing more and more ground every century. Only reason we're not extinct is they're always too busy squabbling to get their act together and crush us."

The priest says, "Hitler came close. Even without us, he wiped out almost all of you before the neurosyphilis got to him and the Incumbents wrote him off and let him fall."

Washington nods. "The Opposition used to be able to field armies, not so long ago. Not big ones, but armies. Now it's a network of cells and a few cities where the totems hold on with their fingernails. Even Seattle is going."

"Why didn't you switch sides?"

"Couldn't. Don't have it in my heart to use what I know to be a wolf. Too much sympathy for the sheep. Can't grind the boot. So I started liquoring and shutting my third eye more and more. I've been waiting for something to come out of the shadows for a long time."

"We're here for you now. It'll be good, and clean—and not at the hands of the Incumbents. You and I—we have cheated them of your death; they will not have it. It will all be over soon."

"I know. Want to sleep now."

"All right." Violetefeld leaves.

· · ·

"Joe, this is Max. We're en route. You're in the Farralons. We're at the Marina. We'll be off the air while we prep for a sea trip. Hang on." Sturgeon jumps out of the panel truck. He, Whitlomb, and Chloe run for his Formosa 51. Arbeiter and Maggie-Sue trail in his wake.

Arbeiter says, "You can't be thinking of taking your sailboat."

"I considered it. At least it has a mortar. But you're right, Kris; go find us a motorboat we can steal."

Arbeiter leaves. Sturgeon, Chloe, and Whitlomb swarm over the craft, grabbing weapons and radio gear. Arbeiter comes back. "Got one." They run to a different slip—Arbiter has already picked the lock and taped the door leading from the sidewalk to the dock—and they run down to a brute of a boat. They pile in.

"Okay. Maggie-Sue?"

"Ready."

"Do it." Water surges under the hull, silently backing the motorboat out of the slip, then turning it east to get out of the harbor and into the Bay. When they're clear, Arbeiter hot-wires the engine and Chloe takes the helm. Throttle full out. The boat howls for the Golden Gate. As they pass beneath, watching the headlights of autos crossing the bridge, Maggie-Sue calls up a massive thirty-knot tidal bore to assist and they go like a bat out of Hell.

"Whitlomb, climb onto the prow and rope down, you're the gunner for this run. Set up the Barrett."

"You couldn't have thought of that while we were in harbor, could you?" In his 1890s finery he presents quite a spectacle clambering over the windshield.

"Arbeiter, when we get there, I want you and Maggie-Sue to go in. This is uglier than I thought, so go ahead and use—ah—extreme measures on yourself before you go in."

Arbeiter cocks his head. "Jawohl, mein Commandant."

"Maggie-Sue, you do what Arbeiter tells you. Don't lift a finger to attack unless he says so; you don't have any quiet ways to take anybody out. I want radio silence from you two unless it's an emergency. I want a nice, quiet, *safe* extraction, you hear?"

"All right."

Sturgeon hurries through the distance and bearing calculations, Whitlomb being otherwise occupied; not to mention very cold. Yells a grid coordinate to Chloe. "Chloe, bring us to within half a kilometer and hold position. Maggie-Sue, when you're in there, try not to get killed, we may need you to get us out of here in a hurry."

.   .   .

Washington is lying peacefully on the sand, looking up at the twinkling stars. There are others scattered around—junkies, whippet-thin cancer patients, a woman dressed like a whore whom Washington guesses has AIDS. And heaps of bones, picked clean and bleached white.

.   .   .

Half a kilometer off shore. They stop. Sturgeon orders, "Maggie-Sue, turn us in place 180 degrees, slow. Perry, come on back, set up on the stern—keep the barrel pointed toward the islands." The boat begins turning as Whitlomb lugs fourteen and a half kilograms of .50-caliber Barrett Model 82 to the stern. For a clean kill, Whitlomb senior's elephant gun demanded a head shot. The Barrett 82 could be pointed at the chest of that same elephant, the trigger pulled, and kill the elephant *behind* it. It can grease kraken with one shot—and has. Perry gets down, swings out the bipod, sweeps the island with the night scope. No vegetation. Just black rock covered with guano.

Arbeiter shakes his head. "Whitlomb, it is positively obscene to watch you fondling that thing. Don't shoot the island until we get Joe out, okay? Then you can put a hole in the waterline and watch it sink." Arbeiter finishes drawing the last component of a particularly hellish brew of substances into a syringe.

Whitlomb grunts. "Would that so simple a solution presented itself." Arbeiter ties off, hits a vein, starts pushing the plunger. It's a lot of fluid. It takes a while.

Sturgeon says, "Okay, folks, let's get this show on the road." Arbeiter walks to Maggie-Sue—she turns around and he puts his arms around her.

She says, "Lean into turns, but not too far. Hold tight. Don't shift your head to the side just to see where we're going."

"Ja, ja, just like before."

"Ready. One. Two. Three. Four." They lift off at great speed.

． ． ．

There is a temple, to what Washington thinks is the west, dimly lit by a few guttering torches. Looks like a dead tree, somehow, although it's a fairly simple classical structure with Doric columns. Or maybe Ionic; Washington can never keep them straight. Black, anyway; many carved representations of vultures. No priests around, though. He heard the radio chatter resume, knows they know where he is. Time to lie here and wait for a man who knows the way out.

． ． ．

Maggie-Sue and Arbeiter arrow over the waves and reach the stone without any trouble. Hide in a hollow, waiting to see if anybody heard them come in. Maggie-Sue runs her hands over a rock. "There's a big hollow space under the island, but it's wrapped in thick metal, and warded, too. I can't dig through it."

"What about shafts, tunnels?"

"Can't feel any."

"This doesn't make sense. Maggie-Sue, if he's down below, there has to be a gap in the metal, in that hollow part you mentioned, or else Washington's telemetry couldn't get out. And there has to be a tunnel for Joe to have gotten here."

"I can't feel any. Could be magically hidden. Or they jumped into a flaring day cage and they just came out."

"Faraday, Maggie-Sue, it's called a Faraday cage."

She looks daggers at him.

"Say it's teleportation. In that case, there's no reason to put the installation under an island. Middle of nowhere would make more sense. Is the hollow space above sea level?"

"No."

"Vulnerable to flooding, then. There must be an entrance on this island somewhere—otherwise, their enemies could dig a mine and let in the water and they'd have no way to get out. So either the HQ is atop the island, or there's an entrance to the underground hollow, and that's the HQ, ja? We need high ground to see. Come on." They creep up the slope of black jagged rock. Crest a hill. "There. Those sheds there. Wait here. I'm going in."

"I'm coming with you."

"You need to cover my way out. And you have to get back to the boat to get them out in case something goes wrong." Maggie-Sue glares at him. "Don't look at me like that. Sturgeon told you to not get yourself killed." Maggie-Sue's eyes almost, but not quite, start glowing. "He said to do what I told you to do, too. Stay here." And Arbeiter is gone.

Arbeiter has half a dozen distinct potions coursing through his veins. He feels like a million bucks. Actually, though, the nominal price for that one syringe probably wouldn't be over 20K—if you could get it for currency, which you can't. He spots the guard with laughable ease. The guard is reading a magazine, his Uzi on the rock beside him. Arbeiter takes a little electronic doodad from his belt. A teeny LED flickers. Motion detectors—the guard could be dead, they'd still spot Arbeiter coming in. He sighs inwardly. Things were so much easier before electronics. He starts pulling tripods and black boxes from his pack. Uses a high-tech thingie to spot all the detector units. Mounts the black boxes the tripods, aims them at the detectors. As he emplaces each one, he powers it up. Clever little silicon brains start building up a synchronous signal. It'll take maybe ten minutes. Arbeiter waits.

Time. Arbeiter sneaks toward the sheds. It turns out that the guard has been looking at pictures in a popular Mobile, Alabama, snuff-porn magazine, entitled *Skinned Niggers,* and has commenced masturbating with his free hand. Ick. Arbeiter waits until he is just about to come, head back and moaning loudly, and then jumps out of darkness and plunges a knife into his heart. Eyes bug out. Mouth gapes open. He comes. Arbeiter castrates him. The guard collapses and Arbeiter leans over and whispers "Hurts a lot, doesn't it?" into his ear as he expires. Grins as he collects the fluid—semen of a dying man is worth a lot. Used to be you had to wait for a hanging to get it. Loots the body for keys. Takes the Uzi and spare magazines in case Washington wants a gun in his hands for the trip out.

Arbeiter oozes into the shed, waving electronic wands. Clean. Idiots. Finds a freight elevator and a stairwell next to it. The door to the stairs is locked and wired. Arbeiter does some illegal things to disable the alarm, unlocks the door, and down the stairway he goes.

Uses a dentist's mirror to peep around corners as he descends. Another guard on a landing, awake and alert, Uzi ready. Arbeiter knows that to guard stairs, with lots of blind corners like this, the right answer is to post *two* guards on adjacent landings—so if one is surprised, the other can hear (or, ideally, see) the deed. So he takes a black sponge ball from his bag, kneads it to break the glass vial within, and rolls it down the stairs. As it rolls, silently, it emits a gas that clouds the mind. Arbeiter follows, zips right past the guard as he stands, confused, and throws a knife into the throat of the one on the next landing. Gets down in time to grab the collapsing body and ease it down, checking for a possible third guard—nobody. Back upstairs and dispatches the first guard. He plugs the bores of the Uzis with Kevlar and cyanoacrylate, glues the magazines into place; instant booby traps.

The door at the bottom isn't even wired—and worse, it has a glass window in it. What a bunch of amateurs. Arbeiter carefully peers through it. Big concrete bay, heavy equipment. Deserted. He unlocks and opens the door. Arbeiter ducks into the bay, stays in the shadows and scopes things out. Catches a whiff of sagebrush, which confuses him. Then a guard appears out of nowhere, bursting around a corner not ten feet from Arbeiter. "Hey," says the guard, raising his Uzi.

Arbeiter raises his hands, says, "Relax. I'm the ninja John sent for. I think there's some trouble on the stairs." Gestures to the guard, turns his back on him, and leads him to the stairwell. The guard follows. Arbeiter turns around and stabs him to death. Shakes his head as he drags the corpse into the shadows and doctors the Uzi.

Enough nonsense. Arbeiter checks around the corner, sees a big room with greasy concrete floors and a variety of vehicles, including the van. Sees a long tunnel going off to the east, flanked by steel doors currently open wide. Notes this fact; they may have to take the tunnel out, fight off anybody at the Yerba Buena house. A corridor leads off to the side, and the smell of sagebrush is stronger. Arbeiter takes it. It goes around a few blind corners, stops being concrete and becomes rough-hewn stone. Around one last corner and Arbeiter is standing in the mouth of a cave in a hill, overlooking a desert night. Becomes very confused. Checks telemetry—still looks like he's in the Farralons. Shrugs. Uses night-vision goggles to sweep the desert sand. Spots Washington. Spots the temple. Notices a man with his own set of night-vision goggles with a rifle to his shoulder. Arbeiter dives and rolls and a bullet smacks into the cave wall. Comes up with his MP5 tracking, walks the stream of bullets right into the cultist. From the way he jumps and collapses, it looks like they didn't even have the sense to put him in armor.

Washington is up and moving for the cave mouth, using a hop, skip, and a jump that eats ground but doesn't look like running. They can hear raucous squawks as the echoing reports of the rifle and submachinegun rouse the cultists. A figure erupts from under the sand, grabs Washington's legs—the old buried-guard trick. Washington kicks his chin and Arbeiter hears the neck snap. Not a hue and cry, yet—just a bunch of voices saying, "Hey! Did you hear that?" and "What was that noise?" Washington makes it to Arbeiter. They skedaddle, Washington taking the Uzi and spare magazines as they depart. As they go, Arbeiter slaps time-delay cyanide limpets onto the walls.

Zap around a corner and right into two priests. Arbeiter knifes one and Washington kicks the other. The one Washington kicked bounces off the wall, his left rib cage staved in. Arbeiter's staggers, hollers for help, and pulls a gun. Arbeiter hoses his face with the MP5. Can't armor your face. He slaps a fresh magazine into his gun as they run past the vehicle pool and toward the stairway.

Well, they almost make it to the stairwell door before lights snap on all over the damn place and Klaxons go off. Arbeiter shoves the key into the lock and turns the door handle. Something is holding the door shut. Washington pulls very very hard. No luck. Must be magic. "Cover me," hisses Arbeiter. Washington gets behind a convenient bulldozer blade and waits for the screaming hordes as Arbeiter starts putting limpets on the door and stringing det cord.

A screaming horde shows up—ten morons' worth. Waving pistols that are either too small to punch through the armor Joe and Kris are wearing, or too big to fire unless you actually know what you're doing. Which this crowd does not. One cultist has a Mac-10 but apparently nobody ever told him that even with a fully automatic weapon you still have to aim. Bullets rain all around Arbeiter. Washington fires on the cultists. A bunch of them fall. One actually manages to hit Arbeiter, who shouts in pain. Washington kills the cultist. Arbeiter is down and crawling like crazy for the dozer blade. Gets behind it. Pushes a button. The door blows up. They run through the doorway. Arbeiter can't help but babble "whoop, whoop, whoop" as he goes—he always liked the Three Stooges.

Run up the stairs, slipping a little in the blood from Arbeiter's earlier kills. The upper door isn't sealed. Zoom out of the shed, yelling for Maggie-Sue. Lights are coming on all over the island. The three of them scurry over the hill to the east shore. They each take one of Maggie-Sue's hands and they bound out over the waves, doing the five-hundred-meter fear-crazed Sea of Galilee boogie. Arbeiter radios ahead as they sprint for the boat.

. . .

"I see them," announces Whitlomb. "They're running over the surface of the water. There are a few cultists coming over the hill, as well, searching for them. I do not believe they've looked out at the water yet. Oops, there they go—they're firing. Let's hope they don't get lucky with a head shot."

It is a very long three-minute wait; Washington's stubby legs slow them down, he can't run too fast. They hear motorboat engines revving. The runners are fifty meters off the stern when the first motorboat slews around the island, searchlight slashing wildly across the surface. Lights on the runners. They hear light machine-gun fire and tracers reach across the waves. Find them. The three of them drop into the drink. Sturgeon curses and jumps overboard, swims east.

Whitlomb is squeezing off rounds from the Barrett, one every few seconds. Manages to nail the searchlight, which cuts off the machine-gun fire. Whitlomb's goggles let him keep shooting as the motorboat closes regardless—a grave error on the part of the pilot, in the sense that it's the last he ever makes. A bullet tears through him into the engine. Another bullet takes the gunner. Washington is holding Maggie-Sue's head out of the water, but Arbeiter is bobbing. Sturgeon gets to him, pulls his head up. Washington and Sturgeon backstroke for the boat. Arbeiter comes to, coughs and struggles, but Maggie-Sue is limp. Chloe is shouting at them to hurry, ready to help haul them aboard.

Tracers start coming from the hilltop, whacking into the water all around. Whitlomb returns fire. Everybody reaches the boat. Chloe drags Maggie-Sue up, savagely flips her over—bloody water gushes from her mouth. Checks her airway. "She's breathing—she just cut her tongue," she says.

Sturgeon and Washington get Arbeiter aboard, who stumbles to a seat and hacks at great length. Sturgeon fires up the engine and takes off. Without Maggie-Sue's help, they can't move at the unnatural speed they arrived with—but Sturgeon figures the speedboat can at least maintain distance.

Another speedboat comes around the island. Whitlomb's rounds don't seem to have any effect. A rocket leaps from it, shatters the windshield as Sturgeon ducks, and flashes over the water to explode seven meters ahead. Through the scope Whitlomb can see a hooded figure, his arms raised high. Chambers a tracer, aims, fires. He can see the bend in the streak where the bullet is deflected a meter out. "They're shielded!"

"Joe! Drop a runner!"

Washington sorts through the piles of equipment, grabs a long, thin metal cylinder. Points it at the speedboat and drops it in the water. Certain lizards of *Basiliscus* go so fast and have such big feet that they can run across the top of the water. Arbeiter and Rider raised a few hundred, once. The torpedo sprouts four legs and dashes away.

Another rocket. This one comes in too low and detonates in the water. The shock wave makes the boat ring like a bell. Whitlomb is soaked. The runner makes it to the speedboat. Big explosion. Much cheering.

■ ■ ■

The sun is coming up by the time they pull into the Marina. Maggie-Sue is alive, barely; her armor stopped the bullet from penetrating, but she has a broken rib that badly scratched her pleura. They pile into the panel truck, haul up the motorcycle, and drive to Rider's loft. Rider and Thiebaud are inside, safe.

Rider grins at them. "Hey gang. Tell me the story."

"You all right?" asks Sturgeon.

"Sure. Wore off about an hour ago. Back to normal."

Arbeiter says, "Or nominal, as the case may be."

They tell the tale as Chloe tapes Maggie-Sue's rib and Arbeiter prepares a syringe of Bone-Gro™.

Rider says. "Okay, easy enough. We go back and blow it to smithereens."

Sturgeon shakes his head. "Al, you weren't listening. Machine guns. Rocket launchers. They probably have artillery or helicopters. Even if we attacked with the Formosa, one sailboat of lunatics couldn't do enough damage."

"Let's blow up the tunnel," rasps Maggie-Sue.

"Well, that'll work once," says Sturgeon. "But Joe saw big doors every now and then in the tunnel—water gets into the tunnel, detector goes off, doors shut before the flood gets any further. Clear out the water and repair at their leisure. Sure, it'll cock up their movements for a little while, and it'd be a smart thing to do just before a frontal assault, but it's not a long-term solution in itself."

"Here's another scary idea," says Arbeiter. "There may be more than one tunnel."

"And by now they know damn well somebody big is on to them." says Whitlomb.

part two

The meeting around Rider's living-room table has gone on for an hour and a half. Chloe dropped batter into boiling oil; took note of the shapes it made. Maggie-Sue stared into a pan of hot bubbling mud. Rider entered *pra*, observed the kinematics of arrows, counted beads on a *mala* rosary, threw dice, watched a butter lamp, and tried to figure out what the sight of two pigeons copulating might mean.

When the sun sets, Washington—who hasn't said anything for an hour and a half—stands up. "Sun's going down," he grates. "I'm going to Colma and ask the dead. Back before dawn."

"You shouldn't go alone," says Sturgeon.

"The dead are shy."

"At least take Maggie-Sue."

"*Fuck*, no," bites Maggie-Sue.

Washington says, "Her least of all. Dead people hate Neanderthals. They already have all the best places."

"Don't call her a Neanderthal," says Chloe.

"You're right. Neanderthals are smarter."

"Fuck you," says Maggie-Sue.

■　■　■

They manage to get some sleep. They're still surprised when they hear the doorbell. Washington tromps up the stairs. Maggie-Sue wrinkles her nose. "You're tracking in mud."

"That isn't mud."

"I know what it is."

Washington sits down. Stands up. "Have to wash my hands."

They wait for him with ill grace.

Washington comes back, sits down again. "Chloe, Max—go sail halfway to Easter Island, then come back. Rider. You've been a Journeyman too long. Become a Master. Whitlomb. Go teach someone something. Arbeiter, Thiebaud, there's a corpse in Marin. Here's the address. The ghost is angry. Go take care of it. Hurry; the police will be there in a day. I'm going back to my shop."

"What about me?" says Maggie-Sue.

Washington looks uncomfortable. "Tell you later."

"Tell me now."

"Go fuck a jaguar."

"Fuck you, too."

"No, that's what they said. Go fuck a jaguar."

"Oh. Okay."

"Wait just a damn minute," says Sturgeon. "*Why* are we supposed to do all these things?"

"I didn't ask."

"WHAT?"

Chloe lays her hand on Sturgeon's arm. "Max, they wouldn't have answered. They're dead."

"They sound like fairly standard building-up-mana things," says Rider. "The dead can only see things in the Bardo, and that's only forty days. They can't tell *why* they're important—just what's going to happen."

"Bullshit," says Washington. "The Tibetans have it wrong."

Whitlomb says, "Both of you, cut it out right there. I'm too old to mediate another clash-of-worldviews argument."

Washington grunts. "You know how this works. I can make their afterlives miserable. I grabbed the first dozen souls and told them to tell me how to avoid getting killed by the Vulture cult—because if they didn't do it, or steered me wrong, I'd be coming after them."

Sturgeon says, "So what if they're steering us into just losing and getting crippled?"

"The dead aren't that smart. And one other thing," says Washington.

"Yes?" says Sturgeon.

"Someone come help me get the dead goats out of my Pontiac and butcher them."

■   ■   ■

Maggie-Sue flies south. Takes off her clothes and walks into the jungle.

Washington sinks into the flow of people. Rides buses back and forth, hearing them live. Offers help when he can—mostly by listening. Sometimes by helping: holding an infant as he mewls, mopping puke. Sometimes by stopping: walking into an argument at just the right time to keep it from going to knives and nines and the .50-caliber Desert Eagles too loud to fire in an indoor range.

Whitlomb sits on a bench in Dwinelle Plaza on the campus of UC Berkeley. Tanned flesh, children striving to resemble *Zombi diego*—although the members of the band tend to be a bit pale from the anemia still going around. Students see him. Sometimes they sit. He speaks. Sometimes they listen. They gather around him. He speaks again.

Arbeiter and Thiebaud are in a Marin bedroom. A corpse lies stiffening under pristine white. Thiebaud whispers a number.

Rider is in the workroom, staring at a great rectangle of marble. Hammer in one hand, chisel in the other. A moth lights on his beard. He shoos it away. It flutters round, comes back to rest on his mustache. He sighs, gets up, tries to find a sweater. No luck. He forms a straight razor from a sunbeam, puts the moth atop his head, and shaves off his mustache, rinsing and saving the clippings. Puts them in a shoe box in a storage room. Puts the moth in the box. Considers. Shaves his head and beard and throws them in too.

Chloe and Sturgeon bring the last load of provisions onto the Formosa 51. Go home and sleep. In the morning they use the motor to back the boat out of the slip. They raise the sails and leave the Bay. Skirting the Farralons and pointing the bow west.

.   .   .

Maggie-Sue is up in a tree, eating. Like the monkeys around her, she eats the best part of each fruit and rains the rest to the earth, reaches for another. It looks wasteful but it's the right way to balance carbohydrates against protein. Besides, other animals eat the rest. Sometimes the meat hunger comes up and she pounces on an iguana, breaks its neck and strips off the skin and feeds.

When she watches a stream she does not think, "My, what a pretty stream." Maggie-Sue doesn't think in words, much, even in the city. When she watches the stream all that is in her head is the way it flows, the smell of the water, the sound of it. When she is hungry you can tell by the way she looks at the trees for fruit or nuts, standing ready to climb if she sees what she wants. When she stubs her toe she grimaces but does not go "Ow."

She sees wounded animals, sometimes. Disease. Her city-heart wants to go to them, soothe them, take away their hurts. She does nothing of the sort. She just watches, looking to see if they're disoriented enough to attack her.

Her skin stays pale, under the canopy. Water beads on it when it rains. The soles of her feet are like leather. Her hair hangs in a single braid. Sometimes she spends hours in the tea brown water, her hand moving every now and again to take a fish. Sits and listens to the birds.

.   .   .

On Sunday Washington stays in his apartment over his junk shop. The store is closed. Flies buzz. Washington waits for evening, keeping his hands busy stringing a necklace of snake vertebrae.

It is Monday morning. Washington inspects his hands—scratches from fighting. No matter.

On Tuesday, around ten, a woman comes. Very dark skin. She's been sent by one of the Tarot-card readers Washington suffers to work his neighborhoods—he lets them scam the foolish, but only if anyone in real trouble gets sent to him. She is pregnant, light-skinned girl inside her. Not rape, but in one sense it might as well be. Washington closes the shop. Goes into the back. She pulls off her sundress. Washington places his hand on her belly. She breathes slowly, her eyes on his as he stares into the distance. Her hand reaches around, closes in his snowy hair.

■　■　■

Whitlomb sits in the dining room of a student cooperative bearing the un-likely name Casa Zimbabwe. Black-and-white-tiled floor. Fluorescent lights. Ceiling fans. The building is all of concrete, two wings around a courtyard. When it was built, it was the first "coed" student housing in America—women in one wing, men in the other. According to legend, there was a duenna named Heidi at the base of the women's wing to make sure men didn't invade. Heidi was a friendly person. Many invaders never made it past her room. It has a waterbed and a huge 1970s wallpaper mural of a sunset. Today, the room bears her name, and coopers reserve it in three-day blocks for visitors or sexual liaisons.

Whitlomb is playing bridge. His partner gets the contract—three no-trump. He gets up. Goes into the industrial-strength kitchen, where work-shifters regularly prepare meals for a hundred people. Makes guacamole, grates cheese over tortilla chips, microwaves them. Comes back, sets down the plate. His partner makes the contract—chubby little dark-haired girl, bouncing up and down a little with excitement when her ten of spades takes the last trick, clobbering the king of clubs and jack of diamonds. The two budding engineers at the table glare and mutter at each other. "You threw away the jack of spades," says the Jew.

"Bite me. You tossed the queen of hearts, what was I supposed to do?" replies the Irishman. They shake their heads at each other's stupidity. Whit-lomb beams at them.

"You teaching her bridge, or telepathy, Perry?"

Whitlomb grins. "I believe that's rubber, gentlemen."

"Yeah, yeah. Next time we do this I'm bringing a laptop for help," says the Irishman.

"You? You couldn't code your way out of a paper bag."

The Irishman stretches. "What time is it? Oh, geez. I'm never making that morning lecture."

"In that case, I guess we'd better just hit the hot tub and drink all night," muses the Jew.

"What a remarkable idea you've just hit on. Perry? Nancy?"

"Oh, no," says Nancy. "No, you all go ahead. I'm all tuckered out."

"Come on," says the Jew. "It'll be fun."

"I'd love to. But I don't have—I mean, I didn't bring up my bathing suit."

The engineers shrug. One says, "Doesn't matter to us. We're geeks. Nudity shorts out our brains and we end up dressing you with our eyes."

She blushes. "But—I mean—"

Whitlomb grins at her. "I certainly hope it is not *me* who is causing you concern. You know what the first thing to go is."

She turns bright red. Perry stands up, holds out his hand. "Come. And if either of these louts gets any funny ideas—well, then, I shall give the blackguard a good thrashing."

"Hmnph," says an engineer. "Can't argue with that. That's his job. Alpha male."

"Yep," says the other. "Silverback."

"Besides," says the Irishman, "where are we going to find a fourth, this time of night?"

She stares at him. "Think we've figured out a way to do it," says the Jew.

So they tramp downstairs and out into the courtyard, take the cover off the hot tub. Lower in a round table. Grab a couple six-packs, dunk 'em into an ice bath, cover the table with a towel and fetch some old cards. The engineers and Perry strip. Nancy comes down in a bathrobe, takes it off to reveal panties and a long T-shirt. She clambers into the tub and they play bridge for a while, gazing at the City lights as the late August breeze whispers through the honeysuckle'd trellis. And then they put away the cards and speak of many things.

· · ·

Thiebaud opens Arbeiter's refrigerator, removes a Chinese take-out-food carton. Opens it and looks within. "What is this, Mr. Arbeiter?"

"Radioactive dog liver. Don't eat it."

Thiebaud puts it back.

"Amazing stuff, dog liver. Did you know dogs are the only animals who can hydroxylate 2,2',4,4',5,5'-hexachlorobiphenyl? That was my senior project, developing a virus to add a sequence that codes for that particular cytochrome P-450 isozyme."

"Indeed. Have you profited greatly from your success?"

"Thanks for the benefit of the doubt. It didn't work the way I expected. Hell of a biowar agent, though." Arbeiter digs through his closet. "Hey, here's my alien detector. Did I ever tell you about the time I had Rider hex it to go off every time Chloe was in the room?"

"Mr. Arbeiter, please. I was present at the time."

"You were?"

"Ms. Lee was quite upset."

"Not my damn fault Sturgeon'd just gotten back from *1000 Airplanes on the Roof*. I'll never forget the look on her face when he pulled the gun on her. . . . Here we go. FBI credentials, Agents Bushmill and Daniel. Bah. Now, this is the sort of thing where humor really *is* a bad idea."

"If I recall correctly, Mr. Rider's first effort produced Agent Black and Agent Tan."

"He should never work when he's thirsty. C'mon, San Quentin awaits."

"I am not comfortable with the prospect of returning to that particular location, Mr. Arbeiter."

"Me neither, brother. But Rider's got that spinning-mercury parabola set up; he'll pull us out if they grab us—even through the wall the Incumbents build around prisons." Arbeiter looks at Thiebaud, who is sewing a teabag. "Do you want to wait in the car, Creedon?"

"Of course not, Mr. Arbeiter."

"All right. Remember, you're one of the good guys, now."

Thiebaud does not answer.

.   .   .

The doorbell rings—it doesn't know who it is. Rider leans out the window, looks down at the door. Nobody. Pulls his head back in. Doorbell rings again. Rider's head comes out—still nobody. Scratches his head. Hears knocking. Goes downstairs. Opens the door. Nobody.

Steps into the street, looks up and down. Still nobody. No, wait, one person visible, about five blocks away. Squints. She looks familiar. She looks damn familiar. Rider drops his chisel. The figure takes five steps, covering a block at a stride; then five more, and raps Rider smartly over the head with a wand made of hiccups. Rider feels very foolish.

"Idiot," says the figure.

"Master," gargles Rider.

"And just what do you think you're doing?"

"What?"

Rap. Rider feels foolish again. "I'm an old woman. I don't have time for this." Sweeps into the building and stomps upstairs. Rider trails behind her. She places her hand on the doorknob and enters, which is something that door was specifically designed to not let people do. Rider shuts it behind her and she whirls off her heat shimmer and appears clearly, right before him. Hits him with the wand a few more times.

"What are you doing here?" he asks.

She squints up—long iron gray hair in two braids, brown Apache face a mass of wrinkles; black blouse and stern skirt. "You forgot your chisel. You always were careless with your tools."

"What? Oh. Wait, I'll go ge—" Rap.

"What's the matter, Al? Ashamed to make an old woman come out of her dotage just to keep an eye on you?"

"No. I mean, yes."

"You saying I'm in my dotage?" Rap. "I am very annoyed, in case you haven't noticed. San Bernardino not good enough for you anymore?"

"What are you talking about?"

"Your Master piece, you dimwit."

"Uh, it's not really a Master piece, not per se," he says carefully. "I don't really have time to get involved in all the academic politics to get the skyskin. I haven't even been a journeyman all that long. I'd no sooner try to weave a heat shimmer that I wou—"

Rap. "Than you would summon a Man-totem *Stenos bredanensis*?"

"I didn't know that's what would come! I was just hoping for a ride out far enough to get away from the destroyer!"

"Ah, yes, the destroyer. Never occurred to you to write us about that, did it? Never even crossed your mind. First thing we knew of it was San Diego foaming and raving about the Dolphin totem because one of their precious destroyers went missing and the water was rotten with cetacean magic."

"Look, Master, all I'm doing here is working on a—"

Rap. "I know what you're working on, you blamed fool."

. . .

Sturgeon wasn't sure about the idea. Sailing is more his gig than Chloe's. But they're both ocean totems. Shore totems, actually—her with the Geoduck and him with *Tursiops truncatus*.

He's not too sure about that last, either. Oh, he took Chloe's drugs and it was a bottle-nosed dolphin he saw—not strong enough for him to be a shaman, of course. But he never felt all that connected to dolphins—cute animals, but so what? And he prefers the deeps to the shore. Standing on the deck, no noise but the creaking of ropes and flapping of sails. And Chloe, when she opens her mouth, which isn't often.

Funny, that. She's such a talker when they're all together, and a shameless flirt besides. But she's so quiet when it's just the two of them. In front of the crew, if the situation demands, she'll peel without a second thought; but out here, she doesn't even get down to a bathing suit. Despite the heat, she's always in tight, thin jeans and a T-shirt. Sweat soaking her. When he teases, she's more likely to smile fleetingly than tease right back. Makes no sense. He remembers when they tracked down the necromancers that had defiled his wife's corpse, how she was then. How she walked into his office and sat down on his desk, legs crossed, short skirt; heavy earrings swaying back and forth. Making bedroom eyes as she introduced herself. But as time went on she got quiet and then got even quieter.

She keeps an eye on him, too. Doesn't bother him any, but he knows that when she's not meditating, she's looking out at the waves that just happen to be in his direction. Unless he's scantily clad, like when he's bathing, hosing himself down with naught on but a G-string. All he can figure is that she's nervous about being alone with him, like he'll get ideas and hit on her. He wants to talk to her about it but can't see how to bring it up.

From these musings, we may safely infer that Rider is not the only member of Sturgeon's cell prone to bouts of intense stupidity.

∎   ∎   ∎

Washington is in his element. So is Maggie-Sue. So is Whitlomb.

∎   ∎   ∎

Days have passed in Rider's loft. He can't figure out when his master sleeps. Every time he wakes up in the middle of the night with his hands itching for tools, she's awake, reading.

There are certain difficult incantations, certain complex spells. In theory, all a synesthetic mage need do is cast one in the presence of reliable witnesses and he gains the title Master. But synesthetic mages tend to a certain artistic pretentiousness, and so they make *things* to prove their worthiness. Traditionally a heat shimmer. Rider's master has ruled his project an acceptable substitute—arguably harder than a heat shimmer. But it is a trip down a path Rider is uniquely suited to take. Rider remembers his master studying the Erlenmeyers of stabilized pain with pursed lips, and an expression that might even hint of approval.

She cannot speak a syllable of Sumerian in the workroom, cannot lay a finger on a single piece of equipment, lest she invalidate his effort. But she can answer questions and guide him, so long as the work is all his own. Rider is honest enough to admit that without her he'd be in serious trouble. At least, he admits it after the fourth time she keeps him from going down a blind alley. The text is damnably obscure, skipping steps and using vocabulary Rider doesn't quite understand—written for a full-blown Master, not a mere senior Journeyman.

The marble block becomes a blurred outline and gains definition as time goes on and the moth lays eggs and the eggs hatch. Rider notices that the new generation eats clippings but do not lay their eggs there—they return to the loft only to eat and rest. Time passes. Generations blur; the moths that flutter in and out are at all stages of development. Still, no more eggs are laid in the shoe box. When he uses open flame the moths do not hurl themselves into it. He doesn't have time to wonder about it. He has bigger fish to fry, as it were, ha ha.

■　■　■

Prisons have airlocks; tiny liminal rooms. The guard buzzes them in; the door shuts behind. Arbeiter turns to Thiebaud, who isn't there. He turns to where Thiebaud is, but he's not there either. Arbeiter shuts his eyes. "Relax, Agent Daniel. Take it easy."

"Forgive me, Agent Bushmill. The sound of the lock startled me."

"Keys and all in the baskets, folks. Check your weapons," says the guard. Arbeiter hands over the 10-millimeter semiautomatic he bought just for the occasion.

Thiebaud places his keys in the basket, turns to the guard. "I am not armed, sir," he says.

"Check your weapons, sir," says the guard. Other guards become tense.

"Please feel free to inspect my person," says Thiebaud.

"Step through the metal detector, sir." Thiebaud does so; it beeps. One guard draws a baton; the other approaches with a wand and waves it over him. It beeps over his chest; the guard draws a small penknife from Thiebaud's breast pocket. Eyes are narrowed.

"I had forgotten I bore such a tool," says Thiebaud. "I regret any discomfiture."

"Daniel, you idiot," yells Arbeiter. "No metal. How many times have I told you that? Now it's cavity searches for the both of us. I hope you're happy. I guess we can just tear up those Giants tickets now, huh?" Arbeiter pulls tickets from his pocket, prepares to rip them asunder.

"I am sorry, Agent Bushmill."

Arbeiter stops. Hands the tickets to a guard. "Here, maybe you'll get some use out of them. Shift's changing soon, right? Let's get started on the search. Where do we go?"

The guard says, "I'll have to call my supervisor, sir."

"All right. Agent Daniel! Sit down over there!"

"Yes, sir," says Thiebaud.

The supervisor's belly arrives, and rest of the supervisor enters shortly thereafter. "These are the Feds?"

"Yes, sir, Agents Bushmill and Daniel; Daniel 'forgot' he had a knife on him."

"Who are they here to see?"

"08964, sir."

The supervisor pauses. "The warden know about this?"

"Yes, sir."

"All right. Bushmill, you can go in. Daniel, you're waiting right here."

"But, sir," starts Arbeiter.

"You have a problem with that, Agent Bushmill?"

"No, sir," says Arbeiter. He walks through the metal detector, and the guards buzz him through the next door.

.   .   .

On the open ocean, the Formosa 51 is silent apart from wind and waves. Chloe's voiceless surveillance is beginning to chill him, and surely the sea cruise is folly. It makes sense to get her to the water and let her meditate, venerate her totem, but what the hell is he supposed to be doing? So he exercises a lot, lifts weights, reads—maybe he's just supposed to ready himself by taking a long vacation.

Chloe, for her part, doesn't understand either. Washington wrought a mighty oracle; when it was done, he gave everybody their instructions. But occult insight does not come with explanations. She suspects that the only reason for the trip is to keep the two of them far away from danger while everybody else is too occupied to guard them.

She's not taking it as well as Sturgeon, she knows. She's in a funk, and she knows it, and knowing it isn't helping her get out of it. Sturgeon is a leader of men; when there is no action to coordinate, the general has no work to do, and doesn't mind remaining idle. Her role in the group is vague— sure, she can fly a plane, pilot a boat, or drive a car with the best of them. But she's always support, a convenience. With great effort she can open her third eye, but she's never used in that capacity unless everybody else is busy. She can administer first aid, tend the ill—but Maggie-Sue is a better doctor and Arbeiter mixes stronger potions; she can shoot a gun, but not a tenth as well as Whitlomb. When Rider stands by his sculpture and derides the strength of the Great Geoduck—stands by synesthetic statuary he makes in pursuit of *art,* for God's sake—she can sneer at him, but in her heart she knows he's right and wishes he'd just shut up about it. Of course, she's included in every plan, but only because the Opposition is too short-handed to waste anything or anybody, no matter how weak or incompetent.

Her only unique skill is vamping, when a female seductress is called for. The Opposition's semiofficial designation for such personnel is "cell whore." Her comrades don't use the term. She's not sure whether she's glad they don't call her a whore or angry they don't feel comfortable enough to say what they must be thinking.

Suddenly it all seems stupid. She heard Washington's conversation with the Vulture priest and it echoed her own thoughts. Seventeen thousand years. What if they do defeat the Vulture cult? So what? The San Francisco infestation is destroyed, saving a few thousand souls from a horrid death, yeah. But it's no more significant than curing the stuffed nose of a patient ridden with arteriosclerosis and Alzheimer's. They're not fighting to save the world. They're not fighting to save San Francisco. They're fighting to save their lives. Big deal. Big, fat, hairy deal. Big, fat, hairy fucking deal.

By the time Sturgeon gets to her the tears are copious and she is shaking as she curses through her sobs. "What's wrong? What's wrong?"

She is incoherent. Fists clenched.

"Don't cry. Please, stop crying."

She glares up at him. "Don't cry? Don't cry?! Damn you men, you always say that. You think I want to cry? You think I want"—sob—"I want to be crying?"

Sturgeon attempts a hug.

She pushes him away. "And that's the next thing, little thing's all distraught, put your arms around her and she'll be all right. Leave me alone. Just leave me alone."

Sturgeon has that gutshot-buffalo expression typical of a Real Man in the presence of a weeping friend. Experiencing deep bewilderment and inadequacy as he tries to figure out what to do. Leave her alone? Stay there? Kiss her? Crack a joke? Give her a drink? Hold her hand?

Chloe ignores him. So there they are, hundreds of miles from nowhere, as she cries under the midday sun and he stands, not knowing what to say. The moment lasts a long, long time.

. . .

Arbeiter enters the interview room. Across the table sits 08964, hands folded. The glint of shackles is visible. The walls are gray and scarred; the table's finish a mass of cigarette burns.

Arbeiter lights a cigarette with a wooden match—no paper matchbooks here, the staple is metal. He tosses the pack to 08964. "You have a name yet?" he asks.

"Naw. But I know yours, Kris," says the prisoner. His eyes don't focus, even with the Coke-bottle glasses. He's small, and pale, and going bald.

"Neat trick," says Arbeiter.

"Not really," says 08964. "The yard. I remember. Together, y'know."

"Oho," says Arbeiter. His fingers close around the haft of a plastic knife, which melts beneath them. Arbeiter yanks his hand up and waves it furiously, trailing smoke and gossamer strands of stinking polymer. "Ouch," says Arbeiter. "I didn't know you could recognize me," he says, scraping charred goop off his hand.

"Well, I can. Now."

"I expect you're wondering what brings me here," says Arbeiter. Sun through dingy window picks out beads of sweat on his brow.

"Release, huh? I know you can do it."

"Exactly. Convince me you're rehabilitated, you walk. The Opposition can use you, eight."

"Got everything I need. Got it all, right here," whispers the prisoner.

"Creedon wants to see you again."

"Naw, he don't."

Arbeiter sighs. "Is there nothing I can say to convince you?"

The prisoner thinks, and thinks some more. Arbeiter's shirt is stained with two circles of sweat. "Naw," says the prisoner.

"Then we don't have anything to say to each other." He rises. "Goodbye, eight." He hits the door with his fist thrice; the guard buzzes him out. Arbeiter walks away.

On his left and his right, the corridor's paint shows its age. There are bubbles, and cracks. Still as a field of ice and twice as cold.

At the corner, more walls; extending without doors into the distance. Arbeiter looks back. No doors visible; dust motes in beams of sunlight. Arbeiter walks faster.

Finally, a steel door. Arbeiter places his hand on the knob, turns. His hand slides without friction. He pulls his hand back; it is slick with half-clotted blood, an obscene pulpy gel. He wipes his hand on his pants and it comes back doubly encrusted. Now his other hand is blood as well. He can feel his arms dying from the ends up.

Arbeiter runs, praying he's just hallucinating.

▪   ▪   ▪

Wade Davis, in *Passage of Darkness,* quotes a Haitian as saying, "Only the truly great work magic alone. For all their talk, watch the hands of the little ones, you'll always see the powders."

Watch Washington's little hands all you like. No powders.

The *l'envoi morts* is not an efficient way of killing a man; piercing his heart with a bullet serves better. And it has the drawback of being prone to backfire; death spirits are not known for their willingness to serve bokor. But if it works . . .

Soon, the seducer's *ti bon ange* is sealed into the calabash. The mind, the memory, the desire is locked up—helpless. The *zombi astral* will serve Washington for a long, long time. Three days later the seducer is dead. Three days after that, Washington disinters the coffin. Calls out the dead man's name. The *zombi cadavre* rises. Washington has no use for it; his friends from his old *vlinblindingue* lead it away.

▪   ▪   ▪

Nancy takes a deep breath, one night, steels herself with cheap wine and a thick slather of makeup, waits for Whitlomb to kiss her. He curses himself for a fool. He's not sure what he's supposed to teach her but he doubts spreading her legs is it.

What does he have to say to her? Nancy Gaoping is an overweight Chinese girl, third generation, army brat, physics major. Apparently brilliant. Whitlomb spoke to one of her teaching assistants. When Nancy learns science, it is effortless—watching her, one would swear she already knew the material, but it had simply slipped her mind and was just coming back.

He talked with the TA for a while. The TA explained a few things about modern geek culture. Women struggling to get a passing grade in a technical class have been known to befriend a smart but socially inept man. She doesn't even have to have sex with him—the fellow is so crazed with lust and full of hope, he will do homework for two, shoulder all the weight in the laboratory. The TA told Whitlomb to come to the next lab session and watch. Whitlomb saw Nancy with a handsome young buck, standing with his hands in his pockets, watching Nancy adjust the laser and write down results. The TA shrugged. "Not the first time I've ever seen it work the other way. Probably happen more if there were more women in the sciences."

Nancy has the social skills of a ewe; is so eager to please it hurts to be around her, sometimes. Her father, a preoccupied colonel; her mother, as close to white trash as an Asian army wife can be. No brothers or sisters. No sense of location—Berkeley is just another base to her.

Her roommates are elsewhere. Whitlomb and Nancy are on an improvised couch, not really big enough for the two of them. He can smell her bucket of perfume; her red-flushed cheeks are close enough to lick. Now her hand has dropped to his lap. She is saying something. He lifts her chin to make her look him in the eye—instead, her eyelids flutter down and she purses her lips.

"Nancy—"

Her eyes open. She has never heard quite that tone of voice before, but she's not stupid. Naturally. What did she expect?

She watches him working his mouth. She knows he's trying to find a way to tell her she's ugly as a boot; and even if he was thirty years younger, she's too gruesome to give him a hard-on. And then he will declaim a homily about loving her like an uncle or grandfather. He manages to begin a sentence but she puts her finger on his lips. "Shush," she says.

"Nancy, I—"

"Never mind. Never mind, Perry."

"Look, it's just—"

She increases the pressure. Something has come into her eyes. "Perry. I think you should go."

Whitlomb has blown it. The whole operation is doomed because Whitlomb has fallen down on the job. Nothing to do, then, but hunch his shoulders and scuttle out; he leaves Casa Zimbabwe through the side door by Heidi's room.

■   ■   ■

The marble is ready. Now it is time for other preparations; Rider gathers materials and chants over them, getting ready. Tens of thousands of dollars of saffron and jade go up in smoke. His master supervises him.

Whitlomb comes in, slumps in a corner. "Trouble?" says Rider.

"Something unexpected came up," mutters Whitlomb.

"Oh?"

Whitlomb clears his throat. "Sex."

"So you got a woody," says Rider. "You're old enough to ignore it, aren't you?"

"I mean she . . . uh . . ."

Rider nods. "And you didn't anticipate this?"

"Of course not. Look at me; I'm old enough to be her grandfather. I think I broke her heart."

"I see. Pardon me for a minute—I need something from the next room."

Whitlomb gets up, peers at the marble block while he waits.

Rider comes in with the wand his master brought, and beats Whitlomb half senseless with it.

■   ■   ■

The moment on the Formosa 51 has finally ended. The afternoon passes in a dragging haze. Sturgeon does sit-ups until he is ill and works very hard at not knowing where Chloe is or what she is doing.

. . .

The jaguar pads off. Maggie-Sue's neck is bleeding. She is spent and crying, on hands and knees on the jungle loam, her shoulders and upper back clawed deep; thighs spread, terrible sweet pain between her legs as she sobs.

. . .

Arbeiter batters at bars with what he has left; the bones of his arms are sponge. He is coughing bile, now; his breath wheezes through bronchioles choked with phlegm and less beautiful suspensions. The light comes from a pinpoint far away, and his eyes tear.

A grid of barred walls extends to infinity, each cell ten by ten, concrete above and below. No doors.

08964 walks through the metal like a wraith.

"Why?" chokes Arbeiter.

"Got nothin' else," says the prisoner. "Got my balls cut off, you know that?"

Arbeiter vomits.

"Should'n'ta slept," muses 08964. "But every cloud 'n all that. Found a way out, don't need balls, don't even hafta go out."

"Out—outside the walls? Even the Incumbent's wall?"

"Just gotta have the right tool."

"I can't believe it," groans Arbeiter.

"Oh, yeah. Once a month, new moon? Two in July, though. Kids in Colma, right there in the graveyards, making out. Dropped 'em screaming right where they could bury them. That's funny."

Arbeiter's arms are shreds of flesh depending from his shoulders. He pisses blood, soaking his FBI-clone blue trousers. He vomits again and his left eye enucleates, rasping on the stubble of his cheek.

"Outside," murmurs 08964. "Any time I want. You fucked me, man, you left me here. You're never leaving now."

"I did miss you," says Thiebaud.

The prisoner turns. Thiebaud reaches for him, and a teardrop splashes.

∎   ∎   ∎

"Agent Bushmill! AGENT BUSHMILL!"

Arbeiter opens his eyes. Across the table, a guard administers CPR to the prisoner as the public address system moans code blue.

"He hit me," whines Arbeiter.

Paramedics rush into the chamber, apply leads. One shouts "Vee tach, vee tach, clear!" and thrice the capacitors bang and the thrice the prisoner convulses. "Intubate! Get IV!" The needle goes in. "Epinephrine push! Hurry, hurry . . . Clear!" The prisoner arches off the floor. "Nothing! Epinephrine and lidocaine . . . Clear! Nothing! Epinephrine . . . Clear!"

And 08964's corpse leaps like a fish in a net.

∎   ∎   ∎

After the doctor comes and the resuscitation attempts stop and the paperwork is over, Thiebaud supports Arbeiter as they proceed to the car. Arbeiter's arms hang limp; he welcomes the pins and needles, agony though they be. And if there's one thing he can count on to be real in this world, it's Thiebaud's arm on his own.

∎   ∎   ∎

Whitlomb is out of ideas. He has to talk to her. Skulks into the physics building, into the lab. The TA looks through him—turns his back pointedly to help another student. Whitlomb walks along the wall, looking for her.

There's Nancy. There's the young buck. He is fumbling with the laser. She snaps commands at him in a low voice. The young buck's brow is furrowed in resentment and incomprehension as he finds out the hard way she's decided not to feed him the answers anymore. She looks up at Whitlomb's approach. Her eyes bore into him for a moment—until she smooths her features into a polite disinterested regard. The kind appropriate for someone too unimportant to bother being rude to.

Whitlomb figures it out. Stumbles out of the lab. Manages to make it out of the building, collapses onto a bench and begins chuckling to himself.

"Ah, the light dawns," he giggles. "A failure? No failure I." Passing students take one look at him and move away in double time.

He spreads his arms and addresses the merciless solar disk. "A failure? Never! I am the finest teacher in all of California! California? Nay, the western seaboard, the continent of North America! Perhaps the world!"

He stands and adopts the pose of a Roman orator. "I am triumphant! No longer will she trust her fellow man! She will prosper!" he roars. "And someday, perhaps, she will stand before the king of Sweden, accept the prize founded by a man in horror of what he wrought, and turn to the crowd. And she will thank the men who taught her math, taught her physics, gave her the grants and provided the equipment and advised the thesis and confirmed the results that lofted her high—lofted her to the very apex of science! And then—and then—and then, perhaps, she will thank her dear old friend, Professor Pericles Claudius Whitlomb—

"Who taught her how to hate."

And his knees give way and the sun stabs his eyes and his heart thunders a hundred beats a minute and he gasps for breath and he fumbles for the nitroglycerine tablets and he sits on the bench weeping—an old, old man; sad as an ugly schoolgirl, weak as a papyrus reed.

.   .   .

Another day at sea. By unspoken mutual consent they have turned the boat around and are heading northeast, homeward bound, away from the tropical sun and toward the chill Humbolt current. It is early September. Some days it rains; it's enough to make one want to stay belowdecks and sleep, sleep until the weather goes away or the ship sinks.

An entirely unsatisfactory arrangement, all in all. They cannot ever be truly isolated from each other, but they cannot talk enough to talk. Simultaneously overcrowded and terribly alone.

A gray, cold afternoon. Not much wind. The water is gray, too, and it is misting rain. Sturgeon decides things have gone too far. Calls out from the stern deck. "Chloe?"

"Yes?"

"Come here. Let's talk."

She comes up from the cabin, eyes perhaps a little puffy. "What's to talk about?"

"You tell me."

She sits down; not with a huff of resentment, nor with a sunny smile. Looks at him. "What's on your mind, Max?"

"You remember a few days ago?"

"Yes."

"Let's talk about that."

"All right."

Long silence. Sturgeon shivers; the sun is setting.

"Chloe, er . . . What . . . Ah, why were you crying?"

"I need a reason? Or permission?"

"Stop it. Talk to me."

She sighs. "Just things, that's all. Bad mood. My period."

"What things?"

"You can't just leave this alone, can you?"

Sturgeon shakes his head. "I don't dare, Chloe. We're going back to the City. There are things there that want us dead. We'll be back with the team again. We have to watch each other's backs. Now, in an ideal world, I could leave you your privacy. I want to. I can't."

"Well, if that's all that there is on your mind, there's an easy solution. I'll go back to Seattle."

"If you really want to go, then you can go. But I don't want you to. We need you."

"Bullshit."

"It's true."

"Bullshit. I'm just another target. I can drive the truck, yeah, great. But I take up more resources than I provide. Max, I know you don't want to say it, but I'm a parasite."

"What are you talking about?"

"Look, when the thin dogs came after us . . . If Rider and Whitlomb could have gone to Treasure Island instead of holing up and protecting me, everybody could have dealt with the attack together. Instead you and Arbeiter nearly got killed before Joe and Maggie-Sue got to you."

"That may or may not be."

She flaps her hands. "Max, quit it, all right? I'm sick of everybody tiptoeing around me, patting my hand! Rider's right. I'm good for nothing."

"Chloe—"

"Name one thing, huh? Oh, wait, I forgot. I'm the cell whore. I'll seduce the High Priest and put Rider's cancer bullet into him."

Sturgeon stands up with a snap, straight into Commanding Officer Pose Number One. "And would you?"

She looks at him. The sun is gone; the air around them is losing heat, and slowly becoming fog. "What?"

"If I told you to do it, would you?"

"Of course. But what are the odds—"

"Chloe, listen to me. You may be saying to yourself you're the least valuable of us and the most vulnerable. You may even be right. It doesn't matter one fucking jot. We still may need you."

She waves him off. "Yeah, yeah. In the battle against overwhelming odds, every bit counts. What difference does it make, though? We're as good as dead, anyway. One of these days they'll find us and stomp us like roaches. Seventeen thousand years, Max!"

Sturgeon's eyes narrow. "Oh, I see. Existential self-pity."

Her eyes flare. "Stop it."

"No, I understand. It's my job to understand my crew's weaknesses and work around them. I always figured your weakness was that you can open your third eye but you don't have anything to fire back with. You can only report what you see and keep your head down. But what I didn't realize is how impotent it makes you feel. Makes sense. You *are* impotent. So you decide before the battle even begins that you're going to lose and you shut that shell of yours and hope the shovel doesn't dig you out and you can live to see one more high tide. I understand completely."

"Damn you."

"Too late. You've already damned yourself."

"I didn't ask to be what I am!"

"But you are what you are now. What are you going to do about it?"

"This is military browbeating. Did you learn this in OCS?"

"I did, actually. I also studied counterinsurgency. That's what you do, you know, when your enemy is an underground. Make sure each and every one of them stops and thinks how overwhelmed they are. Sap their spirit to fight."

"Well, it's sapped. I can't go on. I won't stand with you and wait for it to come. At night, I lie there and I wonder whose head I'll have to cradle while they fight for that last breath, whose blood will soak my skirt and dribble into my goddamn cell whore's cunt. Maggie-Sue's? Perry's? Creedon's? Yours? Who do I see cut down first?"

He shakes his head. "Idiot. Without you, this cell would never have formed."

"Now you're trying to bolster my flagging self-esteem by talking history. Don't pull your big-man shit on me."

"Chloe, listen for a minute. I was talking with Whitlomb about Maggie-Sue. I said she's got a good heart, but she never does anything unless somebody takes her by the hand and shows her what to do. She never shows any initiative—but you do."

No response.

"Chloe, remember when we met? You'd just come to the City, and you realized the mortuaries had been infiltrated by necromancers? And you went looking for a victim, an influential victim, you could use to track them down and take them out?"

"So?"

"I was sitting at my desk. I'd been crying so much I had no tears left. Just a mask. And in you came. You took my hand and showed me what to do, just like Washington does for Maggie-Sue."

"Sure, I opened your third eye. Fine. So what?"

"You gave me hope, Chloe. All I knew was there were monsters out there and I couldn't find them and I couldn't do anything about it. And then you came. I could go on. And then we found Al, and Al knew Joe and Perry, and Joe knew Kris and Kris knew Creedon, and we all came together."

"How sweet. How lovely. Well, the cell is formed and the catalyst can go home now."

"No, you can't. Chloe, I don't know how to say this . . . but I need you. The cell needs you, too, but more than that . . . I need you."

She shakes her head. "Wrong man, Max. The cell gigolo is supposed to keep the cell whore in line, if she gets all anxious. It should have been Arbeiter out here with me. And if I *don't* get back into line, he slaps me around; he'd be perfect for it, he loves it."

"Chloe, fuck the cell. If you want to go back to Seattle, I want to go with you."

She looks at him.

He looks at her.

She comes close. Certain other things are said, overlapping with each other. There are two people under a chill gray sky on a chill gray ocean, holding each other. Four eyes weep. A tiny cell of warmth surrounded by terrible cold.

That evening, Sturgeon finds out where her totemic tattoo is.

■   ■   ■

Rider's doorbell rings—known woman. Rider flies down the stairs, opens the door. Looks. "Hi, Maggie-Sue!" He's glad to see her; but Lord, her face is even uglier than he remembers.

She doesn't say anything.

"Come in, come in. . . ." Stands aside. She enters the building. They go to the loft.

Rider's master looks up. Rider says, "Master, this is—"

She stuffs fingers into her ears and kicks him in the shins. "This is a member of your cell whose name I should not know, boy. It's bad enough I'll have to see all of them and hear their voices. I don't want to know their names. Jackass. It's a miracle you haven't compromised the cell already with that flapping mouth of yours."

Maggie-Sue stares at her. Shrugs. Goes into the kitchen and starts making lunch.

Rider's master looks after her. "Or is that just the help?"

Rider sighs. "Look, just don't ever try to keep her out of the kitchen. I think she's a frustrated short-order cook."

Maggie-Sue gargles. Croaks. Manages to rasp, "Fuck you."

Rider's master says, "Look, you two have some catching up to do. I'm going to go into the next room and put up a sound barrier so I don't hear any secrets, in case the Incumbents get to me."

Rider looks at Maggie-Sue, who is slicing pastrami. "Don't bother, Master. She doesn't talk much. For instance, I have no hope of ever getting an explanation of those cuts on her throat."

"Fuck you."

.   .   .

A few days later, Whitlomb shows up. Then Washington. And finally, Sturgeon and Chloe. Rider's tonsure is mocked. Everybody tells their stories, as Rider's master stands in the next room with the stereo at full blast. Then they commence to wait.

The morning of the third day. Washington is reading the paper. Maggie-Sue is banging dishes around. Chloe and Sturgeon are playing footsie. Whitlomb is polishing his glasses as he argues metaphysics with Rider. Rider's master is staring at Thiebaud, who is poking through the CD collection. She reaches over and taps Rider's arm. "Is that one of the people you were waiting for?"

Rider turns. "Aieee! Jesus, man, don't do that."

Thiebaud gestures towards Rider's master. "May we speak freely before this young lady?"

"Flatterer," mutters Rider's master.

Rider says, "Yeah, she taught me everything I know, but mine is the only name to be spoken, okay? She doesn't want to know."

Thiebaud is reading Laurie Anderson lyrics. "I could not help but notice the remarkable number of moths, Mr. Rider."

"Yeah, well, they're pets. Don't kill any of them, we have a deal going."

part three

It takes a few days to shake the dust of distant lands from their feet. On Friday night they get drunk and argue about just what the Demiurge was thinking when he made the universe. When morning comes and the hungover are through with breakfast and feeling human again, Rider turns to his master and says, "Well, everybody's here. When would be a good time to do the final casting?"

She scratches her head. "Tonight's as good a time as any. We need to rehearse first, though. Al, unlock the workroom."

They all troop in. Chloe looks at the marble out of the corner of her eye. "Er . . . Al . . . how long have you been working on that?"

Rider puffs with pride. "Took a month and a half to carve, even with thaumaturgy to do the rough work."

"It seems," says Whitlomb, in as reasonable a voice as he can manage, "that given the amount of time you have spent, you might have more to show for it than a simple egg."

"It is much more than a simple egg, Gramps."

Whitlomb sighs. " 'Gramps.' Phooey. A pity your master already knows your name. Much merriment could be had devising your alias."

"How about Schlemiel?" says Arbeiter.

Others make suggestions. "Bonehead." "What was that name Sondheim came up with—Hysterium?" "Naah. I say, Good ol' Panic and Freeze." "Let's take a page from Spike Lee—Buggin' Out."

"Get on with it," says Rider's master.

Rider says, "Okay, everybody, see where the tape crosses are? Mustache, right here—Clamface there." Pointing. "Gramps, Shorty, Fuck You, Kraut, and . . . Er . . . Spook. You mind Spook? No? Okay. I'll be all over the room as necessary. My master can't touch anything or speak any Sumerian in here, but she'll be over my shoulder and coaching. I need to teach you what to say. There are only two short phrases, but you'll have to keep them going while I do the final incantations. Okay, now, repeat after me . . ."

．　．　．

It is night. Candles are everywhere. Rider makes last minute preparations. "I wish," he mutters, "we could get a Tibetan band in here."

"Aw, no, Hysterium, not those horrible bone trumpets? The ones that sound like elephant farts?"

"Shut up, Clamface. Everybody remember what to chant and when? We can take another day to rehearse."

"Gods, no," says Arbeiter. "I can't stand another day of hearing you whine about where in the mouth to sound the vowels."

Rider looks at his master. "Have I forgotten anything?"

She shakes her head.

"All right. Positions, everybody. Let's do it."

They lay hands on the great egg—each with their left hand on the stone, their right palm on the knuckles of their neighbor. Rider starts the chant. Everybody joins in. Rider stops chanting. They keep going. He yells at them, horrible syncopated insults designed to break their rhythm. They do not falter. He nods.

Rider stands in a ceremonial robe, staff ready. Rolls his head on his neck. Shakes out his hands, limbers up. Takes a deep breath. Goes to work.

It takes a while. Things are burned. Sumerian counterpoint to the seven chanters. Hands waved. A remarkable dance that makes Maggie-Sue green with envy—she didn't think the effete bastard had it in him. Open third eyes can sense Things moving in the flickering shadows. Rider is sweating freely. Mana crackles in the air.

Rider stands, conducts, gets everybody ready to change to the second chant. And a one and a two and a three. The change is flawless. Now comes the hard part.

Rider prepares the ether. Space warps and flows. Pretty lights. Side effects typical of synesthetic magic: the taste of starlight, glimpses of distant wailing sirens; they hear the night air's dust, and feel the scent of jasmine creeping across their feet. They see mandalas in the backs of their ears: angles that are not square corners, but yet are neither oblique nor acute. The Things in the shadows seem to be chanting, too. The moment approaches . . .

. . . and passes.

Rider stands in shock. Did somebody fail? Arbeiter and Creedon, maybe? No, preposterous; they can't *help* but lurk in the shadows and murder people. Rider quivers—did he miscalculate? He turns to his master, who is looking stricken.

"Now what?" he says.

"I don't know, Al; try to breach it anyway."

Rider tries. The hair stands on the backs of everybody's necks. There is an overwhelming sensation of tension, pushing against an envelope normally invisible . . . and then being pushed back. Now everybody is sweating.

Rider turns to his master. She reaches up and takes his hand."Al, I don't know what's wrong. But try. Keep trying."

Rider grits his teeth, tries again. No better luck.

Rider is shaking. He lets them chant on a while as he gathers his strength. He catches his breath. Tries again, still harder, almost through; nothing. Whitlomb looks over at Rider, whose face is flushed. No, not flushed; nobody's skin can turn that red. Whitlomb realizes Rider is sweating blood.

Rider's master is holding him up as the blood drains in rivulets from his face. More blood drips from his hands. His scleras are completely red from broken capillaries. "It's no use," he groans.

"Try," she says. "Try again. Think like an Apache. Four is the most sacred number."

"Yes, Master." Marshals his remaining strength. Pushes. Pushes harder. Reaches the limit. Keeps pushing . . . and gains a little. Gains a little more.

There is something wrong with the light. There are strange noises. Rider spares a glance around—realizes that moths are throwing themselves into the candle flames. Ten. A hundred. Crawling through the crack under the door. Rider's master props him on his staff, rushes over to throw the door open. A thousand moths. Ten thousand. Coming in great flights, circling in thrumming clouds and peeling off to immolate themselves; protein combustion, the penetrating stench of burning hair. The moths are landing on the egg and flattening themselves, pushing their abdomens against it. Each goes into convulsions, stiffens, dies. Slides off the slick stone only to be replaced by a dozen more. Rider's master is screaming in his ear: "It's all right, it's all right, do it, go through . . ."

They push one more time, eight humans and uncountable moths. They are through. Something fundamental changes, and everybody in the room goes into a deep swoon.

.   .   .

Rider's master recovers in under a minute. Crawls to Rider, who is blanketed with dead moths. She brushes some away, clenches her fist and shouts in Sumerian; his heart begins beating again.

She rocks back on her heels. Catches her breath. Checks the others—out cold, but otherwise fine. She manages to stagger to her feet, gets blankets and pillows, shoves the cushions under their heads and covers them up. Begins sweeping up moths and eggshell-thin shards of marble.

.   .   .

Sturgeon wakes at dawn with one *hell* of a headache. Groans. Rider's master is beside him in an instant with a glass of orange juice. "Everybody's okay, Mustache. Take it easy."

Maggie-Sue sits up. Looks at Rider, who is covered with a fine crust of clotted blood. Crawls to him, checks his pulse. Hisses something incomprehensible to Rider's master. Rider's master says, "He looks bad, but he's all right. Hey, don't—wait, you're not strong enough—" Maggie-Sue yowls at her like a lioness on Biphetamine, slashes in the air with a hand clutched into a claw. Rider's master backs off in shock. Maggie-Sue gathers Rider in her arms, manages to stand up and stagger off to the bedroom. Undresses him and cleans off the blood.

Sturgeon says, "She's a little overprotective. I don't think she likes you much, I'm sorry to say."

Rider's master shrugs. "Elementalist, right? They can't stand thaumaturges, let alone synestheticists. Makes 'em feel obsolete."

Others are coming to. The walking tend the waking, helping them to their feet, feeding them orange juice. Orange juice is the traditional post-blood-donation drink and it's apropos here, too.

Whitlomb says, "What happened to the egg?"

"It hatched," says Rider's master. "The shards of shell are over there."

Whitlomb says, "But it was a solid block of marble."

"Of course it wasn't. What do you think took Al so long to carve it? It was hollow."

"Preposterous. A hollow object cannot be carved from without, unless one makes a hole, however small. It is simple topology."

"Unless you use magic, you senile old coot."

Arbeiter gapes at the hole in the external wall. "Unless it's my imagination, that hole is bigger around than the original egg."

"Think of it more as a gate than an egg," says Rider's master.

Chloe goes in to take a look at Rider and almost gets her eyes clawed out for her trouble before Maggie-Sue recognizes her. "Easy . . . easy . . ." Checks him out.

Maggie-Sue is stringing up an IV of lactated Ringer's. "Blood," she says.

"What?"

"Blood. Compensated shock. Old bitch."

"How? If he was in shock all night he'd be uncompensated by now."

Maggie-Sue shrugs.

"He'll be out for another four, five hours," says Rider's master. "And I would appreciate it if somebody explained to the wildcat in there that I was not neglecting him in the time between the spell and when she woke up."

"She's not somebody you can explain things to," says Washington, rattling the business section.

"Fuck you."

Whitlomb glances across the table at the old man there. Starts. Thiebaud is sitting still, staring into a cup of coffee. Just a dull fiftyish figure in a broad-brimmed hat over a deeply lined face. The gray eyes are not witchy—they're just eyes. *Good God,* thinks Whitlomb. *If he is so debilitated as to appear human, I must resemble the very passport photograph of Death.*

Sturgeon clears his throat. "Ah . . . I don't suppose anybody can explain that business with the moths? Did Al have to summon them and sacrifice them to carry off the spell? He didn't say anything about necromancy when we discussed this."

Rider's master shakes her head. "No. They came voluntarily when they realized they were needed."

Arbeiter stares at her. "They're moths. Moths aren't termites or diatoms; they don't have a hive mind."

She shrugs. "No. But Al fed them with his own hair, gave them a place to rest where they wouldn't be hurt. And there's a hell of a lot of stray mana around here. My guess is those moths were members of a Rider cult."

"Surely you jest," says Whitlomb.

"Oh, it could never have happened with any of *you.* But synesthetic magic is the most advanced means of occult manipulation known."

From the next room, Maggie-Sue hisses.

"Well, excuse *me,* honey. To a moth, we might as well be gods. Their god needed their blood—not demanded, *needed.* They came of their own free will. If the Buddhists are right, they picked up a bunch of good karma. Probably reincarnating as minnows even as we speak."

■ ■   ■

Rider opens his eyes and sees red. Eye damage. Hopes Arbeiter's ointments can take care of that. Blinks. Maggie-Sue is to his left and his master to his right. They are pointedly ignoring each other. "Ack," he says.

They both go to lay a hand on him. Each sees the other. Maggie-Sue hisses. Rider's master draws her wand and looks very angry.

"Gghklk," says Rider. Clears his throat. "Please, last thing I want is to get caught in a cross fire."

"You all right?" says Maggie-Sue.

"Fine, just fine, don't hurt anybody." Looks at his master. "You too."

"The spell worked, Al."

"Couldn't have done it without you, Master."

She slaps his hand. Maggie-Sue hisses and jumps to her feet, eyes blazing. "Help," says Rider. Thiebaud is standing against the wall, guns drawn. "Spook! Get Mustache in here before these two kill each other!"

Rider's master draws herself up. "Don't call me Master, Al. You're not a Journeyman anymore. You can call me by my name, now."

"Christ, I don't even *know* your name."

"I'll tell you later. Somewhere where this wildcat isn't." More hissing.

Sturgeon comes in, along with pretty much everybody else. "Hi, Al. Or Master Rider, I should say."

"Make you a deal. You don't call me Master, I don't call you Lieutenant."

Rider's master sniffs. "Strictly speaking, you can call him by his first name if you want, but he really should call you Master. We have an image to protect." Maggie-Sue hisses. "Will somebody please shut this teakettle up?"

Rider tries to get up. Four hands push him back. "You need to rest, Al," says Chloe, trying to get to him without getting her head bitten off.

"I need to check the egg."

"I've already checked," says Rider's master. "It hatched. There are prints in the concrete and a hole in the wall; you can go look at them later, if you want. Now all of you get out while I tell Master Rider my name. I want to finish up here and go home." Nobody can argue with this, although Maggie-Sue looks ready to try. Washington takes her hand. She slaps his forearm, nails leaving four spots of blood. He ignores it and leads her out.

"Sorry about that," says Rider.

"No problem. It's a good cell. The only thing you hate more than each other is anybody or anything that tries to so much as lay a finger on one of you."

"We don't hate each other."

"Yes you do. Of course, the blond girl has a crush on you."

Rider gapes, then laughs. "Who, her? Her lovers—if she has any—I don't ever want to *meet*. Except Clamface, and I'm not sure that ever happened."

"Is she always like that?"

"No, usually she says 'Fuck you' instead of hissing. Shorty's the only one she really talks to. She can *understand* anything we say, but she's amazingly inarticulate. From what I know of her, it's because nobody ever listened to a thing she said until she left home. She stopped *trying* to talk, never learned to put her thoughts into words. Dyslexia, too, maybe a touch of autism. Her family tree loops in a couple places. Shorty said he saw her trying to read a newspaper once and she was moving her lips and had to go over every paragraph five or six times to get it. I can't imagine how hard she had to work to get her veterinary degree."

"Elemental magic is a throwback to preliterate man; you know that."

"Heh. Well, she's durn near preliterate, that's for sure. Anyway. So what's your name?"

"Laura Stern."

Rider looks at her sideways. "Laura Stern. Laura *Stern*."

"Yes. My name is Laura Stern. You killed my grandson. Prepare to die."

■ ■ ■

Rider almost manages to get a knife to her throat before her laughter and upheld hands register. "Jesus, Master, don't do that. You took five years off my life just now."

"The name is Laura! And sorry. I couldn't resist. Although he *was* my grandson—faugh! Took after my son-in-law's side of the family, you understand. Good riddance."

"Son-in-law? How come you and he have the same name, then?"

"Long story." She starts unbuttoning her blouse.

Rider blinks. "Ah . . . what are you doing?"

"I'm going strip my withered frame naked and crawl into that bed with you. With any luck, I'll conceive."

"But—"

"Oh, don't worry. I may be old, but I'm strong enough to bear another child or two."

"But—"

"Oh, shut up, boy."

. . .

As Rider's master leaves the bedroom and collects her things, she dictates an address. "Al's too lazy to write, so I expect you lot to. Who does computer stuff? Gramps? Okay. Here's an eight-millimeter tape of one-time pads. Use it. I'm out of here. Call us if you need us. Oh, one more thing before I go. Honey? If you ever manage to screw up your nerve, just jump him. He lives for the moment." Maggie-Sue vents a wordless scream and throws a ball of fire at her but she dodges and sweeps into her heat shimmer and leaves in a gale of fiendish cackles. People carefully back away from Maggie-Sue, whose fists are clenched, an uninterpretable expression twisting her already forbidding features. Even the moths duck and cover.

As Chloe plies a fire extinguisher on Rider's wall and rugs, Arbeiter stares after Laura Stern. "Rider lived under the same roof as her for five years?"

"Yep."

"I take back everything rotten I've ever said about him. He wasn't born a jackass. He had jackassdom thrust upon him."

. . .

Rider's vision clears and Chloe's broth and Arbeiter's unnatural aids to healing quickly have him on his feet. Although he is turning an interesting purple-green color all over and his eyes are still red. That, plus the total lack of beard and cranial hair, makes him look rather like a very ugly Krishna. Whitlomb points this out. Rider grins and asks if anybody has seen a hundred milkmaids around anywhere.

"Conference, kids," says Sturgeon.

"Talk, talk, talk, that's all I ever get out of this outfit," says Arbeiter.

"Al, are you sure your . . . project . . . is under our control?"

"It's not under control, no. But it's on our side. We can count on it. Probably. We should wait as long as we can before going in, though. Let it grow."

"Creedon, how much luck have you had gunning for the Vulture-cult field units?"

Without looking up from his book (Oliver Sacks, *An Anthropologist on Mars*) Thiebaud takes a black cloth sack from his coat, sets it on the table. Arbeiter takes it, looks within. Smiles. Spills a few score teeth onto the table. A dentist would note that they are all left upper canines.

People shudder. "Right. So they should be confused and scared."

Washington says, "No. They expect heavy losses at every stage of the game. They grow so fast a few dozen operatives means nothing. They're no weaker than before. Probably stronger. Unless we burn out their base we accomplish nothing."

"Okay. Break out the ephemeris, Perry. They're strongest in sunlight, right? Very well; night raid city. When's the next new moon? Two and a half weeks? Plenty of time to plan, then. Okay, let's suppose . . ."

. . .

Maggie-Sue's watch. She doesn't need the night-vision goggles. Actually, she does need them to see in the dark, but she can't stand to have them on her head all the time. She holds them on her lap.

Maggie-Sue has been having trouble, the last few years. When she was in school she was able to press through by listening to lectures and memorizing diagrams. But now she can't even figure out how fax machines work—why do things get so jaggedy?

Where did Russia go? Ozone is a gas—how can it have a hole in it? How do you get a CD case open without breaking it?

She remembers the brow-ridged magician who found her tending tables in a bar near UC Davis. He'd gotten too old—couldn't read at all, couldn't speak a sentence longer than two words. He'd gotten so bad with machinery he couldn't even change channels on a TV set. He left her with child and took a trip home to England and perished within ten minutes of leaving the airport; looked the wrong way and stepped right into the path of an omnibus.

Damn them, damn all their smugness, Washington with his newspaper and Rider who can read things she can't even recognize as writing and that slut Chloe with all her clever words.

Six months ago she went to Arbeiter and asked him if there was anything that could make her read better. He gave her something. She got halfway through *Huckleberry Finn* before it wore off and the crash was so bad she couldn't remember her name or how to curse, let alone what she'd just read. Good for nothing but wailing like a hurt animal.

And it's been bad since she got back from the jungle. When everybody told their stories she got headaches trying to understand. She vowed then that no matter what stupid schemes they came up with she wasn't ever going to leave the city again. If she went back to the wild one more time she'd never come back, never ever remember how to talk, and she'd end up cowering in the last acre of rain forest, howling at the chainsaws until they came and held her down and put a bullet through her head like a horse with a broken leg.

Sturgeon relieves her. Maggie-Sue goes to her cot and puts the Walkman's headphones in her ears. Tunes it to an all-news station. Maybe if she hears enough talking in her sleep it will sink in again.

■   ■   ■

Maggie-Sue rises early. Goes to slice ham for breakfast. Can't figure out how the knife works. Stares at it. Hisses at it. Hits it. It cuts her; blood flows and she hurts. Makes a horrid uncouth yammering noise. Whitlomb spins around, pointing his shotgun; everybody else bails out of bed, grabbing staves and amulets and guns and knives, looking wildly around for danger. Maggie-Sue stares at them. Points at the knife. Makes an apologetic sound. They all look at her. Some of them look angry. Why are they angry? What has she done? She pisses herself in fear, hot urine spattering against tile as it gushes from her cut-off jeans; cowers against the cabinets, arms waving to fend them off—falls to the ground and rolls onto her back and exposes her throat and belly so they'll stop being angry at her.

"Jesus, Mary, and Joseph," whispers Arbeiter.

"Perry," commands Sturgeon, quietly. "Something's seriously wrong. Move real, real slow. Get a tranquilizer dart. Take her down."

"Max," says Chloe. "Let me try to get close, try to talk to her. I think she's been poisoned or something."

"Go. Take it easy. Perry, get that dart."

Chloe slides forward on her knees, murmuring comfortingly, more for the tone of voice than for the words. The way you'd approach a cowering dog. She wishes she hadn't thought of that analogy, because Maggie-Sue is whining like a puppy riddled with birdshot. Manages to get within a few meters before Maggie-Sue twists her head in her direction; hisses and springs at her.

Chloe is screaming for help, trying to keep Maggie-Sue's nails from her eyes. Washington and Arbeiter dogpile her. It's like fighting a lynx. She keeps throwing them off and trying to bite. She's moving so fast Whitlomb's first shot hits Arbeiter. Reloads. Manages to get her on the second one. Everybody dives into the fray, manage to restrain her until she finally sags limp.

Much swearing and invoking of deities. Hydrogen peroxide flows like wine—everybody has at least a few wounds. Arbeiter checks Chloe carefully—she's the worst off, left eye scratched and bright red, but no major eye damage and nothing deep enough to leave a scar. Finally, he looks up. "Now what the hell was *that* all about?"

"Just a moment?! I put a full seventy-kilo animal dart into you! How is it you're still standing?" says Whitlomb.

"Get with the program and remember, old man; my metabolism's custom, I'm immune to most poisons. What happened?"

Nobody has an answer.

"Joe," says Sturgeon, "you know her best."

Washington shrugs. "She's been weirder than usual since she got back."

They take Maggie-Sue to a cot. They clean her up, and put her in a steel-cable-reinforced straitjacket; strap her down. Sturgeon chains a few convenient ingots of lead to the cot—they've dealt with unnatural strength before.

Rider says, "You know, I was talking to my master about her. I was saying she usually talks more. I thought she was just disoriented from being away from people for so long."

Chloe purses her lips in thought. "She's been . . . I don't know, territorial, lately. Remember how violently she reacted when Rider's master teased her, right after they had sex?"

"What?" starts Rider.

"Shut up, Al, we all heard you two . . . It was like Maggie-Sue was jealous or something."

Rider looks poleaxed. Whitlomb pats him on the arm. "Relax, son. We understand. Witches can induce uncharacteristic behavior, and that . . . woman . . . qualifies as a witch if ever I saw one."

"You know, I bet he's blushing under that bruise," says Arbeiter.

"Anyway," continues Chloe, "that's not like her."

"Maybe she's in heat," says Arbeiter. Chloe slaps his hand.

"No," says Sturgeon. "He may be right. I mean, it's close to the full moon, right?"

Chloe rolls her eyes. "Oh, come on. Women don't all ovulate on the night of the full moon."

"Ah, the full of the moon," says Whitlomb. "That suggests . . .?"

Maggie-Sue screams at the top of her lungs. Thiebaud is by her, looking out the window. There is an angry red boil on her forehead.

"Jesus, Creedon, what did you do?" gasps Rider.

"Silver, of course," curses Whitlomb. "She's a were."

. . .

"We seem," observes Chloe, "to be spending an awful lot of time staring down at sick people on cots."

"Not surprising," says Washington. "Vulture cult accelerates disease."

"So maybe they're sending curses our way," says Sturgeon. "They know by now that mundane measures are ineffective."

"I told you!" crows Whitlomb. "Cold steel and hot lead! Our enemies will quail and fall before us, if only we put our faith in cold steel and hot lead!"

"Shut up, Perry. But the symptoms are all wrong," says Chloe. "Weres get irritable and withdrawn as the full moon approaches, but they don't end up like this."

Washington snickers. "Maggie-Sue, she's irritable and withdrawn at the best of times."

"Wait," says Rider. "Maybe she got bit in the jungle."

"My boy, it is for such observations the scholarly community craves the fruits of your research," sighs Whitlomb.

"No, it makes sense," says Sturgeon. "We had trouble getting through the barrier, earlier, right? So maybe Maggie-Sue did . . . something . . . in the jungle that she thought would bring her mana, but actually drained it. With seven people in the field, it's not surprising that one got unlucky."

"So she did something wrong? Like what?" says Rider. People turn to glare at him.

"I can't wait for that bruise to fade," complains Arbeiter. "I can't see what Al's thinking anymore."

"One way to check," muses Chloe.

Rider figures out what she means. As he studiously avoids looking at Thiebaud it is possible to detect a slight color change despite the bruise. Not that anybody is looking. They all look sick and are turning red themselves and can't meet each other's eyes.

"Creedon . . ." starts Sturgeon. Thiebaud has a wedge of lime to his nose. One can barely detect a slight brimming of tears in his eyes.

People carefully ooze out of the room, to stand awkwardly in the main bedroom; door shut, chattering loudly about nothing at all to avoid hearing Maggie-Sue. Eventually she stops making noise. They slink out. Thiebaud is at the sink, washing his hands. When he turns they can see the tears on his cheeks.

"Ah . . ." says Arbeiter.

"Werejaguar," chokes Thiebaud.

"Sorry to put you through that, buddy," murmurs Arbeiter. Goes to stand by him.

"To hell with him, what about her?" demands Chloe. Thiebaud freezes. Chloe freezes. Everybody else freezes. Thiebaud relaxes. Everybody else relaxes.

"Your concerns are correctly prioritized, of course, Miss Lee," says Thiebaud.

Once Chloe finds her voice, she says, "Never mind, Creedon. But what are we going to do? Another Heroic Journey to Dangerous Parts to get the Esoteric Cure for this Loathsome Disease?"

"O Lord, not again," groans Rider.

"Let us not be too hasty. There *are* certain advantages commensurate with the condition," says Whitlomb.

"Not worth it if it shuts down her cerebral cortex seven days out of twenty-eight," Chloe reminds him.

"Merciful God, what a straight line," says Arbeiter. "But I can't do it. It'd be like shooting fish in a barrel."

"How about a Complex and Dangerous Spell?" suggests Sturgeon.

"Cast by?" growls Washington. "Were-magic is elemental magic."

"All Guns Blazing?" says Rider, dripping irony.

"There's still straight alchemy," says Whitlomb.

"I was afraid you were going to say that. Where am I supposed to get a jaguar?" demands Arbeiter.

■　■　■

"Oh, much trouble. Very much trouble with the visas, senhor."

Rider grins as he sweats. Grimy third-world cubicle and Xuxa posters. Replies in Portuguese. "Oh, trouble with the visas? Oh dear, oh dear. But wait! Foolish me! I have forgotten my papers from the Ministry of Tourism." Hands over photocopies of Penthouse centerfolds wrapped around a substantial bribe.

"Ah, these papers, they will take some study. Please wait here."

As they wait, Chloe stretches. She's been flying twelve-hour days and she's pooped. "I just hope," says Sturgeon, "we can find a boat big enough to carry all our gear and two hundred pounds of jaguar, too."

Chloe nods. "Just our luck captivity breaks jaguars' spirits; it'd be so much simpler to steal one from a zoo."

"Back up a second," says Rider. "Two hundred pounds? Are they that big?"

"Oh, yes, indeed," says Whitlomb. "A healthy male can reach three hundred pounds, perhaps even three hundred and fifty. The slightest mistake and a poor wight has an excellent opportunity to learn to breathe through the sides of one's neck."

"And we're going in there without your dad's elephant gun?"

"Alive, Al, we need it alive," says Chloe.

"Yeah, but what if something goes wrong?"

"He's just trying to scare you," says Sturgeon. "Jaguar are very shy. Almost all the big cats are."

"Except for that unfortunate minority, the savage man-eaters, of course," says Whitlomb, pleasantly.

"'Savage man-eater'?" says Sturgeon. "Don't make me laugh. There has never been a reliable report of a man-eating jaguar."

"But that begs the question, doesn't it? A truly efficient man-eater leaves none behind to tell the tale, as you can see."

Chloe says, "Okay, now *I'm* scared."

The official comes back, beaming. Welcome to Brazil.

As they troop back to the Cessna, Chloe says, "I still don't see why we had to bribe every official in the damn airport. Why not just Jedi Mind Trick them?"

"It leaves psychic traces," says Rider. "We'll probably have to use the Jedi Mind Trick on the way back, though."

"Al speaks sooth. Even the most venial of South American officials is difficult to persuade to overlook three hundred pounds of muscle and claw and big sharp nasty teeth," says Whitlomb.

"Will you stop that?" snaps Rider.

"So how does one go about hunting jaguar, anyway?" asks Sturgeon.

"Well, the textbook approach for tiger (and jaguar are, in a sense, small South American tigers) is to stake out a small animal and lurk in the bushes. The animal of choice is something with a notably high-pitched, helpless-sounding cry," Whitlomb lectures. "No more than two hundred pounds, no longer than three foot from nose to tail, soft and pink . . ."

"Stop it!" wails Rider.

"I think jaguars have better taste than that, anyway," says Chloe.

Whitlomb chuckles. "Really, though, all there is to it is walking into the jungle, wandering around until we find jaguar tracks; follow them, find the jaguar, emplace a tranquilizer dart, and then dig pits, as necessary."

"What are the pits for?" says Sturgeon.

"To bury our dead, of course."

"Right. Chloe, you're the tracker of the bunch. Think you can spot jaguar tracks?"

"Look for fewmets, as well," says Whitlomb. "You can tell jaguar dung by the little buttons and scraps of cloth."

She gives Whitlomb a withering look. "I don't think there'll be any trouble, Max. I'm more worried about one of you men getting a fish up your dick."

Pause.

"I heard about those," says Sturgeon. "I thought . . ."

"Candiru? No, they're real, all right."

"Ah. And what would one . . ."

She grins at him. The three men wince and make motions as though to clutch their genitalia before they remember they're in the presence of a lady.

"Come on, boys," says Chloe, brightly, "let's go see the jungle!"

. . .

As they fly toward the Amazon basin, Whitlomb takes the handset of the occult radio and calls up north to Rider's place.

"Washington."

"Joseph, it's Perry. How are things, old man?"

"Changed on schedule. Cage held. Neighbors complained about the noise. Tomcats came from miles around. Changed back."

"Goodness. Is there any chance she's recovering on her own?"

"Nope. She's not using language. Recognizes the three of us, though. Thiebaud can usually calm her down when she gets excited. We're having some luck housebreaking her."

"What is that noise I hear? Is that growling?"

"Purring. Arbeiter's brushing her hair."

"Ah."

"No trouble getting her into a bath, either. Jaguars must like water."

"Ah. Well, no trouble on this end. We should be able to deliver a specimen on schedule. How are Arbeiter's preparations coming along?"

"Got everything but fresh jaguar blood."

"Good, good."

"Got to go. My turn to make sashimi."

"Right. Carry on."

. . .

"Eeeech," says Rider, stepping into ankle-deep mud.

"Our progress could not be termed significant," observes Whitlomb. "I don't believe we've gone more than ten miles from the river."

"More like five," says Chloe. "We are in trackless virgin jungle, here, guys."

"Ick. Ick. Ick," says Rider, thaumaturging mud off his legs.

"Any sign of a jaguar?" says Sturgeon.

"Nope. Al, you missed a leech on the back of your knee, there."

"Yaah!"

"Don't pull it off. Use your cigarette lighter."

Sturgeon grins. "Al, the next time we walk into the heart of darkness in search of a savage beast, we're leaving you home."

"Promise? Please?"

Whitlomb rolls his eyes. "Chin up, my boy. Open your eyes and observe the beauty of the unfettered birds."

"What birds, Perry? All I see is a whole lot of green. Anyway, you're right. We need to cover more ground. Everybody, I need a piece of your soles."

Sturgeon starts. "What do you want with our souls? Is this necromancy?"

"Your shoes, Max, your shoes."

"Oh." They pull knives, trim off little strips of rubber. Rider washes them off, wraps them in Saran Wrap; covers the bundle with mud. Chants. The mud becomes pseudosolid under their feet. Rider picks up some pieces of vine and undergrowth; chants again. He pulls the bits of plant away from each other, and a path opens up ahead.

"Neat trick, Al," says Sturgeon.

"I'm here to please."

"Got anything for leeches?"

"We shouldn't pick up as many of them if we don't brush against the leaves so much."

"Got anything to call a jaguar?"

Rider purses his lips. "Well . . . there is one incantation. But I'm not sure it'll work. Even the most skilled thaumaturges can't pull it off more than a quarter of the time."

Sturgeon shrugs. "May as well try it, Al."

Rider nods. "Okay. Be quiet, everybody." He rolls his head on his neck, holds up his arms. Takes several deep breaths. Opens his mouth. Intones, "Here, kitty kitty kitty . . . here, kitty . . ."

Chloe throws a clot of mud in his face as Rider dissolves into whoops of laughter. Everybody shakes their heads in disgust and they troop off into the green.

∎　∎　∎

Chloe, on point, holds up her hand to stop them. Squats down to examine the ground. Curses. "Never mind. I thought it might have been jaguar, but these are puma tracks."

Whitlomb squints, bends over and peers at the earth. "Chloe, Chloe. Trust your impulses. We have found jaguar tracks—and unless I am greatly mistaken, up ahead lies a jaguar."

"You're nuts. Those are puma tracks if I ever saw them."

"If you ever saw them? *Have* you even seen them? *Felis concolor*'s range extends to the Olympic Peninsula, but I rather doubt *Panthera onca* sets paw upon the mould over which you raced as a gel. And—I say this with the greatest possible respect, of course—I somewhat doubt you have seen enough of either to know the difference."

"And *I* was not aware jaguar had crossed the Atlantic and taken up residence in Africa. I'm telling you, these are puma tracks."

"You are confused. These are jaguar tracks."

"Puma tracks."

"Jaguar tracks."

"Puma."

"Jaguar."

"Puma."

"Jaguar."

"Isn't this," says Rider, "about when the train comes by and kills you both?"

"How can you tell jaguar tracks from puma tracks?" says Sturgeon.

"Shape. One's more elongated," says Chloe.

Rider and Sturgeon come up and peer at the ground. Sturgeon scratches his head. "Chloe, where are the tracks you're talking about?"

"Right there," she points.

Rider and Sturgeon look at each other. "Yeah, Max," says Rider, "right there. Plain on the nose on your face. Right next to where the centipede went by a week ago, to the left of that spot where the snail sneezed."

"What do you think, one of those poisonous frogs got to them?" says Sturgeon.

"That or the mosquitoes have bled them into delirium."

"Well, that's why we're the trackers, now, isn't it?" flares Whitlomb.

"We may as well follow them," sighs Chloe. "I imagine Perry's infallibility stops at the edge of the lectern, but he may still be right. Al, drop the foliage spell—it damages trail sign."

"Rats," says Rider. "Dinnertime, leeches, come 'n get it."

They follow the tracks through the jungle. Not much sun makes it through the canopy and they are sick of hearing birds.

The come across a stream. Chloe peers at a tree. "Satisfied, Perry? Puma, or I'm a John Bircher."

"What?" says Sturgeon.

Chloe stands up straight. "Our—ahem, harrumph, harrumph, ahem, being as I'm speaking—*Felis concolor* would seem to have happened to have leapt onto the trunk right here. Observe, if you will, the inclawnations, yclept 'scratches' by the vulgar, on this here outer barkean exhumations of this present tree. If we should happen to cross the stream, we'll see the trail resume. Only a hydrophobe would go to such extremes; ergo ergo hoc fucking damn, a puma."

"Hydrophobia?" asks Sturgeon. "Are you saying the thing's rabid?"

"No, no, no," says Whitlomb, testily. "Puma loathe swimming, but jaguar enjoy it. Everybody knows that."

"And that means," says Chloe, "we're in the puma's range. We'll have to get out of it before we have any hope of finding a jaguar. Fire up that spell, Al."

· · ·

Jungle nights are not quiet. The travelers are cleaner than they would ordinarily be after so long a trip, though; Rider makes dirt and damp crawl off their skin and out of their equipment, so they're not as miserable as they deserve to be. They're still pretty miserable.

"We better find something in the next few days," muses Sturgeon.

"Why?"

"We don't want to be in this jungle during the next full moon."

On cue, the howler monkeys cut loose.

Whitlomb starts, then mutters, "A snake, 'tis but a snake disturbing their rest; only a snake and nothing more."

· · ·

Marching along, the next day, Chloe freezes. So does everybody else. She beckons Whitlomb forward. "Jaguar?" she murmurs.

"Definitely," he whispers.

"Why are we whispering?" whispers Al.

"Tracks aren't more than an hour old."

"Ah."

"Al, Max, stay here. If something goes awry, our shrieks should be eminently audible." Chloe and Whitlomb set off into the jungle. Rider and Sturgeon look at the tracks. Shrug and wait.

They return. Chloe is holding a tuft of fur, grinning as she hands it to Rider. He grabs a Y-shaped branch, affixes the fur to the central tip; holds it by the two upper twigs, one in each hand. "Dowsing for jaguar," he smiles. The stick jerks in his hands. "This way. Keep your eyes open."

A few hundred yards later, the stick is pointing up at a ten-degree angle, so they watch the trees. Finally they spot it.

"My God," breathes Whitlomb. "An animal to rival that of Adam's naming gaze primeval. Let's shoot it."

Chloe is peering at the beast through binoculars. "Male . . . about a hundred ten kilograms . . . maybe two years old." Flips through her formulary, measures a dose of tranquilizer into a dart. Loads a few much smaller doses, in case a second or third shot is needed. Hands everything to Whitlomb. "Go git 'em."

Whitlomb gets within twenty meters of the tree before the jaguar notices him and takes off lickety-split. Whitlomb holds his fire.

Everybody else comes forward. "Oh, well. Onward." And they dowse ahead. Magic takes all the sport out of it, really. Suffice it to say they get their jaguar. Of course, when Whitlomb shoots it, it runs off into the bush, but they just dowse after it. Within ten minutes they find a zonked-out jaguar lying on the forest loam.

"Is it out?" says Rider.

"How the hell should I know?" says Sturgeon.

"Draw straws for who goes and finds out?"

"Okay. No cheating, anybody."

Whitlomb glares at the blade of withered grass. "Thunder and damnation. I drew the short straw the last time."

"Go git 'em, O Great White Hunter. Remember, one mistake and you're learning to breathe through the sides of your neck."

"I will thank you to keep your prattling lips secured, woman."

Chloe simpers and makes a kissy face.

Stalking off, Whitlomb is heard to mutter something about Lilith. But he lives; the jaguar is out cold. Chloe draws a little blood from Whitlomb and the jaguar, mixes them in a vial with some Other Stuff provided by Arbeiter, and reinjects the lot into the jaguar. "Hope you like cats, Perry."

"Just how long will this poor creature be unconscious?"

"Another hour, maybe. We should guard him, make sure nothing chews on him before he wakes up. Then it'll be a few days before it takes effect." So they wait. The cat comes to, staggers off. They start the long hike back to the boat.

Nothing much happens along the way. They dowse back to the boat, which is where they left it. Sit and wait for the jaguar to catch up. It is uncomfortably close to the full moon when the cat stalks out of the jungle and jumps up onto the boat. Whitlomb sits with him, scratching him behind the ears, a certain beatific expression on his face.

Two days later they are at the jungle airstrip where they left the Cessna. They Jedi Mind Trick the whole village. Whitlomb, Chloe, and the jaguar climb into the plane, which doesn't leave enough lifting capacity for both

Rider and Sturgeon; they'll have to pair up and make their own way home. Before parting company, Whitlomb calls up north.

"Arbeiter here."

"Kris! It's Perry."

"Hallo, Herr Doctor Professor. Got a cat for me?"

"Yes, he's right here. A glorious animal. We'll be back soon. How's Maggie-Sue?"

"Looking good. Glossy coat; bright, clear eyes . . ." Thump.

"What was that?"

"Lamp. Washington's pulling a piece of string for her."

Rider leans in. "Hey, has she done any damage there?"

"Rider, you ever heard the saying, if cats had hands . . .?"

Rider props his head against the doorframe. "How bad?"

"Well, we broke her of sharpening her nails on your speakers before she damaged the cones. Much. Don't worry, we've kept the door to the workroom locked. She's been pretty good. Although the place is a little dusty, now; she goes crazy whenever we try to run the vacuum cleaner . . ."

"Never mind. I don't want to know."

"Well, you may as well brace yourself. But it'll be a few more days before you and Max can come up, ja? We'll get the worst of the wreckage out before you get here."

▪   ▪   ▪

The doorbell rings. Washington goes downstairs and lets in Whitlomb, Chloe, and a 250-pound jaguar.

Whitlomb grins. "Good afternoon, J—good Lord, man! You look positively awful!"

One of Rider's neighbors, red hair set in curlers, comes around a corner and drops a bowl of Day-Glo orange macaroni and cheese. She flattens herself against the wall as her eyes bulge. "My God! A panther!"

"Oh, come now," says Whitlomb. "Catamounts don't have rosettes on their pelts, now, do they?"

"Actually," stutters Chloe, "it's a very rare breed of domestic dog. Perfectly tame. It's a . . . a . . . a Brazilian Short-Haired Jaguarhound."

"That's no dog! Look, it just extended its claws! Dogs don't have re-tractable claws!"

Chloe sets her arms akimbo. "Oooh, we've been to night school, have we? Well, a cheetah's claws don't retract, right? And cheetah are cats. So this is a Brazilian Short-Haired Jaguarhound, a breed that just so happens to have retractable claws. And, ah, a very long tail."

"You people are keeping a jungle cat in there! I've heard it! I don't care if that lunatic Rider *does* own the building, I'm calling the cops!"

"By the golden nipples of Vulcan's whores," says Whitlomb. He pulls an H. R. Giger print over his face. The woman's eyes go blank and she forgets the last few minutes. They go up to Rider's loft.

The place is a disaster. Arbeiter is sitting in an armchair. Maggie-Sue is curled up in his lap, asleep.

Whitlomb looks around. "If it's not too much to ask . . . What, pray tell, happened to the furnishings?"

Washington slumps against a wall. "Clawed up, mostly. Got rid of the pieces beyond salvage. Had to take down the drapes; she kept trying to climb them."

"Joe," says Chloe, carefully, "why isn't Maggie-Sue wearing anything?"

"You ever try to make a cat wear clothes? Always knew she wasn't a totemist, but we've got confirmation. . . . Some dogs'll put up with clothes, but cats go crazy. Tried wrapping her in an overcoat and putting a leash on her, take her out for a walk, get some exercise. Blew up in our faces."

"You put her on a *leash?* Took her out in *public?!*"

"This is San Francisco. They thought we were S&M freaks or some-thing . . . but then she started yammering and clawing at the buttons. Man-aged to get all the way out of it. Had to drug her and carry her back to the loft."

Chloe looks over at Thiebaud, who is sacked out on what's left of the couch. Even in his sleep he looks just as exhausted as Arbiter and Washing-ton. "When he sees this place, Rider's head is going to explode. Not that I wouldn't French-kiss a gila monster for a front-row seat. Couldn't you three keep her under control?"

Arbeiter says, "How? Keep her in the straitjacket and dose her with

Thorazine every four hours? Lock her in an empty room and throw in a haunch of meat once a day? This happens to be a member of our cell. Besides, it hasn't been so bad. She's very affectionate."

"Oh, no, Kris, you don't mean . . ."

"Of course not. What sort of perverted monsters do you think we are?"

"I get sick just *thinking* about that question!" she yells.

"Quiet, Chloe, don't wake her up. . . ."

"Kris," interjects Whitlomb, "how much of this is she going to remember?"

"I don't know," says Arbeiter.

"None of it, I hope," says Washington. "She remembers me hitting her every time I caught her pissing on the couch, she'll never talk to me again."

Chloe says, "Kris, you don't look very comfortable."

"I didn't know she was going to go to sleep. My bladder's been ready to burst for the last hour."

"Why don't you wake her up?"

"What are you, nuts? This is the first sleep Creedon's had in the last twenty-four hours, what with her crying to go out all the time and him the only one who can calm her down. This place is too small by half to keep a cat her size."

"She's not a cat! Well, anyway, you might as well wake her up now. This is as good a time as any for you to do your alchemy thing. You all have obviously been working real hard, here. Joe, why don't you go crash? Kris, we need, but Kris, Perry, and I can take care of everything."

"No way," says Arbeiter. "She doesn't like needles. It'll take all three of us to get a half pint of blood out of her. Washington, go wake up Creedon."

"Perry and I can help."

"No, you can't. Trust me. Take the cat into the workroom. I'll be there in a minute." Maggie-Sue stirs in Arbeiter's lap. "Go now. She doesn't like strangers. Creedon? Go soak down the blanket."

·   ·   ·

Chloe and Whitlomb have no trouble drawing a pint of blood from the jaguar, who is completely calm and trusting. From the sounds coming from the next room, Arbeiter, Washington, and Thiebaud are having a little more trouble.

"Hold her arms, hold her arms!"

"Easy, girl, everything's going to be all right. . . ."

"Yeeow!"

"Are you all right, Mr. Arbeiter?"

Throughout, Maggie-Sue keeps up quite a running commentary in a dialect of Enraged Feline.

"You got her?"

"Yeah, I—whoa! Grab her!"

"Scheiss, there goes the stereo. . . ."

"Okay, wrap her up, wrap her up!"

"It's all right, girl. . . ."

The tone of the screaming goes from defiant to piteous. "Hold on, hold on, there's a good girl. . . ."

There is a banging on the door, loud complaints. "Creedon, go get the door and shoot the son of a bitch!"

"Forgive us, a friend of ours is indisposed and we fear we cannot receive visitors just now," shouts Thiebaud through the door. "Perhaps you could return at a later time." The pounding continues. They hear Thiebaud unlock the door and open it. Hear gunshots. Chloe and Whitlomb look at each other in horror.

"I believe I have taken care of the problem, Mr. WashingtOOF!!" They have never before heard Thiebaud groan in quite the way he commences to groan.

"Watch her legs! Watch her legs!"

"Gott im Himmel . . . Washington, hold her down while I check Creedon. . . . Creedon, sit down, take off your trousers. . . . Shut up, Creedon, I'm a medic. . . ."

"I'm losing her!"

"Chloe, Whitlomb, get in here!"

Chloe rushes in and tends to Thiebaud, who is in mute agony and bent over double. All the men in the room are feeling stabs of sympathetic pain. "Wow, Creedon, that must have hurt." Thiebaud looks at her. He doesn't look happy. Chloe turns an astonishing shade of red.

Arbeiter, Washington, and Whitlomb manage to keep Maggie-Sue down as the last of the half pint drains from her arm. Arbeiter yells, "Chloe, get Creedon into the next room. Whitlomb, you and Joe will have to keep her down. Watch her legs and her teeth!"

Arbeiter grabs the bag, runs into the workroom, adds a straw-colored fluid to the two bags of blood. Agitates. Pours them together into two large beakers, slams them into Rider's centrifuge and sets it for "high."

More banging on the door. "Open up! Police!"

Arbeiter yells, "Chloe, go Jedi Mind Trick them!"

"With what?"

"Use Whitlomb's mask!"

"I don't know how to use it!"

"Well, do something before they start shooting!"

"You go do it!"

"I can't! I have to monitor the reaction! Go!"

Chloe scampers to the door. "Er, Door?"

"Yes?" says the door.

"I want to go out, but I don't want people out there to be able to come in."

"I'm on it."

"Thanks."

Chloe opens the door a crack and slips out. When the policewoman tries to punch over her head to shove the door open, her hand rebounds from an invisible barrier. The door slams behind Chloe and locks. "Hello, Officer," she says.

The policewoman is staring at her hand. "What the . . ."

"There's no way through, I'm afraid. It's a glass ceiling, turned sideways."

Humanity's survival reflex kicks in and the policewoman forgets. She glares at Chloe. "Open that door!"

"Well, Officer, things are a little complicated . . . you see, there's a very unwell woman in there . . ."

"I can hear that! You unlock that door!" She waves a pistol under her nose. Chloe's eyes cross as she tracks the barrel. The policewoman has turned beet red.

"I left my keys inside! And she's under quarantine! Terribly infectious disease . . . ah . . . Jaguar Fever! Very dangerous! I've had it before, I'm immune, but you can't go in there."

"You can't keep quarantine in a private dwelling! Oh, hell. Murphy, arrest this woman and get her out of my face! Smith, go get a ram!"

Rider's neighbor is screaming from down the hall. "They've got guns! They shot at me!" Chloe is quickly cuffed and dragged out to the street, thrown against a squad car and frisked. Then they stuff her in the back of a cruiser and slam the door.

Upstairs, Arbeiter shuts off the centrifuge, applies the brakes, waits for it to spin down. Drains off a pint of plasma. Adds a reagent, begins titration.

"Arbeiter," calls Washington. "Tranqs?"

"No! She can't have any depressants in her system, this stuff doesn't keep for more than a few minutes, and the jaguar can't stand to lose any more blood for another two months! Creedon, can you stand up?" Hell, Thiebaud can barely breathe.

They hear a ram smashing into the door. Fortunately, it's reinforced with congealed hard gamma and sealed with the stubbornness of a septuagenarian Republican.

Outside Rider's loft, the policewoman curses. "Jesus, Smith, what's this thing made of?"

"What've we got, a crack house here?"

"This is definitely a hostage situation. Get the SWAT team! Get everybody else out of the building!"

Arbeiter is hurrying. Sprinkles in a gray powder until the plasma turns red. Back into the centrifuge. Arbeiter pours a potion down Thiebaud's throat. "This'll keep your yarbles in place. . . . Hang in there, buddy. . . ." Runs out. "I've got three minutes. What's the situation?"

"Heat! Cops!" spits Washington.

The door says, "They're evacuating the building and calling SWAT."

"That doesn't make sense! They wouldn't do that! That's not standard procedure! There's nothing that serious, there's nothing he—oh, no! The fucking Vulture cult's *making* them attack! They're controlled! Doesn't Rider have this place tricked up to deal with that?"

"But how do you turn it on?!"

"Shit, shit, shit . . . Door?"

The door says, "Sorry, I just hang around and swing a bit."

Arbeiter runs into the main bedroom, starts looking for jewels, switches, pull ropes, anything. Finds a concealed panel on the nightstand; flips it open. Curses.

"What?" yells Joe.

"Control panel! But it's in fucking Swahili or something!"

"Kris," calls Whitlomb, "come help Joe hold down Maggie-Sue!" Arbeiter runs out and grabs Maggie-Sue, who is wailing and thrashing like a combine in mud, bashing her head against the concrete floor.

Whitlomb runs to the panel. *Hmn. Cuneiform,* he thinks. *Thaumaturge-dialect Sumerian. Which I don't read. Well, let's see. If we assume Assyrian occult literature shares root words even though the culture was lost . . .*

Tense time. Arbeiter's watch beeps. "Joe, hold her! I've got to tend the plasma!" Zooms into the workroom. The jaguar is sitting there, unconcernedly washing his left front paw.

Joe manages to hold Maggie-Sue for a minute or two, but the wet blanket is drying out and slipping. "I'm losing her!"

The jaguar pads out, cocks its head. Walks over to Maggie-Sue, looks down at her. She freezes. The jaguar makes a sound, kind of like "Mrowrf?" Maggie-Sue mewls at him. The jaguar settles down next to her and starts licking her face. She starts purring.

Washington stares in disbelief. "Whitlomb, you sure that's a jaguar and not a were?"

"Positive!" yells Whitlomb.

"Absolutely!" shouts Arbeiter. "I'm ready! Hold her dow—what the . . . ?"

"Get on with it, you fucking Kraut!" yells Washington.

"This is Lieutenant Johnson of the San Francisco Special Weapons and Tactics Team. We have a negotiator here. Please, we just want you to let the girl go. We're willing to meet any reasonable demands."

Arbeiter sets up an IV. Draws his pistol, runs to stand by the window. Shouts out, "Look, this is all a big misunderstanding. We're not holding anybody hostage! She's just sick!"

"Vulture cult," says Washington. "Vulture cult out there. Got the crowd watching and hoping for bloodshed. Get them away!"

"THIS IS BEN WILLIAMSON. I'M HERE TO TALK. WE'RE GOING TO CALL YOU. PLEASE, WE JUST WANT TO TALK."

The phone rings. Arbeiter gets it. "Uh, hallo?"

"Hello. My name is Ben. Would you like to tell me your name?"

"Yeah, I'm Mother Fucking Teresa. I've got a sick woman in here and you people aren't helping one bit!"

"You say there's a sick girl in there? We can help; we have paramedics right here. We can get her to a hospital in minutes."

"You don't understand! She'll be fine, if you all just go away!"

"We have a doctor on the radio. What's wrong with her?"

"She gets these spells, thinks she's a cat!"

"Schizophrenia?"

"Similar, but the cause is completely organic, a virus, and . . . ah . . . we're administering the specific right now! We would have let you in before, but the stuff doesn't keep well! We couldn't afford to let you come in and interrupt!"

"Who is treating her condition? What hospital?"

"Ah . . . Dr. Bartholomew Stern, out of San Diego!"

"Is Dr. Stern there?"

"No, he sent up the serum and a paramedic. Who we sent out to talk to you, by the way. Is she all right?"

"She's fine. Look, can we come in and check on this woman?"

Arbeiter looks at the jaguar. Not something that can easily be explained. Let alone all the other junk in the loft. "No, she's still violent. We have trained medical personnel in here, we've all been immunized."

There is a pause. Downstairs, the negotiator says, "Bring me the woman who came out." Chloe is dragged over. "Who are you?"

"I'm a friend."

"Perhaps you could be a little more specific?"

"Look," says Chloe. "There's a very ill woman in there. Jaguar Fever. Very rare, very contagious, and very dangerous."

"Why isn't she in a hospital?"

"Treatment takes a long time. She's an outpatient."

"I thought you said it was dangerous and contagious. It's illegal to perform outpatient care under those conditions."

A policeman with a radio yells, "Hey, Lieutenant Williamson? Doc Duc says there's no such thing as Jaguar Fever."

"Shit," says Williamson. "Get this nut out of here." Goes back to the phone. "All right. But we have to come in and check on her eventually. Do you have any way we can contact Dr. Stern?"

Arbeiter sweats. Hits the Mute button. "Whitlomb, you making any progress in there?"

"Hang on, Kris, I've found a dictionary. . . ."

Arbeiter reactivates the phone, "He's probably on the golf course. We can't find his beeper number."

Outside, the radioman yells to the negotiator. "Williamson, we've got an ID on this Dr. Stern. Turned up missing a couple months ago! Suspected homicide!"

"Terrific." Back to the phone. "All right. We've got our people in San Diego out trying to find him. Maybe we can all just go home after all."

"My God," says Arbeiter. "I think they're buying it."

"You fool," says Washington, "Stern is *dead*. Rider killed him himself!"

There is a horrible explosion from the door. Smoke squirts all around the jamb but it holds. Everybody's ears are ringing. "Shit, they just tried to blast their way in!" says Arbeiter. Yells into the phone. "Hey, stop that! The door is reinforced to make sure some robber doesn't come in here and catch the bug!"

Williamson sweats. Nothing—*nothing*—should be able to stand up under an explosive entry. The girl must be dead by now, if there ever was a girl. This is no common bunch of nuts. He can smell the gathered crowd. . . . Has to be some heavily armored and armed terrorist group. He turns to the situation manager and shakes his head.

The captain nods. Radios to base. "Control, we've got some seriously dug in people here. We'll try tear gas but we may need the National Guard on this one. We're going to have to evacuate the surrounding buildings."

Inside the loft, Arbeiter is sweating too. "Hey, you still there? Ben?" No reply. "Shit. They've given up negotiating. Gas masks, everybody! Armor! Whitlomb, just start pushing buttons! They're going to—"

A tear-gas bazooka thumps; a projectile shatters the window and the room is suddenly full of a choking, nauseating cloud. Everybody but Arbeiter goes down. Arbeiter crawls to the bedroom. Whitlomb is vomiting onto Rider's atlas. "Whitlomb! Whitlomb! What button?"

Whitlomb chokes, "Try the big red one."

Arbeiter pushes the red button. The building sprouts wings and flies away.

. . .

Well, that's just plain impossible. The building's tenants watch their home fly off and fall into catatonic shock. The police and the SWAT team stagger; some faint. Control slips; onlookers suddenly go about their business. Reporters wander off to their favorite bars, maybe remembering to call in "false alarm." TV crews turn off their cameras, pack up and leave. The people watching the live coverage begin channel-surfing, marveling at what they can do with special effects nowadays.

Oh, there are going to be a whole lot of UFO reports and nightmares about this one, no doubt. As wind drives the tear gas out of the building, Arbeiter wonders how many suicides will result from this little stunt.

Arbeiter walks over to Maggie-Sue. Washington is coughing, but he has her in a bear hug and she's just whimpering a little. The jaguar's keeping her calm, despite his swollen eyes. Doesn't look like she's choking on her own vomit. The IV bag is empty. Arbeiter pulls the needle from her arm, taps Washington off, unwraps her. She leaps up and hides behind the couch; the jaguar goes with her.

Washington sits up, wipes his streaming eyes. "What happened? Where are we?"

Arbeiter goes to the window and leans out. "We pushed the panic button. And I think we're about fifty kilometers off shore." His giggle has a soupçon of hysteria to it. "And I hope this thing floats, because it looks like we're going down."

"Arbeiter, you idiot. Get Rider on the horn!"

"Huh?"

"Blancs. I have to do *all* the thinking around here." Washington shoves Arbeiter out of the way and goes into the comm closet. "Washington to Rider, Washington to Rider, come in. Emergency." Nothing. "Rider, Rider, come in please, right now." More nothing. "Rider, damn it, get over here and answer the phone!"

"Rider here. What's wrong?"

"Your house is flying into the drink! What do we do?"

"Relax, it floats."

Pause.

"WHAT THE— WHO PUSHED THAT BUTTON? WHAT HAPPENED?"

Washington sighs and begins explaining.

．　■　．

Chloe smiles sweetly at the policewoman and bats her eyes. "You were saying, Officer?"

"You came out of—there was—I saw—Murphy, what are we holding her on?"

Murphy comes over. "Who?"

"Her."

"Huh? Hey, what are you doing in there?"

Chloe smiles again. "You cuffed me and put me in here."

Murphy grabs her by the shoulders and hauls her out. Mutters to himself. "Damn S&M freaks . . . try anything to get themselves hauled off for a strip search." He unlocks the handcuffs, hands them to her. "Take your toys and go on home. I don't have the energy to arrest you right now. Go on."

Chloe goes to her Toyota, scanning the skies. "You know," she thinks, "this would be a prime time for the bad guys to get me. I'm pretty well alone." Tries to raise Air Rider.

．　■　．

Air Rider has just become the Good Ship Rider. Whitlomb feels a little seasick. Washington is still on the radio.

"Gee," says Rider, "I guess I should brief you all on how to work the loft's defense mechanisms."

Arbeiter snatches the handset from Washington. "I GUESS FUCKING SO!"

"Sorry, Kris."

"Sorry my Nazi ASS, you MORON! How the FUCK do we get home?"

"Well, you may be out there for a while, while the field recharges."

"How long?"

"Kris, that button is for extreme emergencies."

"*How long?*"

"Well, making a building fly is no mean trick. Unless we can find a way to speed up the process . . . Kris, it took a year to charge it up the first time."

This narrator will not attempt to transcribe Arbeiter's response.

■   ■   ■

"Hello? Anybody? This is Chloe. . . . Hello?"

"Washington here. You all right?"

"Fine. They arrested me, but they let me go after Rider's building flew away. Neat trick. When's it coming back?"

"Maybe never. Whole building is fifty kilometers off shore, in the Humbolt current, southbound at two, three knots. One of Rider's idiot emergency measures."

"You mean he didn't plan for a way to bring it back?"

"Who are we talking about?"

"Right. How about Maggie-Sue?"

"Resting. Arbeiter thinks she'll be okay."

"And the jaguar?"

"Good. Arbeiter says if we don't get him back to the jungle soon, he's going to bond to Whitlomb. Never go back."

"There isn't much we can do about that."

"No. Rider and Sturgeon just made it to Rio. Flying up soon. Don't know where they're going to sleep."

"Okay. We can always get a seaplane and come pick you up."

"And abandon the building? What about oil tankers? Not made to cope with concrete icebergs, you know. Never mind. You go to the Marina and hole up. And buy newspapers; I don't want to get behind."

■   ■   ■

Maggie-Sue comes to. Washington is by her side, reading Creedon's copy of Sacks. She gets up on her elbows and turns to him. "Why does it smell like cat and the sea?"

Washington unleashes a rare happy smile but recovers quickly. "Cat's over there. We're at sea."

She notices that the building is rocking gently and she can hear waves crashing against something. Her hands feel funny and she looks at them. "What happened? Where did these calluses come from?"

"You got bit by a werejaguar. Allergic reaction or something, shut down your brain. Spent a lot of time on all fours. You don't remember?"

"No, I don't."

"Hey, Joe," yells Arbeiter from the living room, "what'll you give me to keep my mouth shut?"

"Mouth shut about what?" asks Maggie-Sue.

Washington looks very uncomfortable. "Nothing. Tell you later."

She grabs his arm. "What's Arbeiter laughing about?" No answer. "Arbeiter, what are you laughing about?"

"Anyway," hurries Washington, "we were besieged. Pushed a panic button. Whole building flew out to sea. Can't bring it back. Winter's coming."

"Is that why it's so cold in here?"

Maggie-Sue is distracted. Washington will live another day.

. . .

Rider and Sturgeon climb out of the Ford, go down the slip to the Formosa 51. October; late Indian summer. Chloe is sunning herself. Thick sunscreen, though—she doesn't want to turn into a zombie. Rises with a happy squeal, runs and jumps into Sturgeon's arms. Rider makes gagging noises. She takes her tongue from Max's mouth and sticks it out at him.

As they load gear onto the sailboat, Chloe says, "I still don't get how a concrete building can float."

"Well, there's a deep, skinny lead keel bolted to the bottom, for ballast and stability. When the spell went off it inflated these big sort of helium-expanded polystyrene balloons under the basement; injected the basement, ground floor, and most of the second floor with a solid mass of the same stuff. Thank God my renters had already been evacuated. There's one clear corridor going from a window to the stairwell—with the twelve-foot ceilings, you can canoe in. Actually, I'm amazed it worked at all. It's going to take a whole lot of work to make sure everything's as water-resistant as it should be. On the other hand, there are still four units on the two floors left above water. Heh. I can finally have everybody over at once and they can get some privacy."

"Still, it was a Rube Goldberg device, right? I mean, you never figured on making it into a permanent sea base or anything."

"Oh, no. If that's what I wanted I'd build a yacht. No, this won't stay afloat more than a few months, if that. We'll have bring it back into the Bay soon, maybe beach it somewhere on the abandoned waterfront by Third Street."

"Al," says Sturgeon, gently, "there's no way to recover that building. It's been drifting for two days. It's at least fifty nautical miles south by now, probably more. Even if we stole a tugboat, there's no way we have the time to drag it north against the current. And even if we did—the Vulture cult's on to it as a headquarters, and they'd raise another siege. We're going to have to pack up your magical gear and sink the building."

"But—"

"On this trip, Al. I'm sorry."

Rider looks ready to argue, but doesn't. Finally nods. They cast off and head for the Golden Gate.

Sunset. Rider is up on the bow, smoking and watching the water. Chloe comes up and sits with him. He doesn't look at her. "You want to be alone, Al?"

"Yes. No. I don't know."

"It's your home."

"Yeah. It's not just that, though."

"What?"

"The building can't be operated correctly by anyone but a thaumaturge—that's why the panel is in Sumerian. But I shouldn't have set up the panic button to fly the building away."

"It still worked. Al, that spell was a scatterbrained idea in a lot of ways, but it worked. And it was a panic button, for, as you put it, 'extreme emergencies.' Flying the whole building away is a smart response to an 'extreme emergency.'"

"No. I was thinking with my dick."

"What?"

"The biggest, snazziest spell I've got, I put into the panic button. I didn't stop and think what it would mean."

"Well, you lost the building, yes, but—"

"Fuck the building. You know what happened to my tenants?"

"They were evacuated, Al. What are you talking about?"

"What are you, an iceberg?" he spits. "Fuck your I'm-not-involved hard-shelled totem, and while you're at it, fuck you."

She stares. Gets up. "Talk sense or I'm walking away right now. I don't have to take this from you, Rider."

Rider gapes. Holds up his hands. "Wait, I'm sorry. I'm skipping steps, thought you knew what I meant and you didn't care. I should know better. Please, listen to me for a while, I'll explain."

She stands, fists clenched. "Oh, now I'm just the naïve, inexperienced little Geoduck? Haven't seen enough to know what you mean without having it all spelled out for me? Well, to hell with you, and to hell with your patronizing ass."

"I don't mean to imply any of that. I'm not saying what I mean, that's all. Please."

Rider looks unhappy and apologetic. Of course, he can look any way he wants, until he delivers the punch line. She waits for it. It doesn't come. She sits down and looks at him.

Rider runs his hand over his scalp, visibly gets a grip on himself. "Look, the people who live there, most of them have lived there for months, years."

"So?"

"Now, the building is gone, gone in a cloud of the occult. That means *nobody* can remember there was *ever* a building there. For the bankers and the phone company that just means there was a clerical error. But for the people who lived there, there are years of experiences: memories of their home that the survival reflex won't let them recall. I've been following the news, reading the papers, keeping track of them all: three are dead and the rest went into psychogenic shock and ended up in ICUs. The survivors, there's too much in their brains for the reflex to maintain forever. Everybody but my tenants—well, you've seen how people work around the things the reflex won't let them remember; the 'bad records' will be deleted piece by piece from the computers and archives as society knits back together around the hole."

Chloe nods. "I saw it once before, when that football player was carried away by harpies in the middle of the third quarter."

"Exactly," says Rider. "If a mundane finds a James Burana football card, he throws it away without ever really seeing it. Half the inadvertent occultists in the world are people who learned to suppress the survival reflex when their research turned up records referring to things that nobody else can remember. Sightings of those damned Incumbent space elephants, for example."

Chloe says, "So your tenants . . ."

"When their memory comes back, they'll be outside the new pattern. They'll be shunned. They'll be occult creatures themselves—institutionalized for life if they have wealthy families or real loyal friends. The rest will end up out on the street, raving about their home that flew away—and you know how long a human with an open third eye lasts if he doesn't have any way to defend himself against the things that see him."

"I understand."

"All because my panic button made the building vanish. I could have had it animate gargoyles, or something else that would spook people instead of driving them mad. No, I had to think with my dick; figure that my most *impressive* spell would be the one best suited to a crisis. As a result, I've increased the population of street people and mad aunts in the attic by at least a dozen, probably more."

"Al—"

Rider field-strips his cigarette with trembling fingers. "It was a *small* mistake, that's what gets me. When we make a *small* mistake a whole neighborhood becomes raddled with madmen and ghosts. What are we doing? Every day something goes wrong and we hit it with shit we got ready for something else entirely. We plan for everything we can think of, accumulate every weapon and dirty trick we can, but has anything we've ever planned for actually happened? We're playing with dynamite and we don't have the foggiest fucking idea what we're doing!"

"Al—"

"Chloe, I love you like a sister. But go away."

.   .   .

Chloe goes away. Wishes Whitlomb was on hand. Eventually, Max tells Al he should get some sleep. Al says he'll take first watch.

Dawn. Sturgeon wakes up. Goes abovedeck. Rider is at the helm, smoking. "Hi, Max. We should get to the building in another few hours."

"You been up all night?"

"No, I was asleep at the wheel."

"You know you need to sleep. A soldier never passes up an opportunity to eat, sleep, or piss—"

Rider interrupts. "—because he never knows when the next chance will come."

Sturgeon grins, stretches; says "That's right."

Rider nods, watches the waves.

Sturgeon yawns, touches his toes a few times. "Hey, Al? Got a second?"

"Sure."

"Look, it's a loose cell and I like it that way, but we all have to work together on this. It's not sleep I'm talking about here; that's a symptom of—well, I hate to get pompous about it, but still—your irreverent attitude. I have to be able to count on you when we all decide we're going to do something. Just a friendly reminder, Al, okay?"

Rider waves him off. "Shut up, Max; you lost all your credibility when you started sleeping with the cell whore."

Sturgeon takes three steps, grabs Rider by the lapels, lifts him off the deck. "We don't have time for this, boy."

Rider laughs in his face. "'Boy.' Guess you pay attention when Whitlomb's in the room. And my master, too, come to think of it."

Sturgeon shakes him. Rider's teeth rattle. "Now, listen—"

Rider bats Sturgeon's arms away, slams him against the wall with a phrase of Sumerian. "No, you fucking listen, for once, navy man."

Sturgeon gets his breath back. Snarls, "What? What are you trying to do, here? Jockeying for leadership? Pissed that you're not in charge of the cell? Angry Chloe took me instead of you?"

Rider makes a gesture. Sturgeon cannot breathe. The sky is clear; the sun falls on their faces. Rider comes in close. "You naïve, testosterone-flushed sheep. I *can't* lead. That's what I'm counting on *you* for." Rider lets go; Sturgeon collapses to the deck.

Rider waits by the helm. Chain-lights another cigarette. Sturgeon manages to get up, pulls a semiautomatic from his bathrobe.

"Oh, great, Max. Shoot me."

"You're sick. Like Maggie-Sue. Hands up."

Rider waves his hand and the pistol flies out into the waves. "Yeah, Vulture cult's gotten to me, all right. Accelerating what's already there."

"Chloe!" yells Sturgeon.

"She's sleeping like a stone, Max—literally. I dosed you both, but she got double. We have to talk about her."

"You want to kill me, do it already."

"I wanted to, I'd have done so by now."

Sturgeon blinks. Blinks again.

Rider grins. "Pretty rotten company you keep, when that's the most reassuring thing to say there is, eh? Look, I'm sorry I hit you. Can we talk a minute?"

Sturgeon nods cautiously. Rider sits down; pulls a flask of bourbon from his jacket and offers it. Sturgeon shakes his head. Rider drinks deep.

"Max . . ."

Sturgeon says nothing.

"Look, I'm sorry about all that. But if you're going to lead the cell you have to lead the cell."

"So you lead it," says Sturgeon.

"I can't. Leading isn't smarts; I'm smart, but Chloe is smarter than me. It's not power; Maggie-Sue is more powerful than I am. It's not education, or else

Perry would be in charge; it's not dedication, or else Creedon would call the shots, God forbid. Leading is about perspective, the big picture—occultists start forgetting *why* we're running around blowing things up. We need people who still have two feet on the ground, who aren't always looking over their shoulders for ghosts and demons, to tell us what to do, if not necessarily how to do it. Talk to me, Max; if you and Chloe want out, you can go."

"And leave all of you? We don't want out."

"But you don't want *in*, either."

"No, of course not. We'd have to be crazy to want to see all this shit."

"Max, this is going to sound like friend-jealous-of-lover, you know, the way men get when their friends fall in love and don't have time for them anymore. But that isn't it. We don't like each other all that much."

Sturgeon is silent.

"My point is that you're in love with a member of the cell. Like Ian Fleming said—now you've got two hearts. You're going to be watching out for Chloe and Chloe is going to be watching out for you. That's fine. But I don't need Creedon to tell me that all the two of you want is to go somewhere and be safe, together."

Sturgeon maintains silence; he is not looking at Rider.

"The only reason you don't go is there's nowhere safe to go to. But your *planning* is all screwed up. We can't afford that or we're all going to end up dead."

Sturgeon looks at Rider. "Nuts," he says.

Rider looks away, looks back. "Max, what do we do after we pick up everyone else?"

"I haven't worked that out yet. Our plans were all scrambled by having to go to the jungle for the jaguar."

"You've had plenty of time to think about it—in the jungle. But you haven't been thinking about it. You're in love. I hear that love is good, better than anything else. But it gets all crusty and stiff when you're rotting in the grave. Look, it's not just you, you know. Chloe hasn't been using her head lately either. When's the last time you asked why we were still in the fight, or Chloe needled me about using a magic sledgehammer to swat a mundane fly?"

"Then you should be talking to the two of us, not provoking me."

"I hit you, alone, because we need you more. Triage."

∎   ∎   ∎

Chloe wakes up, wonders why it's so bright. Checks her watch. Later than she usually wakes up. Shrugs, stretches luxuriously, sheet tight across her bosom. Wonders if Max has had a chance to talk to Rider.

Dresses. Abovedecks. Sturgeon is at the helm. Rider is leaning against the cabin wall, weaving something with his hands. "What are you doing, Al?"

"Just making a little piece of costume jewelry out of glints on the water. Ring. Want it?"

"No, Al, I couldn't."

"Yours for the asking. I don't give it to you, I'll just trade it for a cask of bourbon. Let me see your hand . . . thanks. We're about an hour from the building."

An hour passes. Chloe climbs up, looks. "Oh, my God! Seaweed-wrapped stucco against gray horizon, that is so cool!" She grins, shakes her head. "Wow. Anyway. I'll put out the bumpers; we can tie up by the stairwell. It's going to be wet going in and out, though."

"I have a canoe in storage," says Rider. "I'll ferry out my stuff."

"Oh, I'll handle the canoe, Al; you go topside and get everything out."

They hail the building; Arbeiter sticks his head out a window and waves. Maggie-Sue maneuvers the sailboat in; they tie off. Much fiddling with the canoe; Rider goes upstairs. "Hi, everybody," he says. "Warm in here."

"Maggie-Sue's contribution to our comfort. The flames of Vesuvius are hers to command," says Whitlomb.

Rider looks around disinterestedly. "Place is a wreck. Just as well we're going to sink it."

"Sink it?" says Whitlomb. "Sink it? But what of your accumulated equipment?"

"No time to move it out. We've got work to do, and besides, it's a foot lower in the water than it should be. I'll need to pack."

"But . . . your sculptures!" Pause. "Al!"

"Someday it'll make an archaeologist very happy. My gift to your profession, Perry." Rider goes into the main bedroom, opens the control panel. Pushes buttons. "Everybody, stay out of the way." Pushes one final button. Stands, claps his hands four times. Yells, "Sumerian fire drill . . . NOW! BUG OUT!" Squeaking and piping shrilly, his books and braziers and bizarre apparati sprout little feet and jump into boxes and suitcases.

Whitlomb watches the commotion. "Neat trick, Al."

Rider grunts. Waits for everything to stop moving. People carry boxes down to the stairwell; Chloe ferries them to the sailboat. It doesn't take long.

"You're leaving a lot behind," says Chloe.

"Not really. The furniture is wrecked, anyway, and cooking gear is easy to replace."

"Your books?"

"Too bulky; I've got all the important ones."

"The rugs?"

"Now you know why I buy cheap things, Chloe. You always have to be ready to walk away."

"I don't," says Whitlomb, "detect a hint of ostentatious martyrdom here, do I?"

"Hint? What do you mean, hint? Am I losing my touch? Anyway, that's the last of it. Get to the sailboat. I have to scuttle this sucker. Maggie-Sue, go to the roof; I'll want a pickup from there, okay?"

They go. Sturgeon unties the sailboat and it moves well clear. They see Rider on the roof, Maggie-Sue beside him, her arms crossed. They wonder why he opens a tin can and dumps the contents overboard. Rider puts his arms around Maggie-Sue and they fly to the Formosa 51. Rider sits on the bow, smoking, as they hoist the sails and depart. The building shows no sign of sinking.

"Hey, Al?" calls Sturgeon.

"Give it a minute," comes the response.

There is a dull thud from the building and suddenly, it sinks like a stone. Moths flutter on the waves; drown, go under. Rider vomits.

．　■　．

They sail back to the Bay, cautious from the moment they can see the Golden Gate. They half expect to find the City in flames, or at least thin dogs standing cheek-to-jowl along the coast in wait. Things are ominously quiet, even when they make quick trips out to various people's places to gather last-minute supplies. Although Thiebaud keeps bringing back teeth from his nighttime strolls.

Preparations are made. Loins are girded. The raid is scheduled for October 29th—as late as they dare without slopping into the Day of the Dead. If the action takes more than thirty-six hours they're doomed, anyway.

They can see things getting nasty all over the Bay Area. The *Examiner* documents a sudden spurt in domestic violence and promptly blames it on the economy, going on to blame that on sex education. Drug-related homicides up. More elementary schools install metal detectors. Riots in People's Park. Malnutrition in the housing projects. The child-abuse units groan under a redoubled caseload. More women carry pepper spray, knives, and guns for fear of rape. A gay bar is bombed. So many street people are doused in gasoline and set ablaze, Holy Cross Hospice cannot take them all; the irony sickens Sturgeon's cell.

Helicopters and speedboats aren't easy to hide, unless you can hoodoo the regulatory agencies. But that in itself leaves traces that Chloe and Max can find. Their job is made easier by the Vulture cult's tendency to use a sledgehammer where a ball-peen hammer would do. There are psychic booby traps all through the city—every time they get close to tracking down a mysteriously missing vehicle, somebody at the DMV blows his own brains out. Arbeiter spends a lot of time breaking into crime scenes and photographing documentation spattered with blood before someone can absentmindedly crumple the paper up and throw it away. Thiebaud is busy spending his nights hunting. They plot his kills on a map, until they realize they're all clustered around transportation arteries—not because that's where they congregate, but that's usually where Thiebaud is when he notices someone in orgiastic schadenfreude.

Chloe volunteers to serve as another stalking horse. She dolls down as a "Goth" getting just a little too old to still be playing with stage blood and ankhs—lets herself get picked up by a rail-thin purple-Mohawked freak. His apartment is filled with death-metal posters and Vulture statuary. She fakes orgasm a couple of times before she starts to lose patience and becomes a little insistent in her queries about, "y'know, the *real* occult stuff." His response is to smile mysteriously, get out a scarf, and start talking about breath control and asphyxiation near orgasm.

She gives up. Sticks two fingers in her mouth, and whistles. Sturgeon comes in and beats the freak senseless while everyone else searches the apartment. Nothing of interest, apart from a box of toes in the freezer Thiebaud says belong to Tenderloin prostitutes that have gone missing. Washington takes charge of them, promising to reunite them with the corpses so their ghosts no longer have to limp. After half an hour of listening to the freak gibber and bite the insides of his own cheeks to spit blood at them, they give up as well—shoot him, and have Washington interrogate his ghost. It spits ectoplasm at them.

■　　■　　■

They've counterfeited currency, taken residence in a cheap Belmont motel. Chloe and Maggie-Sue have pretty much punted their jobs, and Sturgeon has Jedi Mind Tricked his commanding officer into believing the NSA has borrowed Sturgeon to check zoo penguins for electronic bugs. Everybody else is their own boss. The enforced intimacy is beginning to grate—it's been months since any of them have slept in a room by themselves. The waiting is driving them crazy, too, and you can only sharpen your knives so many times. Although Chloe and Sturgeon are pretty happy.

The eight of them are eating lunch at a Denny's franchise. They are surrounded by families on pilgrimage to San Simeon, Telegraph Avenue, Yosemite. Washington is reading a Phoenix newspaper's coverage of the City, just for variety. "Anything interesting, Joe?" says Whitlomb.

"Spate of lye-throwing. Eye-gouging in barroom brawls."

"Boy," says Chloe, "I sure hope things quiet down quick after we take these bastards out."

Washington laughs.

"What's funny?"

"Vulture cult accelerates death and decay. Doesn't cause it. All they've done is moved twenty-first-century headlines back a bit. Won't change back when they're gone."

"You are one cheerful guy, Joe," says Arbeiter.

"Wait a minute. If all these things are going to happen anyway—"

"Looking for an out, Chloe?" says Rider, quietly.

"Cease. Desist," says Whitlomb.

"Well, maybe I am," she flashes. "Are we actually going to prevent anything, or just put it off?"

"If the answer is, no, we're not going to keep anybody from their fate, what would you suggest we do, Chloe?" says Rider.

"Well, get out and wait for it to burn itself out, of course! There's no point in getting ourselves killed for nothing!"

Rider says, "Joe? Maggie-Sue? Kris? Creedon? Same question."

"Alexander Crowley Rider, I tell you now. Do not do this," says Whitlomb, fingers clenched in a peculiar pattern.

Rider shakes his head, cuffs his temple. "Same question, you four."

"Take 'em down," says Washington.

"Fuck them," says Maggie-Sue.

"Bastards are too evil to live," says Arbeiter.

Thiebaud unscrews a jar of mustard and looks within.

"Are we making ourselves clear, you two?" snaps Rider. "We're going to lose someday. We've gone through this a hundred, a thousand times. We're not doing this because it makes sense. We're doing it because we can't live with the idea of not doing it. If you can turn your back and walk away, and meet your own eyes in the mirror afterward, then go. Now."

Chloe and Sturgeon look at each other. Sturgeon stands and holds out his hand. Chloe takes it. They leave.

■   ■   ■

"Terrific fucking stunt, Rider," says Arbeiter.

Maggie-Sue whispers, "No earth, now. Just fire and water and air. We have no base."

Whitlomb grabs Rider's arm. "You fool! You childish, black-and-white idealistic fool! You provoked them, and don't tell me you thought otherwise! Do you know, do you have any idea what you have done?!"

A beat.

"You did not err, Mr. Rider."

They turn to Thiebaud. He arranges five keys into a pentagon. A tear slips from his left eye and trickles down his chin.

"Er . . . Creedon . . ." starts Rider.

"I foresaw her with a dart in her eye. I saw him leave the helm to go to her. Saw the sailboat dashed on a stone, the mortar silenced. Had you not done as you did, Mr. Rider, I would have been forced to employ regrettable steps to motivate Mr. Sturgeon."

"You mean you would have killed one of your own!" gasps Rider. "Why, you son of a bitch! You raving madma—" Suddenly, Rider is looking down the barrels of two Glock 17s. He holds very still.

"Creedon," says Whitlomb. "Put away the guns. The waitress approaches." The guns go away.

The waitress says, "Y'all want some mo—"

"NO!" bellows Washington. She skedaddles.

"Okay," says Arbeiter. "Our plans for the raid are shot—we can't very well kill them and steal the Formosa for fire support. We'll have to think of something else."

"Like what?" barks Maggie-Sue. "No earth. No base."

"Well, why don't you try thinking about the problem, instead of sitting there and hissing at us?" insinuates Arbeiter.

"Leave her alone," rasps Washington.

"Wait, everybody, wait, I beg of you," says Whitlomb. "Let's wait until we're alone before we knife each other, hmn? It will be easier on the survivors. Agreed? Agreed? Yes. Oh, waitress? Check, please."

"I don't like they way you yelled at me," grouses the waitress.

"Here," replies Whitlomb. "A crisp new hundred-dollar bill. I advise you to spend it posthaste, indulging in whatever pleasures you hold dearest, before somebody nails a loop of your intestines to a tree and chases you in an ever-diminishing circle."

"Don't you threaten me!" she screeches.

"A threat! What I wouldn't give for that to have been a threat! No, you eyeless fool, it is a prediction. And by all the saints in heaven, I wish it were the mere ravings of a senile madman."

part four

Max and Chloe go, instinctively, to the Formosa 51. There are still plenty of provisions aboard; and they can fish, and catch freshwater rain with tarps. As they leave the marina, Sturgeon goes below and begins dismounting all the communications gear. They sail into a darkening autumn sky.

. . .

The six of them congregate in Rider and Whitlomb's room. They are heartily sick of the ten-dollar acrylic seascapes hanging over the beds. "The panel truck is still ours," says Whitlomb. "We can coordinate, after a fashion."

"Who?" says Washington. "Can't spare your gun. Other choices are even worse."

Whitlomb shrugs. "I am the least occult. We don't have time to recruit the usual unenlightened idealist. I will don the bullseye."

"Whoa," says Rider. "Guys? They're the *leaders*. They just *left*. They don't think there's any point to this. Doesn't that mean anything to anybody? It's their damn *job* to know when it's time to cut our losses and keep our heads down. Chloe's from Seattle, remember? *Headquarters*, inasmuch as we have one at all?"

Deep, dark silence.

"Bitch," says Maggie-Sue.

"Never thought I'd agree with her on anything," says Washington. "Made mistakes before, though."

"Enough," says Rider. "We've been putting her down since the day we laid eyes on her, and I've been the worst."

Gloom.

Whitlomb says, "This shouldn't be an insurmountable obstacle. I mean, we've lost a driver and our usual leader, but we can work around it."

"Destroy the head and the body will die," says Washington.

Whitlomb shakes his head. "Your negative attitude isn't helping any, Joe."

"Like you said before. It's hopeless. Always has been. All we can count on is to die fighting."

"I was speaking rhetorically."

"No you weren't. I say we plan a kamikaze."

"Yes," hisses Maggie-Sue. "All die. All balance. Only way."

"They've got a point," says Arbeiter.

Rider says, "Hold on—"

"No," says Arbeiter. "Let's be realistic. Now, the raid we planned was marginal at best; the six of us counted on the two of them to shell the island in the Farralons and coordinate us long enough to break in and kill everybody, right? Now, we're under strength, and there's no way we can bring in third-eye-open grunt troops. None of us has the knack. There's no point in running; they'll follow. All we can do is take as many of them with us as possible. Whitlomb offered to lead the cell, but his expendability is irrelevant; because we're not coming back."

Thiebaud is underlining passages in the Gideon Bible. It's heavy going; his tears blur the ballpoint's ink.

Arbeiter says, "For the raid itself, we make Joe coordinate; we can get by without a hand-to-hand man."

Washington grunts, "He's half right. Ignore Maggie-Sue; blanc tart's been trying to commit suicide since she was ten. We'll take a casualty or two if Whitlomb's in the fight instead of me, but this isn't kamikaze time."

"The casualty's probably going to be *you* if we do that, Joe," says Arbeiter.

"I've been dead before; I know the way back."

"That's not going to help if you don't have a body to come back to."
Washington shrugs.

"Just making sure you know what you're getting into."

Rider looks pleadingly at Whitlomb. Doesn't like what he sees.

.   ▪   ▪

Well, they don't have a mortar and they don't have a voice in their ears to tell
them where to go. Still, they have a song in their hearts. Sadly, it's Chopin's
funeral march.

Nobody knows much about demolition, let alone underwater demolition,
but they can mix ANFO and improvise a detonator, Jedi Mind Trick themselves a boat. They position themselves along the line between Yerba Buena
and the Farralons. Maggie-Sue takes off her clothes and jumps overboard.
They roll a fifty-five-gallon drum after her.

"I do wish we could send somebody with her," mutters Whitlomb. "If
she's assaulted by a teratomorph down there, we'll never know."

Nothing attacks her. Thirty minutes later, she bursts from the water, takes
a deep breath. Swims to the boat, boards. Water streams off her skin and out
of her hair in a matter of seconds.

"Neat trick, Maggie-Sue," says Rider. "Must save you time in the morning."

▪   ▪   ▪

Night. Whitlomb is an old man, doesn't need much sleep; so it doesn't bother
him to sit up with Rider as they flesh out the last of their plans.

Not that there's much to plan. Penetrate the bunker, split up, blast everything in sight, rely on radio contact with Washington to make sure everything important gets taken out despite people getting killed or incapacitated.
Washington will just have to take his chances with anyone coming after him
personally.

It is late. October storm; misting rain. The windows are steamed. An occasional roll of distant thunder.

"Al," says Whitlomb.

"What?"

Whitlomb kills his shot of Wild Turkey. Refills. "Al, I never expected it would end like this."

"Like what?"

"Like . . . this. Heh. If I had known last February was the last birthday I'd see . . ."

Rider nods. "Makes sense. Plague, right? Antibodies don't come home either."

"Al, don't play dumb on me. Not now, not tonight." Whitlomb puffs his cheeks. "When I came in . . . it was all a game. Just Erik and me against the Utter Night, eh? Next thing I know I'm Janus, saying one thing to Max and Chloe and another to you . . ."

"You're doing what you have to do, Perry."

Pause. More distant thunder before Rider continues.

"But keeping those two was tantamount to murdering them; they can't handle themselves in a full-blown raid. We're no assault team."

"I never claimed there would be no casualties, and I knew they would probably be it. But that was a quarter of our force, and we count on synergy for effect; now the six of us may well become five or fewer. You must have known that when you drove them off."

"We're not raiders! Not even with all eight of us working together! We're an *underground resistance*. We should be caching supplies and organizing other cells, reveal our presence to the Lizard totemists and warn them what's about to happen. But I seem to be in a minority of one."

"Semantics," says Whitlomb, waving his hand. "The difference between an underground resistance and raiders is just a question of whether or not we come out of the shadows every now and then."

"Opposition types who come out *die,* Perry. Maybe not the first time, or even the third, but it happens. We're here to take targets of opportunity and feed intelligence back to Seattle, remember? Even at that level of involvement, we don't last long—and we're hard to replace."

"You want out, Al?"

"Are you five going in anyway?"

"Yes. Based on Max and Chloe's counts of helicopters and boats, this is still doable."

"If they're relying on technology instead of magic, maybe . . . But it doesn't matter; if you're going in, then I'm going, too. But don't think I haven't considered it. I could make it if I went, go back to the desert. But getting out . . . Max said no when I asked the first time, yes the second. How am I supposed to answer? I knew this would be how I died. I just didn't think it might be over something this pointless."

"Saving San Francisco is hardly pointless. If the Incumbents ever drop a hydrogen bomb on Seattle, we're the backup capital."

"If they drop one, they'll drop two—or ten."

They sit for a while.

Rider sighs. "I don't think either of us are going to make Nirvana this time 'round. So we'll have to wait for the Judge of the Dead to tell us whether it was a crime on my part to try to spare them, or a crime on your part to try to keep them."

Whitlomb mulls this over.

"Besides, it's *still* a game; it's all maya anyway, right? We blow it, the Judge breaks our skulls and scarfs our brains for all the evil we've done, and then gives us quarters for another go." Rider smiles. "I just hope—"

Banging on the wall. "Everybody! Come quickly!" calls Arbeiter.

．　．　．

Whitlomb springs to his feet, pounds on the left wall to bring Maggie-Sue and Washington; Rider runs out and to the next door right, throws it open.

Arbeiter and Thiebaud are statues. Six strangers in black Gothic clothing stand in the middle of the room, grinning to show elongated canines. Their skins are deathly pale. The tallest, a man clad entirely in leather, fixes sparking eyes on Rider. Rider blinks furiously. Looks at Arbeiter and Thiebaud.

Arbeiter looks back as best he can. "The black hand on my heart . . . they made me call you . . ."

"Black hand? What . . .?" But then Rider's gaze drifts back to the man in leather, and loses its focus. He shuffles to stand beside Arbeiter.

Washington rolls out of a somersault into a combat crouch before he notices his three comrades. Arbeiter is saying "Black hand . . . black hand . . ." over and over again, in a voice like a dying whisper. All too soon, Washington stands beside them. When Maggie-Sue enters she doesn't last two seconds.

Whitlomb is the last into the room. He gapes and raises the shotgun to his shoulder. "Vampires," he grates. His finger is curling on the trigger . . . but then he slowly lowers his weapon.

"Ah, my fine cattle," breathes the tall one. "So good of you to flock together into a single herd." He snaps his fingers. "You have my permission to low your distress." Laughter, like the slap of dry leaves on a coffin.

"I should have known," gasps Whitlomb. "Who but vampires would be mad enough to succor the Vulture cult? Are you aware that after they're done here, there won't be enough living blood in this city to fill a thimble?"

"Foolish mortals. Kneel when you address your lords!" Whitlomb falls to his knees.

Rider says, "Look, my doctorate is in quantitative theological epidemiology. I can show you the math. By the time the Vulture cult has killed enough people to satisfy their god, you lot are going to be the top bats in an empty belfry. It's time to reconsider whose side you're on."

"Oh, a clever steer, this one. Placing his trust in crabbed airy theorems. Will you brandish a rubber bible? Smite me with a slide rule?" He strides to Maggie-Sue and runs a finger along her jaw. Her muscles work. A leather-clad woman oozes to Arbeiter and makes bedroom eyes. Her lips are bereft of cosmetics; they are an obscene shade of purplish red.

Washington says, "Kill us if you must. But we will not drink your blood and have your curse in us."

The tall one yawns, upper and lower fangs flashing like a baboon's. "The thought never crossed my mind. For it is not a curse, but the greatest blessing. One we do not bestow lightly."

Whitlomb says, "I imagine you've quite a Utopia planned."

"But of course. Would you like to hear what will become of the world after you depart?"

"Go for it," says Arbeiter, trying to jerk away and thus ease the pinpricks of pain in his neck. "Is it all right if we scoff?"

Lazy smile. "If you find anything to scoff at, please do." He licks his teeth. "The poor deluded mortals who place their faith in their great bird will soon have served their purpose. They know certain rituals that will allow us to drink the blood of the totems themselves. Ah, I see you flinch, my little bruised apple. Yes. We will drink their blood and then the six of us will control cities, nations."

"You'll never get away with it," spits Maggie-Sue, trying to pull away from his hand.

"Ah, but we shall. As you have no doubt guessed, it will be All Hallow E'en when the cult will strike, the night the border between the worlds weakens. They will infiltrate the city with the walking dead; who will notice a few more impeccably costumed zombies? They will whirl through the city, drinking the power of the sweet deaths. We will Ascend and take the power of the animal spirits. And then we will build an empire of the undead."

"No, no, I can't believe it. How did you find us?" chokes Rider. His hand flops on the hilt of a knife but his fingers do not curl.

"Our aerial associates. As you know, the rise of the six of us entails the rise of the six of you. It is the law of karma. A simple procedure with the blood of the six of us, and your pathetic attempt at hiding was revealed."

"But the cult! How did you find the Vulture cult in the first place?" asks Rider.

"A thousand questions. Are you so eager to know the nature of your Nemesis? I assure you, soon you will know us far more intimately than you can imagine."

"I'd like to know who to curse when I reach Hell. If you don't mind?"

"Not at all. It will be sweet to know that your thoughts linger on us." He curls a lock of Maggie-Sue's hair around a finger. Tears start trickling down her cheeks. "Do you recall an author named Edmund Neuman?"

"Nineteen-thirties German author? Wrote rather paranoiac supernatural black humor?" asks Arbeiter.

"Indeed. He has served his god a long, long time. He came to San Francisco in 1990 and his tiny group of followers languished in obscurity for years. But while praying to his bald deity he was granted a vision of my estimable self. He came to me and begged a boon. We have been steering observers away from his activities since."

"Observers? What observers?" says Arbeiter.

"All who would interfere. The Lizard totemists were the most difficult, but my lovely girls soon captured their attentions."

"Remarkable. Who spawned you?" asks Washington.

The tall one smirks. "A foolish old man. In his foul office he revealed himself to me, prattled of some great evil conspiracy. I drove the stake through his heart myself before setting forth to find others equally deserving of the future I will bring."

" 'Foolish old man'?" says Whitlomb from his knees, looking up at the lovely cruel face. "What 'foolish old man'?"

"How many do you know?"

"Indulge me."

"You are not in a position to demand indulgence!"

Whitlomb shudders from stem to stern. "It was Erik Johanson, wasn't it? From the Miskatonic classical archaeology department?"

The vampire smiles. "A friend, I see. Well. Were it *not* the case, I would not say it was—I have no need of lies to hurt you. But as it happens—you may be assured it was."

Whitlomb sobs, "You bastard. You bastard!"

The vampire smiles.

"You are not his spawn! Erik was found with a silver knife wound in his back. You *stole* his blood!"

"He denied it to me! I deserved it!"

"I knew you looked familiar. You're Elwin Tinridge. You're the cretin who tried to excavate an ancient Mycenaean village with a bulldozer, destroyed twenty years of work in an instant."

The vampire grins. "A slight miscalculation on my part—in my *previous* life. I am particularly glad to see you, Professor Whitlomb, colonel of the Van Helsing Society. You have dealt with my kind before. Perhaps, then, this is not the first time you have trembled before one to whom you are worthy only to be a toy." Tinridge holds out his hand and slowly curls it into a fist. Whitlomb coughs, gargles, claws at his chest.

"Stop it! You're hurting him!" wails Maggie-Sue.

The expression on Tinridge's face would have Jack the Ripper applauding. She drops her eyes. "Please. I'll—I'll do anything you want. Anything at all.

Take me, use me, hurt me as much as you want. Only please, please spare my poor father."

"Ah. Filial love. I do understand. Family is important to our kind as well." He opens his fist. Whitlomb collapses to the floor.

More tooth-licking; Tinridge shifts gears. "It is exquisite, isn't it, your helplessness? Soon will come the final submission. Simple rape is so common and over so soon, don't you think? One must resort to odder and odder variations with whatever objects are close at hand; wooden spoons, electric knives, table legs wrapped in live wires. But the healing power of our undead blood lets us take as long as we like; forever, if we so desire. And we do desire so very much. It is all I can do to restrain myself from working our love on this pretty little girl posthaste. Ah, how your faces will twist and shiver when you hear her cries."

Arbeiter looks at Whitlomb. "Enough," he says. "I've been here before; I've done this. This farce has gone on long enough."

"I agree," says Rider, hastily. "One last question, Tinridge, and then we'll let you get on with it. If I may?"

Languorous wave of a long-nailed hand.

"How will you divide up the world? Vampires are notorious for internecine conflicts. One for each continent and two for Asia? Or do you have a horde of lieutenants who'll need fiefdoms of their own?"

"My five friends are my get. We will rule with a single iron fist."

"Okay. Perry, would you care to do the honors?"

Whitlomb gets up, his face twisted into rage. "You son of a bitch. Do you know that you *staked* the man who translated *Gravity's Rainbow* into Latin—on a *bet?*" And slams the butt of his shotgun into Tinridge's jaw.

·   ·   ·

Tinridge sprawls, but rises quickly, hissing. Spreads his arms and grabs Whitlomb by the shoulders. Heaves. Whitlomb doesn't go anywhere.

"Warning shot," says Whitlomb, and blasts Tinridge's right foot into paté.

The other five vampires' mouths drop open. They try staring at the six mortals in the room, but said mortals fail to fall to their knees, run screaming, or commit suicide. Panic begins to appear on pale features. Whitlomb hauls Tinridge to his foot. Throws him into a chair.

"Damn it, Perry," says Arbeiter, tilting his head to pour in eardrops, "are you trying to deafen us?" He hands the bottle around.

"WHAT?" says Whitlomb.

"Hold up," says Rider. "I have to put a Giger print on the door and get some soundproofing up, or else every cop in Belmont is going to be pounding on the door."

"But . . . but . . ." babbles one of the females.

Rider comes back, lights a cigarette. "Nicely done, everybody."

"It was a close thing," says Whitlomb. "I nearly pulled the trigger when first I came in."

"Old habits die hard, Perry. I know how you feel about these leeches."

Whitlomb nails Tinridge's face with a glob of spit. "These hardly count."

"Thank God for the old Black Hand O' Doom convention. Who came up with that, anyway?"

"Max, wasn't it? After he took that counterespionage course way back when. I'm just glad we all remembered it."

Rider puffs. "But I have to ask. Maggie-Sue, where did you get that dialogue?"

"The monkey's filthy movies," she says.

Washington draws himself stiffly erect. "Lies."

"Relax, Joe," says Rider. "I think that was a joke."

A male cries, "But we're superior to you. We're *undead!*"

Arbeiter shakes his head. "You noodleheads, you're not occult *or* undead. You've got chronic viral haemophagimanic pseudoporphyria. One round of Pasteur treatment and you'll be right as rain."

"Not that you'll ever see rain again," giggles Whitlomb, unloading lead buckshot shells from his shotgun.

Rider's eyes slide over. "Easy, Perry. This is no time for hysteria. . . ."

One of the males bolts. Granite walls appear over the doors and windows.

"But I don't understand," mewls a female. "We are too undead. We're supernatural predators of the night. Ellie said so."

"Supernatural? SUPERNATURAL? You want to see SUPERNATURAL?" Washington's grin, although lacking in the canine department, is a horrible thing to behold. "Do you want to know what SUPERNATURAL is? Do you WANT to SEE what it is to be UNDEAD? Well, HAVE A LOOK!" Washington rips his chest open, exposing his pulseless heart. He holds the pose for five seconds; then tears his heart from his body, thrusts it into the faces of the vampires. Two of them faint.

Thiebaud lays a hand on Washington's arm. "I believe that demonstration will suffice, Mr. Washington. We have already gloated more than is advisable."

Washington nods, puts his heart back into his chest. One of the females primly gasps, "Well, it's nice to see that *one* of you has some decency and mercy in him."

"Stop it," says Whitlomb, refilling his shotgun with deer slugs, "stop it, you're killing me! Hee hee! 'Mercy'! Creedon Thiebaud, the Weeping Ghost, 'merciful!' Oh, my poor heart! Pull the other one, it's got bells on!"

He pumps the action, click clack.

Tinridge splutters, "What game is this? What's going on? I have the strength of ten men; how could I fail to pulp you?"

"Maybe you'll find out in your next life," chuckles Whitlomb, and fires a silver deer slug into Tinridge's heart. In the enclosed room the sound is loud enough to slap your clothes against your body; you hear the thunder with your lungs. The other vampires scream.

"But this isn't fair," yelps one of the males. "You're going to gun us down without a word! We answered your questions; please, won't you at least tell us who you are?"

Rider says, "Nope. Sorry. Explaining things to prisoners is against Opposition policy. See you in Hell." And Whitlomb loads another round into the magazine and pumps the action and the room rapidly becomes an abattoir.

■　■　■

Whitlomb lowers the shotgun and fumbles to a chair. Arbeiter rushes to him, takes his pulse, pushes a nitroglycerine tablet under his tongue.

Maggie-Sue flares light from her fingertip, makes sure the fallen's eyes are fixed and dilated.

Rider has to speak up; everyone's ears are still ringing from the shotgun fire. "Perry, what was all that about Professor Johanson?"

Whitlomb shivers. "Erik wasn't well; he knew the end approached, wanted to bring me with him; and so, he requisitioned the live virus from the Twin Cities Center for Occult Disease Control . . . I wouldn't do it . . . he made me promise to keep quiet. . . . He said the wrong thing to the wrong person. . . . Damn him! He never slaked his thirst on anything more sentient than rabbits, as God is my witness!" He draws a shuddering breath.

"He was a friend? A vampire and a friend? I thought you hated vampires," says Maggie-Sue.

"I do; never doubt that! But VHP produces mundane unaging haemophagocity while stimulating mundane psionic activity; their third eyes are open but a slit, they drink blood, but they're not undead. The Incumbents call them pseudovampires and laugh their fool heads off at them; they don't even bother tracking their movements. It's pathetic, really; the poor clots stumbling around thinking they're privy to the dark secrets of eternity when they're nothing but sheep with sharpened hooves. . . ." Whitlomb hunches over. "Erik was younger then than I am now. . . ."

Rider squeezes his hand.

.   .   .

Arbeiter draws a scalpel and cuts the vampires apart, taking bits from them. The smell of blood and dung is thick until Maggie-Sue waves it away. Finally, she says, "Lizards. Stupid bitches. Goth girls flash their tits at them and they grow mattresses on their backs."

"No joke," agrees Arbeiter. "What sort of lummox takes off their talismans? Even to make love? With idiocy like that it's a miracle San Francisco didn't fall a hundred years ago." He begins collecting blood from the motionless hearts.

"We're even dumber," says Washington. "We overestimated their smarts. We get out of this, we make contact and *tattoo* the talismans on them, just like ours, no matter what they say."

"Those sadists were perfect for the Vulture cult," says Rider, chain-lighting another cigarette. "Mundane, so we couldn't smell them; powerful at night, when the Vulture cult is at its weakest."

"And dumb as mud," adds Arbeiter, crushing vertebrae with a nutcracker. "Can you believe the lines they swallowed? I thought my cheeks would rip, it was so hard to keep from smiling. 'Ascension' and 'drinking the blood of the totems'! The six of us rising to oppose them because of the laws of karma!"

"I am to blame," says Whitlomb. "I noted the anemia taking place under my very nose. Half the UC Berkeley band is bled half dry. It did not occur to me to look for mundane vampires as well as occult."

"That is not the case, Mr. Whitlomb. The fault is entirely mine," says Thiebaud. "It is my role to observe our area of responsibility and detect the signs of mundane psionic activity. My lack of attentiveness and—periodic indisposition—has endangered all of us. I must beg your forgiveness."

Whitlomb waves a hand. "Your power and ability is such that we have forgotten the possibility of error on your part. There is no blame to be laid."

Whitlomb shakes off Rider and Maggie-Sue, stands, grins like Baalzebul. "I wonder if Tinridge's diction was as strained before the change?" He bugs his eyes and does a stiff-legged Boris Karloff imitation. " 'Foolish mortals!' Ha! Ha! Ha!"

Maggie-Sue takes hold of him; pulls him down, wraps her arms around him, holds him still.

Time passes.

.   .   .

Rider coughs and says, "Creedon, they *were* telling the truth as they knew it, right?" Thiebaud is assembling a jigsaw puzzle. "Right."

"Who is Neuman?" asks Maggie-Sue.

"Well, now, that's the funny thing," says Arbeiter, dicing ovaries. "According to Rider's thesis—by the way, you might consider reading a few *real* scientific papers; you use ten words when you only need three—Neuman was a Nazi. He was the Incumbent's man on the spot to make sure the Brown Shirts really were wiped out. I'll bet you five liters of wombat snot that he stole every sacred artifact he could, fled Germany after the war, and went on a megalomaniacal kick as soon as he found the right pawns to back him."

Rider nods. "No bet. San Francisco is a good choice; not so full of Opposition that he'd be spotted right off, but not under Incumbent control either. I have old photographs, so we'll all be able to recognize him. How're you doing there, Kris?"

"Almost ready. We drink this stuff, we'll know every last person they ever witched—and we'll inherit their control, for a few weeks. It's great! How come we don't cultivate these dunderheads ourselves?"

Rider starts. "Kris, the moral considerations alone are stag—"

"Oh, I'm just grumbling. Grab a syringe and suck out their vitreous bodies for me, will you?"

Rider would turn green if he wasn't already. "Never mind. I'll get it," says Washington.

"Why did they come?" says Maggie-Sue.

"Well, presumably to suck our—" says Rider.

Whitlomb looks up from Maggie-Sue's embrace. "Wait," he says. She releases him, slowly, as he uncoils and thinks for a moment.

Whitlomb nods. "Maggie-Sue's right. The Vulture cult must know by now that six pseudovampires would be so much Cheez Whiz to us. On top of that, we'll soon have the ability to influence every last soul they once controlled. Yet the Vulture cult delivered them right into our hands. Why send six Achilles' Heels to us?"

"Hrm. Active counterintelligence, maybe? I'm willing to bet that when Joe talks to them, they'll say the Vulture cult has the whole damn city under its sway already."

"Very risky."

"Maybe it was supposed to be more of a fight. I don't think they know how tough we are—the only real toe-to-toe we've had with them, Creedon and I were in Oakland, and Maggie-Sue stayed topside."

"But Creedon's been hunting them. And they attacked your house."

"So what? *Nobody* ever sees Creedon coming, or sees where he goes. And Chloe was there when they attacked, and we *know* they know about her and Max."

"There is another possibility," says Thiebaud. "Recall that I have spent a fair amount of time in their company at the ends of their lives."

"Yes?" says Rider.

"It is my considered opinion that as a class, members of the Vulture cult are prone to utter stupidity. There is a distinct possibility that they have practically no idea what they're doing."

They mull this until Washington says, "Time to find out what they think they know. Are you done with them, Arbeiter?"

"Ja."

Washington nods. "Then they are mine." He borrows an autopsy knife from Arbeiter, detaches Tinridge's head—there is surprisingly little blood, since it all drained out the tunnel smashed through his chest—and sets it on the table.

"Elwin Tinridge," says Washington.

The head's eyelids flutter over the ghastly voids of the bleeding sockets. The lips work.

"I have questions for you, Tinridge."

Those of the assembled who can read lips detect the phrase "Please . . . let me go . . ."

"You desired to enter the realm beyond breath. You have succeeded. But you do not have the kingship you thought you deserved; you are lower than the very worm who will eat your flesh."

The mouth forms "No . . ."

"I will now convince you."

Washington does something with blood, gravedirt, and a bit of wax. The mouth gapes—

And remains open in a scream all the more horrible for its very silence.

"Al told you he'd see you in Hell," whispers Whitlomb.

. . .

"Stupid buggers got around," murmurs Rider.

The South Asian and the Pole blink. "What?"

"Just talking to myself. We've been tracking down people the vampire bit for two days now. Sure, people in this city drop their shorts the way most people drop their hats, but still . . ."

The two of them blush.

"Never mind. I'll contact you later with your orders. And stop rubbing your necks, or else you'll scar."

"Hardly seems fair that the cure leaves a wound when the bite doesn't."

"That's what you get for going home with Goth chicks you should have known were *way* out of your league. Have you picked aliases yet?"

The South Asian says, "I'm Shogun."

The Pole says, "And I'm Son of Heaven."

Rider rolls his eyes. "Fine. Fine. This elderly gentleman, here, will take you to the panel truck and start explaining the equipment to you. Keep Wild Turkey on you at all times—bottles you've checked out to make sure they're all right, if it has a fungal aftertaste it's been ruined by the bad guys—but don't get drunk enough to interfere with your driving or shooting. We should have a comm specialist lined up for you, but learn the gear anyway."

"Right," says Shogun. "We don't have much; us, four bruisers, a few other friends, but we'll help any way we can. You sure our musician friend really did . . . ah . . ."

"Yes," says Thiebaud, tears running down his cheeks.

■　　■　　■

Weeks wind forward. Every now and then they try to hail Chloe and Max. There's never an answer, although the radio does squawk on the seabed and certain rockfish do sense a change in the local magnetic field.

■　　■　　■

Dawn, October 29th. Whitlomb fields calls, fits them into the master plan as best he can. Step one, blow the tunnel between Yerba Buena and the Farralons—which should force the Vulture cult to start running around like headless chickens. Step two, find everything acting like acephalous fowl and stomp them until they stop moving. Step three, raid the bunker. He's got observers all over the Bay Area, and has scattered members of the cell around with various units.

The six severed heads provided floor plans and an estimate of the forces arrayed against them, but they're assuming the Vulture cult sent the vampires to them with as many misapprehensions in their minds as they could inculcate. If the Vulture cult *is* as strong as the heads claim, they are walking into a slaughter. They worry about this. But they're going ahead with the raid—for lack of better ideas.

Three o'clock. Last-minute preparations. Positions are taken. They pick call signs: A3 for Rider, A4 for Whitlomb, B1 for Washington, B2 for Maggie-Sue, B3 for Arbeiter, B4 for Thiebaud. Out at Three C, Son of Heaven checks the engine one last time. Fires it up. In the back, "Ng," the daughter of two old Viet Cong, begins the check-in. Little more than a teenager—but that's how old her parents were when *they* went to war. Everybody responds except the dance troupe, because the choreographer is receiving a blow job. Ejaculation concluded, the last unit comes online.

. ■ .

The sun descends, touches the fog bank as it rolls through the Golden Gate. Son of Heaven leans out the window, watching. As the last arc of daylight fades, he takes out his binoculars and watches the ruddy limb. "Coming, man . . . coming . . . say, ten seconds . . . wait . . . now. Go."

Ng gets on the horn. "Sunset complete. All units, go. Sunset complete. All units go. Confirm." She feels very military.

Confirmations come in.

. ■ .

Down at the bottom of the Bay, a dragon looks up from the sea lion it's chewing for a sunset snack. It stretches. Absently rubs its slightly malformed left front toe—the result of Rider's having sneezed at an inopportune time while carving its egg. Digs a skull from between its teeth and starts circling toward the surface.

. ■ .

The drum majorette pokes her baton into the sky. Whistles for attention. Four precise shrills—the drum section starts. She lets it cycle through three and a half distinct march cadences, gets ready; kicks up her heels as she struts in place. And as the first beat of the second repetition of the first cadence sounds, two hundred left feet hit the pavement. The UC Berkeley Band, foggy about their presence and mission but following an outré compulsion, parades up the Yerba Buena road.

Under the waters of the Bay, there is a mighty flash. Water pours into a tunnel and emergency doors begin grinding shut to the wail of sirens.

Throughout the Bay Area, people with bandaged necks watch. They hold the handsets of pay phones, or finger their cellulars as they wait for occult outbreaks. Forty miles south of San Francisco, a woman at the Mountain View CalTrain station gapes as a midnight black train howls by, going a hundred miles an hour if it's doing five. Phones it in, gibbering about skulls and not-quite corpses hanging from barbed wire before she is overwhelmed; staggers off in search of strong drink, her mind already clouding.

A lonely Farralon island lights up, searchlights probing the waves.

The San Francisco Night Jumpers, their jumpsuits covering their sore necks, watch the streetlights flickering on below as darkness claims the City. A few vaguely wonder why, exactly, they are carrying shotguns filled with rock salt and are planning to parachute into a city; as opposed to, say, a nice flat wheat field.

Big bang at the Richmond Chevron refinery. No real reason; just seemed that while they were planning all this, why not air a few old grudges, too?

■   ■   ■

"Correct," says Ng. "Fire hydrants spewing blood. Not doing anything else, just foaming blood into the streets. People are rushing home."

"Okay," says Washington. "Probably just a distraction."

"A3 here," says Rider. "Band is two blocks from Yerba Buena target. Bright lights ahead; the people in all the houses around us are closing their drapes. Occult's in the air and they're hiding."

Washington nods to himself, legs wrapped around Maggie-Sue's hips as wind thrashes around them. "Ng. Anything more on the train?"

"No. Wai—oh, God, CalTrain 71 is derailed at Hayward Park, completely off the tracks, there are bodies—"

"Take it easy, Ng. B2. Last train station, Fourth and Townsend." They go.

"A3 here. Taking some rifle fire from defenders on the wall, ten or twenty of them; the music from the band is shielding us for now. All conventionaAAA!"

"Ng to A3. You there? A3? A3?"

. . .

Rider is busy. A Circle of Wind and Fire demon has risen from the sewers. Beautiful, if your taste runs to caterwauling masses of burning lavender lungs. Rider's staff moves as if it has a mind of its own, which it does. The air reeks of napalm and halitosis. Whitlomb puts a silver bullet into the demon whenever he gets the chance. Slows it down a little. Rider is dancing around a Ferrari and it is pursuing.

The drum majorette blinks. Remembers the drill. Signals for the Cal fight song. One, two, three, four, and NOW. As the brass blares into the darkening sky and her Lycra cleaves close she goes into a baton routine that would bring tears to the eyes of the finest Texas bimbos.

A little sympathetic magic. Rider's wooden staff goes all silvery and it spins. Spins a whole lot. Rider is dragged along behind it, yawping in fear, as it whirls faster and faster, blurring into a solid disk, pressing the attack. Beats the demon back once, twice, a third time and the gyration surges, staff tips going supersonic with a sound like the Wheel of Kali. Windows shatter for blocks around. It strikes the demon and the unholy thing disintegrates into flaming purple collops of grue.

The defenders on the wall quail. Some throw down their weapons and run for the tunnel or the house. The rest redouble their fire without regard for their diminishing supplies of ammunition.

The fight song is done. She looks at the strange bald man with the staff. He is panting. She looks at the gate. A dark four-legged thing is running for her, unusually thin. She screams—

And another form rushes past her. Claws extend: and Whitlomb's jaguar "disembowels" the thin dog with two mighty sweeps of its rear paws. She shakes her head, tears her eyes from the blur of hide and feline teeth. Time to signal again. One, two, three, four . . .

If one were a Vulture cultist, shivering in the dark and out of bullets, perhaps the last thing one would want to hear at this juncture is the Cal band's arrangement of "Time Warp." Quite a tune. Go get your *Rocky Horror* soundtrack and put it on; try to imagine a marching band performing it with verve and panache, brass bells snapping back and forth.

For additional realism, have somebody dynamite your house, not neglecting worming thrills of light as thaumaturgy shreds what little cover is left. Throw in an archaeologist with a light machine gun braced along the hood of an Oldsmobile; season with a bald synesthetic mage shoving vulture feathers into a railway torch and thereby setting your clothes ablaze. Then try to find a way to retreat and fail to find one. You should probably skip the dénouement, though, unless you have a thing about having your neck wrung.

■　■　■

"A3 here. We're good. Yerba Buena is gone."

"Are you all right?" gasps Ng.

"Fine."

Washington says, "Get me the lizards."

Ng fiddles with equipment. "Lizards on channel seven."

"Lizard totem here," says a woman's voice.

"B1 here. Your location?"

"Marin, by the Well."

"Stand by. Son of Heaven, to Marin, pick up the lizards. Rendezvous with A team by the SF side of the Golden Gate. A team, all possible speed to Marin, wait with the lizards until Three C arrives. After consolidation, come to Fourth and Townsend. Night Jumpers, circle at one thousand feet over South San Francisco grid K12. Confirm."

Confirmations come in.

"Piedmont Dancers here. What do you want us to do?"

"Stand by," says Washington.

"A3 here. What about the band?"

"Any ideas?"

"Send 'em back to the bus. Maybe we'll need them later."

"Do it."

. . .

"You heard 'em, partner," says Shogun.

"I did," says Son of Heaven. "How the hell do we get to the freeway from here?"

"That way. First left."

They go. Radio chatter makes them nervous; calm voices reporting pavement cracking as electrical wires snake out and fry passersby, the Vulture cult killing as many as they can for the mana of their deaths—cars exploding, a nasty spate of 911 calls begging for help as pans turn savage, dump boiling water onto the bare feet of children. Great scalds and puffy blisters. The Son of Heaven takes a deep swig of bourbon and bashes a Yugo into a lamppost. "Oops," he says.

"Next time we do this, I drive."

"Shut up. I grew up driving in LA."

"Give me the booze."

. . .

Three C skids to a halt by the Whole Earth 'Lectronic Link. Many bulky forms pour from the shadows as Ng throws the back doors open. Huge, pale women in leather jackets and heavy boots converge on the panel truck. Some yank skinny, weedy men along; chrome choke collars tighten, feet flex in Birkenstocks. Crowd into the back; Ng barely has room to breathe. Doors slam; pounding on the forward panel indicates readiness to go. Son of Heaven puts the truck into gear, groaning under the weight of grim women and a whole lot of chain.

As the truck passes the midpoint of the Golden Gate Bridge, a rocket arches from the water and grazes the right rear corner of Three C. Son of Heaven punches the nitrous-oxide button, truck leaping forward, and the Shogun screams into his intercom. No casualties, except such minor bruises as one might expect from two dozen people flailing in surprise.

. . .

The panel truck whooshes by; the Olds peels out behind it, Rider at the wheel.

"A4 here," says Whitlomb. "B1, you want us in front of Three C or behind it?"

Washington considers. "B1 here. In front. Have the lizards open a back panel and stand ready with guns. Three C, up gain."

The Olds pulls in front of the truck as they surge for the city.

. . .

A graffiti artist, crossing the tracks at the Twenty-second Street CalTrain station—the penultimate stop on the line—has time to turn and register the presence of the black train before he is obliterated.

. . .

Washington and Maggie-Sue, at Fourth and Townsend, hear air brakes grab and bite, far away. "Three C, bring the Night Jumpers into a circle over Fourth and Townsend. A team?"

"Just off the bridge."

"Hurry." Turns to Maggie-Sue. "Air strike. Now." She runs and bounds into the night sky.

Well, the train gets mighty close—maybe a kilometer—before Maggie-Sue lands a blow on the engine. Washington curses and yells over the radio "Troop compartments! Not the locomotive!" as he scampers south. Long time running along silent halogen-lit heavy rail tracks, stumbling on heaps of gravel. Catches sight of the train—and it's not moving fast. In fact, a phalanx walks before it, automatic rifles ready.

"B1 here. Zombies with assault rifles coming off the black train—nearly a hundred."

"A4. What kind?"

"Necromantic, I think."

As they march forward a cheer of sorts comes from a few decaying throats:

Shift to the left! Shift to the right!
Push down, pop up, byte byte byte!
Shift to the left! Shift to the right!
Push down, pop up, byte byte byte!

You had a good home but you left!

    YOU'RE RIGHT!

Research was there when you left!

    YOU'RE RIGHT!

You had a degree

You beat G.R.E.,

But you wanted a life so you left!

    YOU'RE RIGHT!

Oh, one, two, three!

Oh, one, two, three!

You wanted a bitch from the left!

    YOU'RE RIGHT!

Yet women were there when you left!

    YOU'RE RIGHT!

In dormitories

You tried to spread knees

Of literate cunt you're bereft!

    YOU'RE RIGHT!

Oh, one, two, three!

Oh, one, two, three!

PROJECT LEADER'S TURNING BLUE, SOMEONE PEGGED HIS CPU!

OH, ONE, TWO, THREE!

OH, ONE, TWO, THREE!

SWINGING THROUGH THE B-TREES WITH MY DBX,

I'M A STUPID MOTHERFUCKER, I FORGOT TO TYPE IN HEX!

OH, ONE, TWO, THREE! OH, ONE, TWO, THREE!

Washington says, "Some of the fresher ones sound like they used to be programmers. . . ." He turns tail and runs back, radioing in, "Night Jumpers plane come in from north over Fourth and Townsend; Jumpers out and come south to the station!" In the night sky the plane does as it is told and the Night Jumpers queue up; jumpmaster yells "Go!" and they start leaping out, piloting their parasails, aiming for the deserted street just north of the train station.

Maggie-Sue's fireballs are raining down all around the train; the zombies return fire. Unfortunately, bullets move considerably faster than bolts of flame and her aerial position is entirely too obvious. Washington yells, "Maggie-Sue, cease fire and come south to the station!" She complies. "Jumpers, Maggie-Sue, take cover until all the Jumpers are down." Washington climbs atop a waiting train, flattens himself in the shadows.

"Jumper J9. APC at Third and Brannan, southeast-bound."

"B2, go take it out."

Maggie-Sue runs off, considering. Hides behind a trash can and waits. Lava Nova? Sheet Lightning? Aquae Mortis? The armored personnel carrier appears. She shrugs and unlimbers her LAW. Crude, but effective, No sense in wasting mana. Big noise. The APC isn't going anywhere. A rare smile quirks her lips. "Ugh," she mutters. "Cave woman learn new trick. Ugh. Ugh."

The zombies hear the explosion. Cut loose with a few bursts of automatic fire—what the hell, might as well kill something. Innocent bystanders die in droves. A testosterone-flushed Jumper, disdaining Washington's order to take cover, stands and cuts loose with his shotgun. Bad idea. He gets shredded and zombies run for cover; so much for an ambush. Washington swears—silently.

"Three C, status on the Jumpers."

"All on the ground but three. Want positions?"

"Don't second-guess. I want something, I'll ask." Wishes he wasn't in charge, wishes he wasn't working with raw troops. Better than a kamikaze run, though. "When they're all down, have them come forward to the station, stay under cover." The City is alive with sirens but none are coming this way; the police and fire departments are completely overwhelmed.

The train has stopped at the edge of the switching yard, about half a kilometer from the station proper. The zombies are coming forward by quarters; one group runs as the other three cover the advance. Repeat at leisure. They're getting awful close. "Three C. Your position?"

"Embarcadero and Bay."

"Three C to Third and Brannan and hold position. B2 and A team, wait for them, bring the lizards to the station." Yow, are those zombies close. "Jumpers. Close range, take cover, and open fire."

Figures in the shadows. Shotguns boom. Doesn't accomplish much; the true effective range of a shot shell is maybe twenty meters and the closest zombies are a hundred meters off. But suppressive fire is suppressive fire; it'll keep the zombies from closing until the lizards arrive. Maybe. With a lot of casualties among the Jumpers. But that is ever the fate of paratroops.

And so loads of Tibetan and Haitian salt rain down among the rotting shells; two or three take hits to the face and turn their M16s on their own skulls. The rest take cover and stop advancing. Unfortunately for the good guys, the lurching forms hold up their rifles and rock-'n'-roll; lead saturates the station. People die, screaming, bleeding from tiny holes fronting hideous damage. The stench of urine and feces fills the air, as well as darker odors from bullet eviscerations. A Jumper falls and a conductor snatches up his shotgun, screaming "You BASTARDS! Here's a little PERSONAL SERVICE from AMTRAK!" as he advances, firing wildly. Civilians pelt into the night, crying and bleeding. Washington cannot afford to close his eyes as he yells orders into the radio; he weeps from the top of a CalTrain passenger coach, yellow-sclera'd dwarf commanding others to commit suicide under a sullen dark-orange sky.

"Ng here. A team has the lizards. They're coming."

"Three C, A4, hold position, be ready to move out. A3, drop back to First and Brannan. B2, bring the lizards in. Piedmont Dancers, rendezvous with B3 and B4 by the San Francisco Marina."

A troop of zombies runs for the station, passing not five paces from Washington. They come within thirty meters of the Jumpers and many fall. Two come close enough to rage among parachuters, firing rifles at point-blank range; the rest fall to face shots and rip themselves to shreds. The two are enough; Jumpers cease fire despite Washington's imprecations and run to their comrades' aid. The rest of the charnel horde come forward. Washington is surrounded and he hopes against hope they don't see him.

Washington suppresses a desire to ask where the lizards are. If he reveals himself he's a hundred percent dead, again, and he has no desire to reassume that lifestyle.

The main force is close enough to begin mashing Jumpers, despite their armor and concealment. From the screaming Washington guesses, correctly, that what few Jumpers remain will turn and run. Which brings death that much faster. The command group closes on the concrete buildings of the train station—

—just about the time the lizards open fire. You'd be amazed at the size of the gun a two-hundred-pound woman can carry.

Were Washington fighting an ordinary foe, said foe would fall back and regroup. But this bunch is undead, and so they wade forward. Sure, a few lucky ones make it, bayonet through leather—strong women are down, faces impassive as they bleed to death. But all the others are ripped asunder by machine-gun fire. Washington can hear the locomotive backing away. Maybe six make it to safety aboard the boxcars decorated with the scream-ing remains of chip-room workers as the train churns south in full retreat.

Cheers are voiced.

■　■　■

Rider returns to Three C, waves his staff in his left hand and reaches down with his right to grab Washington by the shirt. "You sent me away from the fight!" he snarls.

"Of course. Knew if I didn't order you directly away you would have gone in and maybe gotten yourself killed. Need you for later."

Maggie-Sue grabs Rider by the belt and shoulder, throws him against the panel truck. Slaps his staff from his hands. "He's right," she hisses. "Get your staff and listen to orders."

Rider grouses.

Washington consults with the lizard commander. "Yes. Anybody who thinks they can come, into the truck."

"Fucking A," she growls.

Ng is staring at the commander.

"What?" she growls.

"How come you've got that fellow on a chain?" says Ng diffidently.

"*She's* on the end of *my* chain," grins the fellow. "Besides, I'm a man; she needs me for my . . . pockets. Spare magazines and tampons, you know."

"Dyke hag," says the commander contemptuously, looking at him.

"Dyke," says the fellow, leering at her.

"Dyke hag."

"Dyke."

"Dyke hag."

"Dyke."

"Forget I asked," says Ng.

Leaning out the window, the Son of Heaven says, "Welcome to San Francisco."

Whitlomb says, "Shogun, Son of Heaven, Ng, out of the truck. You three are the garrison for the City."

The Son of Heaven pales. "What? Just the three of us?"

"Welcome to San Francisco." He climbs into the driver's seat, and Rider gets in beside him.

■   ■   ■

The Farralons are buzzing like a hive of wasps doused with hot sauce. Speedboats circle; helicopters clatter and searchlights flash over anything that moves and a lot of things that don't. Sonar racks the water. Surely there is no way to approach the island.

Deep underground, there is a circle of priests.

"You said," cries an elder, "that without their leaders, they would quarrel amongst themselves and destroy each other. You said," he declaims, pointing at Violetefeld, "that if we gave them the vampires and their false estimates of strength, they would abandon the fight as lost. Well, they *didn't* quarrel, and they *didn't* abandon the fight!"

The others in the circle murmur.

"And now they fall on us! Our warriors have been utterly destroyed! We are mere moments from the final death ourselves! My brothers, there is only one penalty appropriate! I call for the seals to be taken from the bottle of eterna—"

"Enough," says Neuman.

The elder says, "But he has—"

"Enough," says Neuman. "No man here is at fault. There is no blame to be laid."

"But my lo—"

"Enough," says Neuman. "Form the circle; and include Violetefeld; that which we dreaded has come to pass."

"My—"

"Enough," says Neuman.

Violetefeld runs from the place in the circle he held, abandoning the dignity he maintained even under the accusatory finger of the elder. "My lord! I understand what you say, but I cannot flee while you remain! Take what you need of me!"

"I cannot," says Neuman. "What I need has already been lost, long ago. Take your place, Violetefeld. We have failed; let others take this cross from me."

Violetefeld crawls on his hands and knees between two others before he dares stand, looking away from Neuman before allowing himself to weep.

The moment elongates. The elder says, "My lord, hurry now; I beg of you, take your place, that we may proceed."

Neuman says, "I will not join you."

They are staring at him in horror; all except Violetefeld, who cannot lift his head for the tears.

"I'm sorry," says Neuman. "I can't join your circle. Won't do me any good." He smiles. "In a sense, I don't have what it takes."

A cold instant.

"Then flee, lord," implores the elder. "We will cover your retreat. They cannot strike us down once we have joined in the circle. If you will not join us then this place is not safe for you!"

Neuman shakes his head. "No. If needs must, I will cover your retreat. I have nothing to fear from them."

Violetefeld lifts his head. "Let us do as our lord desires."

Neuman stands aside.

The priests link hands—talons?—in a great circle, and chant a spell that was already ancient when Atlantis was three men, a grandmother, and a flock of nervous goats.

Neuman strolls out. Once in the corridor, he begins whistling a cheerful bit of Wagner, and unlocks a small door. "Nope, don't have what it takes, all right," he mutters. "I couldn't *be* that dumb, not if I had another millennium to practice it." He steps through.

. . .

The Marina. The Piedmont Dancers, themselves resplendent in outfits made of entirely too much leather or far too little, clamber into the truck. They're packed in with the lizards like sardines, as it were. There are many entendres on the theme of "Watch what you're doing with that barrel, fellah." Rider wraps the silence of the grave around the truck, but not fast enough to keep from hearing someone trill "Now, who's gone and put *their* pistol in *my* holster?" and a mixture of bass chuckling and girlish giggles. Nor does he avoid hearing someone say, "As one of the token straights here, I assume I have to ride in the *back* of the truck?"

Washington and Maggie-Sue drag a peculiar rectangular construction onto a small-boat launch ramp, chock it to keep it from sliding forward into the bay. It's like three-quarters of a giant upside-down square Frisbee. Some intricate truck-driving work ensues; soon, the rear wheels are on the great alloy plate but the front wheels are not.

Washington cracks his knuckles, squats, and lifts the front of the truck off the ramp.

Maggie-Sue clamps titanic ski runners to the front wheels; Washington sets down the truck. They pass chain through steel loops to lash the truck securely to the plate. When they are done, they have a monstrosity that looks like the offspring of a panel truck, a snowmobile, and a Flexible Flyer. The nose points toward the water. Rider finishes his soundproofing and clambers into the back. Maggie-Sue waves her arms and hisses. Washington is the last one outside; yanks the chocks away and runs to leap into the back before the truck slides into the drink. Doors shut. With an extremely faint "glug" the truck vanishes from view.

So there they are on the bottom. Whitlomb gets on the intercom. "I can't see a damned thing!"

"Inertial tracker. Maggie-Sue, give us a push," says Washington. The truck slides over the mud. Whitlomb fiddles with the steering as Rider fires up the CO_2 cracker. They clear the mouth of the marina and slide down to the bed of the bay. "Speed."

"Six knots."

"Rider, what's the rating on the soundproofing?"

"Mach 1."

"A little faster, Maggie-Sue. Whitlomb, to 275 and hold course." Maggie-Sue sweats with the effort of keeping water out and shoving them forward and the air is thick with a smell like wet ash.

■ ■ ■

The speedboats have stopped bouncing around in fear. Now they are powered down and scanning the water with sonar; cowled cultists are peering over the side.

There is a disturbance. The boatmen do not hesitate; a depth charge goes overboard.

A few fathoms down there is a distinct munching sound. Rather like a Bouvier des Flandres biting through a can of potato crisps.

A cultist cocks his head. From the prow, someone says, "Damn. Sonar went out."

Just under the surface of the water is a yellow eye the size of a fist. It and the cultist regard each other.

"Guys, I think there's something down there," says the cultist, pointing.

The sonar operator says, "Well, I can't tell. This thing is giving me gibberish. Unless whatever it is is the size of an entire sandbank."

"I just remembered something I saw on the Discovery Channel, once."

"What's that?"

"Aquatic animals often have very small eyes, relative to the rest of their bodies."

A sandbank's worth of dragon sticks its head above the water and eats the boat. Depth charges detonate in its gullet as their pressure fuses go off. It belches carbon monoxide and soot, and then swims for the next boat.

■ ■ ■

"We're here. Open the doors."

"You sure this'll work, Maggie-Sue?" doubts Rider. The doors are opened. A membrane of water creaks and bulges but holds.

"Thiebaud, Arbeiter, take point. Lizards and Dancers follow by twos. Everybody else, queue up and go. Maggie-Sue, if things get too rough, drop the waterproofing; I can swim. Go."

Bubbles of air, each holding a member of the Opposition, bulge out and drive for the surface. Thiebaud, then Arbeiter, then the troops. Rider dives for the membrane with an uncouth yell. Off the side of the truck they hear the driver's door open as Whitlomb takes off. Maggie-Sue is left staring at Washington.

"Maggie-Sue, go."

"I won't drop it. As long as I have breath and fire in my body I won't drop it."

"Maggie-Sue . . . I don't even breathe. Remember?"

She drops her eyes. "I forgot."

"Air's not for me; it's to keep the radio dry." He pats her cheek. Maybe that's a smile on his face. "Go on now. Hurry back to me."

She goes.

■　■　■

Great bubbles break the surface. The group stampedes over the surface of the water to shore, dives behind cover. Overheard the searchlights probe. Every now and then, a Great White expresses its curiosity and a capsized cultist screams.

Thiebaud nods to Arbeiter. "I will clear the way, Mr. Arbeiter. Please wait six minutes before following."

"Don't get shot."

Thiebaud is gone.

Patrols walk the island. A northern pack hears a gunshot and a cultist falls. Per doctrine, others rush to aid while the rest hold position and look for forces coming in under cover of a distraction.

A shot here, a shot there. Cultists run in circles and great fans of machine-gun fire riddle the black landscape.

Six minutes after Creedon sets forth, Arbeiter takes point and they pelt forward. The way is clear. A few soldiers wonder why all the corpses they pass look like they saw a ghost just before they died. That is, such corpses as still *have* faces.

.　.　.

A machine-gun nest guards the shaft that leads from the surface to the great bunker. Green flame washes over the belts and boxes of ammunition; primers fire and in a storm of lead the nest is no more. Maggie-Sue nods and gestures Arbeiter to follow.

Maggie-Sue reaches out and the door crumbles to dust. She sends howling wraiths of ice and smog and sand and flame down the stairs. Their wakes are choked with severely abraded slabs of charred, asphyxiated, icy meat. The raiders charge and another door crumbles—

The members of the circle concentrate—

.　.　.

Maggie-Sue bursts onto the great sandy plain, the temple brooding ahead. Gunfire pelts her, like mayflies against a tractor-trailer's windshield, to just as little effect. She spreads her arms, burns to attract attention as Opposition soldiers flow through the corridor and return fire.

The battle is pitched and terrible, but the conclusion is foregone. Cultists come from the temple in droves, but they are badly outgunned. Maggie-Sue decimates them with sheets of lightning and waves of flame; the sand sucks them under and spiked balls of ice hail from the sky. Opposition platoons pour lead and silver on the devotees of the Vulture; return fire is surprisingly light.

Whitlomb is the first to sicken. In the Pacific he witnessed banzai charges: exhausted, desperate men charging into certain death, rushing machine guns with bayonets clutched in emaciated hands. Japanese or gaijin, men scream the same way.

Arbeiter is remembering a story. He thinks the author is Günter Grass; thinks the title is "Bowling Alley." It is a tale of German man, a veteran of World War II, a machine-gunner. He is dreaming of a great pyramid of skulls, piling higher and higher as he sweeps the gun back and forth. And when the skulls roll and bounce off one another they make a sound like a bowling ball rattling pins.

Washington is in an underwater cell. The silence of death surrounds him. The sounds of death come over his radio.

Creedon Thiebaud remembers a summer morning: August 6, 1965. His twentieth birthday. He walked into a Viet Minh village and began shooting. (At the court-martial, the rest of the platoon testified that the village had been rotten with Viet Cong. Honorable discharge.) Creedon can feel the same rage trying to break forth. Anger at their temerity, at their very numbers, at their willingness to come forth and fall like wheat before a scythe. He clamps down hard. If he does it again, falls prey to the thirst to put aside a soldier's humanity and become unto an angel of death, he knows his soul will again be torn from his body. This time, it may never return.

Maggie-Sue is very young; she has never lost a brother or father and she does not know what Thiebaud knows. She is finding out; foam flecked on her lips, eyes glassy as they keep coming and coming.

Their soldiers are finding out too. These were persuaded by alchemy, not hawks and draft boards, and so perhaps when dawn comes the night will vanish from their memories and they can sleep easy. Perhaps not.

And Rider sees thousands of moths pressing against a great egg.

·   ·   ·

"Check fire! *Check fire!*" orders Whitlomb. Blood covers old bones in a jumble of the dead and the dying. The gunfire stops.

"MAGGIE-SUE! CHECK FIRE!" bellows Whitlomb. Maggie-Sue is shaking and sobbing, searing the corpses with hellfire wholly redundant. Arbeiter has to use a right cross to stop her; she sags to her knees and collapses entirely.

Arbeiter squirts fluid into the air from a syringe; revives her. She opens her eyes dreamily. "I had," she says, "the most terrible nightmare."

Arbeiter looks to Whitlomb. Whitlomb looks to Rider. Rider looks for somebody to look to. In the silence, there are moans beginning to build and spread.

Thiebaud is there, cradling her head in his hands. "I am sorry, Ms. Percy," he says. "It was not a dream." Her eyes light on his and tell him to tell her otherwise. "Nor is it over. We must go on, now. Can you get up?"

She can, barely. Whitlomb is looking at the great dark temple. "That was only their first line of last-ditch defense—mundanes, to keep out mundane attack. The generals are untouched. We're going in."

"Are you sure—" starts Rider. Whitlomb and Arbeiter look at him. Rider would prefer them to be glaring, but they are not. They are gazing at him with preternatural calm. "Right. You're right. Never mind. I'm with you, all right?"

Maggie-Sue draws a little closer to coherency. "Lots of troops," she says. "How do we handle them inside?"

"We don't," says Whitlomb. "We cannot. Their battle is over, and we must leave them for now."

She looks ready to argue, then nods. "So we can bring in Joe."

Whitlomb shakes his head. "He has to coordinate their withdrawal. Just us, Maggie-Sue."

"I want to see him again." Her expression is alarmingly slack.

"You will. But not yet. All right?"

"All right."

Rider says, "Kris, get an Oracle Highball into her, yes? Perry, got a minute?"

"As many as you need." Whitlomb and Rider step a bit aways.

"Shell shock, Perry."

"I know. But she's our heavy artillery; we can't let her go. Perhaps Creedon can do something to assist."

"He already did. That's the only reason she's not catatonic."

"Nor do you appear to be your normal chipper self."

"There's one great thing about being a coward."

"Yes?"

"I'm used to being scared out of my fucking mind." Rider looks at the plain. Shakes his head. "Christ, and we're the good guys . . . half of them weren't even armed . . . goddamn massacre . . . Look, we go in, grease the bastards, and take a long, long vacation somewhere sunn—er, somewhere, somewhere . . ."

Whitlomb chuckles. "Sunny beaches, the open sea, and the rain forest; all shot to hell, eh? Perhaps the mountains?"

"Tibet?"

"An excellent suggestion, were it not for the Chinese occupation."

"We'll visit the Dalai Lama in exile, then. And there are some secret monasteries that owe me some favors, anyway."

"Deal."

"Let's go."

Maggie-Sue is looking better; at least her habitual frown is coming back. Whitlomb says, "Creedon, forward scout and wreak unpleasant surprises. Kris, take point. I shall be Hindmost. Maggie-Sue, accompany Al. In the event of trouble ahead, Arbeiter lays down suppressing fire as I come forward; trouble from behind, I shall return fire and Arbeiter comes back. Maggie-Sue, fire on targets of opportunity at your discretion; Al will guard your back and watch for flanking thrusts. Got that?"

"You could have just said Formation 3,8-Echo Stalk," mutters Rider.

"We're penetrating an inner sanctum; watch out for the usual blade traps and Brobdingnagian marbles." Whitlomb chuckles. "You know what priests are like. Let's go."

They step into the temple.

The priests complete their spell.

■   ■   ■

Dunes stretch to the horizon; fine, lifeless, yellow sand. No wind. Hammering sunlight. They stand in their formation, blinking.

"What the hell?" says Arbeiter.

Maggie-Sue kneels and starts playing with the sand. She giggles.

Rider gets down on his knees and puts his arms around her. The other three discreetly turn their backs and study the terrain for a while. When she stops crying and releases Rider, she looks him in the eye and hisses something about women's work that the others don't quite catch. Rider helps her to her feet and tries to stand in Commanding Officer Pose Number One; but since he never served in the military, Rider looks like he's bending over backward and trying to dislocate his jaw.

Arbeiter says, "Nothing on the radio. We're cut off."

Rider waves his staff around. "Pocket dimension, I think. Haven't seen one of these in . . . well, ever, actually. I saw some demos when I was in San Bernardino, but they were just a few millimeters on a side."

"Can't be," says Whitlomb. "You can't rush how quickly the pocket grows. If that horizon's as far away as it looks, this would have to be over five thousand years old."

"So someone got lucky at a garage sale. Besides, desolate ones are easier to make. Could be they just teleported us to the Sahara, of course, but I doubt it."

"No," says Maggie-Sue. "This isn't real earth or real air. Not ours. Not the Sahara."

"Feels hot enough to *be* the Sahara."

"I'll make some canteens and some water."

"Good idea," says Rider. "I think I can make this light into some burnooses, too." The two of them set to work.

"Joe's going to be worried sick," says Arbeiter.

"Not much we can do about that," says Rider. "It's going to take a while to find our way out of here."

"If there *is* a way out."

"There always is. It could be guarded by a dozen titans, of course."

"I don't see an exit—or a dozen titans, for that matter. And that horizon is a long way away."

"We'll have to improvise."

Maggie-Sue finishes a canteen; fills it with water and passes it around. Rider holds up a bolt of rough yellow cloth and starts thaumaturging it into shape.

■   ■   ■

They are fitted with clothing; long robes to keep away the sun and trap humidity. Not as comfortable as shorts and a T-shirt. Still, superior in that wearing a burnoose in the desert does *not* lead the occupant to an agonizing death.

They have fashioned a tent as well. Now they are trying to find a way to acquire food with nothing to work with but sand. Heavy going. Arbeiter found a Mounds bar in his bag and is trying to revive the coconut long enough to get it to germinate. Creedon is hunting sidewinders, although he is somewhat hampered by the complete lack of any indication that a sidewinder has ever passed within a thousand miles. Rider is outside as well, trying to convince himself that the view is a feast for the eyes and working from there. Maggie-Sue has drawn a pentagram and is chanting and hissing in a valiant attempt to summon the God of Soybeans.

The coconut dissolves into a brown goo. "Oops," says Arbeiter. "I think I screwed up the pH."

"I hate when that happens," smiles Whitlomb.

Arbeiter sits down with a sigh and watches Maggie-Sue. An aspect of the God of Soybeans appears in the pentagram—incredibly impressive, inasmuch as a domesticated plant can be—and rustles its leaves at her for a while before vanishing. She sits down.

"What'd he say?" asks Arbeiter.

"Said he wouldn't send his people into the desert. Added a joke about the Jews."

"Ah."

"Smart-ass fucking plant."

Creedon drifts in. Shakes his head.

Rider comes in, coughing. Rinses his mouth out and spits out the door. Flap. Whatever.

"No luck, Al?"

"Looked good. Tasted like sand."

"Aesthetics are hardly a consideration. We can choke it down."

"It *was* sand, Perry."

"Ah."

"We can last at least three weeks without food, though," says Arbeiter.

Rider snorts. "Yeah, but we won't be able to move after one."

"You forgot my little black bag."

"You're right, I did." Rider smacks himself on the head. "And come to think of that, we can be mobile a little longer after that. I can photosynthesize; I learned that when I was an apprentice, back in San Bernardino. If I have to, I can build a sledge and drag you."

Whitlomb laughs. "Well, that's one of us at least. I don't suppose you can lactate as well?"

Rider laughs. The he gets a look in his eyes. Turns to Arbeiter.

Arbeiter stares. "You're out of your mind, Even if I could find a way to do it with just a field kit, it would just mean we'd suck the life right out of you."

"We've got plenty of vitamins, right? In your black bag? I can make sugars out of sunlight and water, so calories won't be any trouble. I'd run out of protein, though . . . let's see . . ."

"Rider, I love you like a brother, but I'd just as soon *continue* to love you like a *brother* for a while, all right? Let's not go overboard on this just yet."

"Hey, I'm not wild about the idea either. Honey."

They compose themselves for sleep as best they can.

In the stifling dim they hear Maggie-Sue say, "I wish Joe was here."

Whitlomb says, "Yes, well. It would be nice to all be together, at least."

Arbeiter asks, "You think we'll ever see him again?"

"Eventually. I have the greatest respect for your philosophy, Maggie-Sue, but I, for myself, must believe in life after death. Even in the worst possible case, we will meet again. Somewhere. As somebody."

Nobody really has anything to say about that.

"It's funny. I hate it to be funny," says Maggie-Sue.

"Hate what?" asks Whitlomb.

"It's not just horrible. Horrible is okay. But it's funny too. Mummies crack jokes while they eat your mind. Those zombies at the train station—that marching chant they had—they were laughing at themselves. I hate it."

"She's right," says Rider. "We're the good guys; it's all right for us to have a sense of humor. But they do too. And hunting them is funny. I mean, you've all been to San Diego, or at least places like it. If you're not paying attention to how horrible it is, you could split your sides laughing. Six-breasted zombies dressed like Madonna. Street jugglers flirting with jackal-faced little girls while keeping five severed heads aloft—and then the heads scream in agony at the puns. And you remember that toxic-waste case who collected paper umbrellas? Flaying people and hiding in their skins to sneak into Trader Vic's and order drinks six at a time?"

"I remember," says Arbeiter. "He spit acid in your face and bit Joe's arm half off and back home, while we were bandaging each other up, we were all laughing so hard we could hardly see straight."

They lie and remember.

"And remember when Al and Chloe wanted to find out how the Seattle game would go?" chuckles Arbeiter. "When the goat got loose and ate one of Al's spell books? And after everything was back under control, none of us had the heart to kill him?"

"I don't want to talk about Chloe," says Maggie-Sue.

That puts an end to it.

.   .   .

Night. They pack up all the gear they've already conjured; never know when your mages are going to kick the bucket. Rider does his thing with bits of sole and sand and Saran Wrap. Arbeiter issues pills.

"And just what might this be?" asks Whitlomb, eyeing the pill suspiciously.

"Casein carrier bound to thaumophosphoric acid, treated to migrate to the mitochondria. The thaumophosphorous sneaks into a phosphate group, and then radiates at 479 nanometers to accelerate over to a adenosine diphosphate molecule and latch on, yielding adenosine triphosphate, over and over again! Terrific, eh?"

"If you say so, Kris."

"Now hold on," says Rider. "That's not what happens when thaumophosphorous gets into your metabolism."

"It's magic, you melonhead. You know how hard it is to culture mitochondria to make this gunk? You ever try to grow human mitochondria in a goddamn ostrich egg? I spent two weeks in the Austin library finding a way to kill bird mitochondria and leave the egg alive. Pop it, for crying out loud."

"Yessir." Gulp. "Any side effects?"

"Slight blue glow. And if danger threatens, don't stick your head in the sand."

"Har de har har. I laugh."

"Laugh as much as you like, Herr Alternativ Universe Magus Master Synesthetic, Herr. Does anybody have any idea which way to go from here? Do we steer by the stars?"

They gaze up at the darkening sky. Continue to gaze.

"Is that Ursa Major, Perry?" asks Rider.

"Indeed. And so we see the truth behind the myth. Imagine, the hunter Orion chasing a great bear, for all of eternity."

"I've never really been able to see animals in the constellations before."

"It helps if they move their limbs. And their bodies are painted in with nebular swirls . . ."

"Guess so. Everybody, stop watching and maybe they'll be still again. If we don't see them, they can't see us; and the last thing I want is to have the whole damn zodiac down here with us."

"So much for astronavigation," mutters Arbeiter.

"We go toward water," says Maggie-Sue.

"Which way is that?" says Rider.

"That way."

"How do you know? Never mind. Stupid question. Any idea how far?"

"At least ten miles—maybe a hundred."

Whitlomb says, "A forbidding distance, but the walk will do us good. Creedon, scout; Kris takes point and I shall bring up the rear. Kris, when you become tired of peeling your eyes, switch with Al. When I get tired, I shall trade off with Maggie-Sue. If anybody becomes fatigued at all, speak up! We'll stop for a break; we have plenty of time. Shall we?"

They go. Fifteen minutes later Arbeiter calls back, "Whitlomb?"

"Yes?"

"Is it my imagination, or is the man on the moon looking down on us with a pitying expression?"

"Just ignore him, Kris."

●　■　■

Around midnight. Rider is on point. As he tops a crest, he sees a body lying in the dip between two dunes. Thiebaud is standing beside it. They cluster 'round.

"Ugly cuss," mutters Whitlomb.

"Just adapted to the desert," says Arbeiter. "Hooded eyes and ears, thick hide with sparse sweat glands, tough hair all over. Why'd you zap him, Creedon?"

Thiebaud lifts an arm. There is a tattoo of a vulture.

"Might just be a totemist."

"Easy enough to find out," says Rider. Mutters in Sumerian. The vulture tattoo fails to glow. "Nope. Mundane or theological. It would've been nice to interrogate him, though, Creedon. Why didn't you take him alive?"

"The individual surprised me, Mr. Rider."

They stare at him.

"Observe his jewelry and footwear."

Rider does so. "Ye gods and little fishes. Blink-of-an-eye ring and cat's-paw boots. They're synesthetic, worth a fortune. What's a lousy desert rat doing with all this gear?"

"He put up a rather *substantial* fight, Mr. Rider. I believe he was a champion of some sort."

Whitlomb says, "Well, we got some loot, at least. Shall we bury the body?"

They stare at him. "Are you out of your mind, Perry?" says Rider.

Whitlomb says, "Come, now. He'll draw scavengers if we simply walk away. Desert peoples watch for vultures, for the warning of approaching thanogens."

"So we won't leave anything to scavenge."

"I beg your pardon?"

Arbeiter begins stripping the body.

"Al? Al, why is Maggie-Sue igniting a fire?"

Arbeiter draws a knife.

"Oh, no."

"Relax, Perry. Think of it as poetic justice."

■　■　■

Their bellies are filled. They've decided to jerk the rest, which will take some time, so they camp.

The sun comes up. They raise the tent and leave the fire going. Post watches and try to sleep.

A few hours after sunset, as they hike through the night, Maggie-Sue says, "There's a stone rill coming up, and an oasis on the other side."

Whitlomb nods. "Creedon, go check it out."

Creedon goes and comes back. He draws a map. They cluster around. "A pyramid, eh?" says Whitlomb. "Makes sense. If this is ancient Egyptian, that explains the size."

Arbeiter says, "No, it does *not* make sense. The Nazis were into distortions of *Norse* mythology."

Rider says, "The Nazis would loot anything they could get their hands on. It's not like they had a philosophy that made *any* sense; I'm sure Hitler would have declared the ancient Egyptians Aryans if it had served his purposes."

"Good point. Any reason we shouldn't just wade in and start shooting?"

"I can't think of one. And we might as well do it now."

"Still, it's nice to be fighting an enemy that's actually *weaker* at night, for once."

"Spoken like a true European. San Diego is strong during the day, too; you've spent too much time hunting down things that go bump in the night."

. . .

They wade in. They don't find anything to shoot.

"Well, this is getting *boring*," says Rider, idly kicking a peahen out of the way. "Maggie-Sue, are there any *other* water sources you can sense?"

"No," she says.

Thiebaud spits out a pomegranate seed.

Whitlomb says, "If we have to search this whole place for secret ways in, we'll be here for weeks."

"Maybe they're just holing up until it's daylight. I say we get some sleep."

. . .

Dawn.

"Sure enough," says Rider. "That hole in the side of the pyramid wasn't there last night. Creedon, you feel like scouting it out?"

Thiebaud draws his Glocks. "Of course, Mr. Rider."

Two minutes later, they hear three gunshots, and Thiebaud calling, "It should be safe now."

The corridor is nothing but simple dressed stone leading to a chamber perhaps twenty meters on a side. Edmund Neuman, one bullet in his gut and one in his heart, is slumped in a stone throne, blood leaking from his mouth.

"Looks just like his photo," says Rider.

Whitlomb says patiently, "Creedon, we don't have Joe with us. Remember? If we want to ask questions, we have to do it *before* shooting."

"Reflex, I fear," says Thiebaud. "I seem to have a knife impaled in my thigh. Mr. Arbeiter, might I ask for some assistance?"

Arbeiter rushes over. "Damn. Nobody's managed to draw blood from you for *years,* have they? Was he that fast?"

Thiebaud shakes his head. "But I attempted to shoot the knife out of the air—and found it is enchanted to pass through metal. Still, all is not lost— as one might expect from one who has not perceptibly aged since the war, his wounds are closing as we speak. I imagine he'll be whole soon."

Indeed, Neuman sits up. "That hurt," he says.

"Yeah?" says Whitlomb. "Eardrops, everyone."

Neuman looks confused as Arbeiter hands around a bottle. "What are you doing?"

Whitlomb says, "You were saying something about being in pain?" and blasts Neuman's abdomen. "How about that?"

They wait until Neuman is able to speak again. He says, "Surely we can be civil about this?"

Whitlomb fires again. They twiddle their thumbs for a while until Neuman heals. Then Whitlomb says, "This *is* civil. You do *not* want to see us when we're irritated enough to be rude. Am I getting through to you?"

"Yes, yes, of course," says Neuman. "You had only to say. I suppose you have questions?"

Whitlomb's shotgun doesn't move. "And I'm sure you know what they're likely to be. Start talking."

Neuman coughs up a little blood. "Well, the good news is you've pretty much flattened my operation in the Bay Area. Your troops hunted down the inner circle of priests. I wouldn't have made it out at all if I hadn't intercepted the mana of their deaths before the Vulture got it."

"How'd you do that?" asks Rider.

Neuman looks crafty for moment, but then shrugs. "I shouldn't tell you—but what the hell, it's not much of a secret, and I have a question of my own for later. . . . Everyone who's worked with the Vulture cult a lot knows the spell I used; the birdbrains are always too stupid to realize they're being used. Take every sixth word of De Sade's *120 Days of Sodom;* translate it into Finnish, then take every third letter and transliterate that into ancient Cretan."

"Got it," says Rider. "So what's the bad news?"

Neuman grins evilly. "I was able to keep you in stasis for several years while I grew back a bit more of my power."

"How long?" asks Rider.

"You'll find out when you go back."

"You're not in much of a position to withhold information."

Neuman snickers. "Why? What are you going to do, kill me if I don't talk?"

Rider draws himself up. "I have worked with people from San Diego before, you know. Even *without* magical regeneration, they can keep people alive for decades while they torture them."

"Go ahead. I've been alive since before the fall of the Roman Empire. Unaging, immortal, immune to disease, et cetera et cetera. Pain still hurts, but not as much as it used to—and every minute you waste here, a score of them pass in the outside world."

"So why are you talking at all?" asks Arbeiter.

Neuman turns to him. "Just a postmortem—a courtesy, really. That and idle curiosity. I always like to get a good look at people I've played with. And I'd like to know how you summoned that dragon. The minute that thing showed up in the Bay, I knew it was time to get ready to leave. That's why I had the cultists send the vampires to you, you know—to set up a set-piece battle so as many people as possible on both sides would die all at once."

Rider says, "I was wondering about that. . . . No particular trick to the dragon; it's an old spell. Any decent occult library should have a copy. You just messed with the wrong people; we had a *lot* of mana."

"Mmm." Neuman nods. "Yes, I was afraid of that."

"Speaking of idle curiosity," says Whitlomb, "what the hell were you trying to accomplish?"

Neuman smiles. "I want to rule the world. It's a hobby of mine."

"Have you considered stamp collecting instead?" says Arbeiter.

"A bit banal, even for *my* tastes."

"What do you mean?"

Neuman stretches. "Haven't you ever heard of the banality of evil? Hitler was a teenaged boy throwing a tantrum; Stalin was forcing round people into square holes; Truman saw the Bomb as a somewhat larger incendiary. Mussolini just wanted the trains to run on time, and he wasn't even able to do that."

Arbeiter says, "So, what, you just want people to read your books?"

Neuman blinks. "What books?"

"Aren't you a writer?"

"Hmn? Oh, writing was just something I did to relax in the late 1930s. Actually, once I became powerful, I never got any useful feedback at all; everybody swore they were the greatest things ever written. It got boring. Except for Goebbels—he was always honest about saying they were just fluff." He looks at Creedon. "Planning on dragging me back to Jerusalem for a trial, Yid?"

Thiebaud blows his brains out. While they wait for him to grow back, Rider says, "I've got a feeling we're not going to be able to do much to stop him, here."

Whitlomb nods.

When Neuman grows back, he says, "No, you're not. I'm not one of the great powers, but what I can do I do very well. Most of my magic is defensive—a rather cowardly trade-off, you might think, and perhaps you'd be right. But I've always preferred to let others do the heavy lifting."

Whitlomb says, "How many times have you pulled this little trick?"

"I've lost count," says Neuman. "Usually it's the Incumbents who track me down. They threw me out of South Africa just a while ago."

Whitlomb grates, "I happen to be *from* South Africa, you know."

"So what? Do you hate me more for it?"

"I didn't think it was possible, but yes."

"Good for you." Neuman applauds. "I think I have a gold star here somewhere I can give you."

"Let me try," says Maggie-Sue. "Cover your eyes." Neuman goes up like a magnesium flare dropped into liquid oxygen. It's a good fifteen minutes before he re-forms out of vapors.

"Not all that effective a bullying tactic," says Neuman. "Third- and fourth-degree burns don't really hurt, you know." He stands up. "Well, unless there's anything else, we might as well all go home. I'd say where I'm going to pop up next, but you'd just warn people, which would be irritating. Don't worry; once I leave, you'll see a portal that'll take you back to the Farralons. I'd kill you if I could, of course, or trap you here, or move the portal to drop you onto the slopes of Mount Olympus, but I can't."

"There is one other thing," says Rider.

"Yes?"

"I think Kris is right. You really need a new hobby. May I make a suggestion?"

"If you like."

Rider fires the .22 derringer concealed in his left hand.

Neuman looks at the hole in his chest quizzically as it closes up. "What . . .?"

"Medical research," says Rider, lighting a cigarette. "If you're lucky, you might be able to find a cure for lung cancer before the pain gets too bad for you to be able to concentrate."

Neuman sneers. "Lung cancer? Please. I had that once—in the *Middle Ages*. I cured myself just fine." He waves a hand over his chest—and freezes. Sweat pops out on his brow.

"The Middle Ages? Tsk tsk," says Rider. "Pre-Colombian. You're in the New World now, old man. With treatment, I'd say you've got five years, tops."

"If you don't care for those odds," says Whitlomb, "you could always track down the Crab totem and apologize for all of Western civilization. If you try, please take notes; we've often wondered where totems go when they die."

"I swear," snarls Neuman, "I'll find a way to destroy each and every one of you."

Arbeiter smiles. "Ah. We're back to the script. Whose turn it is to make a smart-assed remark when we hear that?"

"It is mine, I believe," says Thiebaud. "But I do not have one prepared."

"Well, real life seldom works out like the movies."

"Indeed," says Thiebaud. "Ah, well." He turns to Neuman. "Off with you, then, little nightmare from ages past. I cannot be bothered with you anymore; I have friends to become reacquainted with, and new books to read. Be gone."

Neuman goes.

They step through the portal and onto one of the Farralons. Max and Chloe look up. "Took you long enough," says Max.

Rider nods. "Max. Thought I'd never see you again."

"We had a change of heart. There was a problem in the City—Joe sent your dragon out looking for us, and—well, it's a long story."

"Come on," says Chloe. "Joe's holding a table for us. I won't even argue if you want to cover the pizza with clams."

appendix

THEIR PLACE IN THE SUN:
A brief introduction to *Zombi diego*
Prof. Erik Johanson, Miskatonic University

ABSTRACT

Zombi diego is described, along with a basic bibliography to provoke interest in (and discourse on) the nature of the undead as opposed to the living.

INTRODUCTION

Students of the undead quickly realize that like many of their compatriots in other disciplines, they cannot precisely define what it is they study. Nowhere is this more evident than in the case of *Zombi diego,* aka "San Diego Zombie" and "Miami Pseudolich."

Formally, the undead are "Entities partaking of the natures of both the living and the dead" [Wallace62]; the traditional example is *Nosferatu nocturnus,* the Central European nocturnal vampire. In the process of transformation, the body of the vampire perishes and cools; the heart ceases to beat. But EEGs demonstrate that neural activity continues throughout; CAT scans cannot distinguish the brain of a vampire from the brain of a living man [Grant82]. Clearly, this entity is dead—it does not breathe or maintain a constant body temperature—but as any member of the Van Helsing Society will tell you, *N. nocturnus* is entirely too lively in its pursuit of prey and assault thereof. Ergo, these vampires are undead.

At about this point, an undergraduate desiring ingratiation raises a hand and asks *how much* of the nature of the dead an entity must possess to be considered undead. After all, most of what we can see of each other is dead tissue. The outer layer of skin, the hair, the nails—all of this is necrobiotic. Are we, then, undead?

The lecturer then responds that although he is certain he is not undead, he entertains his doubts about the questioner.

But after the laughter subsides and the class is over, the instructor retires to his study and ponders. Where do we draw the line between living and undead? *Is* there a line? Then, when we meet with our students over pizza and beer, we argue back and forth. And the most cited example—by all participants, arguing every conceivable point of view—is *Zombi diego*.

For the benefit of occultists everywhere, I here attempt to set forth an introduction to the study of this fascinating creature. Is it living, or undead? Human, or inhuman? Buffoonish plaything of the jaded—or parasite sinister as the cuckoo?

PHYSICAL FORM AND LIFE CYCLE

Necro Ego Sapiens Mnenonosa Homosapiens *Zombi diego* is a diurnal endothermic anthropomorph with three distinct life stages [Pend48] [Green77]. As is clear from its species name, *Z. diego* is an undead possessing an undying part, capable of both reasoning and memory, vulnerable to theotoxic salts [Wallace62]. For all intents and purposes, it is encountered only in mixed communities of *Z. diego* and *Homo sapiens* [Woj52]. *Z. diego* closely resembles *H. sapiens,* and so we will concentrate on the differences between the two species.

Most *Zombi diego* appear to be Caucasian, although the species is sufficiently diverse as to evince most ethnic appearances bar that of the red-haired, pale-skinned Celt and the albino [Woj52]. *Z. diego's* skin tone is tan, bronze, medium brown, or peanut-butter-toned (rarely dark brown or black) as a result of extensive exposure to solar ultraviolet [Klas56]. The dermal pigment is mostly melanin, although quantities of photoactive steroids are also present [Klas58]. *Z. diego* is highly resistant to obesity [Green84], a characteristic also found in *Nosferatu* and many other forms of undead [Iijin69]. Adult *Z. diego* females are ectomorphic, although bearing impressive secondary sexual characteristics; *Z. diego* males are mesomorphs, usually well muscled [Green84].

The presexual form is effectively indistinguishable from preadolescent *H. sapiens* unless occult means are brought into play [Pend49], although presexual *Z. diego* tend to be more content and sociable than preadolescent *H. sapiens,* as will be described below.

After ten to thirteen years of life, *Z. diego* undergoes adolescence, assuming a mature appearance after two to four years of transition [Cal53]. Late adolescence is unknown [Young79]. Growth accelerates as per adolescence in *H. sapiens;* primary and secondary sexual characteristics develop [Cal53]. *Z. diego* is highly fertile—96% per year of sexual activity, perhaps even higher given *Z. diego's* normative behavior [Woj52] [Young81]—and has a short gestational period, approximately eight months. Childbirth is easy; contributing factors include the small size of *Z. diego* neonates (2.5 kg on the average, as compared to 3 kg in *H. sapiens* [Cal53],) and the broad pelvis of *Z. diego* females [Young79]. Throughout the entire adult stage, ectomorphism / mesomorphism is retained.

After approximately 33-37 years of life, *Z. diego* enters the postadult stage. This is marked by necrobiosis of the dermis (save the mucous membranes) [Klas56], as well as necrobiosis of the liver and kidneys [Klas56-2] and the bone marrow [Klas57]. These tissues retain their cellular organization and are highly resistant to putrefaction, but are metabolically inactive. The blood thickens and darkens, evincing a high count of dead but un-flushed red and white blood cells. It is not known how any living blood cells can be present at all, given the necrobiosis of the marrow. Renal function continues unimpaired, again through an unknown mechanism [Klas59]. The heart rate drops steadily until approximately the age of 55, at which point it may well cease altogether; cessation of cardiac function is neither crippling nor taken note of. Throughout, breathing becomes labored and the organism exhibits symptoms of chronic oxygen deprivation, notably lack of endurance and impairment of cerebral function [Cal53].

Appetite is radically diminished: in 90% of documented cases, ectomorphism / mesomorphism is retained; in the remaining 10%, the postadult accumulates masses of adipose tissue [Aber82], becoming unattractively obese. The skin petrifies and "tans" as a result of necrobiosis and continued exposure to ultraviolet; the skin of a postadult is visually indistinguishable from thin wrinkled leather. Although the skin heals very slowly, it is highly resistant to abrasions and cuts [Klas56]. Hair growth and sweat production continue unabated: how the skin can continue to heal, regulate temperature, and produce hair without the benefit of biologic processes is under investigation [Klas59] [Mad80].

Postadults retain sexual function as per the adult phase, although fertility drops to approximately a fifth of that of *H. sapiens,* and carrying a child to term results in scarring in the form of "stretch marks" and permanent vaginal distention well beyond that experienced by *H. sapiens* [Young81]. Sexual behavior may be infrequent in the postadult phase [Bord72], although postadults display an evident and undiminished desire to so indulge (discussed below).

Resistance to poisons improves to the point of near immunity; only organophosphates and reptile toxins are capable of harming a postadult *Z. diego,* and even then only after a tremendous period of exposure thereof [Klas59] [Green77]. (*Z. diego* is still subject to suffocation, however.)

Data on the average life span of *Z. diego* are simply not available—an oddity that will receive extensive discussion below.

HABITAT, ULTRAVIOLET, AND GENETICS

Zombi diego occurs only in areas characterized by extensive and intense sunlight [Green84]. In North America, the largest concentrations are found in coastal southern California and coastal Florida [Green77] [Aber82], with smaller colonies along the Gulf Coast [Burke79], and inland southern California and the greater American Southwest [Aber84]. In Europe, *Z. diego* is found in small colonies along the coast of most of the Mediterranean, particularly Greece [Green77]. Information for Asia, Africa, and South America is not available at this time, although anecdotal evidence exists for a South African population [Whit80].

Z. diego is a highly intelligent tool user, preferring to inhabit tract housing indistinguishable from that of *H. sapiens. Z. diego* and *H. sapiens* live side by side in close harmony; members of *Z. diego* do not know they are not part of *H. sapiens* [Green77]. (The implications of this surprising fact are given a more extensive treatment below.) This often results in copulation between the two populations [Young81]; indeed, images of *Z. diego* frequently occur in erotic literature [Gordon83].

Z. diego requires ultraviolet light to remain healthy and active [Pend48]. Preliminary evidence indicates that presexuals and adults utilize UV catalysis directly in a variety of metabolic processes—not only in the synthesis of vitamin D, which occurs in mammals and lizards, but also in the formation of most steroids, including but not limited to testosterone and estrogen [Mad80]. If *Z. diego* is deprived of UV for more than twenty days, a dangerous and often fatal torpor sets in [Pend49]. Depriving a postadult of UV for more than a few weeks results in a potentially reversible hibernation [Pend49]; other than this, the role of UV in the metabolism of the postadult is unknown.

Extensive genetic sequencing of *Z. diego* has been undertaken; to date, no statistically significant differences between *Z. diego* and *H. sapiens* have come to light [Sole84]. (Blood group distribution is identical to that of Western Europeans; all samples thus far possess the genetic markers for aldehyde dehydrogenase and lactase, even in *Z. diego* with an eastern Asian appearance [Yee82].) Preliminary studies of mitochondrial DNA have proven equally unenlightening [Sole85]. Given these facts, it is astounding that the two populations are not interfertile. When sperm and ova of differing species are mixed, the resulting zygote lyses within minutes [Burke50] [Green77]. This procedure remains the most accurate way to distinguish an adult *Z. diego* from an adult *H. sapiens* [Sole84]. Marriages between female *H. sapiens* and male *Z. diego* are generally childless, as affairs undertaken by *H. sapiens* women are rarely carried on long enough to result in issue. Marriages between male *H. sapiens* and female *Z. diego* are usually fruitful, as *Z. diego* is promiscuous and highly fertile [Young81].

BEHAVIOR: SUNNING AND SEXUALITY

The nature-nurture conflict is perhaps the oldest and most bitter in anthropology. Still, there are aspects of *Z. diego* behavior that appear to be constant across culture [Green77], although cross-cultural studies of *Z. diego* are in their infancy [Embeli83]. We will carefully point out those aspects of behavior whose origins are much in dispute.

Z. diego "sunbathes," exposing as much of its skin to the solar disc as it can as frequently as is possible [Green77]. *Z. diego* is often found on the beach, on sundecks, and beside artificial pools; in public areas, *Z. diego* conforms to local standards of modesty, but seems to prefer to go unclad [Green84]. When private sunbathing areas are unavailable, *Z. diego* frequently makes use of ultraviolet lamps, particularly in commercial suntanning facilities, to ensure that all parts of the body are exposed to ultraviolet [Green84]. When sunbathing, *Z. diego* enters a state of semitorpor, neither speaking, reading, nor reacting to most stimuli [Green77]. Efforts to take EEGs of sunning *Z. diego* have, thus far, proven fatal to researchers, as *Z. diego* is as inclined to call for help when approached by a scientist with a van full of electronic equipment as any member of *H. sapiens* is [Grant81].

When sunbathing, *Z. diego* prefers thin fabrics of immodest cut; in feminine clothing intended for outdoor use, the cloth over the central breast and genitalia is often of a strongly contrasting shade, drawing attention to these erogenous zones [Aber82]. Some researchers claim that this is an instinctive form of sexual display; others are dubious, as this behavior is also found in presexuals and the semifertile-at-best postadult [Embeli83].

Z. diego evinces a stimulus-response edge to its sexual activity more reminiscent of the insect kingdom than the higher primates. Approach generally takes place at night or indoors; while sunning, *Z. diego* is disinclined to bestir itself. When presented with an appropriate trigger—generally the presence of a skimpily clad adult Z. *diego* or an attractive, tanned, sexually aggressive *H. sapiens*—eye contact is initiated which quickly leads to: 1. verbal flirtation; 2. genteel, socially acceptable preening / presenting / grooming behavior similar to that of Hominidae; 3. pair removal from the social group [Bord72]. (We assume that after this removal, copulation takes place; but this is fundamentally unascertainable without Orwellian measures [Embeli83].) Z. *diego* is strongly attracted to tan skin tones, blatant display of primary and secondary sexual characteristics, and "aggressive" or "slutty" postures, preferring to ignore *H. sapiens* lacking a suntan, wearing demure clothing, or assuming a hostile or apathetic posture [Cal53]. (Many researchers point out that this is also a good capsule description of casual copulatory activity in *H. sapiens*; they go on to claim that the Z. *diego* "trigger" should be considered a culturally learned behavior [Larson80].)

Intragender sexual approach has been observed in Z. *diego*, particularly in the male; but an exclusively homosexual Z. *diego* has never been documented [Larson81].

Postadult Z. *diego* make eye contact and proceed to flirtation with adult Z. *diego* (as well as *H. sapiens* that could be mistaken for adult Z. *diego* per the previously described trigger mechanisms) as often as adult Z. *diego*, but are usually ignored. It is impossible to determine the normative sexual behavior for mated pairs of postadults; in public, they flirt with appropriate triggers regardless of the presence of their mates—but this has never been observed to result in leaving the mate to go off with the adult [Larson80]. We have no way to know what happens when the postadult mated pair is home alone.

An *H. sapiens* that triggers a Z. *diego*'s sexual reflex is approached, chatted up, and often bird-dogged by the Z. *diego;* given the differing approach to casual sexual behavior in the West between the sexes, this will usually result in a rendezvous only in the case of a female Z. *diego* and a male *H. sapiens* [Larson80].

Z. *diego* do not appear to be inclined to true or serial monogamy, regardless of their host culture. Z. *diego* seldom "marry" another Z. *diego* until both are beginning to metamorphose to the postadult phase, at which point sexual exclusivity is something of a moot point [Aber82]. As noted above, information is not available on the sexual behavior of mated postadult Z. *diego.*

Many Z. *diego* "marry" H. *sapiens* while the Z. *diego* is in the adult phase, preferring to select older H. *sapiens* [Pend48] [Cal53]. Marriage of a female Z. *diego* to a male H. *sapiens* appears to delay the transition to the postadult phase by five to ten years [Klas58-2]. Regardless of gender, a pair-bonded Z. *diego* retains the sexual trigger approach to copulation, which can make for profound mental anguish on the part of the H. *sapiens* [Pend48]. G. Warren Pendragon, a sociobiologist of the old school to the end of his days, claimed that this behavior is selected for in female Z. *diego* through the mechanism of providing a stable homelife for her children (claiming that having an H. *sapiens* guardian increases the chance of the neonate reaching sexual maturity); male Z. *diego,* in this light, are selected for adulterous behavior *so that* they can impregnate female Z. *diego* who are pair-bonded with H. *sapiens* [Pend48]. Opponents of the Pendragon hypothesis point out its misogynistic bent [Larson80], his lack of objectivity given his marriage to a Z. *diego* [Bord68], and the air of paranoia evident in Pendragon's text [Wright50].

INTELLIGENCE AND PERSONALITY

On the Stanford-Binet, Z. *diego* comes in a full standard deviation below H. *sapiens.* (We must remember, of course, that H. *sapiens* wrote the test.) Z. *diego* does somewhat better on nonverbal tests, and, with training, does as well on "learnable" tests such as the SAT as H. *sapiens.* On some tests, such as the Draw-A-Man, Z. *diego* comes out a full two standard deviations higher than H. *sapiens* [Green77]. And yet, the most reliable way to distinguish between adult Z. *diego* and H. *sapiens*—short of exposure to theotoxic salts—is simply to speak to the biped in question. Trained observers finger adult Z. *diego* approximately 80% of the time, although the false positive rate with zombidiegoform H. *sapiens* is 60% [Pend49] [Green84].

What are these observers looking for? I quote G. Warren Pendragon:

In a room full of people, the zombie will be in the midst of a group, all of whom are hanging on every word and every gesture—but when you listen, you realize they have nothing to say and nothing to feel. [Pend48]

Z. diego is not distinguishable from *H. sapiens* on the basis of standard-ized tests. Nevertheless, *Z. diego,* as a species, evinces certain differences:

MATHEMATICAL AND GROSS VERBAL INTELLIGENCE: *H. sapi-ens* scores better on vocabulary and mathematical reasoning. *Z. diego* is more articulate and better able to convey ideas, often despite a severely lim-ited vocabulary, and does better on tests involving short-term memory and mental arithmetic [Manr62].

VISUAL INTELLIGENCE: *Z. diego* outscores *H. sapiens* by a full two standard deviations. Many members of *Z. diego* are capable of producing drawings of phenomenal accuracy, although these drawings often seem "lifeless" to members of *H. sapiens* [Manr63].

AURAL/MUSICAL INTELLIGENCE: No statistical difference, al-though *Z. diego* rarely assumes a performance role [Manr62].

SPATIAL INTELLIGENCE: No statistical difference, although *Z. diego* rarely assumes a professional role (i.e., architect, interior decorator [Manr63]).

KINETIC INTELLIGENCE: There are no standardized tests for kinetic intelligence, but nearly all observed adults *Z. diego* are "good dancers," "graceful," and "good in bed" [Manr63-2].

SOCIAL INTELLIGENCE: In primary school, most *Z. diego* exhibit ef-fective leadership and follower skills, getting along well with peers and in-structors. In secondary school, *Z. diego* is seldom afflicted with adolescent angst and seldom initiates violence, although violence is often initiated against *Z. diego* by *H. sapiens* [Manr63-2]. Truancy is very common, espe-cially when the *Z. diego* does not have an *H. sapiens* guardian. In the 18-35-year range (mid to late adult,) *Z. diego* tends to take a passive role in purely social (as opposed to sexual) interactions, but handles itself flawlessly. In the postadult phase, *Z. diego* tends to become increasingly taciturn and withdrawn [Pend48] [Green77].

COMPLEX VERBAL AND AUTOANALYTICAL INTELLIGENCE: *Z. diego* does not appear to write either fiction or nonfiction for publication; nor have any *Z. diego* authored correspondence beyond that of the thank-you note [Manr62]. All known members of *Z. diego* have claimed to be *H. sapiens,* and thus an emic view is not available [And80]. Members of *Z. diego* reject the view that they are not human, and will respond to a sug-

gestion otherwise with the same degree of bemusement and annoyance an
H. sapiens would evince [Grant82].

OCCULT INTELLIGENCE: No *Z. diego* has ever been observed to
have an open third eye; 68% of adults and postadults avoid those with an
open third eye, evincing discomfort until they are able to flee [Green84].
This behavior closely resembles that of the domestic dog [Kale19], domestic cat [Kale21], Norwegian rat [Kale22], common cockroach [Fleck76],
and sapient mite [Fleck78], leading some to speculate that this is characteristic of species that live in close proximity with *H. sapiens* [Green79].

DEMOGRAPHY

Z. diego is not found in isolation; it occurs only intermixed with certain
populations of *H. sapiens*. San Diego has the highest concentration of
Z. diego in North America; estimates range from 2% of the total mundane
population to as high as 7% [Aber82]. The Incumbents make use of *Z. diego*
as concubines, prostitutes, subjects of medical experimentation / vivisec-
tion, organ donation, and food [Thomp80]. *Z. diego* is a protected species in
San Diego; licenses are necessary to remove *Z. diego* from its natural habitat,
and many populations of *Z. diego* are monitored and cultivated by promi-
nent Incumbents [Aber82].

Elsewhere, *Z. diego* constitutes a mere fraction of the mundane population; perhaps .3% in Los Angeles, coastal California (including San Francisco and Monterey), inland Southern California, and Florida. *Z. diego* is
found in small colonies throughout the greater American Southwest, com-
prising perhaps .04% of the population as a whole; in the specific communities in which it has established a toehold, it makes up approximately .3%
of the population. *Z. diego* is an urban and suburban species; it is not
found in small towns or in rural areas except in the case of transiency
[Aber84].

As noted above, *Z. diego* is not aware it cannot breed with *H. sapiens*. In
this light, its strategy of promiscuous couplings is seen to be the only way
it has to eventually mate with one of its own species [Young81]. Thus,
members of *Z. diego* initiate copulation with anything that *might* be

Z. *diego,* even if they end up spending much of their time making love to the wrong species.

From an epidemiological standpoint, we would expect Z. *diego* to display a high degree of infection by sexually transmitted disease. This does not appear to be the case; Z. *diego* does show twice H. *sapiens'* rate of herpes simplex type II, chlamydia, and mononucleosis, but the incidence of gonorrhea and HIV-positive serum appears to be nil [Gard83]. Early reports that the sperm cells of Z. *diego* can penetrate latex condoms have proven to be in error [Ramone84]. One intriguing possibility is that female Z. *diego* are capable of maintaining Z. *diego* sperm cells internally until ovulation, while destroying H. *sapiens* cells. If this proves to be the case, it is evident that even if a female Z. *diego* enforces the use of contraceptive measures, even a marginal failure while in the company of a male Z. *diego* will eventually result in pregnancy. If this is the case, the true fertility and prolificity of Z. *diego* is astronomical [Ramone84].

SPECIATION

It is hard to guess how Z. *diego* came to be. There are two dominant hypotheses:

The mainstream hypothesis is that under certain conditions of intense sunlight and cultural banality, H. *sapiens* spontaneously shifts to an alternate, undead form—Z. *diego.* This form gains a toehold because it is better adapted to its environment than the ultraviolet-vulnerable, introspective H. *sapiens* around it; and as we have seen above, Z. *diego* is a social creature that does well in mainstream culture despite—or perhaps because of—its unusual mentation and sexual behavior [Pend48].

An alternative hypothesis is that recently, perhaps six or seven thousand years ago, Z. *diego* appeared spontaneously in the Greek islands, speciating within a few generations as a result of artificial selection on the part of the Incumbents, who even then recognized the creature's utility [Sole82]. Records from this period of time are not available, and it is hard to see how speciation could occur so quickly; man has been selectively breeding *Canis familiaris* for at least twenty thousand years, and to this day a Chihuahua can impregnate a Saint Bernard. Further, it is only recently that ectomorphic females have been considered attractive rather than sickly; it is unlikely that *Z. diego* females would have been seen as attractive to the Incumbents in this time frame [Larson83].

ECONOMY

Upon assumption of the adult phase, *Z. diego* prefers to seek independence. *Z. diego* with an *H. sapiens* guardian displace themselves to avoid contact with guardian; *Z. diego* without an *H. sapiens* guardian simply move out [Aber82].

Twelve-to-eighteen-year-old *Z. diego* are frequently truant, spending their time in environments similar to those they will prefer as adults [Jack67]. By the time they assume independence, they already have a good idea how to get along. (Modern *Z. diego* rarely go on to college, although in previous decades some females did so in cynical pursuit of a mate [Jack78]).

Adult *Z. diego* prefer to assume residence in small, inexpensive apartments in company of other *Z. diego* or like-minded *H. sapiens. Z. diego* gravitates to positions of minimal responsibility allowing extensive daytime solar exposure. Many females work as evening- / night-shift waitresses, physical culture instructors, prostitutes, or lifeguards; many males work as evening- / night-shift waiters, parking attendants, amusement park workers, physical culture instructors, prostitutes, or lifeguards. Any position emphasizing solar exposure is possible, including day-shift waitressing in outdoor bars, gardening, construction work, street performance, and transiency. Low-level part-time temporary office work is resorted to when other means of employment are not available [Thomp80] [Aber81].

The employment patterns of postadults are similar, although many of the typical jobs of *Z. diego* are harder to come by—employers preferring those of youthful appearance (particularly in the field of waitressing). Bartending becomes an important means of income, as well as permanent (but still low-level) office work [Aber81].

Statistically valid data on *Z. diego* pair-bonded with *H. sapiens* is not available. Anecdotal evidence indicates that cross-species pair-bonded *Z. diego* often work as physical culture instructors or evening-shift bartenders / waiters /

waitresses [Aber81]. Pair-bonded *Z. diego* often garden during daylight hours, thus increasing their exposure to solar ultraviolet [Pend48].

DEATH

It is not known what happens to aged postadult *Z. diego*. After several decades of existence as a postadult, during which the creature becomes increasingly taciturn, withdrawn, and unresponsive to stimuli as a result of chronic oxygen deprivation to neural tissue, the postadult "retires." Family and friends claim that the *Z. diego* has removed itself to a distant land. Californian *Z. diego* most often cite Florida or Phoenix, Arizona—but *Z. diego* in Florida claim their relatives retire to California. *Z. diego* associates become extremely uncomfortable if pressed for details. Some time after this "retirement," family and friends report having received word that the "retiree" has passed on [Pend48] [Cal53].

We have a single documented case of a *Z. diego* "funeral." I quote G. Warren Pendragon:

We flew to Miami, where Alissa's mother had retired the year before. Alissa seemed to take it well; I had expected her to weep at least this one time, but it seemed that I was more disheartened by the death of her mother than she.

The funeral was in a chapel embedded in a trailer park. I asked Alissa if this had been where her mother retired to; she said yes, and I lost my temper, for when Esteele retired, she moved out of a lovely bungalow in Escondido. I asked her if we wanted our children to ship us off three thousand miles to die in squalor, but she hushed me, as the service was about to start.

When I entered the chapel, I was astounded at the number of people present. Stranger still, all seemed to be couples—and all consisted of a young, tanned person in their early twenties paired with a considerably older mate. I met the eyes of a man my age—and we both looked away. It was like gazing into a warped mirror. Except for a few trivial details of dress, it could have been Alissa and myself.

It dawned on me that there was no coffin. Suddenly, the row of ornamental pottery on the windowsill was revealed for what it was—a full dozen urns of ash. The speaker never mentioned Esteele's name, nor the names of any of the other dead. When it was over, we went to the window and peered at the tiny labels, looking for our loved ones.

Alissa asked me to take the urn; she hardly seemed to care what it contained or what it represented. Returning by automobile to the airport, we quarreled, but she simply shrugged in her infuriating way and would not let herself be drawn out. [Pend48]

What is taking place here is unclear in the extreme. Pendragon hypothesizes a veritable conspiracy of the undead to displace humanity to account for these hijinks; but as has been previously noted, paranoia had manifested itself by the time he put pen to paper [Wright50].

In any event, it appears unlikely that all *Z. diego* travel three thousand miles to die in a trailer park and undergo cremation. There are several colorful but extremely unlikely hypotheses, such as the Gulf Stream Hypothesis (that the *Z. diego* get halfway and drown themselves in the Gulf of Mexico [Barker66]), and Pendragon's Cordwood Hypothesis (that postadult *Z. diego* are stored in warehouses in a state of hibernation for later use as soldiers in a war against the living [Pend48]). We generally assume that "retirement" is a social fiction, and mass funerals as described above are enacted solely for the benefit of pair-bonded *H. sapiens,* who expect a memorial service of some kind [Cal53]. *Z. diego* does not discuss mortality or funeral arrangements except when placed under severe duress, and even then has little to say [Jack64].

A study of morgues, funeral homes, and autopsy records of Southern Californian hospitals revealed no postadult *Z. diego* corpses [Kopyzk71], although it is possible to fail to detect a postadult during autopsy if the body is decayed or the medical examiner is hurried or inexperienced. (There is no way to distinguish a dead presexual *Z. diego* from a preadolescent *H. sapiens,* and the gametes of the sexually mature had already perished, leaving no way to test for the presence of adult *Z. diego.*) This is surprising in and of itself; one would expect postadult *Z. diego* to fall to traffic accidents and random shootings as often as *H. sapiens.* Nor do postadult *Z. diego* crumble into dust at death, as powerful *Nosferatu nocturnus* do, or revert to a fully anthropomorphic form, as weak *N. nocturnus* do [Glass73]. We can only guess at how the life cycle of *Z. diego* comes to a close.

PRACTICAL MEANS OF DETECTION

Exposure to theotoxic salts remains the most reliable way to determine whether an anthropomorph is a zombie or not; but this, of course, results in cessation of the subject when it is in fact of the genera *Zombi* or *Necrozombi*.

Presexual *Z. diego* are vulnerable to theotoxic salts, as above, and are more social than preadolescent *H. sapiens;* but given the uncertainty of the interview process with regards to preadolescents and the unfortunate side effects entailed in shooting a child of any species, presexual *Z. diego* are effectively indistinguishable from preadolescent *H. sapiens* [Green84]. (Exposure to an open third eye is without utility; presexual *Z. diego* do not flee it.)

If a gamete sample can be obtained, adult *Z. diego* can easily be detected by mixing with a known sample [Burke50]. Failing that, subjecting the creature to interrogation by a trained observer can detect *Z. diego* 80% of the time, with a disheartening 60% rate of false positives when the organism in question is a zombidiegomorphic *H. sapiens* [Green84]. 68% of adult *Z. diego* flee an open third eye; this test may be brought into play when a trained observer is not available, with the advantage that the false positive rate is nearly nil [Green84]. Chromatographic analysis of the dermis will reveal the presence of the photoactive steroids characteristic of *Z. diego,* but this technique requires at least a square centimeter of living skin, and thus is not practical. Although adult *Z. diego* manifest a stereotypical response to certain sexual triggers, zombidiegomorphic *H. sapiens* manifest a nearly identical stereotypical response [Larson80].

Postadult *Z. diego* are easily detected through blood test, dermal biopsy, or abdominal MRI [Kopyzk71] [Sole84].

ZOMBIE OR MAN?

Is *Zombi diego* undead, or a living organism? Most hold that *Z. diego* is undead, arguing the following:

1. The postadult stage of *Z. diego* lacks entire systems characteristic of higher vertebrates, notably: a living skin, the liver, the kidneys, and the bone marrow; the circulatory system is highly degraded. In postadults, the metabolism of the nonnecrobiotic organs and tissues is inadequately

provided with nutrients and oxygen; they are maintained through the thaumophagocity characteristic of the undead.

2. *Z. diego* manifests the acutely self-destructive response to theotoxic salts characteristic of the *Zombi* and *Necrozombi* genera.

3. Members of *Z. diego* "act like zombies," in that their response to stimuli is considered uncomplicated and deterministic.

The classification of *Z. diego* in the kingdom Necro is a natural result.

The minority view is that *Z. diego* should be classed as *Homo zombidiego,* right alongside mankind in the kingdom Animalia. The minority argues the following:

1. *Z. diego* reproduces sexually and nurses like a mammal. In this view, the postadult stage is a coda, as irrelevant to *Z. diego*'s place in the kingdom Animalia as the decay of a corpse is to *H. sapiens'* place in that same kingdom.

2. *Z. diego* is thus far genetically indistinguishable from *H. sapiens,* which would indicate a common ancestor (and a very recent one, at that).

3. *Z. diego* considers *itself* an animal, although it does not understand it cannot sexually reproduce with *H. sapiens* and is therefore a separate species.

And finally, the minority has a final, telling argument:

4. *H. sapiens* grafted the kingdom Necro onto the existing fivefold structure because we couldn't stand to admit kinship with the undead.

THE SIXTH KINGDOM

The disagreement between Charles Darwin and Alfred Wallace on the taxonomy of the undead is too notorious to merit much discussion [Muy03] [TDG71].

Modern scholars have adopted Wallace's sixth-kingdom scheme, but there are compelling arguments for Darwin's contention that the undead are not separate species at all. *Nosferatu nocturnus,* for example, is formed when a *Homo sapiens* rises from the dead and becomes haemophagic. At what point does *H. sapiens* become *N. nocturnus*? At death? Or when the vampire rises? Admitted, *N. nocturnus* cannot spawn more *N. nocturnus* through sexual reproduction. But neither can postmenopausal humans—nobody argues that old women are no longer *H. sapiens!*

Wallace maintained that that the undead are sufficiently unlike living organisms to rate their own kingdom. Further, the resemblance between (for example) *Necrozombi homo* and *Necrozombi canis* is much greater than the resemblance between *Homo sapiens* and *Canis familiaris;* to class a reanimated human under the genus *Homo* but leave a reanimated dog under *Canis* struck Wallace as absurd. (As a side note, remember that the notion that the undead should be given a taxonomic kingdom at all was nonintuitive in Wallace's time; many occultists advocated a weakly hierarchical system of technical names, as geologists do with rocks [TDG71]).

At any rate, *Zombi diego* was not recognized as a separate species until 1948 [Woj48], by which time the doctrine of the sixth kingdom was solidly in place. Even *Z. diego*'s modern taxonomy—Necro Ego Sapiens Mnenonosa Homosapiens *Zombi diego*—was the result of long and bitter dispute [Dunhill50].

As you recall, the family taxon of Ego division undead is the full species name of the living organism from which the undead is derived. In the case of undead derived from humans, it is acceptable to abbreviate the formal taxon "Animalia-Chordata-Vertebrata-Tetrapoda-Mammalia-Primates-Hominidae-Homo-sapiens" to "Homosapiens." But we have begged the question. Is *Z. diego* derived from *H. sapiens?*

Until *Z. diego* came to light, no sexually reproducing undead had been described in the literature. (The occasional reproduction of *H. sapiens* via rape by *Nosferatu, Zombi,* and *Necrozombi* has occurred, but the resulting children are indubitably *H. sapiens* [IW61]). The few undead that reproduce at all—notably *Nosferatu* and *Stygiaspectre*—do so by assaulting an *H. sapiens* and transmitting the undead condition through occult means [Young81]. Nearly a quarter of the participants at the Prague conference felt that sexual reproduction alone put *Z. diego* firmly in the kingdom Animalia [Dunhill50]. The controversy continues to this day.

OTHER BORDERLINE CASES

The necromonera responsible for Mummy's Curse (*Necroneisseria gonorrhoeae*) is classed as undead—it has the ability to maintain its metabolism and reproduce even in desiccate environments [Green77]. However, recent research has indicated that *N. gonorrhoeae* can be reverted to the mundane Monera *Neisseria gonorrhoeae* simply by withholding mana [Ting83].

In 1945, the SS occultist Hermann Ausgehoring attempted to produce powerful undead by shriving the undying part of volunteers, while leaving the intellect and body intact. An SS captain, by all accounts a relatively humane man with no appreciable scientific bent or desire for anything but to bring the war to a close, was selected and subjected to the procedure. The resulting monster, tentatively classed Necro Nonego Sapiens Mnenonosa Homosapiens *Ausgehoring horribilis,* found itself (by its own account) suddenly and unaccountably suffused with and sympathetic to the psychic environment it found itself in—to wit, a top-secret Nazi base engaging in unethical experimentation [Gold55]. The first-person documentation of the pseudoscientific atrocities perpetrated by this creature is unavailable to casual researchers, but may be found in the Vatican library and the Library of Congress "Z2" collection [Wink80].

Similarly, *H. sapiens* suffering from partial alienation of the undying part are sometimes considered undead under the genus *Ausgehoring* [Zang58], but few lend this classification any credence [Green77].

PERSPECTIVE

Foucault's work brought home the fact that our naïve concept of gender, under which a person is undeniably a man or undeniably a woman, is suspect; the world simply is not that simple. *Z. diego* does the same for our notions of living versus undead.

In the end, perhaps it is naught but squabblings over semantics; and, truth be told, few outside of academia care whether *Z. diego* is a very lifelike undead or a living creature with a final, highly necrobiotic life stage.

Still, I feel we are prone to a certain overgeneralization. We are the living, and those of us with open third eyes who join the Opposition claim to do so purely on moral grounds; the undead are the pawns of the Incumbents, and are to be dispatched with silver or salt the moment they are detected. As a full Captain of the Van Helsing Society—and I assure you, no hand-to-hand kill is a cakewalk, even during daylight—I often feel this way myself.

But I like *Zombi diego*.

Nobody claims that chimpanzees are saints; Jane Goodall witnessed injustice and murder in chimp society. But we do not *expect* them to be saints; and the fact that they are capable of evil does not make us love them any less. If anything, it increases the wistfulness and delight we experience when we see them content, grooming together with their infants.

Thus it is, for me, with *Zombi diego*. They're not great conversationalists, and the fact that they cannot open their third eyes means they cannot be confidants or colleagues. But I don't need to be able to *talk* to gorillas to appreciate them; I'm perfectly content to watch and marvel. There isn't a primatologist alive who isn't happy to spend six hours in a puddle of mud for the privilege of catching a half hour's view of lemurs at play.

Z. diego ends its life in a necrobiotic shell, the mind draining away as the cerebrum dies; this is undeniable. And throughout its youthful days, *Z. diego* behaves like a foolish, gracile zombie interested only in a good party. But however *Zombi diego* came into existence—whether necromorphism is latent in humanity, or the Incumbents bred an interesting mutant for their own use—a sympathetic observer must admit that we are kin to the heliophilics at play on our beaches. And I, for one, do not begrudge *Zombi diego* their place in the sun.

Erik Johanson
Miskatonic University, Easter, 1985

REFERENCES

Abbreviations:

AOP: Association of Occult Phenomenologists.

JVHS: Journal of the Van Helsing Society.

RSIG: Reform Special Interest Group. (Of the AOP.)

SDIN: San Diego Institute of Necromancy Press.

TCCAOR: Twin Cities Center for Advanced Occult Research.

Aber81: Abercrombie, Justin. *The Economic Role of* Zombi diego. SDIN 1981.

Aber82: Abercrombie, Justin. *Third California Coastal Census of the Occult.* SDIN 1982.

Aber84: Abercrombie, Justin. *Unverified Reports of the Occult in the Greater American Southwest.* SDIN 1984.

And80: Anderson, David. Self-Image and the Occult. Proceedings of the Vienna Conference of the AOP, 1980.

Barker66: Barker, Chaim. *On the Road: Migratory Behavior in North American Entities.* Miskatonic Press, 1966.

Bord68: Bordeaux, Nichole. *Feminism and* Zombi diego. Ascalabotan Press of San Francisco, 1968.

Bord72: Bordeaux, Nichole. *Love Charms: Sexual Behavior and the Occult.* Ascalabotan Press of San Francisco, 1972.

Burke50: Burke, Edward. The Zygotic Lysing Test for *Zombi diego. Popular Alchemy,* December 1950.

Burke79: Burke, Edward. *The Great State of Texas.* Texas Institute of Alchemy, 1979.

Cal53: Calahan, Patrick. *Life Cycle of* Zombi diego. Miskatonic Press, 1953.

Dunhill50: Dunhill, Cyril. Minutes of the San Diego Zombie Special Interest Group meeting of Prague, 1950.

Embeli83: Embeli, Robert. Cultural Absolutism in Modern Scholarship. *Journal of Panoptic Studies,* July 1983.

Fleck76: Fleck, Louis. RAID! *Occult Zoology,* May 1976.

Fleck78: Fleck, Louis. Showers as Genocide. *Occult Zoology,* May 1978.

Gard83: Gardener, Terry. STDs in *Zombi diego.* Twin Cities Center for Occult Disease Control, 1983.

Glass73: Glass, Alice. *Laid to Rest: Eschatology and the Termination of the Undead.* Miskatonic Press, 1973.

Gold55: Goldberg, Laila. Nazi Occult Atrocities. *Protocols of the Elders of Zion,* May 1955.

Gordon83: Gordon, Telemachus. "Those Girls Aren't Human!"; Images of the Undead in Erotica. *Unseen Media,* February 1983.

Grant81: Grant, Steven W. Eulogy. *JVHS* October 1981.

Grant82: Grant, Steven W. Neural Activity in the Undead. *Journal of Panoptic Studies,* July 1982.

Green77: Green, Jessica (editor). *Necrobestiary,* 15th edition. Wallace Foundation Press, 1977.

Green79: Green, Jessica. A Possible Mechanism Underlying the Evolution of Third Eye Avoidance Behavior. *Occult Zoology,* August 1979.

Green84: Green, Jessica (editor). *Field Guide of the Undead,* 37th edition. Wallace Foundation Press, 1984.

Iijin69: Iijin, Mohammad. *Thaumophagocic Processes,* third edition. SDIN 1969.

IW61: "Iridium Woman" (pseudonym). *A Fate Worse than Death: Sexual Assault and the Occult.* Ascalabotan Press of San Francisco, 1961.

Jack64: Jackson, Wayne. Talking to the Undead. *Journal of the RSIG,* 1964.

Jack67: Jackson, Wayne. Educating *Zombi diego:* Barriers. Proceedings of the Phoenix conference of the RSIG, 1967.

Jack78: Jackson, Wayne. Personal communication, 1978.

Kale19: Kale, Brian. *Howling at the Moon: the Eerie Sensitivity of the Common Hound.* Miskatonic Press, 1919.

Kale21: Kale, Brian. *Screaming at the Night: the Wisdom of Cats.* Miskatonic Press, 1921.

Kale22: Kale, Brian. *The Sinking Ship: Prescience in Rodents.* Miskatonic Press, 1922.

Klas56: Klashardt, Franz. *Zombi diego* Dermal Metabolism. *JVHS* January 1956.

Klas56-2: Klashardt, Franz. *Zombi diego* Hepatic and Renal Metabolism. *JVHS* November 1956.

Klas57: Klashardt, Franz. *Zombi diego* Circulatory Metabolism. *JVHS* August 1957.

Klas58: Klashardt, Franz. *Zombi diego* Ultraviolet-Catalyzed Metabolic Processes. *JVHS* March 1958.

Klas58-2: Klashardt, Franz. *Zombi diego* Reproductive Metabolism. *JVHS* November 1958.

Klas59: Klashardt, Franz. Unresolved Issues in the Study of the Metabolism of *Zombi diego. JVHS* special, "Boundaries of Knowledge," Christmas 1959.

Kopyzk71: Kopyzk, Uve. Where are the Zombies? *JVHS* January 1971.

Larson80: Larson, Laura L. Sluts and Slimeballs: Californian Sexuality. *Unseen Media*, November 1980.

Larson81: Larson, Laura L. Flaming Faggots and Desperate Dykes: The Perceived Overaggression of Homosexuals. *Unseen Media*, September 1981.

Larson83: Larson, Laura L. Racy Rakes and Chubby Cunts: An Objection to Solenic's Speciation. *Unseen Media*, March 1983.

Mad80: Madison, Jorge. Recent Work in UV Catalysis in *Zombi diego*. TC-CAOR 1980.

Manr62: Manring, Jesus. Zombi diego: *Fool*. SDIN 1962.

Manr63: Manring, Jesus. Zombi diego: *Artist*. SDIN 1963.

Manr63-2: Manring, Jesus. Zombi diego: *Whore*. SDIN 1963.

Muy03: Muybridge, Eadweard. *The Placard by the Print*. Privately circulated manuscript, penned 1903.

Pend48: Pendragon, G. Warren. *Hearth and Home*. Miskatonic Press, 1948.

Pend49: Pendragon, G. Warren. Hunters Guide to the San Diego Zombie. *JVHS* December 1949.

Ramone84: Ramone, Mark. "Oops." *JVHS* January 1984.

Sole82: Soleinic, April. *Zombi diego* as a Recent Offshoot of *Homo sapiens*. TCCAOR 1982.

Sole84: Soleinic, April. *Zombi diego* Genetics. TCCAOR 1984.

Sole85: Soleinic, April. Private communication.

TDG71: "The Dinosaur Guy" (pseudonym).Wallace's Middle Path. *Unnatural History*, August 1971.

Thomp80: Thompson, Timothy. *The Economy of San Diego*, second edition. Miskatonic Press, 1980.

Ting83: Ting, Eddie. Reversion of *Necroneisseria gonorrhea* to *Neisseria gonorrhea* through Thaumodeprivation. Twin Cities Center for Occult Disease Control, 1983.

Wallace62: Wallace, Alfred Russel. *Taxonomy of the Living Dead*. Privately circulated manuscript, penned 1862.

Whit80: Whitlomb, Pericles. Personal communication, 1980.

Wink80: Winkle, Harold. *Secrets Upon Secrets*, second edition. Miskatonic Press, 1980.

Woj48: Wojinski, Leszek. *Confirmation of the Existence of the San Diego Zombie*. SDIN 1948.

Woj52: Wojinski, Leszek. *California Coastal Census of the Occult,* first edition. SDIN 1952.

Wright50: Wright, John. *Psychological Breakdown of Occultists*. Miskatonic Press, 1950.

Yee82: Yee, Jiong Yang. Genetic Markers in *Zombi diego*. TCCAOR 1982.

Young79: Young, Bernard. *Sexual Development of* Zombi diego. Bivalve Press, 1979.

Young81: Young, Bernard. *Necroreproductive Ecology*. Bivalve Press, 1981.

Zang58: Zang, Mei. *Monsters Among Us*. Miskatonic Press, 1958.

about the author

Stephan Zielinski lives in San Francisco. *Bad Magic* is his first novel.